MASON-DIXON

MURDERS

A Mystery Novel

By
Bob Walsh

To the Honshergon family
Hope you enjoy the book.
Best wishes.
Bob Walsh
13 Apr 06

PublishAmerica
Baltimore

First printing

At the specific preference of the author, PublishAmerica allowed this work to remain exactly as the author intended, verbatim, without editorial input.

ISBN: 1-4137-8679-0
PUBLISHED BY PUBLISHAMERICA, LLLP
www.publishamerica.com
Baltimore

Printed in the United States of America

This novel is dedicated to my brother:

George Eugene (Gene) Walsh
1930–2003

My big brother, Gene, was the role model for the character Arthur in this novel. I tried to make Arthur the same kind of well loved, warm and generous human being that Gene was. Arthur shows some sense of humor, but I couldn't do justice to the jokes that only Gene could get away with in mixed company.

Gene was nearly blind following complications from diabetes and before he died, I would dearly loved to have read to him the chapters about Arthur. It is of much comfort to me that when we last parted, ten years ago, I told him that I loved him and he responded in kind.

Acknowledgments

First of all, I would like to thank my wife, Colette for her enduring patience. Writing this novel was probably one of the biggest tests of our 46 years of marriage. The production started out as simple exercise to try and get several weeks of recurring dreams off my mind so that I could get back to sleeping normally. The ongoing dreams stopped, but refining the story lasted for over three years with the occasional dream coming along to resolve certain disconnects. Many chores around the house were delayed because of this addictive writing project.

Second, I would like to thank, Dennis Orchard, a long time buddy from high school days, for performing the first edit. Dennis, who is a former journalist and semi-retired senior public servant, spent several weeks ploughing through my original manuscript and made many suggestions that eliminated a lot of excess paragraphs and pages (color supplements I like to call them) that were not necessarily connected to the plot. He pointed out several cases of excess use of expressions such as, "Oh" and "Well" at the start of dialogue passages. My main objective for Dennis, apart from a broad technical review, was to see whether the story, "hung together"—so to speak. His Herculean efforts were sincerely appreciated.

Next, I would like to acknowledge the assistance of my good friend, Tony Whittall, for his special efforts in making the manuscript more technically sound. His experience as a former English teacher was severely tested. He ever-so-gently let me know that writing wasn't my strong suit. It gradually became better. Besides performing the detailed editing function, Tony was very helpful in suggesting certain plot changes or clarifications that would make the content easier to read. After a dozen or so drafts, I believe I have a good story to tell.

Although I only presented a few of my chapters at several meetings of a local literary society, I concluded it was not the proper forum. The members' collective encouragement was appreciated. I'm sure my sponsor, Ann Coutts, will pass on my compliments.

I would also like to thank Kurt Myers, Ms Nancy Myers, Penni Bernard, and Shoenna Thomas from the Pennsylvania Bureau of Motor Vehicles for their kind help with state licence plate history. Mr Myers was unaware that his name was similar to an infamous SS General Kurt Meyer, who was a war criminal. He was convicted of killing 18 Canadian Prisoners of War during the WWII battle of Normandy.

Similarly, I would like to acknowledge the extraordinary work and materials provided by Ms. Janice Selig, Anne Ferro, Eltra Nelson, and Linda Blevins from the Maryland Motor Vehicle Administration.

Some acknowledgements should also be made to several of my high school and college classmates (to start a list would be too dangerous) who gave me advice and encouragement via email along the way.

My daughter-in-law, Connie (Keenan) Walsh, deserves her share of credit for doing a considerable amount of fact checking on the Internet.

I must also thank Ida Plassay, a local author, who gave me the advice to try PublishAmerica.com as a publisher.

Believe it or not, I actually enjoyed correcting the host of grammatical errors that both Dennis and Tony pointed out. It is amazing what you don't see when reviewing your own work. My grade school teachers would be impressed by how much I have improved my use of such things as pronoun antecedents and the subjunctive case.

Finally, in order to reduce the production time for this novel, I struck a deal with the publisher, wherein I accepted virtually full responsibility for the editing function. Therefore, in deference to the fact that it is most difficult to proof-read ones own work, I would like to give credit to several military instructors, whose names are long forgotten over my forty years in the service, by recording the following quote, "A few errors may have been introduced to make sure you are paying attention."

Oh! I almost forgot. I must recognize the portrait work of Pierre Bernard. He took the publicity photograph, and like my two manuscript editors, he tried his best to "make a silk purse out of a sow's ear."

Bob Walsh

Foreword

This story is told by two main characters, a father and daughter team of Henry and Heather Macy. Each has certain background bits of information unknown to the other at any given time. It's not that they don't trust each other; it's just that it doesn't occur to either of them to reveal such trivia unless the subject comes up. They tell their stories independently. Each starts out telling their background from their own point of view. When they are together, it depends on what the subject is as to who tells the story. When they are separated, the narration is done by the applicable person.

The tale unfolds in early May, 2003 as Heather returns home after having been away for 13 years during which time she acquired the usual life skills and experiences including becoming a lawyer. As she reacquaints herself with her former teenage surroundings, some references are made to a murder that took place some 30 years earlier and how that crime relates to a more recent murder that happened at the same location a month earlier. Although the story takes place in a mythical city in Pennsylvania and in a small village in nearby

Maryland, it could be a cross border situation between any two states. In this case, the two burial places are separated by the Maryland/Pennsylvania border, otherwise known as the Mason-Dixon Line. Henry's participation generally revolves around his life and career in both the village and the city.

The names of all characters in this novel have been chosen at random and any relation to persons, living or dead, is purely coincidental. There are many clues and characters woven into the story. Some clues and characters are obscure and some are obvious and misleading or have double meanings.

I hope you enjoy it.

Bob Walsh

CONTENTS

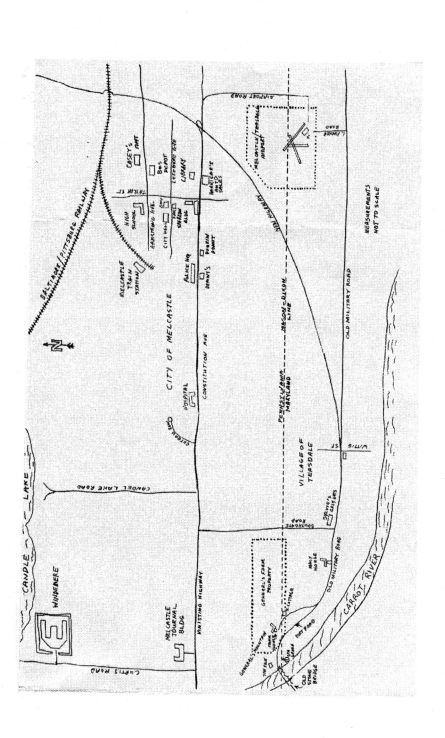

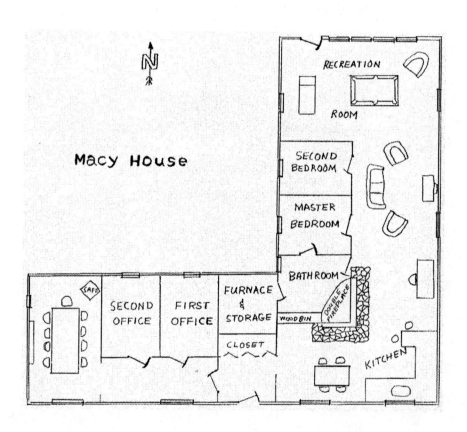

N

Macy House

RECREATION ROOM

SECOND BEDROOM

MASTER BEDROOM

BATHROOM

SAFE

SECOND OFFICE

FIRST OFFICE

FURNACE & STORAGE

WOOD BIN

DOUBLE FIREPLACE

CLOSET

KITCHEN

CHAPTER 1

Back To Normal

My parents, Bonnie and Henry Macy, gave me the name Heather when I was born on April 29, 1973. Little did I know that the date of my birth would be the last day on earth for somebody I never knew. The circumstances surrounding that poor fellow's unfortunate early demise came to my attention some 30 years later.

Last week, Dad and I were pleased to help the police and the FBI resolve two local murder investigations—one a cold case in Maryland and the other in Pennsylvania last month. The last few days had been hectic and we are glad to be back to normal.

Most of the time Dad and I worked independently, but our synergistic efforts were instrumental in linking the two cases. The truth is most of the time I followed the clues on my own, but I frequently needed the help of Dad's knowledge of the people in both communities.

I grew up and went to grade school in a little village called Teasdale in rural Maryland. Our little spot on the map tends to be overshadowed by the city of Melcastle, across the border in Pennsylvania. The state line between the two settlements has historically been called the Mason-Dixon Line.

I recently returned home, after a 13-year absence in Montreal, to work with my dad as his law partner. Dad has an established law office in Melcastle as well as one here in Macy House in the rustic village of Teasdale. Macy House has been the family home for four generations as well as Dad's continuous law office for nearly 40 years.

Today, as Dad and I stood in front of Macy House and watched Sergeant Woznica's police car leave the driveway, we felt confident that our active participation would not likely be required, at least not until the accused were brought to trial. Hopefully, peace and quiet would also return to our village.

Sergeant Woznica's visit had been more than just a courtesy call. He knew that 13 years ago I used to date Casey Clarkin in high school and after graduation I had gone to live with Casey in Montreal. The sergeant had come to warn us that a Canada-wide warrant had been issued for the arrest of my old boyfriend. The Teasdale police detachment had received an info-copy of the warrant because young Mr. Clarkin used to live in Teasdale before he moved to Melcastle for his final year of high school. Unfortunately, the warrant did not contain a photo and after 13 years very few people in the area knew Casey by sight.

After the sergeant finished passing on the routine warning, he casually mentioned some additional details about the two murder investigations to which Dad and I had contributed. Some of this information was new and surprising, but made more sense than my primary theory. Some of the original facts now had new meaning. The details now fitted together in a more logical sequence.

During the discussion with Sergeant Woznica, Dad was obviously pleased that he was the first to figure out that the suspects we helped identify were members a syndicate called SPA-KAL. His satisfaction was short-lived, however, when the sergeant explained that Dad had the correct names but the wrong people.

We waited until the police car had turned onto Old Military Road before going into the house. Dad headed for the conference room at the far end of Macy House and as he went, he commented that he had decided the time had come to dispose of the revolver that Grampa George had kept in the old safe.

I went to my room to see whether I had any pictures of Casey that might be useful to Sergeant Woznica. I dug out an old photo album from the back of my closet. There were several pictures from my high school years, but none with a clear view of Casey's face.

At the start of the blank pages, I found a blurred Polaroid picture of Casey and me that hadn't been mounted yet. The picture was taken the night of Casey's final graduation party. It was an unglamorous picture of two people who had obviously had too much to drink. I folded up the album and went to see whether Dad thought the picture would be suitable to give to the police.

Dad was in his office sitting at his desk. The revolver was in his OUT basket. In his left hand, he held the two Swiss bankbooks he had showed me a couple of night ago. At the same time, he was re-reading the letter from his long lost, twin brother, Arthur, that had provided so many clues about the murder 30 years ago.

I leaned forward and gently turned the muzzle of the revolver sideways in its resting place. At the same time, I asked Dad whether the gun was loaded. There was no answer.

By this time, Dad had rotated his chair partially away from me and was looking out the window. He had assumed a leaned back position in his chair and had that far away look in his eyes. I took that to mean that I should take the chair opposite his desk and wait. He was obviously in another time and place.

I opened the album to the next blank page and slipped the grad party snapshot between the next two empty clear plastic sheets. I pressed the picture into place and stared at it and slowly entered a flashback zone myself. The thirteen years in Montreal flashed by quickly.

CHAPTER 2

Leaving Home At Seventeen

The party picture in the photo album triggered a series of vivid memories starting with Casey's graduation night in 1990. I clearly remember the confrontation the next day. Mother and I had not been getting along very well. I had just turned 17 and I felt the situation was so unbearable I left home—ran off really—with Casey Clarkin. Casey and I had been going together for over a year. He was 19 and we both attended Melcastle High School. He originally came to this area with his parents, but when they moved back to Montreal, he stayed behind and lived with an aunt and uncle in Teasdale. When he was forced to repeat several subjects to pass his final year, he moved into an apartment in Melcastle. He had his own car and had the eye of every girl in town.

I had seen Casey around for a couple of years, but we didn't start dating until after my sixteenth birthday. I thought we were in love. Mother didn't like Casey and we frequently argued about him.

In my younger years, I tended to be a person of few words. One problem with being the laconic type is that when you do say something, your friends sometimes place undue importance on your words. In this case, my comments about my relationship with my mother prompted Casey to suggest that I go back to Montreal with him. I didn't realize he was only half serious.

My mother and I had a big fight for staying out all night after the graduation party. The "discussion" was brief, but heated. I stomped off to my room and fell asleep.

I woke up in the middle of the afternoon, with the sun shining on my face. It wasn't long before my anger returned and I immediately started packing the suitcase my parents had given me for my sixteenth birthday. I remember so vividly the unfunny joke they made that the suitcase was all I needed to leave home. I was expecting more than a suitcase and their laughing about it, made me angry.

I knew I couldn't take all the clothes I had in the closet, so I concentrated on the warmer items, considering that Montreal was such a long way north. The suitcase quickly became full and there was so more that I really wanted to take. I retrieved an old knapsack from the attic above my bedroom. I took two pairs of blue jeans out of my suitcase and stuffed them in the knapsack. That left room for the only suit I owned.

As I took one final look around the room, I thought about taking Coco-Bear, a flat bear that I had slept with since I was a toddler. As I was leaving, I looked back at "my sleeping buddy" propped up against my pillow. I couldn't leave him behind. So I stuffed him in a side pocket of the knapsack.

I was nervous about calling a taxi. I wanted to speak into the phone loud enough to let Mom know what I was doing, but not too loud to reveal any shakiness in my voice.

When the taxi arrived, I was glad Dad wasn't home yet from his downtown office. I was angry with Mom, but not with him. I didn't want to say good-bye to Dad in case he tried to talk me into staying.

I had been to Casey's apartment many times before. Still, it felt strange carrying my belongings up the front stairs and into the lobby. I buzzed his number and it seemed to take forever before he responded over the intercom. When I finally arrived at his apartment, he seemed confused. It was obvious the intercom had woken him up and he was a bit ill tempered.

I was really shaken when Casey asked me why I was there. When I replied that I was taking him up on his offer to go with him to Montreal, he didn't say a word. He didn't seem to remember that we had talked about it the night before. Later, when I offered to help pack his clothes, he declined and said he would rather do that chore himself. It was hard to tell whether he was annoyed or just hung-over.

I stayed overnight at Casey's place and early the next morning we bundled into his old car and left for Montreal. The sun was peeping between the buildings on the eastern horizon as we left the city. By then, my anger with my mother had cooled off and I felt pretty good. I settled in to enjoy the scenery as we left the streets of Melcastle and proceeded onto the interstate highway. I had been to Philadelphia and Baltimore quite a few times, but we soon began to travel on highways I had never seen before.

After a few miles, I began to have uncomfortable feelings that were a mixture of confusion and self-doubt. The previous night at the party my escape plan had all seemed so clear and logical. Now that the deed was unfolding, I wasn't so sure.

Neither of us spoke for a long while as the miles quickly passed. I felt the tense atmosphere had something to do with our assumed relationship. When we did speak, it seemed to me that I was doing most of the talking. In the year or so that we had been going out, I was the quiet one, not only with him, but generally with everyone else as well.

The flow of personal conversations has always fascinated me. As I grew up, I noticed that people, even strangers, would tell me things that they wouldn't ordinarily say to anyone else. Maybe I had a face that told them I sympathized with their anxieties and the person would just keep on talking. They often thanked me for being such a good listener. I noticed the less I spoke the more the other person would keep on talking and their personal secrets would come tumbling out. All I know is that I didn't have any control over who it was or when those mostly one-sided discussions would take place. I used to enjoy most of those conversations. The process seemed harmless enough.

But, as we drove north past Philadelphia, I noticed Casey wasn't responding to general conversation at all. He wasn't in his usual carefree mood, which was what I liked most about him. Something was wrong. As we crossed into New Jersey, he finally came out with what was bothering him.

"I hope you don't think I want to get married or anything like that," he announced. "I like you a lot, but I'm not ready to settle down. I just hope you understand that."

I was stunned. I felt we had developed something special and hoped that some day we would discuss marriage. But what could I say?

"Oh, no. I like you too, but I'm not ready for anything like marriage." I tried not to sound as though he had just kicked me in the guts.

Up to that point, I had thought our love-making was an expression of mutual love. It suddenly became obvious that I had been fooling myself all along.

After a long pause, he said, "Well, that's good."

For a long while after that short outburst, he still didn't respond to any of my attempts to make conversation. I liked it so much better when others did most of the talking. I was desperate to keep my frustration in check, but I felt I had to say something to encourage him to talk.

"You know, Casey, I don't know very much about your parents. What does your dad do for a living?" I asked, timidly.

"Dad is an insurance executive and Mom works part-time at the local library...that is, when she isn't trying to take over the local tennis club or bridge club. I'm an only child and they probably didn't plan on having me. That's why they left me behind in Melcastle to finish high school."

I was glad to hear his voice again. I wanted desperately to have that old feeling back. Maybe if he would open up a little, everything would come back to the way it was. But what he had to say next really startled me.

"Where do you plan to stay in Montreal?"

I couldn't believe that he didn't understand that I had expected to stay at his house. I had to think quickly.

"I had planned to stay with the Simpsons," I replied. "He was Dad's former law partner. He and his wife moved to Montreal a few years ago. I really liked her."

I deliberately paused for a few seconds to see what Casey would say.

"What do you expect to do after that?" he asked.

I really hadn't thought the whole thing through.

"I'm just going to Montreal, that's all. I plan to get a job, find my own apartment and see how it goes from there."

There was no response from Casey for several minutes. I wondered what he was really thinking, but I didn't know how to ask.

I sat and stared out the window for a long while.

I was glad Casey had been back and forth to Montreal a few times because the confusion of highways around New York City was overwhelming to me. Casey liked to exceed the speed limit. That habit contributed to my growing anxiety. The volume of traffic was more than I had ever seen. The highways I had taken with the sports teams were not nearly as crowded as the roads in New Jersey and New York State.

As we drove through the Hudson River valley, the contrast of the sheer rock face of the mountains and the lazy river below was awesome, pretty and frightening all at the same time. I was disappointed that we caught only a few glimpses of Lake Champlain itself as we drove north.

It was nearly dark when we spotted the sign for Plattsburg. It reminded of Mr. Bockington's high school history classes. My favorite teacher was an avid "War of 1812" buff and I'll always remember his description of the naval battle that took place on Plattsburg Bay.

I was still thinking about those days in history class, when we began to see road signs, telling us that we were approaching the U.S. Customs. It never occurred to me that I would miss my country even before I left.

I forced myself to think about how I was going to clarify my relationship with Casey. Since it was clear that I was not going to be living with Casey, my fondest wish was that we would somehow be the way we were in Melcastle. No magic solution came to mind and time was running out.

At the Canadian border, Casey told the customs officer that he was born in Montreal. When I said I was from Teasdale, Maryland, I thought maybe I should have told him it was Melcastle. The officer might have heard of that city at least.

After we passed through both U.S. and Canadian Customs, it was stunning to realize that most of the road signs were in French. With my limited high school French, I couldn't tell what many of the messages were. Casey could speak French, but it didn't occur to him that I might need some translation help.

As we approached Montreal, I really didn't know what to expect. I guess I thought Montreal would be similar in size to Melcastle. Boy, was I in for a surprise. The nighttime skyline of Montreal suddenly appeared across a long, reflective expanse of the St. Lawrence River.

I had envisaged the odd cloverleaf interchange, but the intricacies of some of the three-level overpasses were unexpected. The support pillars made me feel like I was passing through the legs of the table and chairs of some kind of giant's house.

I found myself staring at the nighttime skyline of Montreal. It was fascinating. Some buildings were at least 50 storeys high. When we left the highways and began to travel on city streets, I noticed that all the STOP signs were in French. Actually, most of the stop signs only had the word ARRET on them.

The next thing I knew, we were at Casey's parents' house in a fashionable district called the Town of Mount Royal. We tried the front door. It was locked and his parents were not at home. I found out later that they were away on vacation. It seems they weren't expecting Casey back from school until the end of the month.

We talked the situation over in the car. At first, I suggested that I could look up the Simpsons in the phonebook, but we concluded it was too late at night for that. We decided the best thing would be for me to rent a room at the YWCA.

It didn't take long to travel to the YWCA from Casey's place. I was highly annoyed that he didn't help me into the "Y" with my luggage. As soon as my suitcase was out of the car, Casey muttered something about "a no parking zone" and jumped in his car and took off. No kiss good-bye, no, see ya later—just a wave and Casey was gone. Little did I know that the view from behind in that disappearing car was the last time I would see him. I knew his family name and where he lived, but every time I phoned him after that, all I heard was an answering machine.

In any case, I suddenly found myself alone, at night in a strange city. The sign outside the building simply read YM/YWCA. Inside the gymnasium, a friendly clerk, wearing the company tracksuit, staffed the reception desk. When I asked how I would go about getting a room, I was informed that the YM/YWCA did not provide a residential service in Montreal. The clerk suggested that if I wanted cheap accommodation and a place to eat, I could try the building across and up the street. He added that he thought that it used to be the YMCA before the current organization built the gymnasium. The "Y" had abandoned the rooms-for-rent business long before his time.

"The rooms are nothing to write home about, but the price is right," he suggested.

I carted my luggage across the street. My heart was in my throat as I entered. I had never been in an establishment like it before. I'll never forget the smell and the noises. Welcome to Saturday night in Montreal.

The first thing I had to do was to make a choice. The clerk said the rates were, $20.00 for one night, $100 for a week or $300 for a month. I was pretty certain that I didn't want to stay there very long, but realistically I didn't think I would be able to find anything else in less than a week. That was my first experience at trying to make an important economic decision. I decided $100 was all I could afford.

I figured paying for my room was a good way of disposing of the $100 dollar bill I had, so handed it over. I was surprised when the clerk handed me back the exchange. I was amused by the color of the Canadian money and one was a two-dollar bill. How quaint.

"Welcome to Canada," he said with a big grin. "The exchange rate is in your favor."

I was assigned a room on the second floor. The wire grills on the windows were a subtle reminder that I was in the big city. The first night in my room was pretty frightening. The noise of people running up and down the hall went on well into the night. The lock on the door was pretty flimsy and the one chair in the room didn't reach the doorknob, so I piled my luggage against the door. I slept with my wallet inside my pillowcase.

Early the next morning, I could smell food being cooked in the restaurant, which was right below my room. I had an early breakfast. I don't remember what I had to eat, exactly, except that I was pretty hungry. I walked around the city for a few hours and about mid-day went back and had a soup and a cheese sandwich for lunch.

The cost of food made me realized that I would have to establish some limits as far as eating was concerned. Each morning I would go down stairs and have crepes (like a thin pancake) or toast and apple juice.

A couple of days later, I found a small restaurant a few blocks away. The advertised luncheon special was $3.49. The taste was good, but the servings were meager. At least I had one fairly good meal each day.

I also discovered a grocery store where I bought a daily supply of fruit. I rationalized that going to bed with an apple or a banana, as a late supper would be good for my waistline.

The first few days in Montreal were pretty lonely. In the downtown area of the city, the only people I met were clerks and waitresses. I learned to memorize the nametags worn by the clerks I met each day so that I could address them by name—as though we were old friends. Up until that point in my life, such employees were just people who provided a service.

I was eager to meet the office personnel I would pass on the street each day. Of course, those well-dressed people weren't around at night; so it soon became evident that I was going to have to do something about my lifestyle, i.e. find a job.

As I sat in my room each night, most of my thoughts were about ways to improve my financial situation. The $254 I had when I left home was running out alarmingly fast.

There was one other memorable thing about my life at the former "Y" residence. There was a young man who operated a magazine and convenience stand in the main lobby. As soon as he found out where I was from, he let it be known that he could help a "visitor" obtain a Social Insurance Card and Health Card—for a price. I didn't think I had any need for his behind-the-counter services, so I politely declined the offer.

CHAPTER 3

Life In Montreal

My first five days of living in Montreal went by quickly. I spent most of my time looking for work and thinking about survival. The week I had paid for at the former "Y" was quickly coming to an end. I would have to make a lodgings decision soon.

Thursday morning started the beginning of a string of good luck, although it was well disguised by some unusual circumstances. Oddly enough, my good fortune started with a growing need to do my laundry. On my way into the Laundromat around the corner, I saw a "Help Wanted" sign in the window. The family who managed the operation was fed up running the business around the clock. So, I started that night, on the graveyard shift. The job only paid minimum wage, but for the first time I had money coming in.

The next morning, I went "window shopping" at a supermarket, called a Carrefour. I found myself regaining consciousness on a bench outside one of the shops. Apparently, I had passed out, probably from a lack of food and working all night. In any case, a kindly lady sat there with me until I was able to stand up on my own. She introduced herself as Sister Greenwood. Holy cow! I was being rescued by a nun. What fooled me was that she was dressed in regular clothes. When she asked me where I lived and I told her it was at the former "Y," she offered to put me up for a few nights with some people she knew. I accepted gratefully.

On the way to Sister Greenwood's car, she explained that besides being the principal of a girls' finishing school, she was also responsible for a residence for senior nuns who had retired from teaching. Our first stop was the residence where I found myself carrying in Sister Greenwood's groceries and meeting several other nuns, most of whom wore the traditional habits.

Then Sister Greenwood took me over to meet Bob and Jean Rosser, who lived down the street. The Rossers were on a list of volunteers to take in cases like mine—young and single females on the street, so to speak. Sister Greenwood said that ordinarily she would have let me stay at the nun's residence for a day or two before introducing me to the Rossers. She didn't go through that routine this time because she had to leave the next morning for Ottawa to attend her sibling brother's 40th wedding anniversary.

The Rossers were a wonderful couple. Both in their 70s, they were as lively, friendly and generous as you would ever want to meet. The Rossers even drove me over to the "Y" to pick up my things. I ended up staying with them for about two weeks.

As Sister Greenwood left the Rossers' place, she asked me whether I was looking for a job. She gave me a name and a phone number to call in the morning. She said that the manager of a medical clinic had been asking her whether any of the students at her school needed employment.

At the clinic the next morning, the clinic manager informed me that they were looking for a clerk on the evening shift who could maintain the files, answer the phone and help patients fill in consultation forms. I guess the manager must have been desperate because the she hired me in less than an hour. She wanted me to start work the following Friday.

Naturally, I had to fill in a job application form at the medical clinic.

I gave the Rossers' address and left the space for Social Insurance Number and Health Card number blank, explaining that I had left my cards at home.

The next day, I went back to the magazine stand vendor at the former "Y" and arranged for a Social Insurance Card and a Health Card. He promised me the cards would be delivered in the mail in less than a week. We were so busy at the clinic the personnel department didn't bug me about the missing data. A few days after I started work the cards arrived in the mail. I had the cards sent to the clinic and since I had access to the mail, I was able to intercept them. I entered the numbers on the job forms and never heard another thing about it.

The salary at the clinic was minimum wage, but at least it wasn't the graveyard shift and the manager implied that there might be opportunities for promotion.

Within a few days, I had found an apartment, right downtown. It was the residence of my evening supervisor at the clinic, Thelma Odette, who was looking for somebody to share the rent. She agreed to carry my half of the rent until I received my first paycheque. I was intrigued by the way they spelled that word in Canada.

Thelma was your typical French-Canadian female worker—petite and chic to a fault. She dressed like a model. Thelma's curly black hair changed very little over the 13 years we lived together. You could tell when she became excited or angry. She would prattle away to herself in French. At first, that was a problem until I became more conversant in the language. We seemed to hit it off together. I'm sure we will be lifelong friends.

I worked hard at the clinic and Thelma recommended me for the position of evening supervisor at another clinic within the same company. The new clinic was still within walking distance in the opposite direction from our apartment.

Thelma became like a big sister to me. We went everywhere together. I soon learned that Thelma had a deep passion for mystery novels and the like, which led her to join a local organization called the Midnight Mystery Theatre. One night she invited me to observe a performance. After my first exposure to "participation murder plays,"

I was hooked. We would sit up for hours after each session discussing what we had missed and what each of us had figured out before the conclusions were revealed. Thelma often wrote letters to the organizers to let them know how to improve individual presentations. She eventually became a player.

During those years when we were active in the Midnight Mystery Theatre, I had thoughts about writing a play to contribute to the theatre's repertoire. The handouts the manager gave Thelma were simple enough. Most of them contained only her part and even she didn't know how the mystery ended. Only the manager knew. At the end of the evening, he would come out-of-character to summarize the clues and explain the ending to the audience.

After attending a few plays, I found my sleep was being affected. I began having a series of recurring dreams that wouldn't go away. The dreams were so vivid they would wake me up in the middle of the night. These nocturnal reveries were complicated by the fact that there were two murders that happened on the same spot, but separated by many years.

Every night the series of dreams would start at the common murder scene and branch out in different directions. The location looked much like the floor in front of the Macy House fire place at home in Teasdale. Sometimes one dream would be about the murder many years ago and sometimes it would be about a more recent murder. I could see every detail of the crime scene. As I tried to reconcile the two cases, even the smells of the various places I visited were unforgettable. I could clearly visualize how the victims died and who the murderers were. The nightly sessions became so intertwined and confusing that I was never able to come up with a logical ending.

After two or three weeks of dreaming basically the same set of dreams, I typed as much as could remember on Thelma's computer, hoping that exercise would let me return to sleeping normally. I spent several evenings sketching out the various plot lines and trying to link them all together. After a week or so, the dreams stopped and I was left with about 50 pages of notes that would be interesting only to me. All of a sudden my "play" had become the rudiments of a novel. With my limited skills as a writer, the draft production would take months and the story still needed an ending.

I gave my manuscript to a retired schoolteacher friend, who lived in our building, to assess its potential as a novel. He said that, among other things, I had a real problem with pronouns and their antecedents. He also pointed out a number of major problems with grammar, syntax, logic, punctuation and repetition, to say nothing of a strong tendency to use the passive voice. Apart from that, he allowed that my story was "interesting." I decided my opus could wait for another day.

Meanwhile, my work at the medical clinic began to take on new dimensions as well. As a consequence of reviewing patient documentation forms, I asked questions to clarify certain entries. I noticed some of the clients would tell me things about themselves that I'm sure they wouldn't ordinarily discuss with anybody else. For example, an older gentleman said that he had heard about a personal lubricant that goes on warm. He confided that the cold stuff he currently used causes a loss of stiffness and that was embarrassing, especially with his new wife. I suggested a baby bottle warmer.

My peers were aware that I was interested in furthering my education. One day my supervisor said she noticed that I seemed to have an unusual rapport with the clients. She suggested I should think about going into the professional medical field.

So I enrolled at McGill University as a medical student. I was accepted as a mature student and was able to secure sufficient student loans to cover most of my tuition. I was worried the university would check up on my Social Insurance Number and Health Card, but no one ever did. I may have left a few other facts out of certain application forms, but nobody asked about that either.

Toward the end of my first year at McGill, I changed jobs again. That move was another stroke of luck.

Thelma and I needed a lawyer to settle a dispute we had with our landlord. A co-worker recommended a friend, who worked for a high-profile law firm. We were suitably impressed when we saw her name, Connie Keeman, on the list of the law firm's principals outside the main entrance. Connie helped us well beyond the fifty bucks it cost.

During the visit to Ms Keeman's office, I noticed that there were several desks unoccupied. When I mentioned it, she asked me whether I could type. When I said that I had taken typing in high school, she offered me a job as a typist/ receptionist. The salary was nearly twice what I had been making at the medical clinic, so two weeks later I became a legal secretary. Well, that's stretching the truth a bit, but I learned quickly and did a lot of extra work and research on my own.

After a year or so of typing, filing and learning how the law worked, I decided to switch my university courses from medicine to law. It was a tough slog for almost nine years, working by day and attending classes at night for the most part.

Needless to say, once I started attending university, my social life was limited for several years, at least during the school terms. Most of the dates I had were university students, usually several years younger than me. Still, it was a welcome contrast from repetitive: work; study; eat; sleep routine.

I particularly enjoyed guys who were athletically inclined and took me out golfing, playing tennis or bowling. I even learned to let them win occasionally. Unfortunately, for the first few years, I seldom went out with anyone more than twice.

I guess I had been in Montreal for nearly five years when I met Jean-Guy Bellevance. He spoke English with a heavy French accent. He preferred not to speak English at all. Our relationship gave me an excellent opportunity to improve my French, which was becoming more and more mandatory in everyday life in Montreal. Besides, he showed some promise as a companion. The more we dated, the more determined he was that I should learn to speak French fluently. We went together for about two years and, with Thelma's help, I was well on the road to becoming bilingual.

Jean-Guy also taught me how to drive a car, but I could never convince him that turning right on a red light (which was against the law in Quebec at the time) would improve traffic flow and was perfectly safe.

The relationship with Jean-Guy worked out reasonably well, but we eventually broke up because of his political attitude. He was adamant that Quebec should become a separate country.

I don't know whether it was the break-up with Jean-Guy or not, but I slowly came to realize that I would never be able to pass my bar exams without being fully bilingual. About that time, my roommate Thelma suggested a self-help program for me. We started off with French-only days every Monday, Wednesday and Friday at the apartment. After a year or so, the only time I spoke English was with some of the customers at work.

My next relationship, also a McGill classmate, lasted only a few months. Wesley was probably the best-looking boyfriend I had during my time in Montreal, but a way too strong in his military interests for my liking. Besides attending McGill, he was an aide-de-camp to a Reserve army general. He was full of himself and liked to talk a lot. I wasn't unhappy when he stopped calling.

I wasn't really serious about another boyfriend until my final year at McGill. His name was Robert Hiebert and since his mother tongue was French, the "H" was silent. Robert was also a "mature" student. In fact, he was a graduate of the Royal Military College and then a pilot in the Royal Canadian Air Force. He had completed his compulsory service after graduation and was attending McGill to become a lawyer.

Not long after we met, Robert confided that he was more interested in obtaining a commercial pilot's licence than getting another degree. As part of his air force training, he was qualified as a private pilot but held only a white ticket for instrument flying. He needed a green ticket to fly for an airline. I went flying with him just about every second weekend.

Robert insisted that I attend the weather briefing each time we went up. I eventually became more familiar with cloud formations and weather conditions than I really needed to know.

Robert was serious about my personal preparations for flying as well. He insisted I check my own parachute and that I knew where all the controls on the airplane were and what they did.

Robert eventually passed his green ticket and applied for jobs with several commercial airlines. Just before he graduated from McGill, he received an offer from Qantas Airlines. He left without writing his final law exams. We did communicate regularly by phone and mail for a few months while he was under training in California, but once he was accepted full-time, about six months ago, he kind of drifted away. I don't even have a current address for him now.

After I received my degree, I became a professional staff member at the law firm where I originally started, but I was sent to another location. The articling year passed quickly and was rewarding. I received a lot of help from fellow staff members and assisted them on several cases. As a result, the bar exams contained little in the way of surprises and I was successful the first time.

I had been on staff as a full-fledged civil law lawyer for less than six months, when I was caught in another merger squeeze. It didn't take long to figure out that the newly constituted company had more civil law lawyers than cases. I had an unofficial chat with my supervisor and mentor, who advised me to expect a "downsizing program" to begin in a month.

There was also the not-so-small item of provincial politics and the fact that almost the only language spoken in court was French. I had become comfortable in speaking the romance language, but not enough to handle many of the legal subtleties.

I reluctantly phoned home to see whether Dad would consider taking me on staff. I was delighted when he agreed, but only on condition that I join him as a partner. When I received the official separation notice, my decision was made. I would go home.

My farewell luncheon was a subdued affair. After a few kind remarks, they presented me with a desktop day-timer. It was nice, but what I really liked about it was the pullout notebook. I put the notebook in my purse, but I never did use the larger day-timer. After all, during that last month I wasn't making many appointments.

I said my good-byes to the Simpsons and Sister Greenwood by phone. I met Bob and Jean Rosser for lunch at a downtown restaurant the afternoon before I left. I guess Jean must have liked me because she gave me her secret recipe for the most wonderful banana soup I've ever tasted.

My "big sister" Thelma and I decided the night before my departure that I would leave alone from our apartment by taxi to avoid a lot of tears at the airport. I tried my best to act as maturely as I could once the cab left the curb, but I'm sure my voice gave me away. The driver tried to engage me in conversation a few times, but stopped trying when he saw that I wasn't interested. I had just nicely recovered when the taxi stopped at the departure ramp at Dorval International.

CHAPTER 4

Going Home

My behavior must have seemed odd to a casual observer, as I went through the process of boarding the airplane. The clerk at the check-in counter looked at me quizzically when I had trouble finding my flight tickets. The attendant gave me the same look after I had to pass through the metal detector three times. Needless to say, my anxiety level was up a few notches by then. It was such a relief to finally settle into my seat on the plane.

The giant plane rolled slowly down the runway, gathered speed and finally lifted off. The exhilaration of the takeoff slowly dissipated as the plane settled into a steady climb as we burst through the thin layer of clouds that covered the island city.

I thought about the past few days. My emotions had been alternating between joy and depression. I was happy to be going home, but sad to be leaving a lot of friends from Montreal. Tears welled up again. I wasn't expecting the short flight to Baltimore to be such an emotional event.

By the time the plane made the transition to level flight, the happy side of my feelings began to predominate. The tears of joy that rolled down my cheeks didn't embarrass me, but I turned my face toward the window as a reflex action. I didn't want to talk to anybody for a while. I was delighted that Dad had so understood on the phone; the rest was just plain nostalgia.

Leaving home 13 years ago, I never expected to return, much less be welcomed back. At the age of seventeen, I was more than ready to act as an adult and convinced that my parents were making too many decisions for me without considering my opinions or feelings. As far as I was concerned, their attitude concerning my life and my friends was completely wrong.

Now at the age of 30, I was prepared to admit that my judgment might have been based on too much emotion. Perhaps my decision to leave, the way I did, may even have been immature.

It took me a long time to fill out the customs form as the plane approached Baltimore. I know it sounds silly, but I couldn't remember which day it was. I wrote May 2003 and left a space in front, hoping the day would come to me later. Each entry made me think about how this story all started.

Just before the flight attendant picked up the customs form, I checked my ticket. There it was, Sunday, 4 May. I filled in the missing data and settled back into my seat and closed my eyes.

In general, I would have to say that my life in Montreal had been interesting, but I don't think I would recommend it as a career path— too much of it depended on luck.

As the plane circled the airport in preparation for landing, I wondered how Dad had changed over the years. He would be well into his sixties by now. All I can tell you is what he was like and how he appeared to me then.

Dad was about six feet tall and naturally thin. No matter how much he ate, he never put on weight. When I left home, Dad's hair was light brown, with a hint of a curl on the sides and the back. I dare say it must be fully gray or maybe even white by now. He didn't really comb his hair. He just let it fall forward and to the sides. He had a natural part just off the center of his forehead. He always said that when his hair touched his eyebrows it was time for a hair cut. After a fresh haircut, his right ear appeared to be noticeably closer to his head. Even as a kid, I knew he was sensitive about the shape of his ears.

I remembered his bright blue eyes and his teeth had a yellow hue to them, probably from the pipe that he used to smoke occasionally. Some of his teeth were a bit crooked.

Dad's taste in clothes used to be late Eisenhower or early Kennedy era. He purchased a new suit every ten years whether he need one or not. You might say he was thrifty.

I remember Dad as the most honest man I'd ever met. Really, he was too honest for his own good. You can identify certain generations such as the 'X' Generation or the Baby Boomers. Well, Dad's generation can be identified as those who come to a full stop at STOP sign.

Dad didn't smile much, but he was always cracking jokes, mainly at his own expense. He had what you would call a dry sense of humor. He worked hard and once he took on a case, he never gave up. I'm sure his clients received more than their money's worth.

At least, that's the way I remember my dad. I would find out, soon enough.

CHAPTER 5

The Macy Family

Quite frankly, I was deep in thought when Heather came into my office carrying her photo album. It took me a moment to mentally switch gears from re-reading Arthur's letter to evaluating the quality of the picture she was holding. We discussed the picture for a few minutes including where it was taken. I had to confess I really didn't remember what Casey looked like and the photograph was only slightly helpful. I suggested we let Sergeant Woznica decide. Heather put the Polaroid aside and began to review some of the other pictures in her album.

The truth was Arthur's letter was of far more interest to me at that moment and I must confess my eyes were beginning to glaze over.

Apart from one postcard 20 years ago, the letter that had arrived with Arthur's ashes was the first meaningful correspondence from my twin brother in 30 years. My mind slowly drifted back in time. There were so many things he mentioned that I had to think about and rationalize.

I wondered why and how Arthur became involved in the murder of

30 years ago. The more I thought about the crowd Arthur associated with, the more the letter made sense.

I hoped his letter would answer some questions that I had been thinking about for years. I searched for clues as to why our father and Grandpa George were so secretive about the ownership of the General's Farm. Why did I feel compelled to keep the secret going? Why couldn't my father have told me, before he died, how the General's Farm property taxes were paid? Why had he willed Macy House to Arthur and the General's Farm to me?

As I thought about those questions, I remembered my father telling me when I was a little boy, how this old, stone house came to be called Macy House. "Before houses had numbers," he said, "those built along Old Military Road were referred to by the names of the original occupants." For some reason, that custom didn't seem appropriate for the Hoar family. No one ever called it the Hoar House.

I tried to remember as far back as I could, to see whether anything would help to answer my questions. Things came to mind that I hadn't thought about in years.

My father was always reluctant to talk about his personal life. Other than telling us that our mother died when Arthur and I were born, he said very little. He raised Arthur and me by himself.

The only thing I remember clearly about attending high school in Melcastle was that is where I met my future wife Bonnie Douglass. I also met Vincent Simpson and after he and I attended law school in Philadelphia he became my law partner for a while. Vincent's future wife Lois Auger also hung around with us. Lois eventually persuaded Vincent to join her father's law firm in Montreal.

Lois insisted on the French pronunciation of her surname. So we formed the habit of calling her "Oh-jay" for Auger. It wasn't until after the murder trial involving OJ Simpson that I realized how amusing their wedding announcement "Auger-Simpson" would read in Canada.

After I graduated from law school, Bonnie and I married and we moved into Macy House with my father. He was delighted to have company again. He said it was much like the situation when he and my mother moved in with Grampa George.

The year 1973 was one of significant events for Bonnie and me. Things started to happen about the time Heather was born in April. Naturally, we were all excited about our first-born child and didn't pay much attention to the fact that my twin brother made a sudden decision to leave town to live in western Canada. Arthur had just become a journeyman electrician and lived at various places in the area. My father made no effort to hide his disappointment in the way Arthur lived his life. Arthur kept his reasons secret as to why he left.

Arthur's departure didn't seem important at the time. Arthur hardly communicated with us before he left and, with the exception of one brief post card, not at all afterwards. Immediately prior to Arthur's departure, he had been living with Roger and Ruby Wendelman at the General's Farm. My father would see Arthur at the main building when he went to collect the rent each month.

Roger and Ruby were high school classmates. I was surprised, therefore, to learn that Ruby had been admitted in 1973 to the Windemere Estates, a state-run criminal ward and psychiatric hospital located a few miles west of Melcastle. I discovered she was there when I visited a client at the Estates. I almost didn't recognize her when we passed one another in the hall. She was being pushed in a wheelchair and had a bandage completely covered the top of her head. I couldn't understand why Ruby was in the criminal side.

After I completed my appointment with my client, I stopped at the front desk to confirm that Ruby was an inmate. I visited her occasionally after that, but she never spoke at any time. With Ruby unable or unwilling to speak and a guard present at all times, visits were very short. As for Roger, he disappeared about that time and no one has seen him since.

The final surprising event in 1973 occurred as we were preparing to celebrate New Year's Eve at Macy House. Dad died unexpectedly of a heart attack. Our loss was soon overtaken by the requirements of a growing child and dealing with Bonnie's growing list of illnesses. I don't know what I would have done without full insurance coverage.

I had little time to think about my life in general and how my career turned out. I've been a practicing lawyer in Maryland and Pennsylvania for nearly forty years. Teasdale, Maryland has been my home, but the majority of my practice is in Pennsylvania, mainly Melcastle. My practice has been waning over the last few years and thoughts of retirement have entered my mind fairly frequent lately. The problem is I can't afford to retire. I know I should have been putting some money away each year, but those plans tended not to work out.

There were always some things more important, especially when Bonnie became seriously ill. Initially, she was diagnosed with a deteriorating heart condition and high blood pressure. Eventually, I had to hire a nurse to come to the house during the week, virtually on a full-time basis. Mrs. Mouncey became almost like a member of the family.

I did the best I could to help Bonnie cope with her physical limitations. As time went on, she became susceptible to periods of depression, which became progressively worse. My work became secondary.

Dr. Hammersmyth eventually persuaded me to have Bonnie admitted to the Windemere Estates. I was reluctant at first because of the reputation the state institution for the criminally insane with which medical facility was co-located. It helped that Dr. Hammersmyth, who used to be our family doctor, had become the resident psychiatrist.

There were times when Bonnie barely recognized me during my weekly visits. Fortunately, her ability to remember people and things has improved lately. Medical research has developed more effective medications and Bonnie has longer periods when she is quite lucid and stronger than when she was first admitted. Now, with the use of a wheelchair or a walker, she is able to move around quite well by herself.

Bonnie has been at Windemere Estates for about five years. When Bonnie was first admitted, there were times when she would swing from near normal to childlike in her mental state, and back again—all in a two hour visit. Dr. Hammersmyth's dedication seems to be helping her progress. Bonnie obviously feels comfortable with him. Her mobility was much improved the last time I visited, but she was still somewhat reluctant to initiate most conversations.

Bonnie and I were fortunate to have children at all. Heather was our only child that survived. Bonnie actually was pregnant three times. The first time Bonnie was with child, the pregnancy ended in a miscarriage. Heather survived the second maternity. Bonnie's third pregnancy was a boy, but he died shortly after delivery. Heather knows nothing about the other two pregnancies. The "need-to-know" attitude seems to have become a way of life in the Macy clan.

Heather grew to be a bright, beautiful and energetic woman. She had curly, auburn hair, which she usually wore short. She was always at the top of her class and regularly won French and English prizes. We were sure one day she would go off to an institution of higher learning. As far as Bonnie and I were concerned, it was only a matter of which city. Our only problem was figuring out how we could afford the chosen university, or so we thought.

A major family quarrel flared up shortly after Heather turned sixteen. It mainly had to do with Bonnie's strong dislike for Heather's boyfriend, Casey. Heather abruptly left home shortly after her seventeenth birthday. We made some futile attempts to stop her and it was some time later we found out where she had gone. We were pretty certain she had gone with Casey Clarkin and that he originally lived in Montreal. A phone call to my former law partner, Vincent Simpson, resulted in a return call a couple of weeks later informing us that Heather was living with a female friend in the city and had a job.

The next year, Heather phoned me at my office in Melcastle. It was a short conversation. I'm sure she was as nervous as I was. It seems Heather just wanted to let us know she was well, had a full-time job as a supervisor in a medical clinic and was planning on attending McGill University in the fall as a medical student. It wasn't until after she hung up that I realized that it was her birthday.

I never told Bonnie, but I used to receive phone calls at the down town office from Heather about once a year. We never spoke for more than one or two minutes each time. Whenever I would ask Heather where she was living or working, she would say everything was okay and would change the subject.

CHAPTER 6

Macy House

It wasn't much of leap from reviewing my family history to my draft response to the letter I recently received from the Teasdale Historical Foundation requesting input on the historical background of Macy House. My first draft was sitting on the corner of my desk. As I wrote it, I remember being concerned about not revealing any clues as to the Macy family ownership of the main house at the General's Farm.

I glanced over at Heather. She seemed to be off in her own little world as she gazed at the open photo album that was cradled by her crossed legs.

I quickly re-read my hand-written notes on Macy House.

Macy House was built just after the First World War, by my Grandfather, W. George Macy. The construction of

Macy House was based on the same floor plan and materials as the 150-year-old main building at the General's Farm.

My father, W. Horace Macy, ably assisted Grampa George in building Macy House. My father obviously learned quite a bit from Grampa George because he eventually became a successful general contractor and land developer himself.

Grampa George was a stonemason by trade. He was also a part-time carpenter, electrician, plumber and general handyman. According to my father, Grampa George was responsible for building most of the houses along Old Military Road and a few buildings in the city of Melcastle.

The last major repairs made to Macy House were to upgrade the plumbing and the wiring in 1954. Both my father and grandfather were frugal people. I was in my early teens at the time and my help really wasn't required.

I had the porch and parts of the roof replaced a few years ago because the carpenter, who was also a client, knew the source of the special slate tiles the job required.

A half acre lot on a low hill on the north side of Old Military Road was chosen as the site for Macy House because of the unobstructed southern view. Most of the lots directly opposite were unsuitable for housing due to the flood plane of the Carrot River.

Few trees can survive in the rock and clay mixture along Old Military Road. The soil becomes rockier closer to the General's Mountain. The Wye oak tree is Maryland's state tree and the Union Army probably planted the trees along Old Military Road before the Civil War.

There is a common split rail fence, stacked about three feet high, between many of the houses and behind most on the north side of Old Military Road.

The U-shaped driveway at Macy House is squared off in front of the house to provide parking for about five cars. The old flagpole on the lawn between the "In" and "Out" lanes hasn't carried a flag since I was in high school.

Macy House looks like a typical hip-roofed bungalow from the front view. Two ornamental pillars flank the double front doors, noticeably offset to the right of center. Six square windows, in pairs of two, face the street. The 18-inch thick exterior walls are constructed of quarried stones, held together with pinkish cement. The old-fashioned gray slate roof provides an overhang of about two feet along the front and back of the house.

Inside the entranceway there is a relatively large reception area. The house is divided into two halves, domestic and business. The business entrance is made apparent on the left by a set of double doors with clear glass on the upper half. Through the glass, two offices can be seen as well as the entrance to a conference room at the end of the hall.

On the right, one enters the domestic portion through the "PRIVATE" door. The living quarters is basically another bungalow, set at right angles to the front of the house. The overall floor plan is L-shaped.

The most impressive feature in the living quarters is the double fireplace made of quarried stone similar to the outside of the house. This massive stone structure is really two fireplaces offset by 90 degrees (one facing south and the other facing east) and served by a common fire-pit. The smaller fireplace is seen first, immediately on the left. It was originally designed as a baker's oven, but was closed up to improve the efficiency of the larger one. The main fireplace is around the corner facing the living room. Its opening is about five feet high and six feet across with a ten foot mantelpiece.

The continuous apron in front of both fireplaces is constructed of common fieldstone extending out about four feet on all sides. Inlaid hardwood flooring extends beyond the apron and throughout the rest of Macy House.

Past the double fireplace are a combination kitchen, dining and living room. The window over the kitchen sink provides a view of the parking lot, glimpses of the Carrot River and the mountains in the distance.

A cathedral ceiling runs all the way from the kitchen to the back of the house. Around the corner on the left, the wall formed by the main fireplace and the bedrooms extends to the peak of the house. The enclosed space above the bedrooms is used for storage.

The bathroom is located behind the fireplace and next to the master bedroom. A few years ago, I had a door installed between the bathroom and the master bedroom. The objective of that door was to avoid having to go through the living room to move from one room to the other. The logic of that never seemed to have occurred to my grandfather.

The only other enhancement was the television cable we had put in several years ago. We had to pay extra because there aren't that many houses along Old Military Road once you're outside the village of Teasdale.

CHAPTER 7

Why The Ownership Secret?

I really can't explain why I never told either Bonnie or Heather about the Macy family ownership of the General's Farm. It was just something I grew up with and never seemed terribly important. All I can say is that the farm was among the several bits of property and businesses in which Grampa George and my father made investments in the local area. The only property I ever remember them talking about was when they bought the General's Farm.

It wasn't until I visited the General's Farm as a teenager that I understood their fascination with that particular piece of property. Every month-end my father would go to collect the rent. I would accompany him as often as I could. Sometimes as a treat, my father would take me out to the balcony. The unobstructed view was always spectacular at any time of the year. My father explained to me that when the army constructed the building, the site location was most important as an observation post.

Grampa George and my father apparently purchased the land and buildings during the great depression. Taxes on the General's Farm had been in arrears for many years and it was eventually expropriated by the city. Because there were so many municipal properties and abandoned private estate sales taking place at the time, the city administration conducted some property sales by mail. As a rule, anything that belonged to the city would have a minimum bid limit contained in the specifications when those particular properties were put up for disposal.

Somehow, the General's Farm was advertised as an estate sale, with no minimum bid. When Grampa George and Dad noticed it had "no minimum bid," they put in a token bid and apparently nobody else bothered. I don't know what they paid for it, but Grampa George and Dad would laugh every time the subject came up.

When Grampa George died, the deed papers and the survey maps for the General's Farm were passed on to my father. After I finished university, I persuaded my father to make up a will. He had me list the General's Farm as an asset worth $2,013. I found that to be an odd figure, but I didn't question it. He put the will with the other papers in the safe in the conference room.

My father never revealed the details about the General's Farm ownership. Perhaps the reason the two of them kept the purchase a secret was because they were worried that if the error were ever revealed, the transaction would be rescinded.

Dad did say one thing shortly before he died: "Don't worry about the taxes, Henry. I've set up a trust fund and the interest should cover the taxes forever. It's a financial arrangement with a corporate lawyer from Baltimore. The fund was his way of paying for a summer cottage that I built for him at Candle Lake."

I know the farm used to cost Dad about $65 a year for the taxes back in 1973, because after he died I would annually receive a letter with a receipt for the taxes paid. It came in an odd shaped envelope had no return address, just a string of numbers on the top left hand corner.

A year or so after Dad died, a fire completely destroyed the Land Records Office in Melcastle. Apparently, whatever backup system the city had was either destroyed or non-existent. After the fire, the city administration had more important problems than verifying the ownership of the General's Farm. The city finance department was content to know that the taxes were being paid. As long as the money kept coming, the officials weren't terribly interested in who actually owned the property.

The operation of the Land Records Office was in disarray for many years after the fire. The only official way the city administrators could tell who owned any particular piece of property was to have the people who claimed ownership, to come in with certified deeds and have a copy placed on file. My guess is that less than ten percent of the lots in Melcastle and district were identified that way. All others had to be certified by obtaining affidavits from four immediate neighbors. Even today, I receive requests from clients to do property certifications.

The name "General's Farm" started at some point during the Civil War because an army general occupied it. Military recruitment and training arrangements have changed considerably since the nineteenth century. I'm told the soldiers, who were generally farmers, kept their animals by the Carrot River while the animal's owners were paid for serving in the army at that post. That was an agreeable arrangement, until the Civil War broke out and the soldiers had to be prepared for battle.

The main building on the farm was said to be haunted by ghosts of prisoners who didn't survive the Civil War. I've been meaning to ask Bill Hird, the Teasdale Historical Foundation Research Director, whether Civil War prisoners were ever held on-site. Come to think of it, Roger Wendelman, who used to rent the main building from my father, disappeared without a trace some 30 years ago. Maybe his ghost still haunts the place.

The buildings on the farm are located about three-quarters of the way up the General's Mountain, which isn't really a mountain at all. In fact, the land formation is just an unusually high riverbank; with scrub bushes covering most of the Maryland lower level and trees on the Pennsylvania crest. The land on the other side of the mountain's crest slopes gently toward Melcastle, the main population center. Friends tell me the city is starting to encroach on the north side.

The city of Melcastle used to provide property administration for several rural areas immediately surrounding the city. At the time of the fire, the Pennsylvania portion of the General's Farm property was too far out of the city to be of much interest to the city administration. In fact, the General's Farm didn't officially become part of the city of Melcastle until the early 1990s, when several surroundings municipalities were amalgamated into the Greater Melcastle Area.

There are actually two buildings that make up the General's Farm: the main building and a cottage. The main building is all that can be seen as you approach the site, going up Old Military Road on the Maryland side of the mountain. The cottage is hidden in the woods about 50 feet away from the main building, off to the east and a bit south. You would have to know exactly where the cottage is in order to see it.

The cottage has been occupied by Albert McClelland for as long as I can remember. I have always assumed that Mr. McClelland was a descendant of the original resident. My father rarely spoke about the old man.

At one time, both the main building and the cottage were entirely on the Pennsylvania side of the border. That apparently changed just after the turn of the twentieth century, when the boundary was redrawn to place the border line thirty feet farther north, putting most of the cottage in Maryland. Two British surveyors, by the names of Mason and Dixon, did the original survey in 1767.

The main building was constructed with the same materials as Macy House: mainly quarried stones and a dark gray slate roof. The right hand portion of the farmhouse (equivalent to the domestic part of Macy House) is built back into a ravine. The army probably kept its horses in a passageway underneath. The ravine forms a natural corral behind the building.

Because of the steep slope of the mountain, the rear portion of the rest of the building is dug into the mountainside. Even so, the front of the main floor is significantly elevated above the road. A portico constructed on the front gives the farmhouse the appearance of a two-storey building. Four matching columns made of cement and small, rounded stones support the portico. There's a narrow driveway underneath the portico. A massive stone stairway, centered under the portico, leads to the main floor.

The balcony on top of the portico, estimated elevation about 300 feet above the Carrot River, provides an even better southern panoramic view of the countryside than you experience at Macy House. From the balcony, one can see the giant bend in the Carrot River as it comes from the northwest side of the mountain and passes to the southeast. It's good for the soul to watch the changing seasons from up there.

After my father died, old man McClelland paid the rent for his cottage for a few months and then stopped without explanation. I wasn't going to make a federal case out of $15 a month. Maybe I should have because that was 30 years ago and that money would have added up to quite a tidy sum by now.

When I inherited the farm in 1973, I had one more reason not to take any further landlord-type action against Mr. McClelland for non-payment of rent. Back in my early high school days, I was rather fond of his daughter, Ruby. She was my first love. As fate would have it, she married Roger Wendelman and the two of them moved into the main house, where they lived for about 10 years. Roger never held a job. They lived basically on Ruby's salary working for the city.

During the summer of 1973, there were several rumors about the Wendelmans. The most credible one was that Ruby Wendelman was found by the police, repeatedly scrubbing the floor in front of the fireplace and unable to communicate with anyone. She was taken to Windemere. All we know for sure is that Ruby was pregnant.

The rumors suggested that there was some connection between Roger's disappearance and Ruby's incarceration at Windemere. How and why she admitted was all kept very quiet. No one knows what happened to the child Ruby was carrying when she was admitted. All I know is we were more concerned with the birth of our first child, Heather, about that time.

Several years ago I discovered evidence that someone had been staying in the main building periodically. I first noticed a backpack on the floor beside the little fireplace and a pair of muddy boots at the top of the stairs.

A few months later, I suddenly came face-to-face with a young man who appeared to have made himself at home. He glared at me, as though I were threatening his territory. At first, I was too frightened to challenge him. He looked menacingly at me as he stood near the kitchen with a small log in his hands. We were in a kind of a Mexican standoff for a few moments. I asked him what he was doing there, but he didn't answer. He just threw the log into the smaller fireplace, stroked his short beard and watched the log catch fire. He seemed mesmerized by the fire. Without saying another word, I slowly backed down the stairs. I had ghastly visions in my mind of him attacking me and disposing of my body in the fireplace. Because of my secret ownership, no one would think to look for me at the General's Farm, except maybe Albert McClelland, the hermit who lived in the cottage next door.

The next time I went back to the farm, the young man wasn't in the house and his possessions were gone. However, it wasn't long before he was back again. Eventually, we came to know one another a little better, but still we didn't talk much. When he did speak, he spoke with great difficulty—halting like a frightened child. I never did learn his name or where he came from. I felt sorry for him more than anything. Lately, he seemed to have become used to my visits and didn't give me that penetrating stare that frightened me at first.

During the past year, I found myself visiting the main building at least once a month. I would even go up to the farm when the road was hardly passable. He would often join me on the balcony. Out there, neither of us would say very much. We would both stand there for five or ten minutes and look out over the countryside. I always left the balcony first. As I drove down the hill, I would watch my "guest" in my rear-view mirror, but he never returned my wave.

As I approach retirement age, the view from the balcony has become more and more a part of my daily thoughts. I have often wondered what it would be like to live up there permanently. I also thought about the fact that when the Pennsylvania Heritage Society was successful in getting the main building designated as an Historical Site would that make them my quasi-landlord? But, that's getting ahead of the story.

CHAPTER 8

My Career And SPA-KAL

I have always been suspicious about the affairs of a clandestine property management syndicate called SPA-KAL. The syndicate has kept the identity of its membership private ever since it appeared on the scene at least forty years ago.

I didn't know it at the time, but the nefarious SPA-KAL group had been attempting to buy the General's Farm even before it came into my possession. Perhaps that's another reason why my father and Grampa George went to great lengths to keep the ownership secret. I was stuck with the secret and didn't really know why. It took 30 years and two murders to determine which party would give in first—SPA-KAL or me.

The first incident happened a few years after I opened an office in Melcastle. SPA-KAL bought the building my first office was in, tore it down and made the land into a parking lot.

A similar eviction happened a few years later to an old college classmate of mine, Vincent Simpson in the village of Kinistino. I had made a graduation-day promise to Vincent that if he were unsuccessful in setting up a practice in his hometown, I would set up a partnership with him. He moved into the second office in Macy House and brought a small list of clients with him.

My practice was modest, but looked as though it would grow. However, it wasn't long before Vincent and I realized that we needed more clients. In order to qualify for Pennsylvania government contracts, we knew we had to establish an address in that state. So we opened up a small office in Melcastle. I agreed to work in the city half days.

Business did improve significantly, but it wasn't enough as far as Vincent's wife, Lois, was concerned. After she and Vincent moved to Montreal, I worked alone for a couple of years. I continued to rent the tiny office in Melcastle and bid only on those contracts I could handle by myself.

About ten years ago, another lawyer approached me with an offer I couldn't refuse. My new partner and I ended up renting a suite in a brand-new, eight-storey building we called the "Sparrow Building," named after Murdock Sparrow, a prominent businessman and mayor of Melcastle for many years.

I was concerned at first about the overhead expenses of the new quarters, but my new partner convinced me that income growth, based on steady business from his government sources in Pennsylvania, would more than cover the extra expenses.

The arrangement was that my partner and I would have a double office, rent-free for the first year—if we signed a ten-year lease. That was fine for a couple of years, until my partner skipped town with a sizeable amount of money from our clients. It took me two years to clean up that mess. I survived and business did increase enough to eventually support the lease.

The office in the Sparrow Building also brought me in more frequent contact with Judge Jack Sewchuk. Jack's old law firm was in the Sparrow Building. I had a dislike for Jack dating back to high school days. We never did hang around with each other very much. We came from totally different social backgrounds—he from the elite establishment of the grand city of Melcastle and I from the tiny little Teasdale. Jack was an arrogant and snobbish SOB even then.

We both became lawyers and, as you might expect, attended different universities, me, to law school in Philadelphia, and he, to Harvard. After graduation, he joined his father's firm in Melcastle. I had to spend most of my time in the early years building my practice, whereas Jack didn't.

I always considered myself at least the equal of Jack Sewchuk when we both were lawyers, but he became a judge early on in his career. As lawyers, Jack and I came face-to-face in court on two cases only. I'm pleased to say I won both cases.

It wasn't long after the second case that Judge Buck Meller died and the race was on to fill the vacancy. Six months prior to the election, the Sewchuk family, and the Byrd family that Jack married into, used their collective influence to have Jack appointed acting judge. Most of us in the legal community thought Jack, having lost several high profile cases, wouldn't even enter the election, let alone win it.

There were certain other improprieties in Jack's background. He had several "driving while intoxicated" convictions, but the most significant item was an affair with "another woman" that resulted in a child. In spite of all the negative elements, Jack put his name up for election. His opponents failed to factor in the political influence of the Byrd family and their connections with the so-called higher society. I believe even Jack was surprised that he won.

I had thought of entering the competition for the vacant judge's position. My father was well known and I had won quite a few high profile court cases. But my lack of financial resources forced me to sit and silently cheer on the opposition.

It was just as well that I didn't enter because Bonnie was pregnant and due on the day of the election. As it turned out, she had a miscarriage during the middle of the campaign.

I must say Jack probably wouldn't have done as well without the help of several other prominent citizens outside his considerable family connections. He had no shortage of money. Terry Andersen-Koop, the soon-to-be Senator from Melcastle, virtually managed

Jack's campaign. Val Albertson and her sister, Cynthia Leblond, both wives of wealthy businessmen, provided active support. And, of course, there was Jack's wife, Rose. She managed the Melcastle Journal, which gave Jack full endorsement. Rose and her sister Lenore inherited the Byrd family fortune, which included a string of newspapers around the country.

One could say the high school relationship between Jack and me slowly turned from adolescent competition to cordial distrust.

I'm not sure how much the rivalry had to do with what happened about four years ago. I signed a contract to conduct background research of various property holdings in the area. I didn't realize when I started that most of the addresses I was assigned had recently been purchased by SPA-KAL.

A tall, balding man, with a considerable paunch, presented the contract. He approached me in my office and introduced himself as, Pierre Barnard. He asked me whether I would be interested in doing some property research. I had a lot of experience in that field, so I said I probably would.

At first, Mr. Barnard wouldn't even tell me the firm he was representing. The proposed job was a simple offer. I could work at my own pace, tracking the history of individual property sites in the greater Melcastle area at $125 per site. He estimated that each "case" would take about two hours to complete. I would be expected to complete a quota of at least four assigned addresses per week. At the end of the brief conversation, he left me a plain business card that read:

Pierre Barnard:
Hal-Burton Property Development Corp.
Pennsylvania Division.

I discovered an odd note on the reverse side of his card. There was a casual, hand-written entry: "Washington office." Below that was a 1-800 number. Curiously the first three characters of last seven were the letters "FBI" instead of "324." At first, I dismissed the letters as somebody fooling around with the numbers and accidentally transformed them into those particular letters. Curiosity eventually overcame me and I dialed the number. When the person at the other end of the phone line answered, "Federal Bureau of Investigation," I quickly hung up.

Other than the initial meeting, my only contacts with Barnard were by phone. He usually responded to my requests for a personal conversation within the hour. Otherwise, I was instructed: "Drop off your weekly report at Room 303 in the Sparrow Building." He also informed me that the sign on the office door would be marked, "Harold E. Burton, Property Development Corporation" or "Hal-Burton" for short. "Those who know the founder call it Hal E. Burton," he added, with a little smile.

I found the instruction strange at first, because I knew the FBI had a highly visible office that you could see when the elevator happened to stop on the second floor. The entrance was complete with security guards and an electronically controlled glass door.

Each week when I turned in my report, the receptionist would give me a supply of questionnaires, compilation instructions, and a new list of assigned addresses to research.

After a while, I became familiar with the whole routine and Barnard and two or three months would pass between calls. That was fine with me. The checks, with the Hal-Burton logo in the top left-hand corner, came in the mail as regularly as my reports were submitted. The address on the checks was Washington, D.C. and the phone number was the same as the one on Barnard's business card, except the digits 3, 2, 4 had replaced the hand written FBI letters that had been on the back of his card.

The few property owners who owned their homes prior to the 1973 fire were the easy ones to document. For the rest, I had to visit the new Land Records Office, one or two real estate offices, and at least one lawyer for each time the property was sold. Some cases were very time consuming.

The "special contract" work had become a staple part of my income for over the last four years. At times, I found myself working a lot at night to fill the quota of four clients a week.

As time went by, I noticed that more and more of the assigned addresses were now owned by SPA-KAL. I became suspicious that SPA-KAL was the real target of my contract.

Up until I started working on the property research contract, the only thing that SPA-KAL meant to me personally was that the syndicate owned the Sparrow Building. I, like most people, believed Murdock Sparrow's money financed the construction of the building and the letters "SPA" of the SPA-KAL logo stood for Sparrow. The other speculation was the "KAL" stood for Ben Kalloway, the syndicate lawyer.

I never gave the logo much thought until I realized that Murdock Sparrow has been dead for about seven years and Ben Kalloway had been retired from his law practice almost as long. The burning question: "Who were the principals of SPA-KAL today?" My gut feel was that Jack Sewchuk and Harvey Parslow, the former chief of police, were involved. The association between Jack and Harvey went back at least 45 years. My guess was that if Jack and Harvey weren't the owners, they knew who were.

While documenting the sites that involved SPA-KAL, I detected an undercurrent of apprehension that I was unable to capture in my reports. The tension was most noticeable on the faces of immediate past owners who sold their properties to the SPA-KAL syndicate directly. When I asked those owners, whether they felt they had received a fair price for their property, they hesitated and then replied in the affirmative. I'll never forget the look on one man's face as he replied to my question. He stared directly into my eyes with a kind of pleading look that I didn't understand. I also noticed that some of the verbal answers by the former owners sounded almost rehearsed.

As a wag once said, "it doesn't take a rocket surgeon" to notice that most of the "persuaded" properties were located just off the new highway interchange on the eastern approach to Melcastle. If the houses were removed, the amalgamated land would make an ideal location for a fairly large shopping mall. The only successful mall in Melcastle was in the west end and it was not owned by SPA-KAL.

Four years of property research contract work made me feel more like an undercover agent than a lawyer. I became increasingly concerned that the persuasive tactics of the SPA-KAL organization were suspect. I secretly hoped that my efforts on the contract would eventually force SPA-KAL to reveal their membership.

CHAPTER 9

Heather's Return

One morning about a year ago, I was surprised when Heather called to say she had graduated from the McGill Law School and had a job with a large law firm in Montreal. She had completed her articling assignment, written her bar exams, and was sure she had done well. She was expecting to be called to the bar in a few days.

I had no idea Heather was even interested in the legal profession. I congratulated her and wished her well. When I asked her where she was living, she didn't answer directly and gave me the impression she wasn't ready to let me know that information just yet.

Then, two months ago, Heather called to say she had passed her bar exams and had been called to the bar. She also added that her firm had recently been taken over by another firm and she had been given the unofficial word that her chances of staying on with her current employer were slim. The newly created firm had more than enough civil law lawyers. "Besides," she said, "the politics and bilingualism problems in Quebec are starting to bother me."

"You're always welcome here, you know," I assured her.

"I'm glad to hear you say that, Dad. Does the offer of a partnership still hold?"

"Certainly does."

"That's very nice of you, Dad, but it will depend on whether the company lets me go and the kind of settlement is offered."

"It kind of looks like we'll be seeing you in the near future."

"Yeah, I guess you're right, Dad. I'll phone you when I'm ready."

I couldn't tell whether her good-bye was one of happiness, excitement or resignation. I thought about it for some time after she hung up and concluded that it was probably a mixture of all three.

It was Saturday, the third of May, just before noon, when Heather called again to say she and her law firm had come to a financial settlement and she was coming home. She advised me she had picked up her severance check and all she had left to do was finish packing. She said she would be on the morning flight to Baltimore—arriving at noon.

I spent the rest of Saturday afternoon getting ready for Heather's arrival. I drove into Melcastle to pick up a few supplies for the house. Heather's return would certainly change my bachelor-like existence. I spent a few hours that evening scurrying around tidying up the house.

Ever since Bonnie was hospitalized, I've had to hire someone to keep the house at least halfway clean and respectable. The cleaning lady I've employed for the past seven or eight years only comes every two weeks. She wasn't due until Monday and the house was in obvious need of her expertise.

On the way to the airport on Sunday morning, I couldn't help thinking about the day Heather left. I've thought about that day many times and wondered whether I could have done anything differently to prevent her leaving.

It had been 13 years since Heather went away. Heather didn't know it, but on the day she left, I was approaching our driveway as her taxi was leaving. When I went in the house, Bonnie told me, through a flood of tears, that Heather had left home without saying good-bye or where she was headed.

I had an idea where her boyfriend, Casey Clarkin lived. I drove by the apartment building in time to see Heather carrying her suitcase and knapsack up the front stairs. I parked my car around the corner. The elevator doors had closed by the time I entered the lobby. I checked the names on the registry to confirm there was a Clarkin listed. I knew that Casey came from Montreal and now I was reasonably certain where Heather was headed. I stood there for several minutes considering whether or not I should press the "call" button for his apartment. I had to make up my mind quickly because another tenant was entering the front door.

Assuming Heather had gone up to Casey's room, I decided against confronting them. If I had caught Heather before she went in, my powers of persuasion might have been more effective. My intrusion at that point would only have inflamed Heather's anger and she would more than likely have reacted negatively, rather than consider our side of the situation.

On the way home from Casey's apartment, I concluded, as parents, our only hope was that Heather would have enough common sense to realize that running away was a big mistake and that she would come home on her own.

When Heather didn't show up the next day or the day after that, Bonnie and I were forced to conclude that she really wasn't coming back.

A few days later, I ran into some friends of Heather's at the restaurant in my office building. As far as they knew, Casey was heading for Montreal after graduation and that Heather had talked about going with him. The kids joked that their memories might not be too accurate because they had all been drinking pretty heavily. The way they spoke and rolled their eyes told me that they wouldn't miss Casey all that much and only tolerated him because he was with Heather. I didn't tell them why I was asking, but I'm sure they figured it out.

With plenty of time to spare, I parked the car in the airport parking lot. I was pleased with myself for remembering to look up at the nearest light standard for the symbol to make it easier to find the car on the way home.

The arrivals monitor in the terminal gave me the first hint that things weren't going as planned. It showed "Delayed" opposite the Flight 119, the only flight from Montreal. I inquired at the passenger assistance desk and found out that there had been a major thunderstorm at Montreal and all airplanes had been held on the ground until the weather cleared.

I wandered around the airport retail area. As I walked, I looked for something to pass the time. I had a coffee in the cafeteria, visited the novelty shop and then the bookshop.

I checked the arrivals monitor again and continued to walk aimlessly around the airport. I noted the many changes since the last time I was there. I thought about buying *USA Today* to check the weather map, when I bumped into another customer near the newsstand. He was Stewart Logan, the mayor of Melcastle. He was a few years younger than me, but I came to know him fairly well through various municipal matters and social functions.

"Hi Stewart. What brings you here?"

"Hi Henry," he replied, as we shook hands. He seemed to be preoccupied.

There was a lengthy pause. It appeared as though Stewart wasn't interested in talking. I thought I should say something.

"I'm here to pick up my daughter, Heather, but I'm afraid her plane has been delayed."

"Is she coming from Montreal?" Stewart asked.

"Why yes, how did you know?"

"I'm meeting Dorothy Sparrow. She's coming from Montreal and as you know the flight has been delayed."

"And how is Dorothy?"

"She's fine. She was visiting her daughter in Montreal. The daughter is recovering from a bout of that flesh-eating disease."

"Necrotizing Fasciitus," I responded. "I trust she's recovering?"

"She's coming along fine, now. Thank you. I'm surprised you've heard of that disease. It's rather rare, I understand."

"Yes, my secretary's son came down with it a couple of years ago. She's a single mom and I became fairly involved. As soon as the young fella left intensive care, I volunteered to act as an attendant a few evenings. His condition was pretty touch and go for a few days. He was pretty badly scarred up, but fortunately the plastic surgeons did a good job and most of the scars will be covered by his normal clothes."

"Yeah, I know what you mean. Dorothy's daughter is really upset with her scars. Apparently they're visible around her neck and shoulders." Stewart looked away, as though he didn't want to talk about it any more. I suspected he was close to tears.

The next few moments dragged by again. Both of us spent the time looking for something else to talk about. The fact that Stewart and Dorothy were dating wasn't widely known. Their ages were a lot closer than most people thought. The illusion was fostered by the fact that Murdock Sparrow had been much older than Dorothy.

Finally, I thought of an appropriate subject, "Wasn't that a shame about Dorothy having to sell the big house after Murdock died? I thought Murdock was well-off and she wouldn't have to worry about things like that."

"I'm not sure what happened there," Stewart replied.

"Dorothy hasn't said anything?" I asked.

I guess I asked the right question, because Stewart began talk non-stop for several minutes.

He paused and said, "You're a lawyer, Henry, right?"

"Yes, I am."

"I'm fairly certain old Murdock had plenty of money at one time," Stewart began. "But right after he died, Dorothy's friends persuaded her to invest in some cockamamie real estate scheme with SPA-KAL. She lost most of her money, I understand. Then she had to sell the big house to make ends meet. She's sure the SPA-KAL syndicate just put the Sparrow name on the building to buy some moral conscience."

I shared Stewart's suspicions, but I didn't want to say anything.

"I can't convince Dorothy to take legal action and try to recover some of the money," Stewart continued. "After Murdock died, I started going out with her because I knew her since we were kids, but lately I think we're getting a little more serious.

"I know her older daughters, Val and Cynthia, fairly well, but I'm not acquainted with her daughter, Carole, from Montreal at all. I think Dorothy might be bringing Carole along today to meet me. What do you think?"

While Stewart was talking, I was trying to decide whether he was a man in love or someone who didn't know where to turn. I was surprised by the sudden question and didn't answer right away.

"I mean—are there any lawyers you can recommend for this type of case, Henry?"

"Well, I suppose I could recommend one or two."

"I sure would appreciate it, if you could," he said forlornly.

"You might be best to hire somebody from out of town," I suggested.

After that, the conversation generally switched to the weather and baseball. Finally, the flight monitor showed an arrival time of 15:35 hours.

A crowd began to gather at the baggage carousel and I lost track of Stewart.

Few passengers disembarked Flight 119. I recognized Heather even before she smiled. I was not only pleased to see her returning home, I was proud of what she had become. She was carrying her purse and briefcase, and a large duffel bag. She was probably bringing home all her worldly possessions.

With her shoulder-length auburn hair and big blue eyes, Heather looked much like her mother when Bonnie and I were first married. Her dark blue business suit, with a red and white silk scarf bordered by gold maple leaves, gave her a smart and professional appearance. When we embraced, I caught a whiff of a familiar fragrance in her hair. It reminded me of the perfume that Bonnie once used.

"Welcome home, my dear. Do you have any baggage to pick up?"

"Yes, I have two suitcases. I had to borrow one from my roommate, Thelma. She's going to send the rest of my shoes when she can find a suitable box. This bag is her brother's hockey bag. I'll have to send it back."

At the baggage carousel and later on the trip home, Heather talked all about her experiences of the past 13 years. I heard all about the plane delay; her first job; her roommate, Thelma; the mystery club; going to university; her experiences with the legal profession; her boyfriends; and, of course, the downsizing.

I responded with the occasional question or comment, but it was obvious, normal conversation was going to be a bit one-sided for a while. We really didn't have that much in common.

After dropping off Heather's luggage at home, I realized neither or us had eaten since early morning. In Heather's case, breakfast was just a croissant and juice on the plane. I suggested a country restaurant in the old part of Melcastle where we ate and talked for the rest of the evening. The sun was just setting on the horizon when we left the restaurant and headed for home.

Near the Maryland-Pennsylvania border, we drove past an old building on Southgate Road. There was a sign out front that read: Mason-Dixon Murder Mystery Museum. Although the sign had been up for years, it was new to Heather.

"Murder Mystery Museum? What's that all about, Dad?"

"It seems that somebody needed a place to store the artifacts from various unsolved murders or border feuds."

"There must have been quite a few 'unsolved murders' to justify a museum."

"The border wars didn't stop when the location of the boundary was finally settled in 1903. The descendants of the Calvert and Penn families kept on killing one another just the same. Perhaps they weren't all clan related, but there were a few unsolved murders when I was a kid."

"That must have been scary."

"Yeah, but we all knew who to stay away from."

"Mind telling me who they were or are they all dead?"

"I guess it's safe enough to reveal the names now. I don't know if the fathers are still alive, but the sons are respected members of the community today."

"Who are they, Dad?"

"Jack Sewchuk's father was a ringleader on the Penn side and father of the senior Harvey Parslow was his sworn enemy on the Calvert side."

"How did the two clans eventually resolve their differences?"

"I don't know really. Perhaps the Second World War made them come together. Bruce Sewchuk and Dale Parslow were in the same outfit and after the war they came back with a different attitude, I understand."

"How about the Judge Sewchuk and Chief Parslow, were they friends when they were young?"

"They never really came together until high school. Harvey was like me he went to grade school in Teasdale. Jack and Harvey were both top athletes and played on the same rep teams so I guess you could say they were able to tolerate one another's company."

"Interesting."

Back home again, I parked the car and retrieved Heather's suitcases and duffel bag from the trunk. As I was going in the house with the suitcases, I noticed the duct tape I had put over the hole in the little window vent on the back door of the car had come loose on the trip back from the airport. When I pressed the loose tape back into place, my hand went all the way through the window. I opened the door and pushed the tape back in place as best I could and promised myself I would have repairs done later. There wouldn't be time in the morning because I had an appointment at ten o'clock.

I put the excess duct tape in the garbage. The full garbage can reminded me that I needed to take the garbage out to the curb. Monday is garbage day in Teasdale. One of the reasons why Grampa George built the U shaped driveway was to make it convenient for the garbage truck to drive all the way in without having to back out. The village stopped providing personalized service about 20 years ago which means I have to cart my containers over 100 feet out to the road.

CHAPTER 10

Starting Over

When I stepped out of Dad's car, I had expected the quarried stone exterior of Macy House to be the same, but the wooden trim around the windows looked as though it could use a fresh paint job. I had expected the lawn to be green, but it was a yellow brown and the earth in the flower garden was dry and cracked. Obviously, there hadn't had much rain lately.

As I entered the residence part of the house, I expected to be greeted with the comforting smell of fresh cut firewood drying beside the small fireplace. The recessed woodbox beside the fireplace was empty. The air in the house was decidedly stale. I had to assume Dad didn't use the fireplace much any more.

I thought about what a home and family meant to me when I went to my old bedroom. I was the fourth generation to live in this house, but it wasn't until I sat on my old bed that I appreciated how comforting an old house can be.

My old trophies and medals were still on the shelves beside my bed.

I fingered the awards and tried to recapture the feeling I had when I won each one. Some I couldn't remember receiving, especially the medals. Some had dates but didn't mention the place or the event. I remembered how proud I was at the Melcastle track meet where I entered seven events and won five medals.

It had been a long day and sleep came easily.

I deliberately slept-in the next morning. I really had no plans for that day, other than discussing the working arrangements of the partnership with Dad. I knew he had an office here in Macy House. I wondered whether he still had the tiny office in Melcastle where I sometimes used to stop in for a ride home after school. I wasn't sure, but I assumed Dad preferred to work alone. After all, the last time he had a partner that I knew of, was at least 15 years ago.

I stumbled to the kitchen and looked at the "old-fashioned" electric cuckoo clock that was still mounted over the window above the kitchen sink. The pop-out bird mechanism had quit working long before I left home. Dad had tried to fix it several times. The hands stood about a half inch away from the Roman numerals, which made it difficult to tell the time anywhere but directly in front. The time was somewhere around eight-thirty.

It wasn't long before the gears of the clock made those sounds that meant it was time to push the long-inactive, little bird out the door. I didn't even have to look at the clock; it was exactly eight-thirty. Dad should be up and around by now, I thought. When I was going to high school, he was always either in his office or out of the house by eight o'clock.

The thermometer, glued to the window, already registered ninety degrees, but that was because the sun was shining directly on it. The true temperature wouldn't be reflected until the shadow of the overhang crossed below the window.

As I became used to my surroundings again, even the smell of the house gave me a comfortable feeling. But, I had to admit that the kitchen and living room were even drabber than I remembered. The old wagon wheel chandelier was definitely from another era. The paneled walls had turned a darker yellow and the curtains on the windows had faded with age.

Strangely enough, the living area seemed to be relatively neat and clean. I expected to see a lot more dust and clutter, considering Dad has lived alone for quite a few years.

Come to think of it, I really didn't know how long Dad had been living alone. I kept in touch with friends in Melcastle, but they didn't tell me when Mom was admitted to the hospital.

Through the kitchen window, I noticed the sky had cleared. The normal haze to the southwest was lighter and made the view of the blue hills of West Virginia sharper and closer, but still there was that distinctive blue coloring. Over to the southeast, I always imagined that with a powerful telescope I could see all the way to the ocean or at least Chesapeake Bay.

I thought about what I was going to have for breakfast. I had become used to cereal, toast and coffee ever since I moved in with Thelma. I couldn't remember what I used to eat for breakfast when I was living here in Teasdale.

I opened the bread drawer. The plastic bag of bread had only two slices in it. I took out one and left the other for Dad. I put it in the toaster.

I checked the "best-before-date" on the milk carton and discovered it was good until next week. That was a good sign. The spoons were in their usual place in the jar on the table.

The toaster shattered the silence when it popped. One side of the toast was more black than brown. The other side was almost white. I scraped the black stuff off in the sink, which made both sides cold by the time I applied the butter. I made a mental note to discuss with Dad the possibility of getting a new toaster.

As I ate my cold toast, I wondered about the good friends that I didn't have much of a chance to say good-bye in my haste to leave town, especially my girlfriends. How would my old high school buddies remember me? How many of them would still be around?

As I put the dishes in the sink, I looked out the window. I saw a woman cycling up the driveway. She was dressed in a yellow windbreaker and black slacks. She parked her bicycle against one of the pillars and not too long afterwards the doorbell rang. When I opened the door, I obviously startled her. She was attempting to put a key in the lock.

"Ah…ah…I'm Christine Wilkinson. I'm Mr. Macy's cleaning lady. I have a key, but I always ring the doorbell in case he's with somebody in his office."

"Hi, I'm Heather Macy. Come on in. I presume you know where things are and what to do?"

"Pleased to meet you, Heather. Yes, Mr. Macy keeps everything behind the laundry room doors," she replied.

As I returned to the kitchen to rinse the burnt toast scrapings down the drain, I spotted a man half jogging and half walking up the driveway. It took a few seconds to realize it was Dad.

As Dad came through the door, I said, "I didn't know you were a jogger!"

"I call it a modified jogging…I used to jog…when I first started,…but I found it…too hard on the knees…It helps me sleep…I think," he panted.

"Well good for you," I smiled.

"Oh…I see you've met…Christine," he gestured, as he passed between us. "I'll be in the shower…if anybody is looking for me."

"I'll alert the media," I commented, borrowing a line the Dudley Moore movie. Dad looked puzzled.

I went back to the kitchen. Dad went off to take his shower. A few minutes later the noise of the shower stopped and the next sound was the exhaust fan. The fan had just started its drone when the telephone rang. Although Dad had finished showering, I assumed he likely hadn't heard the phone.

"Hello this is Judge Sewchuk," came a rather gruff and official sounding male voice. "Is this Heather?"

"Yes, it is," I replied.

"Good, you're just the person I wanted to talk to. I heard you were back in town and have become a lawyer. Congratulations and welcome back."

"Thank you."

"I'll come right to the point. I have an assignment that I think you might be interested in."

"As long as it's in the civil law field. That's the only experience that I have, you understand."

"That's perfect. This is a property settlement case. It's a routine assignment and shouldn't take more than a few days."

We agreed to meet at ten-thirty.

"Sure, I'll be there. Where is your office, Your Honor?" " M y chambers are on the fifth floor, north wing of the Sparrow Building, twenty-nineteen, Constitution Avenue. You can't miss it. It's the only eight storey building in town."

As he spoke, I wrote the address on a pad by the phone.

The way he terminated the conversation was very abrupt. Perhaps he recognized my lack of experience. Surely, my reference to his office instead of his chambers was not that serious of a mistake. Then I thought, no, he was probably extremely busy and didn't care too much about being polite, especially with someone so junior and inexperienced.

I felt a little bit of panic, not really knowing how long it would take me to drive into town. I had never heard of the Sparrow Building, but I knew Constitution Avenue well. What was that he said? "Twenty-nineteen, Constitution Avenue—fifth floor—eight storey building." I repeated the note out loud, as though hearing the numbers would ensure the accuracy. That shouldn't be too difficult. I reminded myself to take the note with me.

I called to Dad through the bathroom door. I wanted to confirm that the car was available. He said yes, but I had the feeling he really didn't hear me too well over the noise of the fan. The additional noise of the electric razor made any further communication difficult. When the noises stopped, I tried to condense the content of the phone call from Judge Sewchuk as best I could, but it was hard to tell how much I was able to communicate through the closed door.

His voice at times was barely audible. He had obviously moved away from the bathroom door. He shouted back that the keys were hanging behind the bifold doors in the entranceway. He said he didn't need the car because he had an appointment here at ten.

My next problem was what to wear. I held up a few skirts and jackets to see which would be the most presentable. I decided the suit I wore on the plane yesterday would be the best, but it needed to be ironed.

I was glad to find the steam iron was still stored in its usual place. I gave the pants and jacket a quick press. No one would notice the creases in the new blouse I had just unpacked last night. A little scarf would hide everything but the collar. Besides, I didn't want to push my luck with the iron.

About the time I finished dressing Dad emerged from his bedroom.

"I thought you were still in the bathroom," I declared, rushing past him into the bathroom.

"Sorry about that," he said. "My, you seem to be in a hurry."

"Yes. My appointment with Judge Sewchuk is at ten-thirty. I just have time to brush my teeth and wash my hands."

After I completed my ablutions, I went to the front door and picked up my briefcase. I put the judge's address in my jacket pocket and headed for the car. Dad handed me the keys as I went out the door.

CHAPTER 11

Victor Gabler—Mr. Hal-Burton

Monday Morning

The morning after Heather's arrival, I overslept. I'm usually up well before seven o'clock. The excitement of her return caused me to toss and turn all night and I didn't really get to sleep until near daybreak. Seven-thirty was late enough that I even considered not taking my morning jog. I decided to just have a banana for breakfast and see whether I could cut some time off my usual hour-long route. By the time I left the house it was nearly eight o'clock.

En route, I thought about the gentleman named Gabler who phoned from Hal-Burton last week to make an appointment to see me at my Macy House office. After four years of making contact only by phone, I wasn't sure whether I was going to meet an FBI agent or a legitimate member of Hal-Burton. Over the phone the caller sounded diplomatic and businesslike.

I was still uncertain about the Hal-Burton organization. Even though I did some research and learned that it was one of the largest property development corporations in the world, I couldn't convince myself the local office wasn't a clandestine FBI operation.

Even with a few shortcuts, my exercise trip took a little more time than expected. That meant I had to rush to prepare myself for my appointment at ten o'clock.

As I completed my jog and turned up the driveway, I noticed a bike leaning up against the pillar by the front door. Another senior's moment, I had forgotten to mention to Heather that, Christine, my cleaning lady, would be coming. It seemed to me the best way around that embarrassing situation was to make an "excuse me" comment and rush into the bathroom and take a shower.

While I was in the bathroom, I tried to remember the Hal-Burton chap's first name. A letter of confirmation of the appointment had arrived on Friday, complete with a business card. The letter had a colored, embossed Harold E Burton Property Development Corp (U.S.A.) logo, listing their worldwide offices. I reminded myself to check the letter before my guest arrived.

When I finished my shower, I could hear Heather on the phone. A few minutes later she spoke to me, but I couldn't hear her very well because the exhaust fan was on and I was brushing my teeth. As near as I could understand, Heather had an appointment with Judge Sewchuk in the city. Apart from that, all I could gather was that she was asking whether she could use the car.

When I emerged from my bedroom, Heather was waiting outside the bathroom door. She seemed a little annoyed that I hadn't let her know the bathroom was free.

We talked a little more, while we jostled for position in front of the mirror by the front door. I usually wear a suit and tie every weekday, however, this morning I found it particularly difficult to make the ends of my tie come out even.

Heather continued to fuss with her hair and rub imaginary lint off of her slacks. She looked very professional in her suit. With her naturally curly hair, she really did look attractive.

As Heather was getting into the car, I thought that since she was going to be in the city, we might as well meet for lunch. I usually go into the city, around noon to meet with my secretary before she leaves for the day.

"Heather, why don't we have lunch after you're finished with Judge Sewchuk," I said, as I leaned out the door.

"Good idea. I'm going to some place called the Sparrow Building. Are there any good restaurants around there?"

"I'll meet you at the La Gondola restaurant. You can't miss it."

As Heather backed out, a sleek two-tone brown van entered the inbound lane. I waved to Heather and stepped back inside the house. Through the spyglass in the door, I could see the van pulling into the spot Heather had just left. The vehicle looked more like a tourist bus, but with smaller tinted windows. It looked impressive with two large, sliding doors on the passenger side, an array of antennas on top and a satellite dish on the back.

A balding man in the passenger seat was putting his hat on as the vehicle came to a stop. The male driver, also dressed in a jacket and tie, was wearing the traditional chauffeur's cap.

I spotted the letter from Hal-Burton on the table beside the door. I quickly flipped it open and noted the name Victor Gabler on the signature block. I slipped the business card out from under the paper clip and put it in my shirt pocket.

I just had time to open the louvered doors and select the jacket that matched the suit pants I was wearing.

I peeked through the tiny spyglass again in time to see my guest exit the van and approach the front door. I assumed he saw me saying goodbye to Heather, so I opened the door to greet him. He was a tall man dressed in charcoal gray, three-piece suit. He wore a fashionable hat with a short brim and carried a hard-covered briefcase. The immediate effect of the penetration of his steel blue eyes was disconcerting.

"Good morning Mr. Macy, I'm Victor Gabler from Hal-Burton Property Development Corporation, United States Division," he said, as he removed his hat. "You *are* William Henry Macy, I presume?"

With the opening question, he presented his card. The card was more elaborate than the one I had put in my shirt pocket. This one had multiple colors running through the Hal-Burton logo. In the sunlight, each color glistened separately as the card was tilted. In the middle of the card, under his name, which included a string of degrees, was the title "Vice President, United States Division."

"Pleased to meet you Mr. Gabler. I'm afraid my business cards are in my office. Please, follow me."

We proceeded directly to my office. I had a holder of cards on my desk. I took a card out of the middle to ensure the one I gave him was not disfigured in any way.

Mr. Gabler studied my card for a few seconds, as though he were passing judgment on its authenticity or the quality of the printing shops in the area. I offered him a seat across from my desk. He sat on the front edge of the chair. Still studying my card, he began to speak.

"I have come to solicit your services in the purchase of the General's Farm." He spoke slowly with a warm smile on his face and stared directly into my eyes.

Obviously, he wanted to get down to business right away. The mention of the *General's Farm* as his first order of business startled me. I wasn't expecting to discuss the subject of the General's Farm at all, so I felt the best thing to do was to say nothing. I pretended I was taking my time getting seated. The pause was a little too long to be polite.

"Yes, how can I be of service in that regard?"

"My company has been doing research on the General's Farm and the surrounding properties," he declared. "And we have determined, through our international contacts and private investigators, that only a certain number of people could be the owners of that property. We have concluded that you are either the actual owner or have firsthand knowledge of who is."

"What makes you think I would be the owner or any more informed than anybody else?" I asked. As I was speaking, it occurred to me that I had probably contributed to some of his research.

"We have virtually eliminated all the other candidates. We are left with only one or two people, besides yourself. At first, we thought the most logical candidate would be Mr. McClelland. We also considered

Mr. Hird in the village of Teasdale. He is one of the more knowledgeable persons from a historical point of view."

"Yes, Bill Hird has lived in the area a long time and is a good reputation for being a historical buff," I commented.

"Agreed, but we kept coming back to two facts that have been consistent for over 30 years. First, the annual tax assessment for that property is sent to a Swiss bank every year. Second, we also know, through our Swiss contacts, that regular annual correspondence within one week after the release of the annual tax assessments, is addressed to William H Macy at 3155 Old Military Road. That is or was your father I believe. It is our contention that these notifications were confirmation that the taxes had been paid."

"Sounds pretty circumstantial," I said, as I looked away to avoid his riveting gaze.

"We also considered Ruby Wendelman because she used to work at the Land Records Office before her unfortunate incarceration. As you know, she is the daughter of Mr. McClelland, who lives in the cottage beside the main building at the General's Farm. We have concluded that both their incomes together were insufficient to cover the initial purchase let alone the annual taxes. We are aware that you and Ruby McClelland went together during your high school years."

"I don't see what my relationship with Ruby has to do with the ownership of the General's Farm," I interrupted.

"Probably nothing, but her name came up during our research of each possible candidate. We had to confirm that she didn't conspire with anyone else to buy the property, using her inside knowledge from the Land Records Office. There is even the possibility that she set the fire to cover up the sale."

"I find that a little hard to believe," I said. "Besides, she was in Windemere when the fire happened."

"Perhaps I should attempt to eliminate the more likely candidate, other than yourself. Mr. Hird has a reputation of being an authority on the subject. We have confirmed, simply by asking him, that Mr. Hird does not know who the owner is."

"And you believed him, just because he said so?"

"Yes, we did. Besides we were pretty certain who the real owner was at that point," Gabler replied. "We also know that you visit the Farm or the area on a regular basis. Shall I go on?"

I had kept the ownership of the General's Farm a secret for over 30 years and my father and grandfather before that. The thought of actually acknowledging ownership would require a serious mental adjustment. I was desperately thinking of something to say that would avoid answering the question of ownership.

Gabler kept his gaze on me, waiting for an answer. After a few seconds, he reached into his briefcase and pulled out a thick file. Clipped to the outside of the file was a single sheet of paper and a check. He separated the two items and laid them on the desk beside the file, but kept them in front of him. The positioning was obviously meant for me to see the content. I could see the check was made out to William Henry Macy for $10,000 and the paper was a Letter of Offer.

"I have been authorized to offer you a retainer in the amount of $10,000 for legal services to be specified later," he said slowly, as though he was expecting me to interrupt. "Basically, Hal-Burton is looking for documentary evidence of whomever is the owner of two thousand and thirteen acres of property known as the General's Farm in the states of Pennsylvania and Maryland." As he finished, Mr. Gabler's lips were drawn back in a tight smile. He was obvious waiting for me to comment or ask questions, but I wasn't sure what he wanted me to say.

"What legal services do you expect me to perform?"

"I'll come that in a moment."

"I have no idea how much the property is worth," I said, still trying to avoid the obvious question.

"Hal-Burton is prepared to offer $550 for each acre of the property that is suitable for housing or commercial development," he read. "We estimate the developmental portion of the property to be approximately 2,000 acres. We are offering $100 for each of the other 13 acres. The main building and the cottage are located on the latter 13 acres."

"What about the heritage groups?" I asked. "They seem to have a tremendous amount of control over development of such lands, particularly the buildings."

"Our offer includes a one time grant of $15,000, over the next five years, to each of the heritage groups for restoration and preservation of the buildings, specifically the main building and the cottage.

"We are mindful of the disparity of the fund-raising efforts put forward by the two groups and will negotiate an arrangement to donate matching dollars for each dollar they raise privately, for the next five years.

"Hal-Burton is also prepared to negotiate a similar gift towards the restoration of the Old Stone Bridge."

"You seem to have covered just about everything."

"Except your admission that you are the owner," he responded sharply. He was now all business. The smile had disappeared.

I paused for a few seconds.

"The property was owned by my father," I announced casually.

Considering the length of time I had been holding on to the ownership secret, I had expected a greater feeling of relief or resignation. Over the years, I had imagined several scenarios for the eventual revelation that I owned the General's Farm, but none of those thoughts included the scene that was literally staring me in the face.

It took me a moment to realize that instead of relief, I was feeling euphoric. I couldn't concentrate. Disjointed thoughts were racing through my brain.

Then I realized, although I had admitted my father owned the General's Farm, that statement didn't necessarily mean it now belonged to me. For all Gabler knew, the farm could have been willed to my twin brother. I wondered what other evidence Gabler had. My anxiety level was rising. For a few seconds, I couldn't put my thoughts into words.

Gabler's expression suggested he was confident he knew the identity of the present owner. He searched through the file again.

"There's one more thing," he said in a softer tone. "We are aware of your attachment to the mountain. If within the next five years you should decide to sell Macy House, a house of the equivalent size or style will be provided to you, including one half acre of land." He sat back in his chair and waited for me to speak.

In my excitement, I'm afraid I didn't hear all of what Mr. Gabler had just said, but I was confident that everything was in my favor. It was obvious that he had done his homework and was serious. I decided there was no longer any point in keeping the secret about my ownership of the General's Farm.

"Well, what do you think, Mr. Macy?"

"Yes, the General's Farm belongs to me, but I'm not sure whether I want to sell it."

"We were pretty certain you were the owner. We pride ourselves in being thorough," he responded, his back straightening as he spoke. "I think you'll come to understand that our offer is better than any you'd be able to obtain on your own."

"Okay then, I guess it's time to show you my 'documentary evidence,' as you call it."

"Do you have the documents here on the premises?"

"Yes, they're in to the conference room."

I stood up and gestured toward the door. Gabler put his papers in his briefcase and picked up his hat as I led the way down the corridor past the other office.

I fumbled nervously through my keys as I prepared to unlock the conference room door.

The furniture in the conference room has always been strictly utilitarian—a six foot by twelve-foot table, ten mostly unmatched chairs and my grandfather's safe. The safe is the old four-foot-high kind.

I turned on the lights and opened the curtains and gestured to Gabler to sit at a chair at the corner of the table nearest the safe. I sat in the chair across the corner of the table from him and attempted to dial the combination lock. It took three tries before the handle finally dropped and the thick door opened.

I withdrew two files: one marked "Last Will and Testament of William Horatio Macy" and the other marked "The General's Farm." The latter contained a few oversized survey maps that stuck out all around the folder. I placed the folders on the table and pushed the Last

Will file to one side. I started by unfolding the maps from the General's Farm file. The papers crackled as though they were about to shatter.

Attached to the top of the maps were a series of legal papers, complete with a circular imprinting stamp. The one on top was the bill of sale from the Loraas Estates Auctioneers. The second document was an original copy of the deed. The other documents had to do with survey details, mineral rights and outstanding liens. Attached to the inside of the file cover was a receipt for a lawyer's fee for $30. It was marked—"Received with thanks"—and signed by Herb Murphy.

"I must admit I've never opened the survey maps," I said. "I had no idea the property contained over two thousand acres. I'll take your word that it is that big. All I knew was that it contained the Farmhouse, the cottage and a lot of trees. I never realized how much land was involved."

I passed the property documents to my guest.

Gabler looked closely at the deed and survey maps. He turned over each document that had an intaglio stamped image to confirm that it had been made by an impress device commonly found in a lawyer's office. He went back and forth between the detailed map and the larger survey map. After a few moments he spoke.

"These documents *appear* to be genuine," he declared; with a slight emphasis on the word appear.

"Thank you. I have no reason to believe they aren't genuine."

"In fact, some of these papers have the Land Records Office stamp on them and should be returned to that office. Only the ones marked 'duplicate' were meant to be in your possession."

He separated the documents as he spoke.

"Obviously both sets of documents were in my father's possession from the time of the sale. I guess the whereabouts of the original documents was the least of the worries of the Land Records Office staff at the time of the fire."

"I suggest we deal with document custody issue later. Now, according to these documents, the land and buildings were purchased by William George Macy and William Horatio Macy. Can you prove to me that the ownership was officially transferred to you?"

"Well, I have my father's will here. It was witnessed by Mrs. Griffin, my next door neighbor, but I'm afraid it has never been registered," I said sheepishly.

"I understand," he mused and paused for a second. "You were afraid it might compromise the secret of the ownership, right?"

"I suppose that's how the secrecy started. I assumed title fell to my father when Grampa died. When my father died, his will gave the farm to me and my twin brother was to receive this house. My brother has not lived in the area for many years."

I handed the will to Gabler to inspect. He took a few seconds to flatten out the creases and closely inspected the legal imprint stamp. He quickly glanced through the will and then went back to the property documents.

"Do you know this lawyer...Herb Murphy?" he asked.

"Yes, he was a new lawyer in town at the time. Dad wanted to make sure that certain legal things were done outside the family."

"Can you provide me with his phone number or address?" he asked, as he retrieved a notepad from his briefcase.

"Certainly, but I don't think he maintains a law practice anymore. Although, I believe he still lives at his original address in Melcastle. It's right beside the high school on Armstrong Avenue at Taylor Street. His phone number is 523-2594. I can remember his number because it's just two digits away from the private number at my downtown office."

Gabler wrote down the phone number and the cross streets of Herb's address in his notebook.

"What should I do about the survey maps and land title deeds?" I asked.

"We can deal with returning the documents once we have settled the other details."

"What other details?"

"Now that the ownership of the General's Farm property has been verified, our property acquisition team can turn its attention to contiguous properties that can now be validated by these maps. We're particularly interested in the ownership of the property in Maryland, south and east of the cottage."

"Why should that area attract your attention? There's nothing there but a steep bank of rocks and scrub trees."

"We believe there have been several attempts by a syndicate that goes by the name of SPA-KAL, to acquire the property all along the southern perimeter of the farm. The Cottage itself is not important to Hal-Burton, but in order to present a complete package to the civic officials and heritage groups, we would like to clarify the status of all the land surrounding the farm."

"That shouldn't be too difficult with the resources at your disposal. Is there anything else that I can help you with?"

"There is one more item—the payment of municipal taxes. As I said at the beginning, our research pointed to you as the owner. We would appreciate confirmation that our theories are correct. How were the taxes paid?"

"My father told me the interest on an original deposit at a Swiss bank would pay for the taxes each year. When father died, I found it was easy just to do nothing. The letters from Switzerland assured me that the taxes were being paid."

"Those letters plus the will and the survey maps makes you the official owner. Would you happen to have a copy of one of those letters?"

"We'll have to go back to my office for those," I said.

"That takes care of the taxes on the main building. Now, what about the taxes on the cottage?" Gabler asked.

"I have no idea how the taxes on the cottage were paid. Now that I think about it, the cottage has been in Maryland since the resurvey in 1903 of the original Mason-Dixon survey. I guess the cottage taxes should have been paid to the Teasdale municipality."

Gabler nodded and then pulled out a document from his briefcase and handed it to me. It was a Letter of Understanding in two copies.

As I read the Letter of Understanding, I was curious about the fact that only the State of Pennsylvania was mentioned. I wondered whether there would be more paperwork for the cottage.

When I finished reading, Gabler asked me to sign and date the second copy, which I did. He then handed me the retainer check for

$10,000 and one of the copies.

Then Gabler presented me with the Letter of Offer that he had discretely let me see back in my office. It was also in two copies. I noticed that the offer used the expression "approximately" in front of the five hundred and fifty dollars per acre for the property suitable for housing development. After I had read the Letter of Offer, he took it back, signed both copies himself and returned one copy to me.

As I accepted the Letter of Offer, I came to realize the magnitude of what we were doing was about to change my life.

"I'm curious. What is it about this particular piece of land that suddenly makes it so valuable?"

"To the experienced land developer, that's easy. The city of Melcastle is being severely restricted on the other three sides. The city is bound on the south by the Maryland state border. On the east, you have the joint Melcastle/Teasdale airport, plus the highways and railway yards. And on the north, it is blocked off by the Windemere Estates and Candle Lake. As you know, the lake area has been completely developed for years and Windemere is federally and state owned. That only leaves the property west of Southgate. The Pennsylvania portion of the General's Farm north of the ridge is ideal for housing development."

"Hmmm. I never thought of it that way."

"The final selling price is dependent upon the ability to maintain stable market values on all properties in the immediate area. If word of this deal gets out, property values in the area may rise. I'm authorized to spend only a certain amount of money on this project. If the other properties go up, then the amount we pay you must come down. You do understand the need of secrecy, I'm sure."

"I understand."

"If all goes well, I expect to be in a position to call a press conference at the end of the week. The secrecy also applies to Heather," he concluded, with his friendly, but hard stare.

"You have my word, sir."

"By the way, I have a photocopier in my van. Would you mind if I made copies of the property documents?"

"Sure, whatever you like."

Gabler selected the four or five pages of the survey maps and will that he needed. On the way out of the conference room, I stopped by my office and picked up the latest copy of my annual correspondence from Switzerland. At the van, he opened the rear panel door and handed the papers to someone inside. The sliding door was open just far enough for me to see the person was a young woman with bright red hair and dressed in a dark blue suit.

"Would you make a copy of these documents please, Shirley?"

Shortly after that I could hear the copy machine whir into action. When "Shirley" handed the papers back to Gabler, I could see an array of equipment that would put most commercial offices to shame.

After Gabler and his van left, I did a quick calculation on my office calculator to make sure my mental arithmetic was accurate. A rush of adrenaline came over me as I realized that in a week or so, I could be a millionaire. I noticed the $10,000 retainer check was a Hal-Burton check drawn on the First Union Bank in Philadelphia and not on the Citibank like those I had received for my work with Barnard. I could only recognize the bold signature of "Victor Gabler" but the other signature was hardly more than a line with a squiggle at the start. The check was dated last Friday. I guess they were pretty confident.

I looked at my watch. It was hard to believe it was just after 11 o'clock. I had planned to do some work at home this morning, but I reasoned by the time I started, it would be time to head off to meet with my secretary, Roma Dowler for our usual noon exchange meeting.

Then I remembered lunch with Heather. I phoned Roma to see whether she would like to stay a little longer today to meet Heather. Roma said she had anticipated Heather's arrival and had made arrangements for her son, Alex, to stay at the day-care center for and extra hour. I thought it was clever of me to hide my excitement over the General's Farm deal by telling Roma that I wanted to bring Heather up to see her after lunch.

I looked out at the driveway on my way back to the conference room and suddenly realized I didn't have a car. I suppose millionaires can take taxis.

As I was making room for the property paper files in the safe, a small, brown envelope slipped out of one of the other files on the same shelf. I put the files in my hand on top of the safe and opened up the envelope. It contained a large man's watch. I had forgotten Dad had given Arthur and me each a Bulova watch when we turned twelve. Arthur had left his on the bathroom sink the day he left. Dad kept the watch in the safe, expecting Arthur to write and tell us where to send it. Arthur never did write and Dad forgot all about it. I noticed that Heather didn't wear a watch. Maybe she would appreciate it. I put the watch on top of the safe to remind myself to offer it to her.

As I was about to close the safe door, I noticed a couple of official-looking certificates sticking out of the Last Will and Testament file. The documents turned out to be death certificates. The first was inscribed to "Shurlie Irene Macy, 12 November, 1938." The shock of seeing my birth date on my mother's death certificate put a different perspective on my special date. The other death certificate read, "Baby Macy (Boy), 12 November, 1938—pronounced dead at birth, due to umbilical strangulation." Wow! My brother and I actually started out as triplets! Man, that information was quite a revelation. I looked at both certificates a long time before I put them away.

While I had the safe open, I thought about looking into the small box-like arrangement hanging from the top corner. It was locked, but the key in the lock also served as a handle. I have always avoided looking in there because I knew that was where Grampa George kept an old revolver. I have always had a strong fear of guns.

I opened the box door and on top of the gun I discovered two Swiss bank account passbooks. Inside each passbook were the instructions on how to identify the account and how to make inquiries. At the end of a string of numbers on each, there was a personal identity code. The identity code on the first book was W-H-MACY and on the other was MACY-W-H. I figured one of the passbooks must be for the taxes on the General's Farm. As for the other one, I had no idea.

I closed and locked the safe and went back to my office. It felt strange calling a taxi.

The cab arrived in a few minutes and I was relieved that I didn't know the driver, which meant I didn't have to worry about making conversation. All I had to say was, "The Sparrow Building, please."

CHAPTER 12

Judge Sewchuk's Chambers

Monday Morning

Dad always kept his cars in good condition. As near as I could tell, this car was at least ten years old. The engine sounded smooth when I started it. That was good. I adjusted the rear-view mirror. As I shifted into reverse, the knob came off the handle. Not a good sign. I put the knob on the dashboard beside the sunglasses holder. The gas gauge showed a quarter tank. I hoped that would be enough to make the trip into town and back.

As I was backing out of the parking area, Dad stuck his head out the front door and suggested we meet for lunch at La Gondola Restaurant. I hadn't heard of that restaurant, but I felt I could figure out its location later. I was more concerned that I was running late for my meeting with Judge Sewchuk.

I mildly regretted accepting the appointment time on such short notice, but what the heck, a job is a job and what better place to start than with a judge?

As I headed out the driveway, I noticed the van approaching on the in-bound lane. Oh yes, Dad did mention he had an appointment. I guessed that was his visitor.

As I drove into the city I had noticed that Dad's car was sadly in need of a spring-cleaning. The driver's-side floor area had salt stains and crusted mud. The back seat was littered with McDonald's wrappers, a multi-times folded city map, a blanket and a throw pillow. There was a pair of muddy rubber boots stuffed behind the drivers seat. The duct tape on the rear window vent probably covered a cracked glass. Dad must have been in some pretty rough country recently.

I pulled the piece of paper out of my pocket and placed it in the glasses holder: 5th Fl, N. Sparrow Bldg, 20-19 Const. Ave.

It just seemed natural to take the old familiar route—left on Southgate Road. Just after the turn, I glanced to my left, out of habit, to see how the General's Mountain looked this morning. I recalled seeing this view many times when I was riding the school bus to the high school into Melcastle.

After a short distance, Southgate Road passed through an old wooden arch. A barbed wire fence came right up to the arch on both sides of the road. Kids riding the school bus with me used to say that was the Mason-Dixon Line. We had studied about the history of the border disputes between the Penn family and some other family. My guess was that the final settlement put the boundary between Maryland and Pennsylvania about where that arch and fence were.

The first mile or so along Southgate Road was the only stretch where I could travel over 30 miles per hour. I was just getting up to 50 when I noticed a sound like a window was partially open. I quickly concluded that it was coming from the duct tape on the window vent behind me. The noise wasn't loud, just annoying. It wasn't like Dad to leave defects like that unrepaired. The house could fall down around him, but not his car. Maybe it was just the car was getting old and Dad didn't care about his car the way he used to. His age and living alone might have something to do with it too.

My next revelation was seeing that the city had spread so far west.

There were two or three new housing developments on the east side of Southgate Road.

As I turned right on Constitution Avenue, the sun, which had been behind me, now was shining on my lap and felt nice and warm.

There was a large shopping mall with big-box-stores on the Constitution Avenue corner. The A & P caught my attention because that chain had pretty well disappeared in Quebec a few years ago. The A & P chain lost out in a series of nasty grocery chain "store-wars."

Most of Constitution Avenue was unchanged. After a few blocks, I had to come to a quick stop at a traffic light at Coteau Avenue or "Coteau Row" as we used to call it. That row of houses was always the most popular place where we used to go after sports events.

As I sat at the light, I wondered whether I could still remember the names of the families along the giant crescent ending in a cul-de-sac. The first house was the Andersen-Koops, then the Albertsons, the Watkinsons, the Fordhams, the Galens, the Pladsens, the Leblonds, the Carswells and the big Sparrow house…

H…O…N…K   H…O…N…K

The car horns were blaring behind me. The light had obviously turned green. I roared through the intersection. I resisted the urge to panic by telling myself all I had to do was look for an eight-storey building.

Soon a series of larger buildings downtown started to appear. Thankfully, for my purposes, there was only one with eight floors. It looked even bigger than I had imagined because it was shaped in the form of a giant L. The side along Constitution Avenue took up the whole block. I could see now what Judge Sewchuk meant by his chambers being in the north wing. You could see the end of the north wing sticking out. That side of the building would be along Taylor Street, if memory served me correctly.

The parkade in behind the Sparrow Building was nearly full. I had to go to the fifth or sixth level to find a space. It was so close to the top level that I could see the sun shining over top of the Sparrow Building.

That helped me keep my directions straight. I kept repeating to myself the judge's instructions, "fifth floor, north wing."

I was lucky; the spot I found was near the parkade elevator. It was also immediately in front of the internal corner of the building. When I passed through the space between the parkade and the rear entrance, I noticed there were reserved parking spaces at street level surrounding the elevated parking.

As I entered the building, I saw a large sign indicating the Justice Building was to the left. It wasn't until I entered the short passageway that I became aware that the "north wing" was actually a separate building. The north wing elevators were located immediately at the end of a short covered passageway.

Upon arrival at the fifth floor, I was surprised when the doors opened on back of the elevator. Straight ahead, all you could see was a large, elevated reception desk in the middle of the hallway. There were three clerks seated at the desk and a phalanx of three or four security guards standing behind them. The floors all around were gleaming and the smell of paste wax permeated the air.

I introduced myself to the clerk at the center of the reception desk and asked how I might find Judge Sewchuk's chambers. I was asked to provide three pieces of identification. I wasn't too sure the clerk would accept my Canadian driver's licence, my Quebec Law Society membership and my Canadian bank account cheques. After I signed in and put on my clip-on badge, one of the security guards stepped forward and escorted me to the judge's chambers.

I was introduced to a middle-aged lady, in a dark gray woolen suit. Her greying hair was rolled into a bun. Her eyes were large and dark brown. The nameplate in front of her read: "I. Burgh." I was willing to bet when she was in school the kids used to call her Ice Burgh.

Ms Burgh directed me to a chair in the hall opposite her desk and went about her work, but you could tell she wasn't really concentrating on anything.

"Judge Sewchuk is running late this morning," she offered. "His last case was late getting started."

"That's fine. I have lots of time."

"He's usually punctual, but sometimes his cases are a little trying. Oh, I'm sorry. I didn't mean that to sound like a pun." My guess was she had used that line before, just to see how visitors would react.

A few minutes later she opened the judge's door and spoke a few words. Then she turned to me and announced the judge would see me now. She led me into his chambers. To my surprise, there was no one there! Ms Burgh retreated, leaving me standing alone. I had to assume the judge had gone back into the courtroom through the door on my right and would return in a moment. It gave me a chance to look around his chambers.

There were numerous certificates and diplomas mounted on the oak paneled walls. Several framed pictures sat on the right hand side of the judge's desk. I recognized the judge in one of the pictures in front. The color photograph showed another man assisting the judge in putting on a baseball jacket. The judge was much bigger than the man assisting him. The smaller man's face was partially turned away from the camera, but he looked familiar.

I noticed the same jacket that was in the photograph hanging on a coat rack in the corner. I took a step closer to the rack. My attention was drawn to several large discolored spots on the jacket sleeve that weren't visible in the photograph. The pink spots stood out on the white leather sleeves. The red shoulders had some discoloration marks that weren't as obvious. It looked like someone had done a poor job with a spot remover.

At that moment, Judge Sewchuk entered the room. Although I was expecting him, he startled me as he burst through the door like a fullback heading for a touchdown. He was just as I had remembered him, a tall, barrel-chested man. He approached me with that big politician smile of his—the one that looks like a one-slot toaster with teeth. His hair, what little there was of it, had turned almost completely white on the sides. Obviously, he was in the habit of combing his hair across his head to hide a bald spot, which was more noticeable later when I saw him from the back.

When we shook hands, I felt a couple of flesh colored band-aides at the base of his thumb and forefinger. His grip was weak, unusual for a man of his size and athletic background. At the same time, I couldn't help but notice that his left hand was almost completely wrapped in a tensor binding covering a white cotton bandage. Just the tips of his fingers were exposed.

"How are you, Heather? I haven't seen you in years. To tell you the truth, I just found out a few days ago that you obtained your degree in Montreal. How did you happen to end up there?"

"I'm fine, thank you, Your Honor. Montreal is a long story."

"How's Henry? I haven't talked to him for quite a while. I see him now and again in the lobby and at a few social occasions. It's too bad we don't associate much anymore. I miss his dry humor. How's your mother, Betty? Haven't seen her in years."

I immediately bristled and wanted to inform him that my mother's name was Bonnie, but I thought it best just to respond to the question about Dad.

"You know Dad. He never changes," I responded, trying to cover as much of the territory as I could with a simple response.

We continued in this multiple-question, simple-answer routine for several minutes.

I was somewhat put off by this whole facade and I began to wonder whether the assignment was really genuine or something nobody else would take on. Finally, he walked around to a high-back, leather-bound chair behind his desk and gestured with his bandaged hand to a chair opposite for me to sit.

"Well my dear, there has been a long simmering dispute over the property known as the General's Farm."

The judge opened a folder of papers on the side of his desk.

"Yes sir. Up on the General's Mountain," I threw in, trying to show some enthusiasm.

"The bank of the Carrot River is quite high at that point," he commented, "but I wouldn't call it a mountain, certainly not looking at it from the direction of the city." He seemed to enjoy lecturing me.

"Yes, sir," I responded, dutifully.

"The senior judge from the Teasdale county in Maryland and I have agreed that the dispute between the Pennsylvania Heritage Society and the Teasdale Heritage Foundation has gone on far too long. They're still arguing about where the Mason-Dixon line passes through the property. The consensus is the main building is in Pennsylvania and the cottage is in Maryland. It seems the heritage groups would rather argue than co-operate."

"Okay," I interjected quietly, not knowing whether I should say anything more or not.

"Judge Brothwell and I have agreed that both sides are to be represented by counsel. Your appointment would be to represent the State of Pennsylvania. I would appreciate it if you could reach a settlement as soon as possible. The assignment is routine and should give you a nice income for a few hours work. The contract calls for up to one hundred hours. You shouldn't need anywhere near that much time, but Judge Brothwell insisted. I think that's because Pennsylvania is paying for the lion's share."

"I'm quite prepared to put in as much time as it takes to resolve this issue, Your Honor, but I'm concerned I won't have any standing in court, if it should ever come to that."

"I doubt if it will ever go to court," said Judge Sewchuk. "Should it require court appearances, you could always ask your father to sit in for you. I would expect you to keep your father informed as you go along."

"You mean like a paralegal, Your Honor?"

"I would say a little better than that. I assume you'll be applying to write the Pennsylvania bar exams this July. By the way, send me a copy of your application, including a copy of your membership in the Canadian Bar Association or whatever it's called up there, and I'll write a letter of recommendation for you."

"That's very kind of you, Your Honor."

As I sat there, the feeling became stronger that I was being set up. His instructions and answers were all too quick and at the same time lengthy. Maybe he just liked to hear the sound of his own voice.

"Judge Brothwell is from Teasdale and he has already named the lawyer representing the State of Maryland."

"Judge Brothwell, I've heard of him," I responded, "He lives in Naicam, I believe." I wasn't really sure where the judge lived now. He may have moved to Teasdale during the past 13 year for all I knew. I was feeling frustrated and wanted to correct the judge on something.

"The Maryland lawyer's name is Dennis Archard," the judge said as he rummaged through the pages in the file. "I would suggest you meet with Mr. Archard as soon as possible. "He lives at 2118 Old Military Road, in the metropolis of Teasdale."

I bristled at the "the metropolis of Teasdale" comment. I attempted to disguise my reaction by getting my notebook and pencil out of my briefcase to record the name and address.

"I shouldn't have any trouble finding Mr. Archard, considering that I live with my father on the same Road," I said, trying not to reveal my growing sense of frustration. I hoped the judge wouldn't notice the edge in my voice.

"The Pennsylvania Heritage Society and Teasdale Heritage Foundation have agreed to hold a joint meeting for the first time, this Wednesday night, at seven-thirty, in the city hall auditorium."

I repeated the date, the time and the place, in a low monotone voice as I wrote the data in my notebook. Hopefully, I had recorded it correctly.

The judge spoke for a few minutes about how nice it was to have me back in town and how he hoped this assignment went smoothly.

At the end of our little social discussion, the judge pressed an intercom on his desk and asked his secretary whether the paperwork was ready on the General's Farm assignment. Ms. Burgh entered and handed the judge a folder and left. After examining the contents briefly, the judge signed once on the top paper and a couple more times on other sheets underneath. He flipped several pages back and forth a few times and then handed the file to me.

"Just sign there on the bottom of the first and second sheets and you're in business," he said. "And initial my copy attached to the cover, please."

"There," I commented, when I had finished signing and initialing.

"You are authorized an hourly rate of $50, not to exceed $5,000. I don't expect you'll need anywhere near that amount, but, as I said, Judge Brothwell insisted," the judge commented, as he extracted his copy and handed the remainder of the file to me. He then placed his copy in his "OUT" basket.

"And now, if you'll excuse me, I'm due back in court," he announced, as he abruptly turned and disappeared through the door he had previously entered.

"Thank you, sir," I said, as a knee-jerk response. I'm sure he didn't hear me.

I was stunned that he would assume my acceptance of the assignment without any discussion or clarification. In Montreal, I was taught to identify what would be accepted as the "completion of an assignment" at very least. I found the judge's whole demeanor more than a little arrogant. I felt angry and frustrated. Were my feelings clouding my judgment? Perhaps I was making too much of the whole thing. All kinds of conflicting thoughts were going through my mind. Something wasn't right. The feeling in my stomach was similar to the way I felt during the Mystery Club sessions back in Montreal, only this was real life and a property dispute could hardly be compared to a murder mystery play.

I wandered out of the judge's chambers barely able to contain my frustration. I wasn't sure whether Ms Burgh saw me leave or not. She was talking to another woman down the hall.

It was only eleven o'clock—far too early for lunch with Dad.

After I dropped off my security badge and stepped into the elevator, I figured a little shopping might help settle my nerves. I recalled seeing a small ladies shop near the stairs. Just as the elevator doors opened, I thought I should convert my money to U.S. dollars first.

I proceeded to the Constitution Avenue entrance. Through the glass doors, I could see the First Union Bank across the street. My thoughts of visiting the bank were cut short because it was raining quite hard. That persuaded me to wait for another day and then I would be able to take my time and open a bank account, deposit my severance check and exchange the Canadian cash I had in my wallet.

I decided that since I had plenty of time, I would do some browsing in the rest of the shops on the ground floor. I was pleasantly surprised by the quality of the clothing they had for sale and the prices were lower than I had expected. Then I remembered the amounts were in U.S. dollars.

I explained my situation to the sales lady and persuaded her to let me try on some shorts and blouses. I had the feeling as soon as I mentioned Dad's name that she knew him. She even offered to put my selections aside for me.

I was looking around the ladies shop and feeling good about my new "lay-away" plan, when I noticed a neon sign over what looked like a restaurant across the concourse. Because of the glare, I had to read the letters underneath the lights one by one. The sign read: "L a G o n d o l a." Oh, my goodness! That was the restaurant Dad mentioned where we should meet for lunch. The clock behind the sales counter said it was five after 12. So much for the thought of having a drink while I waited for Dad.

CHAPTER 13

Lunch With Heather

Noon Monday

The drink I had been nursing was just about empty when Heather appeared at the Maitre d's station. I stood as she was escorted to my table.

"How come you're sitting in the smoking section, Dad?"

"I've been coming here ever since the place opened. My favorite table happened to be where they put the smoking section when the bylaw was passed."

I was still recovering from the excitement of the meeting with Victor Gabler. I was concerned that Heather would notice something in my behavior and force me to make up some excuse to hide my recent good fortune concerning the General's Farm. Then I thought Heather suspected something by the way she opened the conversation.

"Celebrating something special…like my return home…or a new partnership, maybe?" Heather asked playfully.

"In a way," I replied, and let out a breath I didn't realize I had been holding. Relax! Relax! I told myself.

"Your drink is almost empty. Have you been waiting long?" Heather asked, as she put her briefcase on the floor and adjusted her chair.

"Only about five minutes or so. I thought I'd better order something or they would wonder what was happening and then I'd have to give them a song and dance about your coming home. So I ordered a drink."

"Okay, I guess we're ready to order…on second thought, I'm not all that hungry today," Heather added, as she smoothed out her napkin.

The waiter arrived and while he was taking our orders, he hinted that I should introduce him to Heather. I was reluctant because I knew that would trigger a visit from Mr. Spagnoli later, which I wasn't too keen on right then. I was nervous enough as it was. Heather ordered a salad and I ordered a medium-rare steak. I guess all the excitement had made me hungry. Then I remembered I hadn't had much for breakfast.

"How did your visit with Judge Sewchuk go?" I asked as a way of deflecting the conversation away from myself.

"Boy, is he a long-winded fellow."

"Always has been I'm afraid."

"I told him I was concerned about my legal standing in court, until I can establish my accreditation," Heather commented, as her salad arrived.

"Surely that won't be a problem. I realize you'll have to write the Pennsylvania and Maryland bar exams, but I should be able to help you with any court appearances until then."

"No, it's not that so much. I don't really know what it is, but Judge Sewchuk seemed to have everything all worked out. He even offered to write a letter of recommendation. He assured me my lack of legal status was just a formality."

"That's interesting, but you must admit it was nice of the judge to offer," I countered, trying to take a positive outlook.

"I don't know. It all seemed too rehearsed," Heather demurred, as she pulled a file from her briefcase and handed it to me.

"Perhaps you're reading too much into it…meeting him

professionally for the first time and all," I suggested, as I accepted the file.

"The file even contains a letter of introduction, which gives me authority to demand access to various files and things. Note the letter is dated last Friday."

I checked the various pieces of paper in the file. The contract itself was neatly summarized in the covering letter, which gave her and her firm, "full authority to bring to resolution all matters between the States of Pennsylvania and Maryland and in particular the Pennsylvania Heritage Society and the Teasdale Heritage Foundation and the owners of buildings and property known as the **General's Farm**.

The words *"General's Farm"* stood out like a neon sign to me. I was stunned and I guess it showed.

"You seemed surprised, Dad. Is there anything wrong?" Heather asked, with some concern.

I cocked my head and I tried to look as though I was mulling over a point of law or something.

"Not really. As you say, it's curious that he should date the letter last Friday. I don't know as I've even seen Jack since I received your phone call on Saturday," I replied, trying to control myself and hoping the length of my answer would cover my reaction to seeing the General's Farm as her assignment.

"Well, in any case, I'm happy it's an assignment I can do and you can help me with. I thought of your experience in handling property settlement cases and your knowledge of the history of the farm," Heather added, as she started into her salad, which had just arrived.

The conversation that followed was mostly one-sided on my part. I'm afraid my description of the General's Farm became a rambling dialogue. I remember talking about the Wendelman couple who used to live there; how Roger disappeared and his wife Ruby was admitted to what used to be called the Hospital for the Criminally Insane— probably in connection with Roger's disappearance. The more I talked the more detail I couldn't help slipping in. I even mentioned the fact that Ruby was pregnant at the time and it was rumored the baby was given up for adoption because of Ruby's condition.

Finally, my steak arrived. I quickly seized on the opportunity to stuff my mouth and let Heather do the talking. Every time she finished saying something, the only thing I could think about was my meeting with Victor Gabler.

I was desperate to switch the conversation, so I mentioned how much Heather looked like her mother when Bonnie was young. I commented that her mother was so pretty and so popular that I often wondered why Bonnie picked me to marry.

I didn't mean it as way of bringing Bonnie into the conversation, but it turned out to be as good a way as any to bring the subject out in the open. Heather showed genuine concern about her mother.

Heather confided that she had heard from friends in town, that Bonnie had been admitted to the hospital for long-term care. She knew that Bonnie had been away from home for several years, but I could tell she thought Bonnie was still in the hospital and didn't know that I had placed her in the then brand new place called Windemere—a long term care facility collocated with the criminally insane.

I gave her a brief history of Bonnie's medical condition. I assured Heather the services were much better at Windemere than the hospital. I could see the negative impression of Windemere in Heather's mind was going to be a problem. I had to explain the dual set-up at Windemere and that her mother was not classified as either criminal or insane. I told her that my hope was that one-day Bonnie would be well enough to come home. It was important to me that Heather understood that. I also wanted Heather to know there were encouraging advances in medicine and that Bonnie was showing signs of recent progress.

When I finished speaking, I was totally unprepared by Heather's next comment.

"I was wondering whether it would be all right if we visited Mom?" Heather asked, as she reached out and touched my hand.

"I think that would be great. I could consult Dr. Hammersmyth to see whether it's okay. If you are really interested, I'll call him and we can make arrangements to visit tomorrow, if that's all right with you."

"Sure, tomorrow is fine by me. By the way, I guess I should think about getting a car of my own. Any suggestions where I should start looking?"

"I suggest that you try John Barrigar at Barrigar's Auto Sales just down the street. I've bought my last three cars there."

"I can assume that he's been in business for over 30 years then?" Heather chuckled, as she poked me on the arm. "Perhaps we could make a better deal if we bought you a new car too, Dad."

"I take it you aren't too impressed with my 86 Olds?"

"Eighty six? I didn't think it was that old," she laughed.

"Yeah. I guess maybe trading the old car in isn't such a bad idea. Shall we go?"

"Judge Sewchuk also suggested that I meet Dennis Archard. He's the lawyer representing the State of Maryland."

"I've heard of Dennis, but don't know much about him, except that he's young and good-looking. I think he has been involved mostly with wills and pre-nuptial agreements and the like. Oh, and property settlements."

"Interesting combination."

"Want to flip for the bill?"

"Would you mind catching this one, Dad? All the money I have is Canadian. I still have to open a bank account and convert my money to that dull American money," she said with a wink.

"We'll have to hurry if we're going to meet my secretary...sorry, our secretary. Roma just comes in during the mornings. She's a single mother and only works part-time. It works out fine. I work at home during the mornings and come here around noon and she leaves shortly afterwards. She picks up her son at the day-care a couple of blocks away."

"Good. I'm looking forward to meeting her."

"I've had my Pennsylvania office in this building since it opened about ten years ago. It's a bit more luxurious than I need, but at the time, my practice was much bigger than it is now. Perhaps it's fortuitous, that with your arrival, the business may start to grow again."

As we were riding up in the elevator, Heather asked where I park my car.

"My parking spot is at ground level. It goes with the office rental.

It's right by the rear entrance doors—very handy."

"Darn. I parked in the parkade. I had to go up about five or six levels to find a spot."

"I should have told you about my reserved spaces."

"Reserved spaces?" Heather questioned. "You have more than one spot?"

"Yeah, two of them. They came with the original ten-year lease for my partner and me at the time. It didn't cost me that much to retain the second one, so I keep it as a convenience for my clients."

"I should go and move the old car into one of your spots."

"I would suggest you do that after you meet Roma. You can move the car while I finish some work that has to be done today. My spaces are marked 8C and 8D."

"I hate to bring up the subject again, but could you lend me some money? I doubt whether the ticket booth-person will accept my Canadian money."

"Here, take a couple of twenties. That should hold you until you complete your banking," I said as I paid the lunch bill.

As we exited the elevator on the eighth floor, I pointed to a window at the end of the hall.

"You can see Barrigar's Auto Sales. It's a block down and across the street. It maybe obscured by the big Wye oak trees."

"Ah yes. I see it. I was looking for a parking lot full of cars," Heather replied, as she went to the window.

"Oh, he has lots of cars. It's just that you can't see most of them from here."

We returned to the reception area where I introduced Heather to Roma.

"Hi Heather!" Roma exclaimed. "I'm so pleased to meet you. Your father called on Saturday afternoon and said you were coming home."

"I'm pleased to meet you, Roma."

"I'm sorry I can't stay long, Heather. I have to pick up my son at the day-care."

Roma didn't depart right away as expected. She looked uncomfortable and seemed to have something on her mind.

"Mr. Macy, I was thinking…on the weekend…after you phoned with the news about Heather.," Roma stammered.

"It's okay Roma," I interjected. "You're among friends here."

"I didn't want to mention it, but…I was wondering whether it would be proper for me to ask…whether you were considering having me work full-time now that…I mean when Alex starts kindergarten…"

"Full-time sounds like it could be a good possibility," I agreed.

"That would be great. I know what the finances of the firm are like and I really didn't want to ask. It just kind of blurted out of me. I'm sorry."

"Don't give it another thought, Roma. You have been with me for years and you are entitled to speak your mind. You've helped me out of tight spots many times and I appreciate it. Heather and I will come up with something."

"We can always work something out," Heather added.

Then I remembered the offer from Gabler.

"In fact, I think you should receive a raise effective as soon as Heather moves in," I announced. "After all, there is bound to be more work."

After I made the announcement, I realized I could finally think about being more generous, not only because of my recent good fortune, but to reward a loyal employee.

"Thank you, Mr. Macy," Roma said, blushing with excitement and tears beginning to form. "Now I must be off to pick up my son."

After Roma left, Heather and I turned to survey the rest of the office.

"That's my office back there." I indicated. "Nothing too spectacular. My partner and I decided on the office space when we first moved in and I was never motivated to change it. Besides, mine is closer to Roma's desk."

"Nice!" Heather said, as she stepped inside the second office. "I guess I can start moving in anytime then."

"Okay by me. There are no keys for either your door or mine, just the outer door. We'll have a key cut for you today and go over the case files starting tomorrow. As for the partnership, how does a 50/50 split sound?"

"That's more than generous, Dad," Heather replied.

We shook hands awkwardly.

"Now, I have to finish some paperwork for a Philadelphia client. Why don't you look around and see what needs to be done before you move in."

"I'd better move the car. Then I'll have a closer look around here."

"Sure. By the way, the office next door may be coming available in a month or two. It's a lawyer's office and the current resident looks like a sure bet to win the election for a new judge's position that has recently opened up. Kathleen Crowsfoot Armstead is the odds-on favorite to win."

"Kathleen Crowsfoot Armstead?"

"I'm not kidding. That's her second name. She goes by Kay Armstead, but I know about the Crowsfoot name because she asked me to witness her application papers for the election."

"Maybe you shouldn't have told me. By the way, I noticed your graduation diploma is made out to William Horace Macy. Why your father's name? And how come it isn't in color?"

"That's a long story. That's a photocopy. The original is in the office at home. I wrote the university many years ago, but never received a reply. The mail comes as William H Macy which is fine, but I'd like the diploma corrected to read 'Henry'."

"Is there any way I can have a look at the vacant office?"

"I have a key to the outer door. It's in my office."

When Heather returned, I was still composing the Philadelphia client's letter on Roma's computer.

"I see you haven't finished yet. I think I'll go look at Crowsfoot's office," Heather chuckled. "You said you had a key?"

"Yes, it's in the top right-hand drawer of my desk. I'll be about a half an hour yet. By the way, please don't use the name Crowsfoot."

"Sorry, I was just trying to add a little humor."

The letter for the Philadelphia client was coming out of the printer, when Heather returned. The case was one I had lost and I was trying to persuade the client not to appeal, without saying as much.

"What did you think of Kay's office?"

"It's pretty much the same as my office. Both are kind of dark."

"You could always redecorate," I suggested. "You would be surprised what Roma can do for an office."

"Is there a Staples in this building?"

"No. SPA-KAL wouldn't allow them in."

"SPA-KAL—I've seen their signs on several vacant lots and buildings on my way into town. What kind of outfit are they?"

"All I can tell you is they are a powerful, local syndicate. They own quite a few buildings and various properties around town. The word is they've overextended themselves. They're trying to sell some holdings to recoup some cash, but their prices are a way too high for most people around here."

"Sounds like a mysterious bunch."

"You don't know the half of it. We're standing eight floors above the lot where old Tony Whitehall's filling station used to be."

"I remember them," Heather added, reacting to a familiar name. "He and his wife Christine used to run the place together."

"The SPA-KAL people muscled the Whitehalls out. Tony eventually sold the property to SPA-KAL, but I doubt whether he received a good price for it. Shortly after the sale, the filling station was demolished and this building took its place."

There was more to the SPA-KAL story, but I let it go. Heather seemed preoccupied.

"How have you managed to run two office locations with so few law books in this one?"

"I've discovered over the years that you don't really need as many of those books as the Law Society and the publishers would like you to believe."

"I guess we'll have to take an inventory of what we have in both places and go from there," Heather concluded.

"I'm surprised you didn't suggest we subscribe to a law library on the Internet."

"That's a great idea. I think I'll make that one of my first priorities, once I'm settled."

"Good. What else did you do while I was working?"

"I took your advice and opened up an account at the First Union Bank. I deposited my severance check. Man! I knew there was a premium on the U.S. dollar, but I lost more than a third of my severance check," Heather fumed.

"Well, that's the way it goes, I'm afraid," I commented.

"I don't know—but seeing the dollar value on my check shrink by more than one third just gave me an empty feeling. I was so stunned. I didn't think I ordered any blank checks. But, I must have, because the teller asked me whether I wanted birds on my checks. Apparently I'm getting checks with birds on them."

"All set?" I asked, as I selected the office key from my key ring and headed for the door.

"You know, when I saw the Brinks truck out side the bank it reminded me of every time a boyfriend of mine in Montreal would see one of those he would say, 'there's a mobile crime scene' and he would laugh to himself."

"Must have been some boyfriends you had up there."

"I didn't mean that, the way it came out. You would have liked most of the boys I dated."

We had a new office key cut at the combination hardware and convenience store on the main floor. While we were there, we had an extra key cut for Macy House.

As we exited the back door, Heather stopped and looked at the separation between the north wing and the main building.

"When did they move the courthouse from the old building on Galloway Street to this building?"

"That's a long story. The old courthouse had been crumbling for years and was going to cost millions to repair or build a new one. That debate was raging just as SPA-KAL was about to start construction of this building. The architects just made a few design changes and the courthouse has been attached to the SPA-KAL Building...I mean...the Sparrow Building ever since."

"There must have been some not-so-gentle arm twisting to make that deal."

"I'm sure Judge Sewchuk had a hand in that. I'm convinced he's connected with SPA-KAL somehow."

"I can see where they separated the buildings, but isn't that odd to have to go into one building to enter another?"

"The courthouse actually has three other entrances and another set of elevators. The passageway elevator was meant to be part of the main building. It was obviously cost effective just to move it back a few feet and build a covered walkway."

"I suppose it's convenient if you are a lawyer and have your office in the Sparrow Building," Heather said, with a wink.

I started the car.

"By the way, what is the telephone number at the office?"

"That's a neat arrangement we had installed. The downtown office and home phone number are the same. The phone rings at both places at the same time. Either Roma or I can answer it. She usually lets it ring three times before she picks it up. If neither of us answers after four rings, it automatically goes to the answering machine."

"Good thinking. That means I won't have to remember two numbers."

"I also have an unlisted number in my office," I added. "It's the second button on all three phones—Roma's, mine and now your phone."

"That's good. I'll make a note of it tomorrow."

As we approached Macy House, Heather brought up the subject of the offices again. I had the feeling she had something else on her mind.

"Did Crowsfoot…I mean Kay Armstead…did she have a partner?"

"Yes she did, she and her husband, Herb Murphy, were partners for quite a few years. She has always gone by her maiden name. Not that it matters, but they are now separated. He moved out several years ago."

As we pulled into our driveway and I was about to turn off the ignition, I remembered a problem.

"I was thinking—there isn't much in the house in the way of food. Should we go out to eat?"

"Good idea. Where would you like to go?"

"How about the newest restaurant in Teasdale?" I suggested. "It's a service station slash restaurant called Sylvie's. I've tried it a few times and the food is pretty good."

"All I want right now is a hamburger, French fries and a Pepsi," Heather announced. "But maybe I'll have to change my style a bit. That's what I always used to have when I was a student."

"I know what you mean. Now I've pretty well settled on some form of seafood or chicken fingers. I never seem to notice any reaction when I ask for boneless chicken fingers."

"Dad! You used to use that line 13 years ago."

"Yeah, I guess some things never change."

"Yeah, well there's always hope."

"By the way, the owner/manager of the restaurant is an old classmate of yours, Sylvie Spagnoli."

"The same Spagnoli family that runs the restaurant in the Sparrow Building?"

"That's correct."

"Sylvie Spagnoli? I'm not sure she was in my class, but there was at least one in every year ahead me and several more in the lower grades."

"They're a big family that's for sure."

"Aren't they the Italian family that used to live in Teasdale and moved onto Coteau Avenue?"

"That's the ones. They had about ten kids, as I recall."

"I remember Sylvie fairly well," Heather commented. "But all I remember about the family is that no matter how hard they tried they just couldn't fit in with the crowd on Coteau Row. They obviously had loads of money because the house was the really big one right on the end of the crescent. Maybe it was because they had so many kids. I don't know…interesting."

"I guess papa Spagnoli wanted to set his daughter up in business and Teasdale was as good a place as any. I know Sylvie works there during the day, because I stop for gas once in a while and she sometimes serves the cars herself. We'll have to see whether she is on tonight."

As it turned out, Sylvie wasn't working that night. Supper was basically uneventful except for two rowdy teenagers at the next table. It was obvious that they were trying to attract Heather's attention. After several minutes of their loud banter, and liberal use of foul language, I had had enough. I suggested, my voice just short of a rage, which they might find some better place to carry on their adolescent conversation.

"And who might you be, Gramps?" one of them asked.

"I'm her father," I retorted.

"Well, why don't you take her home then, Gramps?" the other one chimed in. They both laughed.

"You know, the more you try to act grown-up the more childish you sound," I declared, my voice getting louder as I spoke.

"Let's get out of here," the first one said.

"Yeah, who needs this?" the other asked, as they left.

The woman at the cash had noticed the commotion and came to our table.

"Thanks for your help with those two," she said.

"No problem. They're a couple of the Spagnoli kids aren't they?" I suggested.

"Yes. They come in here all the time because their sister owns the place and they think they have special privileges."

"I thought so. I've known their father for quite a few years."

"Thanks. I'll mention it to Sylvie when I see her."

On the way out, I asked Heather whether she recognized the two teenage punks.

"No, should I have?"

"They're the Spagnoli twins that you used to baby-sit. You often mentioned that the twins were the worst, as I recall."

"You mean Ronald and Reagan?" Heather asked dumbfounded.

"I can imagine their father will be quite upset when I tell him how his boys behaved this evening. I see him just about every weekday at La Gondola restaurant."

"Dad, if those two were the Spagnoli twins, then one of them is a girl," Heather giggled. "Ronald and Reagan."

"Ronald and Reagan?" I mused. "I guess old man Spagnoli really was a Republican."

As we left the parking lot, Heather suggested we buy some groceries.

116

"There's a Piggly Wiggly on Constitution Avenue between Southgate Road and Coteau. That's where I usually buy my groceries."

"Ah...right, I saw it this morning on the way into town."

"You went in by way of Southgate Road, I gather. There are too many traffic lights that way for me."

"Yeah, I haven't tried the new highway yet and don't really know how to use it. I'll try it next time. In the meantime, let's solve our groceries problem."

I started in on the usual list. "I guess we need just about everything: milk, bread, a few frozen TV dinners, eggs, frozen pizza, tube steaks..."

"What are tube steaks?" Heather asked, as we turned right on Southgate Road.

"Wieners," I replied, with a chuckle.

"I might have known."

By the time we arrived home and put the groceries away, I was ready for bed. Heather found a pencil and some paper and started writing.

"What's on the agenda for tomorrow?" I asked, as I headed for the bathroom.

"I thought I'd go up to the General's Farm and take a look at what I'm getting myself into. I still can't understand why Judge Sewchuk chose me for this assignment."

"I wouldn't worry too much about that. Jack often sends work my way without any obvious reason. I always felt I had to accept the jobs or he wouldn't send any more. Quite frankly, I've depended on those contracts for a fair percentage of my business."

"What are your plans for tomorrow, Dad?"

"Not too much. I guess I'll call Dr. Hammersmyth and see when we can visit your mother."

One important thing I planned to do was deposit the $10,000 check. I also had to do some work done on my property research contract.

"I think I'll stay up for a while. I want to finish off my application for the bar exams and draft that letter of recommendation Judge Sewchuk offered to sign."

"If you need any help, don't hesitate to ask."

"Is it okay if I ask Roma to type it up?"

"Sure, she won't mind."

"Will she deliver it to the judge's secretary, as well?"

"Sure," I said, bubbling through my toothpaste.

CHAPTER 14

Visiting The General's Farm

Tuesday Morning

As the General's Farmhouse came into view, I wondered whether Dad's old Oldsmobile would make it up the mountain.

You used to be able to see most of the building as you rounded the bend of Old Military Road. The trees and undergrowth had pretty much obscured the farmhouse from a distance. It didn't look nearly as impressive today with just the roof ridge and the big chimney sticking out.

Technically, Old Military Road was classified as a paved road. The surface was reasonably intact near Macy House, but west of our place it had suffered the ravages of time. If it weren't for the crown of Old Military Road as it branches to the right, you would hardly be able to tell it from the gravel road that continues straight a head. My guess is that the gravel road used to be the main thoroughfare between Teasdale and Kinistino, the little village across the Carrot River. The U.S. Army probably applied better maintenance to Old Military Road as it branched off the main road because it was undoubtedly used to bring in construction materials and military supplies to the farm.

I presumed the gravel road straight ahead still led to the Old Stone Bridge. It was comforting to see bridge again, but the arches were barely visible over the bushes as I approached the junction that led up to the General's Farm.

I slowed down a little in order to make the gentle turn to the right. At the same time, I knew I had to keep the car's speed up to make the climb easier. As soon as I completed the turn, I pressed my foot as hard as I could on the gas.

I had never made the trip up to the General's Mountain in a car before. All my other visits were by bicycle. I remembered the incline being really steep for a bike, especially the first part. When we cycled up there, we invariably had to walk our bikes the last hundred feet or so until the road leveled out.

The paved part of the upper section of Old Military Road was really old. In that remote part of Maryland, the last time the people living along that road saw a paving machine was probably around the President Kennedy years. The so-called pavement was more like a loosely connected series of potholes.

As the narrow road hugged the steep mountainside, I took a quick peek up the valley toward the northwest. The view was enchanting. There was a light blue haze hanging over the far side of the Carrot River, making the scene like look like a picturesque postcard. Fluffy clouds were obscuring the sun at that moment and the sun's rays shining through looked like giant straws drawing moisture from the earth.

The road was not as steep as I remembered, but steep enough. My apprehension of driving off the edge eased as the road leveled off and widened out. The right side of the road branched off and became the entrance lane to the farmhouse.

As a kid, I always felt like an intruder going up that road. I had never actually been inside the farmhouse. I wondered how much truth there was in the rumor of it being haunted by the ghosts of tortured prisoners from the Civil War.

There was something familiar about the big square windows of the house. The fact that they were undecorated with curtains or blinds definitely made the place uninviting. I was glad I had a legitimate reason for visiting.

As I slowed the car to a crawl, I noticed the farmhouse was well constructed of quarried stones similar to Macy House. The most impressive thing about the structure was the portico over the driveway. The top of the portico also served as a balcony. Bushes and trees obscured both ends of the house.

Old Military Road widened out even more beyond the house. At that point, Old Military Road became a two-rut dirt path with grass growing in between and eventually became a single path leading down to the golf course clubhouse. You could see why the farmhouse hadn't been built any farther up the mountain. The angle was much steeper where the two-rut dirt path ended.

I had intended to drive right up under the portico, but I could see as I approached that a yellow police tape blocked off the driveway:

"Police Lines—Do Not Cross"

One continuous tape was strung between three of the four pillars that supported the portico and the other end was tied to the gate in a stone archway under the right-hand side of the house.

I allowed the slope of the hill to slowly let the car come to a stop under a small bush at the extreme right side of the road. I applied the parking brake, opened the car door and stepped out. The brilliance of the sun was temporarily obscured by the cloud of road dust that I had stirred up.

You could tell the police tape had been in place for several days because it was drooping close to the ground and dust-covered. It was then that I noticed a police car parked, facing me, on the other side of the portico. There was no one around and the radio was silent, so I retraced my steps towards my car.

Through the opening above the gate in the stone archway, I could see there was a passageway underneath that end of the building. The interior looked dark and foreboding. If I ever had to go in there, I hoped it would be with another person. I stepped over the police tape and peered over the gate. On both sides of the passageway, which appeared to be about 40 feet long, there was what looked like stalls for animals or storage areas for firewood. The passageway looked more like a barn with a low ceiling. A series of stilts, similar to the pillars holding up the portico, but not as thick, held up the middle of the ceiling or floor above. Shorter stilts held up the left side of the ceiling. A quick glimpse of that area was all I needed.

I caught my foot slightly on the police tape as I stepped over it. The tape remained secure on the gate. The crime scene was intact. Nervous or not, I continued my inspection around the east side of the house. A two storey, stonewall ran the length of the right hand side of the house. There was a thick growth of underbrush up against the wall. I went just far enough to see that the mountain out back opened up into a narrow ravine.

I returned to the driveway. I cautiously stepped over the police tape again. Under the portico, a rather impressive set of stone stairs led up to the farmhouse proper. To arrive at the main floor, I had to go up eight or ten steps to a landing, make a 180-degree turn to the right and then another half dozen steps. The semi-sheltered space was much warmer than I had expected.

I opened the balcony doors and went out. The more than 180-degree view of the river valley below was gorgeous. You could see for miles from northwest to southeast. It reminded me of the view from the kitchen window at Macy House, only much higher up. From that height, you could even see the varying depths of water in the Carrot River.

I went right out to the railing and took a long pause to appreciate the northwestern view and the haze over the river and the blue hills of Virginia in the distance. As I turned my gaze to the southeast, I figured that Macy House should be down there about a mile off to the left. The end of the line of stately Wye oak trees was clearly visible, but the houses along Old Military Road all looked pretty much the same.

Back inside, I could see two or three rooms through the glass in the door to the west on my left that might have been bedrooms at one time. The layout looked more like a motel with its common corridor on the southern side. I guessed that those rooms were the sleeping quarters where the general's staff slept and perhaps the general himself.

As I opened the solid door on the east side of the landing, warm air rushed out. At the same time, my nose was assaulted by a sharp, musty odor that made my head recoil and my eyes blink. There were footprints in the dust and debris on the floor.

To my left there was a stone fireplace similar to the small fireplace at home.

Some sunlight managed to pass through a pair of dirty windows into what was obviously a kitchen. It was complete with an icebox and wood-burning cook stove. The sink had a few dirty dishes in it and a five-gallon pail underneath to catch the dishwater.

The kitchen and main living area beyond were littered with candles, crudely mounted on inappropriate things such as jam can lids, saucers and even a small pail.

The feeling began to grow that I had seen that place before. As soon as I saw the second fireplace around the corner, I realized that the layout of the main floor was basically the same as Macy House, only much older and laden with dust.

The cathedral ceiling above the bathroom and bedrooms gave the farmhouse interior the appearance of spaciousness. In Macy House, the space above those rooms was closed in to form an attic. The differences in the rest of the house were personal touches, especially the furniture and articles on the plaster walls.

The items over the main mantelpiece included an old bugle, a musket and a ceremonial sword. The sword was complete with a scabbard and gold aglet. The pointed knobs that hung from the elaborate cords of the aglet were obviously made of real gold as they glistened even in the dull light. It reminded me of one of my boyfriends in Montreal was a general's aide-de-camp. When he wore a similar aglet to a military ball he took me to, everybody, especially the females, had to hear about it.

123

Until I saw the aglet over the mantelpiece, I was under the impression that particular decoration was strictly a British tradition. But, I guess in the Civil War days U.S. generals wore pretty well whatever they wanted to. If the sword were a genuine Civil War piece, it could be worth a small fortune.

As I walked toward the rear of the building, I felt the springiness of the wooden floor in front of the fireplace. The lively condition of the flooring was logical, given that the building must be over a hundred and fifty years old. The mill-planed planks, covered with several coats of varnish, were uneven in width. In some cases, the ends of the boards still contained some traces of the bark. This made the cracks quite pronounced at the ends where the bark was no longer in place.

At the back of the living and sitting room area, a row of windows looked out on the ravine I had just seen down below. As I approached the door to the left of the windows, I noticed the hand railing beside the short set of stairs outback could use a major repair job. The two stone steps looked safe enough.

Suddenly, a man dressed in a suit came bounding up the steps. He must have been in the ravine when I was examining the passageway.

He seemed as surprised as I was. He was tall and good-looking with an athletic build. My guess was that he would be about my age.

"Excuse me ma'am, may I ask what you are doing here?" he asked sharply.

"My name is Heather Macy," I responded defensively. "I'm a lawyer and I'm here doing some research on the General's Farm. I've been assigned by Judge Sewchuk to act as the lawyer representing the State of Pennsylvania in the dispute between two heritage societies."

"Well ma'am, I'm Detective Turcot from the Melcastle Police," he asserted. "This is a murder scene and no one is supposed to be in here."

"I'm sorry. I haven't touched anything. I've never been here before and I'm just trying to familiarize myself with the property."

As I spoke, Detective Turcot had moved around to a better light. His face seemed familiar and the way he spoke triggered some old memories.

"Say, don't I know you?" I asked. "Is your first name Louis?"

"Yes, it is. You seem familiar to me as well."

"Did we go to school together by any chance?" I asked.

"Perhaps. I only went to high school here for my final two years, before I left to attend Police College."

"What years did you attend good old MCCI?"

"1989 to 1991."

"I left in 1990," I said.

"I guess we could have been together in...Grade 11 then," he ventured.

"I was going with Casey Clarkin in Grade 11."

"That name sounds familiar."

"Were you on any sports teams?" I asked.

"I was on the boys' basketball team."

"That's what we have in common. I was on the girls' team."

"That's right. I remember you now. Olshin was the coach of both the boys' and girls' basketball teams. That made joint practices much more fun."

"For some I guess, but I was only interested in Casey."

"So, you left town and became a lawyer?"

"Yeah, I'm back here working with my dad."

"Well, that's great. Perhaps we'll see more of you. I trust Casey Clarkin is no longer in the picture. At least, I don't see a ring."

"No, no. Casey is long gone. How about yourself? Is there a Mrs. Turcot?"

"There was, but we were divorced after about a year. We were too young."

"So Melcastle is in good hands then."

"You might say that, but we do have the occasional murder."

"Let's hope there aren't too many of those."

"The body we found a week ago is the first murder we've had in years. A hiker stumbled over a shallow grave, a hundred feet or so back in the ravine."

"Ah yes, back in there," I said and as he spoke I was hoping this was one of those occasions when the other person would keep on talking and tell me more.

"Yes, the victim was a male, about 30 years of age, who had been dead approximately ten to twelve days. The technician at the forensic lab said that the murder probably occurred about 17 April."

As Detective Turcot was speaking, I heard Thelma's voice in my head saying, in her quaint little French-Canadian accent, "Those are good clues, ma cherie."

"Wow! That's pretty accurate."

"Actually, the 17th of April was an estimated date, give or take a couple of days. The body was buried in a shallow grave and wrapped in plastic sheeting. We suspect the victim was killed in this building. Whoever buried him didn't do a very good job. The frost was probably still in the ground back in April. The spring run-off and the animals had pretty well uncovered the whole body."

The 17 April date resonated with me because that was the day I found out I was terminated from my job in Montreal. My curiosity cried out for more details. I was reacting like Thelma and I used to during our Mystery Club adventures.

"You seem to be worried about something. Is there a problem?"

"Just a few details that don't add up," Detective Turcot replied. "We know the victim lost a considerable amount of blood…from seventeen stab wounds…probably a knife. Even though the wounds were small, they were deep."

"Seventeen stab wounds. That's a lot," I commented.

"We figure the victim must have come to his demise in here," he said and pointed to the fireplace area. "The floor in front of the fireplace has obviously been cleaned recently."

Detective Turcot slowly moved toward the front of the house. I repeated to myself, "17 stab wounds—17 April." When he had his back to me, I sneaked an envelope and pencil from my purse and quickly scribbled, "17 stab—17 Apr."

"You'll notice the bleached look of the wooden floor in front of the fireplace and there are spots on the stone apron as well," Detective Turcot said and spread both hands indicating an area about five or six feet wide.

"Yes. I can see the difference, now that you point it out."

126

"We did the standard luminol and fluorescent light test which showed a lot of blood had been spilled."

"Ah yes, I've seen that on TV."

"The room still smells of Javex. The smell was much stronger a week ago when we were first called in."

"You're right. It gives the dust in the air a peculiar smell that I hadn't noticed before."

It really just smelled musty to me.

"We still haven't located the murder weapon, but according to the coroner's report it was long and thin, like a carving knife. We found blood on the underside of the cracks in the floor, right near the stone apron. We had to go downstairs and scrape a sample from between the planks."

"I still don't see what the problem is," I interjected politely.

"The problem is the DNA analysis on the sample from the probable scene does not match the victim's blood. It was 'close enough to be a relative, but no cigar.' That's the reason I'm back here today to search for more blood samples."

"I understand the crime labs can do wonders with DNA analysis these days," I said.

Detective Turcot obviously concluded from my comment on DNA analysis that I had an interest in the subject and took the opportunity to impress me. I listened carefully because I still felt a little guilty about invading his crime scene. He informed me that the Pennsylvania state police had recently opened up a new multi-million dollar Centre for Forensic Sciences in Melcastle and the DNA scientists had their own wing in the building. Analysis that used to take anywhere from four to six weeks can now be done in 48 hours or less. He added that in the past the technicians used to need several cubic centimeters of blood to do the complete test. Now only a tiny piece of material or blood is needed and it can tell you ten times as much as the old way did.

"Now the Melcastle lab can do testing on blood, saliva, semen, skin and hair all at the same time. The lab boys can even tell you a person's age, gender and ethnic origin. Not only that, they have started keeping computer records that will automatically match previous DNA tests from other criminal cases. The computer matching with other non-active cases takes an extra day or two, depending upon your priority. Pennsylvania is also linked with similar centers in several states across the nation. Soon all 50 states will all be on-line."

By that time, we were near the front door and Detective Turcot gave me the distinct impression he had more work to do and that it was time for me to leave. I apologized for taking up so much of his time and made my way outside.

CHAPTER 15

Meeting Mr. McClelland

Later Tuesday Morning

From the gloomy interior of the farmhouse, I stepped out into the bright sunshine. I was surprised to see an old man, his back to me, standing in front of Dad's car. He had a grade school scribbler in one hand and a pencil in the other. As I approached, he didn't appear to notice me. I could hear him complaining about not being able to read the licence plate in that location, as though it was my fault. His mutterings also included something to do with the fact that Pennsylvania only issues one licence plate and that he was glad my Maryland car had two plates, which saved him a trip around to the back of the car. I had the impression I could have lessened his troubles if I had parked under the portico.

I said "Hello" as a warning that I was approaching. He didn't respond until he had finished writing in his scribbler. Over his shoulder, I could see that he had written the days' date, May 6, 2003 and in extra large characters, "PAW 6797," the licence number of Dad's car. When he closed the scribbler, I could see the word "**DIARY**" in bold letters across the cover.

He was a small man, at least 80 years old. His white hair was tossed by the light breeze.

I tried to step around the old man, but just as I moved he turned toward me. He stuck out his chest and squared his shoulders as if to indicate he was protecting his territory. Apart from that initial challenge, I soon discovered that he was really a timid man. I learned later that he was just checking to see whether I was with the police. Perhaps my navy blue jacket and gray slacks looked like a uniform to him and that was his conditioned reaction to people in authority trying to hassle him.

We stood there for a few seconds, facing one another, not saying a word. The old man spoke first.

"I like to record the licence numbers of all the vehicles that come up here," he said quietly.

"That's nice. Do you have many visitors up here?" I asked.

"No, not many," he replied. "There are a lot of cars that stop at the junction where the road splits."

"That's interesting." I said.

"Some drivers come up and look at the farm house, but stay in their cars," he continued with more confidence in his voice. "I don't bother recording those numbers."

"That would be tourists," I suggested and moved a few steps to his other side. He remained in the same spot, but turned his body toward me. I guess at that point he had concluded that I meant him no harm.

"I don't know, but they're usually from Maryland or Pennsylvania, as near as I can tell by the color of the plates on their cars. I can't read the numbers too well away out there," he said pointing to where the road widens opposite the pillars."

I glanced to where he was pointing.

"I would have to move my telescope and I don't want to do that. The range is all set for that spot," he said, pointing at the area between the portico pillars and the stone steps.

"I see," I said, but really didn't understand.

"I'm glad both states went to reflective plates recently. It makes it easier to read the numbers. The multi-colored Pennsylvania plates, where one color fades into the next, makes it easier to distinguish one state from another. Still, I wish Pennsylvania cars had two plates."

As I moved around to his left side, I noticed the car was sitting at an odd angle. The passenger-side bumper was actually touching the ground. The right-hand front wheel appeared to have dropped into a sharp depression.

"It looks like my car is stuck," I declared.

"Sure does."

"I don't suppose there's a phone around here I could use?"

"Sure. I have one in the cottage," he said, pointing into the trees.

I looked to where he was pointing, but I couldn't see anything that might be called a cottage.

"There's a cottage in there somewhere?"

"Sure is," he chuckled. "Follow me."

He turned sharply and walked around and through some bushes. I followed at a distance and sure enough, a small building became visible under some larger trees. If you follow his footsteps, you could actually walk upright. We crossed a small bridge with a low railing on one side. A tiny stream below made a faint bubbling sound. I stopped on the bridge and looked back. I could see the area by the pillars of the portico and the front corner of the car's bumper, but definitely not the rear licence plate.

The cottage looked to be about a storey and a half high. It was only about 75 feet from the portico, but was located on the other side of the ravine that ran behind the main house. The front part of the cottage appeared to be an add-on. The wall that faced south toward Old Military Road was made up of side-by-side, tall windows from corner to corner. On the near side, the upper half of the front door was all glass. Two tall windows on either side of the door extended from about two feet off the ground to the roofline. The overall impression was that it originally might have been a greenhouse. The rear portion of the cottage was built into the far side of the ravine.

My host invited me in and stood holding the door as I entered what appeared to be his kitchen. There was just enough room for both of us to pass inside and close the inward opening door. In spite of the large number of windows, the atmosphere inside was rather dull. The outside vegetation had obviously obscured the light from the sun.

The other obvious thing was the smell of the place. I could tell that my host hadn't finished his spring-cleaning yet.

The room appeared to be rather cramped. The overhang of the roof made the cottage appear bigger than it really was.

The old man pulled a chair away from nearest side of the oilcloth-covered table and gestured for me to sit. From the wear on the tablecloth, I could tell the kitchen was where he spent most of his time. There was just enough room between the table and an overstuffed chesterfield on the right to a pass to the back of the kitchen where there was another door.

As I sat down, I noticed there were two half-finished cups of tea on the table. Perhaps two people live here, I thought.

The old man picked up the teacups and put them in a tiny sink in the corner on the other side of the far doorway. From the sink, he was only a step from the phone located on other end of the table.

The phone was one of the old rotary-style, black models. He extracted a telephone book from underneath and searched for the number of the towing company. He then moved the phone itself up onto a shelf above the table. As he dialed the numbers, he turned away so that I couldn't see his face.

I took the opportunity to look around the room.

On the other side of the sink, there was a large, two-piece, top and bottom cupboard-set. It looked unusually large for the room. It was all white and at least seven feet high and four feet wide with a counter-shelf in the middle, which contained a hotplate. Next to the cupboard-set, there was a small wood-burning cook stove.

Along the continuous bank of windows on the south wall, there was a large chest-high safe on which was mounted a four-foot-long telescope. The ancient observation piece was pointed at the window beside the door we had just entered.

The slow clicking of the telephone dial ceased. I checked to see that my host was still facing the wall, ready to speak into the phone. He was obviously a secretive person.

He held this pose for several minutes. Long enough for me to stand up and inspect the telescope. It bore a large, brass plate. The engraved letters were only partially legible, some were clear and others were completely worn away. I could make out "Presented to," but not the name underneath. The surname looked like it started with the capital letter 'M' followed by eight or ten lower case letters. The only part of the date that could readily be seen was the first two characters of the year "18—."

As I checked my host again, I caught a quick glimpse over his shoulder of a woman moving from one room to another. By her stature and the clothes she wore, I could tell she wasn't young.

As I returned to my chair, I noticed a small television set mounted in a recess in the wall above the table. It seemed to me a better place to put a TV would have been on top of the safe, but I presumed that space had been reserved for the telescope.

Quietly, the old man hung up the phone and turned around with a shrug and a sigh of frustration.

"I guess I dialed the wrong number," he snorted.

My first reaction was that perhaps he had difficulty reading the number of the towing company. It didn't help that the phone was on the shelf and the phone book was on the table.

He handed the phone over to me, turned the phonebook partially around and pointed at the advertisement in the yellow pages. I gathered that he wanted me to dial the number.

I dialed the number carefully. I had never used a rotary phone before and was amused by the slow return on the dial. It took the towing company several rings to answer.

"James Tire and Towing—would you hold please?" said a female voice. Before I could respond, the next thing I heard was music from a local radio station.

As I waited, I realized I didn't know my host's name.

"What address should I give to the tow truck company?" I asked.

"Just tell them it's the Albert McClelland residence, 3255 Old Military Road. That's McClelland with a 'd,'" he emphasized.

The 3255 number was easy to remember because the Macy House address was 3155. I repeated the name Albert McClelland to myself. That could be the name on the telescope, I thought.

Meanwhile, Mr. McClelland nervously puttered around the room and the music continued to play over the phone.

After a few moments, the old man, who had been holding his "diary" under his arm, set the scribbler on the table. He carefully spread it open at the last entry. He then turned, opened the safe and took out another scribbler from a pile of ten or so on a shelf inside. He placed the second scribbler beside the first and studied them. After a while, he spoke.

"PAW 6797 has been a regular up here for many years…an older gentleman…now."

He made a double clucking sound, shook his head and looked at me quizzically.

"In fact, that car was up here about three weeks ago. Yeah, there it is…PAW 6797," he declared, triumphantly.

I knew it was my father he was referring to, but I thought it was odd that a man of his age should refer to my father as an "older gentleman." I could tell he was fishing for the connection.

"PAW 6797 is my father's car," I volunteered.

By now, I had been waiting on the phone for about five minutes. The old man's attitude had warmed considerably since we met in the yard.

"You can't expect very good service, way out here in the boondocks, especially if they think they're going to a Maryland address. James Towing is a Melcastle company."

Mr. McClelland was obviously trying to be friendly. He even offered me a cup of tea. I declined because I didn't think I would be there very long. Besides, I was more interested in his diary.

"I see you keep a lot of scribblers, Mr. McClelland," I said and nodded toward the open safe door.

"Yes, I've been keeping them as a diary for about 30 years now." He placed the two scribblers on top of the pile in the safe and closed the door.

"Thirty years! That's impressive. I gather you do this as a hobby."

The way he reacted, I had obviously struck a responsive chord. He quickly opened the safe door and pulled out the entire pile of scribblers, which he set on the table and slipped out the bottom one. He held up the badly skewed scribbler for me to see and opened it to the first page. I stared at the front cover.

"I started my diary on the night of April 29, 1973," he commented. "The weather was mostly cloudy all day, but cleared off by supper time."

I didn't know what to say or think. The shock of hearing my birth date affected whatever else he said for few seconds. I continued to stare at the cover—*April 29, 1973*—in bold characters on the top right hand corner.

"Two vehicles stopped at the General's Farm. The first one was licence number...T 41973. That truck had been here most of the day."

He read from his notes with some noticeable agitation, which carried over to his comments afterwards.

"That truck used to come up here regularly, but I haven't seen it since."

He repeated, "...haven't seen it since," as though he were trying to figure out what had happened to the truck. Then he looked up, his head cocked to one side. Something was puzzling him. At first, I thought he was just having trouble with his memory. Perhaps he was letting me know that he knew more, but couldn't put it into words.

Then he returned to his diary and resumed speaking, but I couldn't tell how much was reading or how much was ad lib. In any case, his tone was excited.

"But, back in 1973, it was the car I really noticed...it was SLE 360. That car wasn't one of the regulars that used to come around. I was sure something mysterious was going on at 3257 Old Military Road and SLE 360 had something to do with it."

I could hear Thelma's voice in my head warning me to remember the details. I couldn't remember the licence number of the truck except I think the first two characters were—T 4 followed by four or five other numbers. I concentrated on repeating SLE 360 a few times in my head.

"What do you mean, 'something mysterious was going on'?" I asked, hoping he would repeat all of what he had just said.

"Them two drivers had been inside the house for quite some time, when all of a sudden the they came out carrying a heavy, rolled up rug and put it in the back seat of SLE 360. Then, they drove off, one guy in the car and the other in the truck. As soon as they were gone, I left right away to report it. I didn't have a phone then, ya know."

I tried desperately to think of something to say to have him repeat some of the details. But by now there was a faraway look in his eyes. After a few moments, he spoke.

"Haven't seen Roger since…Ruby went into the nut-house that same night."

The old man was in a zone. I might as well not have been there. He just kept talking. I tried to interrupt a few times, but he wasn't listening. He only wanted to talk about the driver of the car, describing him as being "short and kind of stout" and wearing a short, brown jacket with a crest. It was clear Mr. McClelland harbored a certain animosity toward that man. Perhaps he knew the car driver. The only name he mentioned clearly was somebody by the name of, "Roger," but that person didn't appear to be one of the drivers.

I was hoping the lady from the towing company wouldn't pick this time to come back on the line.

For reasons known only to him, the old man began to talk about birds. The birds obviously made him angry. He especially didn't like sparrows. They were around all the time apparently.

Then he went back to the car—SLE 360 again. To help me remember, I made up a mnemonic to help me remember it—State Law Enforcement: **360** degrees. I was hoping he would mention the truck licence number again. How would Thelma have handled this, I wondered?

Meanwhile, on the phone, I could hear the radio station playing a song by a certain female singer from Quebec I detested. In Montreal, we were inundated by her music and quite frankly; I had tired of hearing her screeching voice day and night. I held the receiver away from my ear and tried to ignore her voice and concentrated on the old man's disjointed conversation.

Mr. McClelland didn't seem like he was going to repeat the truck number without prompting. I figured the only way I was going to obtain that information was to ask for the number specifically.

"What did you say the licence number of the truck was, Mr. McClelland?"

He ignored my question and went back to talking about the birds. I though maybe a change of subject might help bring him back to reality. I looked around the room and seized upon the first object that came to mind.

"Haven't seen a rotary phone like this for years," I said.

To my surprise, he immediately picked up on my comment.

"Had the telephone quite a while now. Cost me an arm and a leg. Just because we live a little off the beaten track is no reason why they should be able to gouge us like that. Still, sure wish I'd had it the night Roger Wendelman disappeared. Had to walk down to the corner store in the village to make that phone call. Don't like to go out after dark, ya know."

"Who's Roger Wendelman?" I mused out loud.

He ignored my question. He didn't seem to understand that I wasn't terribly interested in his opinion about the telephone company. He continued talking as though I were hanging on his every word. He reminded me of a few professors at McGill.

Then he suddenly went back to the licence numbers again. Maybe my question about the truck licence number had worked.

"Most of the time I can read the licence numbers from here using my great-grandfather's telescope," he said and automatically stooped and grasped the telescope with his hand over the engraving plate. He was looking toward the driveway.

"Yes sir, SLE 360. I'll never forget that number."

As he spoke, I looked out the window to where the telescope was pointed. I could clearly read the licence number on the police car on the other side of the portico. It was obvious why Mr. McClelland used the telescope for his preoccupation with licence numbers. He needed glasses.

"What did the police say about your observations?" I asked, thinking how unreliable his testimony would be in court once it was known he didn't wear glasses.

"What police? They never even spoke to me. Besides, I don't like the police around here. There are too many shady things going on with them, for my liking. I wouldn't tell them nothin' anyway."

I realized that this was probably more conversation than the old man had had with a stranger in some time. He continued to shuffle around his little kitchen and out of habit he turned on the TV. The picture was black and white and quality was poor.

"The cable was only hooked up about a year ago," he commented. "Cost me a bundle for that too. I couldn't believe what it cost to have the cable hooked up."

"I agree," I said quietly, not wanting to set him off again.

The towing company dispatcher finally came back on the line. As I spoke to her, the old man's monologue suddenly reverted to the body discovered in the ravine last month. I'm pretty sure he mentioned two more licence numbers and vague descriptions of the drivers. I seemed to remember he said one driver was a big man with short white hair and the other one was short and "kind of" stout. For some reason when he mentioned the big man, I immediately thought of Judge Sewchuk and his bandaged hands. I think he mentioned a brown jacket and crest again. I couldn't be sure. I missed a lot of the detail because I was having trouble understanding the dispatcher's questions. After I gave her my name and address, the "location of the service to be provided," and the phone number, which was in the middle of the rotary dial, she estimated the tow truck would take about 35 to 40 minutes.

When I hung up, Mr. McClelland was bad-mouthing the police and the judicial system. When he started in on the lawyers, it looked like a good time to leave. I thanked him for the use of his phone and said I wanted to explore the property some more. I informed him that the tow truck would be along in about half an hour or so and left. He followed me out of the cottage for a few feet and then turned around and went back inside. I stopped on the little bridge and shouted my thanks again, but he probably didn't hear me or see my wave.

I wanted to take a better look under the main house. As I crouched under the police tape attached to the gate hinge, the weight of my hand easily pushed the wooden gate inward.

Before I stepped through the gate, I noted that the police car was still parked on the other side of the portico. I felt more comfortable knowing Detective Turcot was probably still upstairs. The Detective's DNA remarks made me curious about the underside of the floorboards, particularly in front of the main fireplace. I noticed the floorboards were supported by big logs that ran under the kitchen and living room areas. The span between those support beams had to be nearly 15 feet. No wonder the floor was so springy.

From underneath the house, the ravine still didn't look too inviting. I went just far enough too conclude that the ravine wasn't a normal hiking trail. I wondered who would take such a difficult hiking route. Who was the hiker was that found the body?

I retreated back into the sunshine. The lush green of the golf course down by the river seemed a better place to waste the remaining half hour or so until the tow truck arrived.

Beyond the end of the two-rut road past the portico, a rough path branched off toward the Old Stone Bridge. A few large rocks provided convenient hand support. I didn't realize how steep the path was until it was too late to retreat and go down via the road I had driven up.

CHAPTER 16

New Golf Course, Old Body

Later Tuesday Morning

I wasn't expecting the tow truck for at least 30 minutes. A quick look over the golf course on the way down and you could tell the owners had put a lot of time and money into its maintenance. The color of the fairways and greens was much richer than the surrounding farmlands.

The Carrot River, which cuts through the middle of the golf course, flows south from Pennsylvania and makes a giant curl around the General's Mountain before heading east. The land next to the river had become part of the Hylands golf course long before my time and the Old Stone Bridge was now just a cart path between holes.

Except for unusually high spring floods, the gravel road and the Old Stone Bridge were built high enough to allow traffic to pass year-round. The bridge and the road were about 20 feet above the water for the rest of the year. The gravel road was fairly wide at the junction with the Old Military Road, but closer to the bridge the road surface narrowed and had deteriorated significantly over the years. I wondered whether anyone had ever considered upgrading the bridge.

As I neared the bottom of the rocky slope of the General's Mountain, I noticed a white car and a small truck parked near the east end of the bridge. About 100 yards away, I could see the distinctive blue piping on the car denoting it belonged to the Maryland police. There were several men milling about.

A gentle breeze carried the unmistakable smell of freshly excavated earth. Several pieces of earth moving equipment were sitting idle nearby. The machines must have stopped when the police car arrived.

Even from a distance, I could see the bridge was in severe decay. The stone arches looked to be intact, but the road surface on the bridge seemed to be strewn with rubble. There was a large sign posted at each end of the bridge with the word "WARNING" visible from a distance. My guess was that the signs contained warnings to the golfers to use the bridge at their own risk.

As I moved closer, I saw the Maryland police had cordoned off an area from the bridge, along the gravel road and completely surrounding the sixth green, including the sand traps.

The men I saw on my way down had formed a line and were systematically searching the cordoned off area. They carried short sticks and wore masks to prevent inhaling the dust they created as they probed the long grass.

Off to the side and giving directions to the crew, was a tall, wiry man dressed in police officer's coveralls. The three chevrons on his sleeve indicated the rank of Sergeant. On his head, the Sergeant wore a beach hat with a sunshade built into the brim—not regular service issue headgear I'm sure. As I approached, the Sergeant stepped toward me and pulled down below his chin the surgical mask that he was wearing. His face broke into a natural wide smile.

"Hi there, I'm Sergeant Woznica from the Teasdale Police. Can I help you?"

"Hi, I'm Heather Macy. I'm over at the General's Farm, doing some legal work on the disposition of that property. I live down the road and thought I would take a look at the old golf course where we used to pretend we were playing golf when I was a kid."

"Then you're not connected with the body that the Melcastle Police found at the farm a few days ago."

"No, I just hope it doesn't affect the case I'm working on."

"One thing I've learned in my fifteen years on the force is that dead bodies have a way of affecting everything around them."

One of the searchers interrupted our conversation.

"Come on Toley, help us out here. We have a lot of ground to cover and we brought some nice Polish sandwiches. You used to be one of us you know."

"Hey kid, you know why Polish people have a 'ski' on the end of their names, don't you?" Sergeant Woznica retorted. "Because they don't know how to spell toboggan."

The gang all laughed, especially the guy who spoke up.

"Toley, that's an unusual name," I remarked.

"Yeah, it's a nickname I've used all my life. Besides, I'm afraid of what they would come up with if I insisted on Anatoley."

I was curious to know what they were searching for, but didn't want to be too forward in asking. I turned as if to leave.

"You say your name is Macy?" Sergeant Woznica inquired.

"Yes, why do you ask?" I stopped and turned around.

"A Macy family use to live on Old Military Road, just around the corner."

"That would be our place. I lived there when I was growing up."

"You're back now, I take it?"

The sergeant smiled as he moved closer. His smile dominated his face.

"Yes, I'm a lawyer now. I've joined my dad's law firm, Macy and Macy," I replied, using an instantly created name for the firm.

"You know the more you talk, the more I remember you."

The sergeant evidently wanted to pursue the conversation. He was obviously curious about whom I was. As he continued to talk, I wasn't sure whether he was just overly friendly because I was a female or just enjoyed talking.

"You seem to have quite a few men out for this job. What happened?"

He seemed only too happy to respond.

"The people who own the golf course were remodeling the holes around the bridge the weekend before last. When they were moving some earth, they uncovered some human remains."

"Meaning a body that has been there for a long time?" I asked.

"The new forensic lab in Melcastle tells us the remains had been buried for about 30 years. The victim was a male approximately 30 years old. He was wrapped in a hemp rug, which obviously retarded the decaying process. In fact, when the excavators informed us they had found some human remains, I expected to find bones only. These remains were fairly well preserved and almost recognizable. The victim was about six feet tall and some time during his life had broken a leg."

"How can you be so sure of the age and the amount of time the victim had been buried?"

"The technicians can be pretty accurate in the forensic lab, but in this case they gave me a range of 25 to 35 years on both counts. I use 30 years old and 30 years under ground to simplify conversation."

Detective Turcot seemed more than willing to talk about his case, so I decided I would see how far Sergeant Woznica would go in providing more information on the golf course case.

"What else did the new forensic lab tell you that you otherwise wouldn't have known?"

"Well, the individual probably died from a loss of blood. He was shot through the carotid artery in the neck. A 32-calibre bullet was recovered from inside the back of the skull. We're searching for the gun now."

As he finished speaking, he cocked his head and gave me a questioning look.

"Now I know where I remember you from," he exclaimed. "You were a classmate of my step-sister, Jessie Stewart. She used to talk about you all the time. I seem to remember you and Jessie were very competitive, particularly with boyfriends."

143

"Yes we were. But, I didn't realize you and Jessie were related."

"Yeah, my mother remarried and Jessie isn't a bad kid-sister if you have to have a sister," he joked. "She really liked Casey Clarkin, but you kind of won that battle as I recall."

"You could say that, I suppose," I replied, taken aback.

"What ever happened to Casey?"

"Well, that's a long story that doesn't have a happy ending," I responded curtly, not wanting to pursue that line of conversation. "Let's just say we parted company shortly after I left high school."

"I see," he winced and the smile disappeared.

"Yeah, I went to Montreal and obtained my law degree and here I am starting a new career."

"Congratulations. It's nice to see people make it better for themselves," he responded, as he reached inside his jacket pocket and handed me his business card.

"The same goes for you," I commented, as I looked at his card. "Making Sergeant isn't too bad either. I'm sorry I don't have my business cards yet."

"That's okay. It has been nice seeing you again, but I'd better start working," he announced. "It has taken me five days to gather these guys for this search. I have to make the best of their services while I can." He touched two fingers to the brim of his makeshift headdress as a casual farewell salute.

I thought about the trek back up the mountain toward the old man's cottage. It had taken me only about five minutes to come down, but the return trip along the same route was going to take considerably longer. I decided to follow the gravel road back to the junction and walk up Old Military Road.

On my way, I reflected on how excited Thelma would be if she were here; two murders, separated by 30 years, discovered in the general same area. I know exactly how she would say it: "You'd better write down all the details as soon as you can, before you forget them, ma cherie."

As I trudged my way up the steeper road, I realized that the outside edge of the road was not as secure as I had thought it was. There were

144

several large spaces where guideposts used to be. The original post had obviously slid away. I decided to move over to the inside part of the road.

I had just reached the steepest part of Old Military Road, about 200 feet from the farmhouse, when the tow truck passed me. By that time, my breath was decidedly labored and I took my time the rest of the way.

By the time I arrived, the tow truck driver had hooked a chain under the rear bumper. Mr. McClelland was in front, supervising you might say, with his diary in one hand and a pencil in the other.

Pulling the wheel out of the hole was simple enough and took only a few seconds. The car slowly rolled back, gently stopping as it hit the truck's oversized rubber bumper. The chain sagged to the ground.

The tow-truck operator, assuming I was the driver, asked me to put my parking brake on so the car wouldn't move when he backed up the truck again. My legs felt weak from my recent climb. I stepped on the parking brake as hard as I could. The driver backed up his truck a few feet and stopped. The car didn't move.

"See the nice square hole?" he asked, and pointed to the area where the front wheel had been a few moments earlier. "Your wheel fell through an old wooden culvert that probably was installed by the Union Army *before the Civil War*."

"I guess that fits with this location—being the General's Farm and all," I sputtered, gesturing toward the farmhouse.

"Yeah, I guess you're right," he chuckled. "It's not everyday you come face-to-face with history."

He picked up his logbook from the truck's cab and began to record some data. He seemed to take an inordinate amount of time for such a simple towing job. I moved close enough to see that he was sketching the site. He had drawn a curved line representing the road leading to the farmhouse and marked an "X" where the hole would be. He then drew a red dotted line above the "X" and below the farmhouse. Undoubtedly, the line represented the Maryland and Pennsylvania border. I wondered whether the location made a difference in the rate he would charge.

"I'll report this hazard to the Department of Highways. The whole culvert will eventually have to be replaced," he commented, as he finished his entries.

I offered to pay the driver.

"It's all part of the service," he said, pointing out the AAA bumper sticker on Dad's car. "Sorry it took so long, but I had to deal with a four-car accident on the Old Military Road at the intersection with the new highway."

I was glad I didn't have to deal in cash. In my shock over the currency exchange at the bank the day before, I had forgotten to withdraw some American money. From the $40 Dad had given me, I had only one twenty and the change from the down payment I had made on the parkade. I didn't want to part so soon with what little cash I had.

The driver threw the chain into the back of the truck, made a simple three point turn-around by the portico and sped off down the road. I was extra careful when I tried the same maneuver later. I didn't want to end up stuck again on the other side of the road or worse still, go over the edge.

As I reached the level part of the road at the junction, I thought about Mr. McClelland's Diary. I decided right then and there that I would start using my notebook as a diary. I pulled over and parked.

I pulled out my notebook and recorded as much as I could remember about everything I had just learned:

Heather Macy's Notebook

Tuesday, May 6, 2003

Met Det. Turcot—Melcastle Police
- Body found in ravine—approx 30 years of age—stabbed 17 times

- Dead approx 3 weeks   Apr (17), 2003
NOTE: Check sword over fireplace?
-DNA from body does not match with blood found at Gen's Farm
 "Close enough to be a relative"

Met Albert McClelland (with a "d")—3255 Old Military Road

Mr. Mc C keeps a DIARY
- His diary started—29 Apr 1973
- Licence No SLE 360—driver short & stout
- Wore brown jacket with a crest on it
- Licence No—T4 ? ? ? ?" (Truck) Mr. McC believes it was Dad—
- A regular visitor   (Note: SEE MR McClelland again)

- 3 weeks ago— (approx 17 Apr, 2003)
- PAW 6797 (Note: Calls Dad an older gentleman)

- 2 or 3 other licence numbers? Connected with ravine body?
- One driver was really big   (J U D G E SEWCHUK?)
And the other short and stout.

- - - - - - - - - - - - - -

- Met Sgt. Woznica (Toley)—Teasdale Detachment
- Human remains dug up on golf course—30 years of age
- Shot through carotid artery—probably bled to death
- Buried approx 30 years (wrapped in hemp rug)
- 32-cal. slug lodged in skull

CHAPTER 17

Windemere Estates—A Family Again

It was shortly after one o'clock by the time Heather returned home from her visit to the General's Farm. I was preparing lunch.

"I don't want to rush you, but I spoke to Dr. Hammersmyth this morning and he thinks a visit could be a good thing. He said he would like to be present—to make sure everything goes well. He suggested this afternoon at two o'clock. I took the liberty of accepting. If you can't make it, I'll go by myself. I haven't been for a visit for a week or so anyway."

"I'd like to go today," Heather said. "And I'm glad Dr. Hammersmyth will be there. I appreciate his concern."

"Dr. Hammersmyth mentioned he prescribed a new medication a few days ago and the first indications are it could be the appropriate one for Bonnie. He suggested a short visit of a half hour or so."

"That's good. I must admit I've felt guilty ever since I found out

Mom was in the hospital. When you told me she was at Windemere, it put a whole different perspective on it. I was worried Mom was never going to come home again."

"Dr. Hammersmyth and I believe that Bonnie is making real progress with her depression, which I believe is her worst ailment."

"I knew about her heart condition, but isn't depression supposed to be triggered by something emotional?"

"They're not sure. Your leaving home didn't do her any good, but it wasn't likely the direct cause. According to Dr. Hammersmyth, it's probably a genetic thing or a chemical imbalance. He has been researching the subject for years and he's now leaning toward the chemical imbalance concept."

"I don't know whether that is a good thing or not," Heather mused.

"What do you mean?"

"It could mean that's what I have in store for me somewhere down the line."

"Let's assume it's good news…at least the new medication is," I suggested.

We finished our soup and sandwiches.

"We have half an hour until visiting time and the drive to Windemere usually takes me about that long. It's only about 12 miles, but Curtis Road was under construction last week."

"It would be nice if we could use the Old Stone Bridge," Heather commented. "That would save several miles."

"You'll have to take that up with several levels of government and the heritage groups," I said.

I drove because I knew the way and it's a little tricky, especially the turn off Curtis Road near the Melcastle Journal newspaper plant. Besides, I didn't know how well Heather drives.

We had just turned onto Southgate Road when Heather pointed out the noise caused by the broken rear window.

"How long have you had the broken window, Dad?"

"About a week. I tried to fix it Sunday night, but I guess that just made it worse."

"How did it come to be broken?"

"Somebody broke in one night in Melcastle."

"Are car break-ins common around here?"

"It's not so much that the car was broken into, it's the way it happened that was curious."

"Curious in what way?"

"I had a meeting with a client one evening out near the old drive-in theater. We were in his backyard concluding our conversation, when I heard a noise like the sound of a champagne cork, and the sound of glass breaking at the same time. I was still a long ways from my car when a young man jumped in a pickup truck and sped away. The street lighting wasn't good and I was only able to describe him as a white male with dark clothing."

"Did you reported it to the police?"

"Yes. The investigating officer took the case more seriously than I would have thought. He searched the car and dug out a slug from the door panel on the other side. The fact that it was 32-calibre slug seemed to be significant to him."

"Was anything stolen?"

"Just some paper files I had in one of those expandable folders. Fortunately, most of the data that was stolen was also on the Mac back at the office."

We didn't talk much for a while. Heather seemed to be more interested in the landscape and cloud formations.

"I'm glad you're driving," Heather said, as we turned into the Windemere Estates grounds. "I would never have known to turn into that opening in the trees to enter the Estates."

"Yeah, the entrance is a bit obscure," I responded. "Actually there's a sign, but the shrubbery has grown up around it over the years. The whole route seems second nature to me now."

We drove up the long, tree-lined driveway to the parking lot outside the perimeter wall. The only entrance is through an ornamental archway with a double iron gate.

It was routine for me, but I could see that Heather was under impressed by the building's austere interior. A large desk on an elevated platform dominated the reception area. There are benches for visitors along the walls on both sides. I was glad that I had informed Heather during Monday's lunch that the criminal inmates were housed on one side and the medical patients on the other.

As we approached the reception desk, I noticed there was a new supervisor's nameplate beside the office door behind. The new nameplate read:

"Mrs. Dawn Greisler."

I had come to know Dawn well over the years as one of Bonnie's nurses. I assumed a promotion must have occurred during the past week.

Heather seemed to be focusing her attention on the criminal side to the left of the reception area, which was barred by a large, floor-to-ceiling iron gate. I'm not sure whether she noticed the guard seated in the shadows in the alcove inside the gate.

After we signed-in, the desk clerk went back to the supervisor's office and spoke to someone inside. Mrs. Greisler quickly emerged and followed the clerk to where we were standing.

On this day, Dawn wore her usual pale blue uniform dress that had been starched and steam pressed many times. The condition of the uniform was a telltale sign that Dawn had been working at Windemere for many years. Her ample chest supported a machine-embroidered nametag on her left side. The oval badge was sewn on and had been pressed flat over time. Her slightly greying hair, swept-up in the back, was becoming to her. On this day, Dawn was pleasant, but all business.

After the introductions, Dawn said that Dr. Hammersmyth had advised her of our visit. I explained that Heather had been away for a few years and was now back in town.

Dawn escorted us through the large wooden doors on the medical side to our right. As we entered, I could see that Heather was still looking curiously at the austere appearance of the iron gate on the other side of the reception area. I had been on that side several times before on business and I wouldn't recommend it as a place for a casual visit.

It was a short distance down the first corridor to Bonnie's room. As we approached the doorway, a tall thin man in casual slacks and yellow cardigan sweater emerged to greet us. I hadn't seen Dr. Hammersmyth in person for several months and I didn't recognize him at first. As we shook hands, I said I was surprised to see that he wasn't wearing his customary white smock coat.

I introduced Heather to Dr. Hammersmyth and he made the usual small talk about how much she had changed. I could tell that Heather barely remembered him even though he had been our family doctor since before she was born. Then I remembered that it was about the time Heather left home that he had started to specialize in the care of seniors.

As we entered the room, Bonnie was sitting on a settee by the end of her bed. She didn't rise until we were quite close. I embraced her as usual and announced that Dr. Hammersmyth and I had a surprise for her.

Heather approached her mother and said, "Hello Mom, how are you feeling?"

"Hello dear," Bonnie replied, with a bit of tremor in her voice. "I'm feeling much better, thank you."

Bonnie smiled vacantly and appeared nervous. Perhaps Dr. Hammersmyth hadn't fully briefed her about our visit.

As the four of us stood awkwardly in front of the settee, Dr. Hammersmyth sought to break the ice.

"Heather is just back in town and thought she'd like to see how you're doing, Bonnie."

Bonnie reacted by saying; "It's nice to see you back, Heather. You've been away along time."

"Thirteen years," Heather replied cautiously, looking first at her mother and then at me.

"And what have you been up to all this time, my dear?"

"I've been in Montreal, getting my law degree."

There were a few more exchanges like that, but we still weren't exactly sure that Bonnie had realized who Heather was. As the conversation when on, Heather seemed to relax. Bonnie's attitude took a bit longer to soften. The tenseness in Bonnie's voice dissipated noticeably when an orderly arrived with a pitcher of iced tea and some glasses on a tray.

"Would you like something to drink?" Bonnie offered, as she turned toward her bedside table. "Dr. Hammersmyth was so kind to provide some iced tea for us."

Bonnie's offer may have been rehearsed, but it was a positive sign. Dr. Hammersmyth helped pour the iced tea. After Bonnie and the good doctor delivered the refreshment, we all sat on some folding chairs obviously provided for the occasion.

For several years, it had been unusual for Bonnie to initiate much in the way of social conversation. She startled the doctor and me by asking Heather where she was staying. Heather replied that she was, "staying with Daddy."

Bonnie seemed pleased and her physical appearance changed visibly. Her shoulders relaxed and her eyes moved from person to person. The more the conversation referred to Macy House and us as a family, the more Bonnie seemed to join in. She looked at Heather several times and studied her intently. When I mentioned that Heather was now a lawyer, Bonnie said, "Good, perhaps you'll be able to work with your dad."

I was delighted with her use of the phrase "work with your dad." I'm sure Dr. Hammersmyth noticed as well.

Still, we weren't prepared for what happened next.

"You know, doctor, I have been having the strangest series of dreams lately," Bonnie began. "The dreams are all connected and started a week or so ago."

None of us said anything, so Bonnie continued talking.

"Each dream starts at the same place, in front of our fireplace at Macy House. In the first dream, there was a young man holding a baby in front of roaring fire. The next night, the dream began the same way. Only this time, the man carrying the baby walked straight into the fireplace and disappeared. The flames didn't disturb them at all.

"The next night, as I watched, a different young man appeared— coming out of the fire place. The fire was out. This man looked much like the first, but had a short, blond beard. He turned around and just stared at a spot above the mantelpiece.

"The following night, the man with the beard went out the front door. The door led a balcony where our driveway is. I was overcome with the strangest feeling as I followed him. I looked out over the balcony. It was early evening and a few lights were shimmering in the far off hills.

"Last night, the young man with the beard and I went out onto the balcony again. He seemed to wave at someone below. I couldn't see anybody, but I noticed there were tears running down his face."

We all sat silently for a few seconds. Then Bonnie spoke again.

"What does it all mean, doctor?" Bonnie asked, with tears in her eyes. "Am I going crazy?"

"No, no, Bonnie," Dr. Hammersmyth said, as he reached out and gently touched her hands. "Dreams are sometimes a way of telling ourselves there are things going on in our lives that we can't explain. The fact that you feel comfortable enough to talk to us about your dreams is as a positive thing."

Bonnie nodded and suddenly appeared to have become tired. She went over and sat on her bed. Dr. Hammersmyth took that as a sign that Bonnie was due for her medication and suggested that Heather and I leave and come back another day. Our departure was a bit mechanical. I gave Bonnie my usual hug and kiss. Heather approached Bonnie as I backed away. She and Bonnie shook hands and said how nice it was to see one another again. Heather said that she would be back as soon as she could. The two of us waved and left. Dr. Hammersmyth backed out the door and said he would be back after he had escorted us out. Bonnie turned and fluffed up her pillow.

On the way out, Dr. Hammersmyth commented that there had been some strain during the visit to be sure, but Bonnie obviously had recovered some social skills and seemed to recognize Heather towards the end. The medication was obviously an improvement. He was also considering some other new drugs to build up Bonnie's stamina. He said he would continue experimenting with the dosage levels. The medication and more visits might help Bonnie connect with us. He was pleased and sounded hopeful.

I waved to Dawn and as we passed by the reception desk. You could see the clerk entering our departure time.

On the way out of the building, Heather and I were both evidently reflecting on the same thing—Bonnie's dream sequence. Heather was the first to put her thoughts into words.

"Dad, has Mom ever visited the General's Farm?"

"Not that I know of—at least, I never took her up there."

"Part of Mom's dream sequence sounded like she was familiar with the balcony."

"Yeah. I sure hope Dr. Hammersmyth is right...about it being a good sign, I mean."

We walked out into bright sunshine. The temperature had climbed well into the nineties. We opened all four doors of the car to let the heat out and took off our jackets. As Heather undid the top button on her blouse, I was reminded of Dorothy Sparrow and her daughter's problem with visible scarring. I thought I should warn Heather about what Roma's son had been through.

"By the way, Heather, Roma's son was stricken with that flesh-eating disease a couple of years ago. You'd never know it, the way he runs around today."

"Necrotizing Fasciitus," Heather added.

I said I was surprised she would know of the disease and its clinical name.

"I guess I didn't tell you," Heather said. "The nun who helped me out when I first arrived in Montreal—has a sister, her biological sister, in Ottawa whose grandson had the disease about four years ago. When I called her, just before I left, she said the little guy was fine."

We drove home in silence for a few miles. Our discussion about the flesh-eating disease made me think of Dorothy Sparrow's daughter again and then Mayor Logan's request for legal assistance for Dorothy.

"Heather, would you make a note to remind me to phone Carl Wickland, please."

"Who is Carl Wickland?" Heather asked, as she took out her notebook.

"He's a lawyer friend that I think could help Mayor Logan or at least

156

Dorothy Sparrow."

"Stewart Logan was a city councilor when I left. I gather he is the mayor now, but who is Dorothy Sparrow?"

"She's Murdock Sparrow's widow."

"Oh yes," Heather nodded. "The guy the Sparrow Building was named after."

On the way out of the estates, neither of us said anything for a few moments. Then I remembered Heather's visit to the farm. As she was writing the note about Carl Wickland, I asked, "By the way, how did you make out on your visit to the General's Farm?"

"That was quite interesting," Heather replied. "Altogether, there was a body, some human remains and two crime scenes. The body was discovered in the ravine behind the farm. Detective Turcot, from the Melcastle Police, was working on that one when I arrived."

I immediately wondered whether my squatter-friend could have been the body found. I needed to be discreet about what I said.

"You say there was a body found. Was it a murder?"

"Yes. There were multiple stab-wounds and a great loss of blood."

"And the human remains...?"

"The human remains were buried near the sixth green beside of the Old Stone Bridge. That person had been murdered as well."

You could feel the excitement building in Heather's voice.

"Will either of the murders affect the General's Farm assignment?"

"I don't think so, but Sergeant Woznica said that murder always has a way of affecting everything around it. Even one that happened 30 years ago."

"Who is Sergeant Woznica?"

"He's the police officer in charge of the Maryland murder, on the golf course."

"That's convenient. I mean, that two murders just happened to be separated by the state line."

"And separated by 30 years."

"Interesting," I mused. "Very interesting."

"It *was indeed* interesting," Heather added, as she referred to her notes. "I also met an old man named McClelland—his first name was

Albert, I believe. Did you know he started a diary the day I was born? He even mentioned you drove a truck back then."

"I know Albert McClelland quite well. In fact, I ended up paying for the installation of his cable TV. He put up a big fuss about the cost at a town council meeting before the line was installed along Old Military Road. At the meeting, I thought I was speaking on behalf of the township, when I said, 'we would cover all costs.' I had been elected by the residents along Old Military Road to speak on their behalf, but I didn't represent the town council, which the Teasdale mayor told me in no uncertain terms. When it came time to pay the hook-up charge for his place, old Albert still gave the council a hard time, so I paid his fee."

"That's strange. He gave me the distinct impression that he paid for the TV cable himself because he said it cost him 'an arm and a leg' to use his words."

"Well I have the receipts to prove it. I was kind of forced into making good for his share because I had given my word."

"Sounds like you."

"I'm sorry. I interrupted you. Tell me more about your visit."

"Detective Turcot told me about their new forensic lab in Melcastle and how it has helped him with his case."

"I've heard of Detective Turcot, but I can't say I know him."

"In any case, Detective Turcot gathered some blood samples from the scene at the General's Farm, but it didn't match the body they found in the ravine. He made a curious remark, something like the DNA was 'close enough to be a relative, but no cigar.' He was looking for more evidence. I'm afraid he was annoyed that I had intruded upon his crime scene."

"That's interesting, because about 30 years ago Roger Wendelman was living in that building when he disappeared without a trace. But that couldn't be the body they found recently. Foul play was suspected 30 years ago and Roger's wife Ruby was committed to the state hospital in Windemere Estates. I believe it was partly because of Roger's disappearance. I understand she's still in custody there."

We both thought about the situation for a few seconds.

"Could the blood sample that Detective Turcot recovered be

Roger's blood from 30 years ago, I wonder?" Heather asked.

"I don't know. The blood could be from Civil War prisoners for all we know," I suggested.

"Yes, but it would be quite a coincidence to have blood that was so closely related buried in an adjacent murder scene," Heather noted.

"Wait a minute, are you thinking the blood sample that Detective Turcot found could be from the human remains that Sergeant Woznica was working on by the Old Stone Bridge?"

"That's one explanation," Heather suggested.

Heather's comments jump-started my memory.

"Did the Sergeant at the golf course happen to mention that the human remains had a broken right leg?"

"I think Sergeant Woznica mentioned something about a broken leg, but I don't know if he mentioned which one."

"Still, I doubt whether the hospital would keep X-Ray records back that far."

We both fell silent again. I was impressed with the way Heather made the possible connection between Roger's disappearance and the blood sample that *was* obtained.

It had always bothered me that Ruby Wendelman was locked up and never charged with anything.

Heather took out her notebook again and began to make notes.

CHAPTER 18

Arthur's Ashes

Late Tuesday Afternoon

Heather and I were sitting down to eat a pizza that I had heated up in the microwave oven, when the phone rang.

"Good afternoon, this is the McCosham Funeral Home in Baltimore calling," began a female voice. "Are you William H Macy?"

"I'm William *Henry* Macy," I replied.

"Is your address 3155 Old Military Road?"

"Yes," I responded slowly. The introduction sounded like one of those telemarketer calls.

"And you are a relative of William Arthur Macy?"

"William Arthur Macy is my twin brother."

I looked at Heather. The "twin brother" remark had caught her attention.

"William Arthur Macy has died and his will specified he was to be cremated and his ashes be sent to…Macy House…in Teasdale,

Maryland…for internment by the flag pole at 3155 Old Military Road," the voice quoted. "The urn containing his ashes has been shipped by the Dawsay Funeral Home in Melfort, Sask-at-che-wan, Canada. It arrived last night."

I could tell by the way she labored through the word Saskatchewan that she had never heard of it before.

"Couldn't you just ship it to my address?"

"I'm sorry it must be signed for and witnessed, you know," the disembodied voice intoned.

I wondered how many phone calls of that kind does a funeral home employee make in a day?

"Please bring three pieces of identification. There's a large sealed envelope which must be signed for and witnessed, as well."

"Okay," I responded.

"Do you have our address?"

"No, I didn't catch it. Would you mind repeating it?"

"That's—the McCosham Funeral Home at 12911 Kirkland Street in Baltimore."

I repeated the address as I wrote.

"We would appreciated it if you could be here before 11 o'clock. That's when our sessions usually start. My name is Andrea Dietz. That's diet with a 'Z' on the end."

"Diet with a 'Z' on the end. Dietz," I repeated

"That's right," she said and hung up.

By now, Heather was intrigued by what she could hear on this end. She couldn't wait for an explanation.

"What was that all about? Who is William Arthur Macy? I didn't know you had a twin brother."

"I guess it's time to tell you about your Uncle Arthur," I suggested. "Arthur is or rather *was* my twin brother. As brothers, our looks were the only thing we had in common. Otherwise, we were as different as night and day. You already know that my mother died when I was born. What you don't know is the birth was twins. The delivery was over a month premature and the onset of her labor was very sudden, prompting my father to take her to the hospital in the village. Had he taken her to Melcastle she might have had a better chance of survival. My father had to live with that decision for the rest of his life."

"But why the big secret?" Heather asked plaintively.

"We decided not to tell you about Arthur mostly because there wasn't much point. I didn't associate with him outside the house and Bonnie didn't like Arthur at all. In any case, Arthur suddenly left town shortly after you were born. He just jumped in the pickup truck and left. I don't think he even asked Dad whether he could take the pickup. Dad never said anything. He just shook Arthur's hand and wished him well."

"Where did he go?"

"Arthur was a journeyman electrical lineman. He told us he saw a job poster from Saskatchewan Power at the Melcastle office, advertising jobs for linemen to build a power grid in northern Canada."

"And you've never heard from him since?"

"We only received one short postcard from Arthur. The card said that he was married and had five children and that's about it. There was no return address, so we couldn't reply."

"Sounds like Uncle Arthur was quite a guy."

"Arthur had his moments. His marks in school could have been better. He seldom studied and he spent too much time running around, playing sports. I'm afraid Arthur considered himself a much better athlete than he really was. He always hung around with the top athletes like Jack Sewchuk, the Parslow brothers and Roger Wendelman. 'The gang,' Dad used to call them. Arthur was more interested in being considered part of the crowd, which included lots of girls."

"I know the type."

"There was one event that made Arthur stand out from the rest," I suggested. "It happened at a backyard pool party. Roger Wendelman was discovered unconscious at the bottom of the pool. Arthur was inside the house and by the time he started to help Roger, several minutes had passed. Arthur forced the water out by pushing on Roger's back, rolled him over and applied mouth-to-mouth resuscitation. Roger survived and Arthur was a hero."

"At least that's a nice story."

"Unfortunately, Roger was never the same afterwards. He had difficulty speaking. His friends tried to help him back into sports, but he broke his leg playing football. It was horribly disfigured and never did heal properly. Roger had been a star athlete in many sports and the accident pretty well finished any thoughts of an athletic career. He eventually dropped out of school."

"How did Roger wind up at the General's Farm?"

"Ruby McClelland had a lot to do with that. Ruby was at the pool party and somehow felt responsible for Roger's welfare. The fact that Ruby hung around Roger full-time after that night bothered me. Roger and Ruby eventually married. Old Albert McClelland arranged for them to move into the General's Farm. Ruby and I had dated a few times before the near-drowning incident and I was kind of taken with her. In a way, losing Ruby was a blessing because a few weeks later I met your mother. I knew right away Bonnie was the one for me."

"Well, I'm glad for that," Heather mused and nodded her head.

That made me feel better. The visit with her mother seemed to have a positive effect on Heather. I decided it was a good time to fill in some more blanks for Heather and the best place to start would be with the ownership of Macy House and Dad's will.

"I guess the phone call settles the ownership of Macy House."

"What do you mean?" Heather asked. "I always thought you owned this house. Is...I mean was Arthur a co-owner?"

"In fact, in Dad's will, he left Macy House to Arthur. Dad never bothered to change his will before he died. Even though I've been paying the taxes and the upkeep all these years, I always felt that legally Macy House belonged to Arthur."

"Seems a tad unfair. Perhaps your dad felt you would inherit Macy House in the end."

"Perhaps," I responded.

After a few minutes, Heather asked in a mocking tone, "What do you mean by upkeep?"

"A few years ago I hired a contractor to repair the roof. It was expensive because that kind of slate is hard to find. In order to maintain the secrecy, I had to have the contractor start out repairing the roof on this building first and then a few days later quietly do some repairs on the main building at the General's Farm," I replied.

Suddenly, I realized I had let the General's Farm secret out of the bag.

"Maintain what secrecy? What do you mean? Do you own the General's Farm too?"

Heather was now completely baffled.

"Yes, Dad willed the General's Farm to me. That's why I wasn't too upset about Arthur getting Macy House. I didn't think it was such a good deal. But, what could I say? I was getting free rent at the time."

"Well, I'll be."

"By the way, I would like to keep the ownership of the General's Farm a secret for a few more days, please."

"Why do you Macy men have this need for secrecy?" Heather asked and shook her head in wonder.

I just shrugged. I really couldn't answer that question and I didn't want to pursue that subject any further. Instead, I turned the conversation to what I had found in the safe.

"While I was going through Dad's will yesterday, I discovered that I was not only a twin, but apparently Arthur and I started out as triplets," I said. "The death certificate says Baby Macy was pronounced dead at birth."

"Are there any other secrets I should know about?" Heather asked with beaming eyes.

I hesitated. "There's one secret that not even I know the answer to," I announced. "I guess it's about time to show you the combination to grampa's safe while I'm at it."

With that, we went to the conference room. Heather turned on the lights and I pulled up a chair in front of the big safe.

"The combination is your birth date. The first number is 29 left, and the second number is 4 right, and the third number is 73 left," I instructed, as I rotated the dial.

The door of the safe opened on the first try and I retrieved the two Swiss bank account passbooks.

"One of these passbooks is for the property taxes on the General's

Farm. The interest from the original deposit has paid for the taxes ever since Grampa George and my father bought the General's Farm. My father kept the secret of how the taxes were paid until just before his death, but he didn't tell me where he kept the passbook. I didn't even know there *was* a passbook until yesterday."

"Which passbook is for the property taxes?" Heather asked.

"I don't know. I have no idea what the second passbook is for. Maybe nothing. I guess I'll have to go to Switzerland to find out. Perhaps we could both go."

"I could go for that," Heather exclaimed, with a big smile.

"The other stuff in the files includes survey maps and Dad's Last Will and Testament."

"Should I be interested?"

"No, not really," I answered. "Say, I noticed that you don't wear a watch. My brother Arthur left his in the bathroom, the day he left. It's one of those watches that automatically winds itself as a function of your arm movements. That was a big thing before they came out with watches that operate on a battery. You could consider it a belated birthday present from Arthur and me. Would you like it?"

I handed the watch to Heather as I spoke.

"Thanks Dad," Heather said, as she admired the watch. "Professional women wearing a man's watch is the 'in' thing today."

Heather gave the watch a few shakes and held it up to her ear. Then she set the time by looking at my watch.

She put the watch on her wrist and admired it some more. "Are there any other secrets I should know about?"

"No, not that I know of," I replied, knowing I would eventually have to tell her about the visit by Mr. Gabler.

"Good," Heather pronounced.

As I put the passbooks back into the little box in the safe, Heather noticed the handgun.

"Is that a gun, Dad?"

"Yes. It belonged to Grampa George."

"I didn't think you liked guns."

"I don't. I've just never gotten around to getting rid of it."

"As long as it's not the 32-calibre revolver that Sergeant Woznica is looking for."

"It might be a 32-calibre. I don't even know how to tell what size it is. But, I can assure you it isn't the one your Sergeant friend is looking for."

I shut the safe and locked it and we quietly went back into the living room.

It was our first full evening together at home. We watched the Stanley Cup hockey playoffs on TV for a while. My favorite team was the New York Rangers and they weren't playing, so I wasn't much interested. Heather said that she had become partial to the Montreal Canadiens. She was pleased the "Habs" were making a comeback after a few lean years.

Before I went to bed, I reminded Heather I would be making a trip to Philadelphia tomorrow.

"What's happening in Philadelphia?"

"The Philadelphia trip is one I've been putting off for several days. It's the final paperwork for a client who lost a libel case and he has since moved his business to Philadelphia. What I'm concerned about is the possibility of an appeal. I don't want to proceed with the case mainly because he wasn't honest with me in the first place."

"Is it something that I might be able to take on?" Heather asked. "As you know I came into this partnership with a zero case load."

"No, I don't think so. He's from one of those rich families in Melcastle with more money than brains. He was more offended by the lawsuit than damaged by it. He case was with old Mr. Zubiac who was an old friend of my father's. It's a good thing the case happened after my father died, otherwise Dad would never have let me take it on."

"Whatever you say."

"I also have another reason for going to Philadelphia."

"What's that, Dad?"

"I thought it might be a good time to stop in at the university to correct my name on their records. Want to come along?"

"No thanks," Heather replied. "I think I should look after getting a car and finish my banking business. I would also like to stop somewhere and buy some linens. The towels in the bathroom are frayed and the tea towels are worn out as well."

"Guilty as charged," I confessed. "I've been living alone too long, I guess."

"Good night Dad."

"Good night dear. Want me to drop you off in the morning?"

"That would be nice. What time are you leaving?"

"Seven-thirty-eight o'clock. I want to be on to the Interstate as soon as I can. I'll have breakfast on the way."

"That's good because I made an appointment with Mr. Barrigar for nine o'clock. Perhaps I should have mentioned your name?"

"It shouldn't make any difference. There's only one Macy in town. However, you may find he's not terribly punctual at that hour."

"Why's that?" Heather asked. "I thought all car salespersons were on the job at the crack of dawn."

"He probably does, but I happen to know he meets his wife for breakfast before she goes to work at nine o'clock."

"Okay, I'll show up after nine then."

CHAPTER 19

Meeting Dennis Archard

Wednesday Morning

On the trip into town, Dad took the new highway; at least it was new to me. We drove by a row of small planes parked next to the fence.

"I didn't realize the new highway came so close to the airport."

"Actually, they had to modify one or two of the runways to accommodate the highway. That was quite remarkable considering the whole arrangement involved two states, which meant joint funding, planning, design and construction."

Soon we were at the Melcastle City exit, where the city council had erected a sign:

WELCOME TO MELCASTLE
THE CITY WHERE YOU ARE
ONLY A STRANGER ONCE

"Where would you recommend I have breakfast, Dad?" I asked, as we quickly entered the commercial area of the city.

"That's a good question. I always have breakfast at home. Perhaps you should try Denny's. It's two or three blocks west of the office on Constitution Avenue."

"That would be a good walk afterwards. I need the exercise. Besides, I would like to arrive at Mr. Barrigar's after nine. They say meeting a car salesman early in the morning gives him too much of an advantage."

"He's okay. I saw him on the street last Saturday and told him if he played his cards right, I might send you over to look at a few cars. My meeting him did have another advantage. All I had to do was tell him you were returning and the whole town would know shortly."

Dad pulled up besides Denny's and let me out.

"I should be back around four o'clock," he said as he drove off.

Denny's had a reputation in Canada of being charm-free. On this particular morning, the service was fast, the food was good and the place was clean. In addition, I didn't expect decaffeinated coffee, but a steaming cup was delivered cheerfully. I decided to have a second cup, which nicely took care of the extra few minutes until nine o'clock.

I was getting ready to leave when I saw a number of police officers, rush out of the Dunkin Donuts next door and run across the street. Then I realized they were heading to the police headquarters, probably for a roll call or something. It reminded me of an announcer on a radio call-in show in Montreal who used to say: "Besides the two things in life that are certain: death and taxes, we also know that there are two things you will never see. One is, you'll never see a robbery at a donut shop and the other is no airline will ever use 911 as its flight number.

I took my time walking the five blocks to Barrigar's Auto Sales and arrived close to nine-thirty. The car lot was much bigger than it had appeared from dad's office window.

As I opened the door to the sales office, a tall, young man with short blonde hair, almost a brush cut, greeted me. He appeared to be in his mid to late twenties.

"Hi, my name is Dennis. Can I help you?"

I had been expecting to meet a man about my dad's age, but Dennis was a good substitute.

"I was hoping to speak with Mr. Barrigar."

"My step-father is away for breakfast. He should be back in a few minutes."

"Well, I suppose we can start. I'm interested in a car, preferably four or five years old, automatic with low mileage."

"Good. We have several models on hand that might do the trick," he said, as he opened a side door to the sales lot. We walked along a row of cars backed against a page-wire fence.

"Do you have one of those cars with the seat belt on its radiator?" I asked casually.

"Seat belt on its radiator? I don't understand."

"I'm sorry. That would be a Volvo. A friend of mine in Montreal used to refer to the Volvo that way. He was always partial to that make of car and I thought when the time came to buy a…" I was too embarrassed to finish the sentence.

"No, we don't have any cars with 'the seat belt on the radiator,'" he chuckled.

"That's too bad," I replied.

"Do you have a price range in mind?" he asked, as we approached the far corner of the lot, where two rows of cars came together.

"Not really," I said, trying to sound as though I could buy any car on the lot without straining my budget.

"The best buy on the lot is this Chevy Lumina right here. It's six years old—in excellent condition. It has air conditioning, remote door locks and trunk release. It was fitted with new tires less than one year ago and has been cleaned and certified." He rhymed the features off confidently.

He opened the hood and talked about the engine and various other features it had. I had just opened the driver's door, when Mr. Barrigar arrived.

"You must be Heather," he said, all out of breath. "I'm John Barrigar. Delighted to meet you. Sorry I'm a little late."

"It's nice to meet you too, Mr. Barrigar. Dad recommended your establishment as a place to buy a good used car."

"Please call me John. Dennis sometimes calls me Mr. B. I kind of like that too. Your dad is one of my best customers."

"Dennis was kind enough to show me this car, which he says is the best buy on the lot."

"There is a good reason for that. Whenever Dennis needs a car, this is the one he usually takes. I'm sure I've missed a few opportunities to make a sale because he was using it," he said as he arched an eyebrow in Dennis' direction.

"I'll take that as my cue to leave," said Dennis. "Good luck with your car buying, Heather. It's been nice meeting you."

"Nice meeting you, Dennis. Thanks for your help."

After Dennis left, it was Mr. Barrigar's turn to do the sales pitch. While Mr. B. spoke, I could see him looking over my shoulder in the direction of the sales office.

"I see Dennis is still here. Would you like to take it for a test drive?"

I said sure and settled in the driver's seat while Mr. B. went for the keys

Mr. B. came bouncing back and soon we were driving through areas of the city I had never seen before. Mr. B. was a non-stop chatterbox.

"Your father and I have doing business for more years than I care to remember." He spoke and gave directions at the same time. "He told me you were coming home and that you had become a lawyer. Your father really is a good man, you know."

"I think so, too."

"Speaking of becoming a lawyer, Dennis is a lawyer by profession. He's my stepson. He just covers for me occasionally. He has helped me out quite a bit lately, ever since I lost my partner a few months ago in a car accident."

"I'm sorry to hear about your partner."

"Thanks," he said quietly.

"Dennis must be a pretty handy person to have around, I gather," I commented, as we turned down Constitution Avenue and headed back toward the car lot.

"I meant to give you his business card earlier," Mr. B. said as he handed me Dennis' card. "Dennis would be mortified if he knew I was handing out his cards. I give the cards to my customers, in case they might need his services. He's just starting in business and every little bit helps."

I took the card and glanced surreptitiously at it as I left the car. I found it interesting that Dennis' last name was Archard not Barrigar. Then it struck me that Archard was the other lawyer in my new assignment.

"I notice Dennis' last name is...Archard," I commented,

"Yes. I married his mother when Dennis was only 13 and he preferred keeping his Archard name."

"Is the price on the sticker the price of the day?" I asked, as I parked the car near the spot from which we started.

"I think we can take a few hundred dollars off that," he replied, nodding in agreement with himself.

"Okay then, I'll take it," I responded, all too quickly. An experienced trial lawyer wouldn't have accepted the first deal offered so quickly, I thought.

"Good. I'll go in and start the paperwork. How soon do you want your car?"

"As soon as possible. Dad dropped me off this morning and he'll be away all day. I have to run some errands for a few hours, but I'll need some transportation home."

"Speaking of getting home, I assume you'll be living with your dad on Old Military Road?"

"Yes, why do you ask?"

"Your plates will have to be registered in Maryland. Next, I need to know whether you want the Bay Series plates."

"What are the Bay Series plates?"

"It's a project the Maryland government started to encourage people to contribute a little extra to help cleanup Chesapeake Bay."

"How much extra?"

"I don't really know. Nobody from around here ever ordered them. I see them quite often though. That just tells me they're from the Atlantic coast area."

"How can you tell them from the regular plates?"

"They're multicolored with a long-legged bird standing in the middle, replacing the state seal. There are some reeds and grass growing up around the numbers and letters. Kinda pretty."

"I think I'll stick with the regular kind for now."

"Okay, then. I'll take the forms over to the Maryland MVA for processing as soon as I can."

"What's the MVA?"

"Motor Vehicle Administration," he replied, with a chuckle. "We call it the Bureau of Motor Vehicles in Pennsylvania. I guess the two states title them differently to avoid confusion."

"Sounds more like bureaucracy to me," I commented, as we left the car and headed to the sales office.

"You're probably right. Where can I reach you...at your dad's office?"

"Yes, I'll be there until at least noon."

"That's fine. I interviewed a fellow yesterday to be my assistant. He's supposed to be in by ten o'clock. Assuming he shows up, I should be able to have your licence done by noon."

"Okay, I have several things to do at Dad's office and some shopping. If I haven't heard from you by noon, I'll give you a call to see how it's coming along."

"We're lucky that the Maryland MVA is close by."

"Where do you have to go for that?"

"There's an MVA outlet over in Teasdale. It's too bad you don't live in Pennsylvania because I have a good friend working at the Bureau of Motor Vehicles," he added, with a wink and a grin. "I sometimes call her to accelerate the process, but that doesn't apply in this case."

Obviously he was dying to tell me something, but I knew I would figure it out in time.

"I see my new assistant is here now. He'll be able to look after the place while I take care of your plates. If you would sign a Bill of Sale, please, Heather."

As I sat down, I noticed that Dennis had taken off across the street. While Mr. B. was filling in the forms, I took a closer look at Dennis' business card. His office was located in Room 509, 5th Floor West, 2019 Constitution Avenue—the Sparrow Building.

After I finished signing the paperwork for the car, I decided to meet with my "assignment colleague" on the way to dad's office.

Room 509, was just that—one room, not counting the vacant reception desk immediately inside the entrance. An empty aquarium separated the two desks. I see what Mr. B. meant when he said that Dennis was a struggling lawyer. The hall door was open and Dennis was sitting at the second desk.

Naturally, Dennis was surprised to see me. I thought I would have a little fun with him.

"Hi Dennis. My name is Heather Macy. I understand you're representing the State of Maryland on the General's Farm case. I'm representing Pennsylvania. I'm new in town and haven't had time to order business cards."

"Hi Heather, I had a feeling I would be running into you again," he responded, as he slowly rose from his desk. "I just didn't know it would be this soon or that you were the other lawyer on the General's Farm case."

"Judge Sewchuk suggested I meet with you to discuss how to handle the assignment."

"I noticed the name Macy on my step-father's appointment book, but Judge Sewchuk never told me who the other lawyer was."

"It took me a while to relate the name Barrigar to Archard as well, but your step-father explained it all to me."

"I have a standing arrangement of filling in for my step-father each morning while he goes for breakfast. I've been helping out for the last couple of months. He comes in at seven o'clock and goes for breakfast about eight-thirty," Dennis said nervously. "Until his new assistant arrives, he has nobody to look after the place while he's out. The new fellow should arrive today. Mr. B's partner was killed a few months ago and I help out as a favor."

I blinked and waited for the explosion of words to end.

"Every once in a while, he allows me to use one of the cars on the lot. In fact, I drove the Lumina just yesterday and I really do recommended it."

Dennis' face had become quite flushed as he spoke. He finally paused for a full breath.

"Yes, I know. I just bought it," I said, as I showed him my copy of the Bill of Sale.

"Well, good for you," Dennis said. "That makes me feel better. I never know what he thinks of me, using his cars like I do."

"You don't have to worry about that. He really thinks a lot of you, you know."

"Okay, let's do some General's Farm business," Dennis said, more as way of changing the subject. He sat down and pulled several file folders from a drawer and handed them across the desk to me.

"Here are most of the documents you'll need," he continued. "Those are your copies. I did a little research after getting my letter of authority from Judge Sewchuk last week. I took the liberty of making a photocopy for the other lawyer assigned."

I guess that explains why my contract letter was dated last Friday, I thought. Both letters were probably done at the same time.

"I appreciate that. This should help me bring me up to speed. I wasn't looking forward to going in cold to the joint heritage meeting tonight."

As I checked the titles on the various files, Dennis continued.

"First of all, I don't see the two of us as adversaries on this project," Dennis said. "Those files contain copies of minutes of the meetings of both the Pennsylvania Heritage Society and the Teasdale Heritage Foundation. Apparently when the commission in 1903 redrew the original Mason-Dixon boundary line a small strip of land changed from one state to the other. Presumably, that's what the current dispute is all about."

"1903 you say?"

"Yeah, I used the Internet and found out a bit about the Mason-Dixon survey and the boundary dispute. If you're interested, the library might be helpful for some of the local clan history stuff."

"Thanks again," I responded.

Neither of us knew what to say for a second.

"I guess I'd better start my reading," I commented, as I fingered the files and wondered what treasures they held.

I stood up and took a step toward the door. Dennis was quick to follow.

"By the way, if you need anything from the Bureau of Motor Vehicles, my mother works there," he said, in the same high-speed manner as before. "She started working again in 1974, right after I was born. She lost her job at the Land Records Office when it was destroyed by fire a few years earlier. As you probably figured out her married name is Barrigar now."

Dennis spoke as if he were trying to pass on as much information as he could in a minimum amount of time.

So, that's what Mr. B was getting at when he said he had a friend at the BMV, I thought.

"Thanks, I'll remember that," I said as I used the reception desk to put the files in my briefcase.

"In case you were wondering, my dad died in a car accident when I was 13. I also have a younger sister who is taking Pre-med at university. She goes by the name Lois Barrigar. She has spent the last three summers working at the state adoption agency in Melcastle. She sometimes helps me with my paperwork, too. My step-father has no children of his own."

"I'm an only child," I responded, "and my father is a lawyer and has an office in this building on the eight floor." I found myself speaking quickly as though I was trying to match personal histories and references.

"Yes, I've seen your father many times, but I doubt he would know me."

"We'll have to correct that won't we?" I said, thinking this guy is worth a second look.

"There's a William H Macy involved in my becoming a lawyer," Dennis added. "He helped sponsor my university tuition."

"Can't be my dad. He never uses the first name, William."

"That's too bad, I wrote my sponsor a letter, but whoever my sponsor is he never acknowledged it. I guess I'm just a grateful lost soul."

"Speaking of lost souls, the police were working on the case of a murder victim found in the ravine behind the main building."

"That's all we need."

For a moment neither of us could think of anything else to say. Then we both spoke at the same time.

"This assignment should…" Dennis began to say and stopped.

"I see by your diploma…" I started to say and stopped.

"Go ahead," Dennis gestured with a sweep of his hands.

We both laughed nervously.

"I see by your diploma—that you graduated from the University of Philadelphia. I also noticed that you don't wear a graduation ring." Or any rings at all, I wanted to say.

"I ordered a ring, but it came inscribed as D. Orchard and not Archard—a common mistake. So I sent it back. That was over a year ago. I guess I should inquire what happened to it."

"My dad has had the same kind of name problem, only in his case they substituted his father's name, Horace, for Henry," I commented, as we stepped out into the hall.

"By the way, my main office is in my house in Teasdale," Dennis said almost apologetically. "I don't spend much time here."

"We do the same thing," I responded, as I headed for the elevator and pressed the up button.

"As I started to say earlier, this assignment should give us an opportunity to get to know one another better."

I thought about shaking hands as though we were concluding a formal business meeting, but somehow it didn't seem appropriate. Fortunately, the bell for the elevator sounded and the doors sprang open. I stepped in without checking to see whether the UP or DOWN arrow was lit up.

"Yes, it should be an interesting case. Let's hope it will be one where everybody wins," I said through the closing doors. I was relieved to feel the elevator going up.

It had been a pleasant and promising meeting. I tried to convince myself that I didn't want to become too friendly with opposing counsel.

I made a quick plan for the rest of the morning—a side trip to Dad's office, (I'm going to have to get used to calling it our office.) After a short talk with Roma, I would read the files Dennis had given me. Maybe, I could squeeze in a trip to the library. That should take care of the remaining hour and a half before my car would be ready.

As the elevator came gently to a stop at the eighth floor, I realized certain things were starting to bother me. Why was I, a rookie lawyer in town, selected for the General's Farm assignment and on such short notice? Similarly, why was Dennis Archard given the job? Was he a charity case or was he part of a set-up? Did the body found behind the main building have anything to do with the property dispute? Was that body related to the human remains found on the golf course? Why was Mr. McClelland so agitated about what went on that night 30 years ago and in particular SLE 360? Why was there no follow-up police interview with him?

Before I could write the questions down, I wanted to talk to Roma. As a reminder, I fished out my notebook and held it in my hand on the way into the offices of Macy and Macy.

"Hi Roma. How are you fixed for time?"

"Hi Heather, I'm not busy at all. How much do you know about the Mac?" she asked, as she swiveled her chair around.

"Not much. I just used one for word processing in Montreal."

"Your father always used to say that he could only type forty words a week, but I would say that he's a little faster than that," Roma commented, with a big grin.

"Obviously, I'll have to have a computer to work on. Do you think we can convince Dad to spring for another Mac?"

"I don't think you'll have too much trouble. He certainly knows the value of having a computer around."

Roma proceeded to show me several packages she was using including a financial package featuring the company books. I was soon overwhelmed and looked for an excuse to move on.

"I know you'd love to show me more, Roma, but I have some reading to do," I said, as I stood up and backed away toward my office.

"I hoped you don't mind, I took the liberty of setting you up with some stationery and things. Let me know if you need anything else."

"Thanks Roma. By the way, I picked up an assignment yesterday representing the State of Pennsylvania in settling the General's Farm dispute."

"Isn't that nice. Here less than two days and already you've brought in some business. We sure could use the income. I hope you don't think I was too forward yesterday with your dad?"

"Not at all, Dad obviously thinks very highly of you."

"Thanks. If there's anything I can do for you, please don't hesitate to ask."

"As a matter of fact, there is. Would you mind typing these two things for me? They're straightforward. One is an application to write the Pennsylvania Bar Exams and the other is a draft letter of recommendation for Judge Sewchuk to sign. Be sure to date them in April, as I've written them."

I handed the draft documents to Roma, along with my Quebec Law Society membership.

"No problem. I should be able to do them tomorrow morning. Is that soon enough?"

"Sure, thanks. By the way, would you mind delivering both and a photocopy of my bar membership to Judge Sewchuk's secretary—after I've signed them, of course?"

"Sure thing."

My new office looked much brighter than the day before. Roma had done more than just add some office supplies. The Venetian blinds were pulled up to the top, letting in the north light. That helped. I hadn't noticed the curtains on the windows before. There was even an extra set of lights turned on near dad's wall.

Along with my nagging question concerning the General's Farm assignment, I also wanted to make a list of things to buy for our offices. First would be new computers and a coat rack. Then I entered the questions that I was thinking about coming up in the elevator.

I sat down and reached into my briefcase for the folders Dennis had given me. I started with the Pennsylvania Heritage Society file reasoning that the smallest one would be the easiest.

All of the Pennsylvania (Melcastle Chapter) Minutes were laid out the same way. Meetings were held on or near the first of each month and the locations were rotated among the member's houses.

The agenda each month was standard. There was the usual reading of the minutes of the previous month, followed by a moving and seconding. The only interesting parts were the reports from executive members. They tended to be sketchy. Once a year, the Finance Director would report the receipt of a $2,000 annual grant from the State Finance Department. The Melcastle Society had a total of $3,911 in the bank as of the end of last month. There seemed to be a lot of emphasis on who provided the "refreshments" each meeting.

The chairperson apparently looked after most of the reporting on the status of the five or six heritage sites in the area. Actual site visits were rare. Some reports appeared attached to the minutes of the following month. The minutes file went back about five years. Over that time, the membership of the executive never changed.

As I recalled when I was growing up, the chairperson, Lenore Andersen-Koop, was also active or at least visible in several other high-profile associations, such as the Mental Health Society and the American Red Cross. I'd heard of most of the other members of her committee by name, but didn't know them personally.

Doreine Pladsen was listed as the Immediate Past Chairperson. I remembered her from pictures in the paper. As far as I was concerned, she always had white hair. She was probably a generation older than her contemporaries on the committee.

The next three members I didn't know at all, except say that their families all owned big houses on Coteau Avenue. Janet Fordham was listed as the Secretary; Betty Galen as the Social Director; and Dorothy Watkinson as the Treasurer.

Shirley Posnick-Carswell was the Fund-raising Director. This was a name I remember from her athletic background. Some of Shirley's high school and state records in track and field were in the glass display cabinets, when I attended.

Cynthia Leblond was listed as Special Projects Officer. The Leblond family was among the wealthy class. The Leblonds probably

180

had the largest mansion on Coteau Avenue. I was in their house once, after one of our famous after-event parties. After consuming a tidy sum of the host's alcohol, we were asked to leave. I remember being impressed with the three-car garage, complete with a panel of three electronic garage door openers. A house with one door opener was a big deal back in the 1980s.

I concluded from the Pennsylvania Historical Society minutes that this committee was top-heavy in redundant positions and more oriented toward social standing than achievements. They were all at least a generation or two older than me and, with the possible exception of Janet Fordham, not one of them had ever held a real job. The heritage society was really just a social club and not only were the members all female, they all had the same common address—Coteau Ave.

The minutes of the Teasdale Heritage Foundation were quite different. A small executive group held meetings every two or three months, always at the Teasdale Town Hall, at 111 Old Military Road, East. There was no indication the foundation received any money from the State of Maryland. Nevertheless, they had set aside $7,000 for the General's Farm project. The last bank statement showed $9,755 cash on hand. If refreshments were served, there was no mention of it. It was clear that the Teasdale group relied heavily on fundraisers such as raffles, bake sales and the like for their primary source of funds. Each set of minutes contained the results of the fund-raising events since the previous meeting.

I recognized most of the Teasdale members as friends or acquaintances of my father. I only knew one of them personally, but Dad had often spoken about the other members.

The chairperson was Mrs. Val Albertson. She was a former schoolteacher in the village. She was no longer teaching by the time I went to grade school in Teasdale, but her reputation was well respected. The Albertson family she married into was said to have lots of money. I never quite understood how they decided which place to live in because they kept both houses—the one by the river in Teasdale and the other on Coteau Ave. in Melcastle.

Mr. Tom Whiteside was the Secretary. A former official at the

United Nations headquarters in New York City, he was retired and now living in Teasdale, his hometown. I felt I knew him fairly well because he and Dad went to school together.

Mr. Larry Scotten was the Finance Director. He had been a Chartered Accountant for as long as I could remember and often worked with Dad on cases that had a financial aspect.

Mr. Bill Hird was the Research Director. I knew him as the owner of the little store in the village. I understood he used to teach history at Melcastle High School, before he went into the grocery store business. When we drove around the area on Sunday night, Dad said that Mr. Hird had recently sold the little store and was now retired for the second time. I figured he must be 75 or 80 by now.

The Recording Secretary was listed as Georgia Bean. That had to be the same Georgia Bean who went to high school with me. It would be nice to see her again. I wondered what she was doing hanging around with that crowd?

The Teasdale minutes were much more comprehensive than the Pennsylvania minutes. In most cases, the responsible member for each project provided a summary report for the minutes with a full report attached. I didn't have time to read all the reports, but I gathered the projects were fairly numerous.

In one of the papers, Mr. Hird presented a detailed history of the cottage at the farm. I skimmed through that report. It seemed like the officers lived in the larger building and the general in the cottage.

I knew I was running out of time, but I noticed several entries in the minutes where the members discussed the estimated costs of refurbishing the cottage and the practicality of rebuilding the Old Stone Bridge.

Just then, Roma stuck her head in my door.

"Is there anything I can do for you before I leave, Heather?"

"As a matter of fact, there is. Could you tell me where I might find the city library? I doubt the old one still exists."

"The new library is just down the street—across from Barrigar's Auto Sales. Do you know where that is?"

"Yes I do. I'm going to Barrigar's to pick up my new car there shortly."

"Good for you. You're lucky. The new library just opened recently. Two months ago you would've had to go over to Fennell Street."

"That's great. I have some more research to do on this assignment," I replied. "I have a key. I'll lock up."

"Will I see you tomorrow, Heather?"

"Either Dad or I will be here. I'll have to let you know."

"Before I forget, some man called to advise your dad that the Hal-Burton Property Development Corporation press conference would be held on Friday at two o'clock in the high school gymnasium. You might be interested, because the subject has to do with the General's Farm."

Roma leaned back to her desk to retrieve the telephone message.

"Hmmm that's interesting. Let me write that down and I'll leave the telephone message slip on Dad's desk."

"I can do that on my way out," Roma suggested.

"By the way, Dad won't be in this afternoon. He's in Philadelphia for the day."

"Yes, he left a note on the Mac," Roma said as she took the message slip and left.

Roma was gone before I remembered that Dad wouldn't be in on Thursday either.

The duty librarian at the front desk found a synopsis of the Mason-Dixon subject for me in the Encyclopedia Americana and offered to make a photocopy. I thought 30 cents a page seemed a little steep so I made a note of the salient points of the article in my notebook:

The dispute over the drawing of the boundary between Pennsylvania and Maryland was essentially between the Penn family and the Calvert family. Large land charters were granted by the British Crown to encourage inland settlement. These grants were loosely defined, but who owned exactly what became important for the protection of the settlers and, of course, payment of taxes. Armed conflicts between the tax collecting authorities from both families and the settlers became as worrisome as the Indian threat.

Huge parcels of land were granted to the Calvert family, who settled in an ill-defined area including most of present day upper Maryland, upper Virginia and parts of West Virginia and some parts of southern Pennsylvania. The Calvert clan also claimed parts of Delaware and as far up the Delaware River as Philadelphia.

The Penn family represented the area now generally known as Pennsylvania. The Penn family settlements also overlapped parts of northern Maryland.

The boundary was supposed to have been

settled, when two British surveyors, named Mason and Dixon, were hired in 1760 to survey a boundary between the two extended families.

The Mason-Dixon Line, as it came to be known, was originally established in 1767. It remained in dispute until another survey was completed in 1903. Even then, there were still minor disputes, such as the area known as the General's Farm. The respective Heritage Society and Heritage Foundation were not satisfied because the 1903 survey moved the boundary 15 yards farther north, thus putting the cottage entirely in Maryland, whereas before, all but the south-eastern tip of the cottage had been situated in Pennsylvania.

In addition, the new boundary now split the Old Stone Bridge through the center. Neither side had the money to restore the buildings or the bridge, but it gave each side an excuse to argue rather than co-operate.

I now felt much better prepared for the joint meeting of the heritage groups, but there was still a lot I didn't know. I was curious as to who were the movers and shakers in each group. I had hoped I would have a chance to talk to Dad before I went to the meeting. Maybe I could even talk him into going with me.

Even though I was just across the street, I phoned Barrigar's to find out about my car. Mr. B's assistant said the car wouldn't be ready until about two-thirty. In the process of getting the licence, Mr. Barrigar remembered the air conditioning had to be upgraded before the car could be sold.

La Gondola seemed like an appropriate place for lunch.

CHAPTER 20

Unfinished Business In Philadelphia

Wednesday Morning

I knew roughly where I was going in Philadelphia, but I was a little uncertain about some of the latest highway interchanges. The new signs and overpasses made me nervous.

What was I going to say to old Mr. Chipman? I needed an excuse to ease my way out of continuing his case, should he decide to appeal. I couldn't quite come up with a plausible conversation line. I even thought of turning the case over to Heather. At least she wouldn't have the emotional baggage that bothered me.

As it turned out, my worries were for naught because Mr. Chipman had left early. His secretary gave me the impression that she didn't like the whole idea of the case in the first place. She didn't say it exactly, but the way she commented on the case, she left no doubt in my mind about her feelings. She promised to do her best to keep the subject from his attention. The tone of her voice told me it was time to leave for the university.

The trip to my old campus only took about five minutes. Mr. Chipman's office was on Broad St. and the cross streets were still familiar. I drove slowly down Lombard St. I was concerned that administration offices may have moved in the intervening 40 years since I had been there last. Fortunately, the "old fortress" was easy to spot. Luck was on my side and I found a visitor's parking spot close to the front door.

It was near noon as I approached the main reception desk and asked whether I might speak to the Registrar personally. I gave my name to the young man at the desk and he seemed annoyed when I insisted that Macy was spelled without an E. A blank look came over his face when I told him the nature of my visit.

"A 1960s administration problem you say."

The clerk asked me to wait and made a waving gesture to some chairs a few paces down the hall. As I picked out a chair, the clerk disappeared. Within a few moments, a tall woman with distinctly greying hair emerged from an office behind the reception desk. She wore glasses and was dressed in a gray pantsuit with an off-white blouse.

"Henry!" she cried. *"Henry MACY."*

I was stunned to say the least.

"Don't you remember me?"

"I recognize the voice and there's something familiar about you, but…"

"Patricia MacNeil! We were in law school together."

"Of course, I remember now. We were in the same study group. How have you been? What are you doing here?" I inquired, as we embraced. Patricia always was the tactile type.

"After I left law school, I worked in my father's law office in New York for a few years and then the university asked me whether I would like to take on the Assistant Registrar's job. A few years later, I moved up to the Registrar's position and I've been here ever since. What have you been up to?"

"Oh, I've been practicing the Black Art in Melcastle ever since I graduated."

"That's cute. I haven't heard that expression for years. What brings you back to Philadelphia? Are you going to increase your endowment fund?" she asked, with a nudge and a wink.

I didn't really understand what she had just said. I heard the words, but I didn't know whether she was just kidding around or not.

"No, I'm back to have my name corrected on my diploma and mailing address, and on whatever else you may have me incorrectly identified."

"Well, you've come to the right place. With my experience and your money, we should be able to make short work of that minor problem."

"Your money? Endowment fund? You have me confused."

"The William H Macy Scholarship, of course," she exclaimed, with a bemused look.

"I'm sorry," I said. "I'm not aware of any William H Macy Scholarship."

"Well, that's a new one," she snorted. "Your father established the William H Macy Scholarship the year we graduated. I could look up the exact details, but in general, I can tell you the Macy account receives an annual check from a bank in Switzerland. There's enough in that account to fund the tuition for one student for at least four years."

"Well, I'll be…"

"As a matter of fact, I just happened to know, there's sufficient growth in that particular account to think of sponsoring a second student. Which reminds me of the peculiar caveat your father attached to the tuition instructions."

"And what was that?" I asked, still trying to recover from the news.

"Our instructions were to alternate the chosen student between law and engineering each year. That has always puzzled me. Why did he want to provide for an engineering student?"

"That's all news to me, Patricia. My guess is that Dad was always interested in becoming an engineer himself. He was self-taught and perhaps he had secret plans to enroll himself. Who knows? He was a very secretive man."

"Listen Henry, I haven't much time right now. I have a meeting first thing this afternoon. I was planning to eat lunch at my desk. On second thought, why don't we pick up a sandwich for you at the cafeteria and we can talk for a few minutes while we eat?"

The sandwich I ordered at the cafeteria looked good on the menu, but turned out to be some kind of "mystery meat," as Patricia called it. We sat at our table and talked.

The next hour flew by in a blizzard of questions and answers. Toward the end of our conversation, Patricia confided that she had never been married, but had one child, which had been given up for adoption. The affair happened in New York City while she was working for her father's law firm. She was suspicious her father had arranged for her employment at the university because the assistant's job had been created just before she arrived.

On the way back to Patricia's office, I told her about Heather's return home and supplied more details of the purpose of my trip to pique her interest.

Patricia enjoyed our chat so much that she decided that she would have her assistant take over the meeting. She picked up a file that was on her desk and handed it to her assistant who was just entering the conference room. At the same time, she announced to those gathering for the meeting that she was going to take care of an urgent administrative problem and would try to be back before the meeting ended.

"This calls for some research." Patricia stated, as she grabbed my arm. "Let's pay a visit to the Archives Building."

She led me to one of the even older buildings on campus.

"I used to work in the 'stacks' during the summers, while I was a student," Patricia announced, as she opened a heavy steel-clad door.

We descended a narrow set of stairs and entered a large room filled with at least 20 rows of six-foot-high open shelves, filled on both sides with file folders.

"Yes, I remember that. It seems to me you worked after classes during the school year, as well," I added.

She knew exactly where to go and entered between the rows marked "M-N."

"I don't see the William Henry Macy file. It should be right near here," she commented, as we neared the far end of the dimly lighted shelves.

"I wouldn't know where to start looking," I said.

"My own file is on this shelf and MacNeil and Macy should be almost side by side," she suggested, as she placed her hand on a file near the end of the row. Her surname was printed on the vertical tab, in large letters.

"Yes, I can see your name quite clearly."

"Your file should be here between MacNeil and Melnechuk," she said as she put a finger between the two files. "You remember Eilene, she was the home coming queen one year."

"How could anyone forget Eilene Melnechuk? She was the one with the big…"

Patricia and I exchanged knowing smiles. At the same time, Patricia subconsciously pulled the lapels of her suit jacket together, fastened a button and returned to the task of searching the shelves.

"Your file," Patricia continued, "should have an orange tag on it indicating you were a student and a green tag indicating that you graduated."

"You're right. It's not there," I said, trying to help.

"Your father's file, with the letter "H" in the middle, should be in the next section."

"What do you mean 'your father's file'?"

"As the source of a scholarship fund, your father is automatically a patron and every patron has a file, flagged with a red identifying tag. You can look down the row and see several red tags."

"Ah yes, I see them."

"Okay, let's see if we can find your father's file."

Patricia quickly moved to the next section. Her hands jumped from one red flag to another and after a few seconds, she pulled out a file marked William H Macy. The file in her hand appeared to be much thicker than others on the shelves.

"Sponsors' files are always much easier to find. I was working here when your father's file was opened," she said and tucked my father's file under her arm.

"So that's how you were so familiar with Dad's donation," I suggested.

"That and the fact that the investment, which my office monitors, has grown over the years."

"Would my record not be on a computer somewhere?" I asked, as we moved back toward the entrance of the row.

"True. In fact, all hard copy records are on microfiche as well, but neither of those systems shows the color-coded flags. In my experience, the physical records for those graduating prior to the early 1980's would likely be more accurate anyway. It must be here somewhere."

"I suppose you are right."

The light was better at the front desk where Patricia opened up Dad's file and placed it on the counter.

"Aha! There it is. Someone has placed your file inside your father's file," Patricia announced.

"So, my trip wasn't in vain."

"Not only that, someone placed your orange tag on the front cover of the file instead of the back and as the file became bigger over the years the orange tag didn't stick up as far. Therefore, because your file was inside your father's file it wasn't visible."

"A combination of filing errors," I volunteered meekly.

"But, that still doesn't explain why there isn't a green graduation tag on it," she mused.

"Surely we can just add a green tag."

"Yes we could, after we have confirmed that your graduation documents are enclosed and…" Patricia's voice trailed off.

"What's the problem?"

"There's your green tag," she exclaimed. "It was never put on the cover. Someone must have been in a hurry and just placed it inside."

"Must have been some summer student," I suggested jokingly.

"I suppose, in a way, you're lucky you received your diploma at all."

"I guess you're right. Even I can see how the problem originated."

"There, the graduation tag is on your file and they're separated so the confusion will not happen again."

"I should have brought my problem to your attention earlier and you could have straightened the files out sooner."

"I doubt it. Who else would have known your father's file was even there to find yours?" she confided.

"Good point."

Patricia signed out both files at the desk, saying nothing to the archives clerk about the tagging errors. She explained to me as we left that she would still have to confirm the computer records matched the hard copy files.

"It will likely take several memos, and probably personal visits to Lord knows whom, to have a diploma reissued. I'll handle the paperwork personally."

"Thank you. I don't suppose I could have two copies of my graduation diploma? I would like to hang one in my second office at home."

"I don't see why not. I will include it in a memo to the Chancellor explaining the mix-up and reiterating the point that the William H Macy Endowment has been in place for over 40 years. I will stipulate the university has made a gross error and that it should be corrected immediately with an apology."

"I appreciate your help."

"I don't want to jeopardize any endowment fund let alone one that has the potential to expand to include another student. By the way, if the fund is increased ever so slightly, we could fund both an engineering student and a lawyer."

"I hear you. Please let me know the details on that," I added. I was already thinking about what I might do with the proceeds from the General's Farm.

"I will also forward a copy of my correspondence to the University Alumni Association and the Law Society and have them amend their records."

Back at her office, Patricia peeked into the conference room to see how the meeting was going in her absence. Without saying anything to them, she returned to her desk.

"By the way, I happen to know that quite a number of students, who have been helped by your father's scholarship, have written thank you letters. Your father's instructions were to keep any such letters at the university. You might be surprised by the names of the people your father's scholarship has helped over 40 years."

Patricia opened Dad's file to a list of recipients of the scholarship. I noticed that one of the names was, Dennis Archard. I had seen that name on the Sparrow Building list of tenants.

"Do you happen to have a letter from this one?" I asked, pointing to the Archard name.

"We keep the letters in a file down the hall. I'll have a look."

"Don't bother now. I know you are anxious to attend your meeting," I suggested. "I'd appreciate it if you would leave the letters where they are for now. I'll take care of them later."

"I have your address and here's my business card. It has my Email address on it. We should keep in touch. I'll write my home address on the back," she added, with a coy smile.

"Thank you very much for straightening out my problem."

"You're most welcome."

"It certainly has been nice seeing you again," I said, as we embraced.

On the way home, I wondered how difficult it would be to persuade Heather to outfit our offices with computers. Roma has certainly convinced me of the efficiency of preparing a wide variety of legal paperwork involved in day-to-day office work. To tell you the truth, I'm too afraid of the technology. I had heard that you could have a whole legal library on line, complete with a "keyword search" capability. Somebody mentioned that phrase to me a little while ago.

I also pondered what to do about the surplus in the William H Macy Scholarship Fund. Perhaps I could start one in Heather's name. Maybe Heather will want to take some post-graduate courses.

It certainly made the trip home pass quickly.

CHAPTER 21

Police Headquarters

Wednesday Afternoon

I thought about my baby-sitting days with the Spagnoli family as I entered La Gondola restaurant. Lunch was uneventful, except for the Maitre d' who kept hovering around. He was obviously curious about the solitary person who was taking up a table in his restaurant for over an hour.

As I lingered over my salad and second cup of tea, I reviewed my notebook. I had to tell somebody about what I had discovered concerning the two murders. The most important item was to suggest the DNA blood sample that Detective Turcot had gathered, might be that of Roger Wendelman. It was obvious that neither police force knew about Mr. McClelland's diary, including the licence numbers and the suspects' descriptions. I wondered whether Detective Turcot had checked for DNA evidence on the sword over the fireplace.

I wondered whom the chief of police might be these days. When I was in high school, it was Chief Parslow. He had a fierce reputation for being tough on teenagers. That shouldn't matter because now I was an adult. If Parslow were still the chief, it would be a good test of my ability to function in this town. But first, I had to pick up my new car.

When I arrived at Barrigar's Auto Sales, Mr. B. couldn't apologize enough for not remembering that all cars over five years old had to have the coolant replaced. He gave me the impression I was supposed to feel guilty because he had to pay for the upgrade.

I drove to the police headquarters and parked my car behind. When I was in high school, we had toured the building, so I knew the chief's office was on the second floor. I filtered my way through the crowd in the "bookings" area and went up the main stairs as though I knew what I was doing. No one challenged me, so I kept going.

I couldn't help but noticed a huge wooden carving of the Melcastle Police crest hanging on the wall at the half-landing. It was nearly as wide as the stairs and about two inches thick. The clear lacquer finish made the beautiful wooden grain stand out.

The secretary's desk, unchanged over the years, was semi-circular and stuck out in the middle of the main east-west corridor. A young, good-looking woman was standing between the desk and an open filing cabinet. She tilted her head and cradled a telephone receiver against her left shoulder. She was searching the files with both hands and talking on the phone at the same time.

The newish-looking, slide-in cardboard nameplate on the desk made me wondered how long the chief's secretary had been employed in this position. The nameplate had "Ms R. Hannas" on it.

I was standing there for several minutes, when I spotted a big brass nameplate on the office door on the other side of the secretary's desk, which read:

"Harvey Ivan Parslow II, Chief Of Police."

My heart started pounding. My bravado quickly melted with each beat. I though seriously about turning around and leaving.

At that moment, Ms Hannas terminated her conversation. She hung up the phone and slammed the filing cabinet shut in one dramatic movement that suggested displeasure with the person on the other end of the phone.

I meekly asked whether I could speak to Chief Parslow. My inquiry was returned with a curt and mechanical response that Chief Parslow wasn't in at the moment, but was expected back momentarily. I gave her my name and the now-rehearsed line that I was there on a legal assignment concerning the General's Farm, which she dutifully recorded on a message pad. She directed me to a row of chairs about 20 feet behind me in a short hallway at right angles to the main corridor. I selected a chair right on the corner, where I could see Ms Hannas and the chief's door at the same time.

I heard footsteps coming down the main corridor behind me, but I didn't realize it was Detective Turcot until he was past me. As he walked, he was concentrating on putting some papers in an already overstuffed expandable file folder. He hurried past the secretary's desk without saying a word to Ms. Hannas. He knocked on Chief Parslow's door, entered and closed the door behind him.

I expected him to come back out as soon as he realized the chief wasn't there, but he stayed for several minutes. He emerged carrying a single piece of paper and hurried back down the corridor. He was obviously preoccupied and still didn't notice me. I raised my hand to greet him, but I was too late. After he had gone by, I wondered what was he doing in the chief's office? The expandable folder also piqued my curiosity. What are the odds of it being Dad's folder? How paranoid I had become.

I occupied my time for the next few moments just looking around. There were half a dozen pictures of past chiefs of police on the north wall of the main corridor. I was fairly certain the one nearest the stairs was Chief Parslow's. The stern looking faces were accentuated by the service caps they wore. The uniform tunics had changed styles over the years, but remained basically the dark brown jackets. The crests on the caps were all the same. It was hard to tell from a distance, but the crests probably were the same words and design as the wooden crest on the stair landing.

197

Mounted on the south wall, there were a number of different shaped items. I stood up and took a step out into the main corridor to take a better look. The array was an odd collection of framed items and banners mounted in a random fashion, and continued between the doorways down to where Detective Turcot had gone. These items were obviously from sporting events and other memorabilia.

My gaze was attracted to an unusually large, framed item near the corner behind the chair I had been sitting in. I moved around the corner to face it squarely. Under a covering of glass, was a black and white almost full page from the Melcastle Journal. It was yellow with age and contained a nearly full-length picture of a much younger and smiling police officer Parslow. He was dressed in his two-tone, summer uniform with three big stripes on his sleeve. As he stood with one foot on the bumper of a car, he appeared to be a little more heavyset than the sullen portrait across the hall would suggest.

The newspaper headline read:

COP CAR DONATED
TO MUSEUM

The subhead added:
Sergeant Parslow saddened(?) to see old friend leave
The car was a gleaming all-black police car, probably an early-to-mid 1950s Ford. It had no sirens or crests on the doors, as opposed to the brown and blue cars the Melcastle police drove today. The article underneath mentioned this car was one of the first in the state equipped with a two-way radio and was the fastest vehicle on the road when it first went into service. It added: "The recently promoted Sergeant Parslow personally drove this car for most of the 200,000 miles on the odometer." The article went on to state that 1974 Chevrolets were replacing all older model police cars.

In the picture, Sergeant Parslow had a big smile and wore a uniform baseball cap and hip-length, dark-colored jacket, both bearing police crests. Now that I could see it up close, the crest was made of the words, "A DUTY TO SERVE AND PROTECT" stacked pyramid style. There were some Latin words inscribed on a ribbon underneath. The ribbon was overlapped and curled up at the ends.

I studied the smiling face for a while. There was something odd about the angle of the baseball cap. Then it struck me. The face was the partially obscured image I'd seen in the picture on Judge Sewchuk's desk. Why would the chief be presenting a jacket to the judge?

The jacket recollection set in motion a series of thoughts. I wondered whether Judge Sewchuk could be the "big man" driver that Mr. McClelland recorded in his diary. Then I wondered whether the "short and kinda stout" driver could be the chief. The more I thought about the possibilities, the more convinced I became that I was on to something. It didn't take me long to decide that a meeting with Chief Parslow wasn't such a good idea after all. I cancelled the appointment.

"Done," declared Ms Hannas, with a forced smile. I noticed she drew a line through the message, but didn't throw it away.

"Thank you," I said. "Could you please tell me where I might find Detective Turcot's office?"

"Far end of the corridor, last door on the right."

On my way to Detective Turcot's office, I took another look at the newspaper clipping on the wall. Ever since talking with Mr. McClelland, I found myself fixated with licence plates. Unfortunately, the frame cut off the bottom half of the letters and numbers. I couldn't be certain about the first three characters. The camera angle didn't help the visual acuity either. The characters could have been SLE 360 or just as easily CIF 360.

I leaned my head closer to the covering glass, but I couldn't see any more of the characters below the frame. The lighting was poor and a bench prevented me from getting much closer. I hoped the Melcastle Journal would have a copy of that paper, or better still, the original picture.

At that moment, I heard someone bounding up the stairs behind me. From the reflection off the glass covering the newspaper article, it looked like Chief Parslow. He was definitely shorter than me and the rotund body looked like it could belong to the portrait of the chief on the wall. I pretended to be looking at the other items on the wall and waited for him to pass. He walked with a spring in his step, even athletic for a man his age.

I wondered whether the chief's secretary was aware that I was only a few feet away. I moved to my right slightly so that I could see him in the glass reflection as he passed by the secretary's desk and turned towards the chief's office. Ms. Hannas was talking on the phone so she just handed the message slips to her boss as he went by. The chief grabbed the messages and barely broke stride. He glanced at the pieces of paper briefly. I was relieved he didn't appear to have noticed me.

When I heard his door close, I made my way toward Detective Turcot's office. On the way, I reminded myself to look at the donated car picture before I left the building to see whether there was any publication date visible.

At end of the main corridor, I leaned my head around the corner of the last door and discovered it was really an entrance to two more doors. Detective Turcot's name was printed on a large cardboard form and mounted on the closed door on the left. I was about to knock on the opaque glass portion of the door, when I noticed a brass nameplate on the other door, which was halfway open. The nameplate read:

"Inspector John A. McGillivray,
Deputy Chief of Police."

I recognized the name, but I wasn't sure why. I glanced into the room, more as a reflex action than trying to be nosy. For that split second, while I was trying to figure out why that name was so familiar, a voice rang out.

"Heather, is that you?" asked a male voice from the dimly lit room.

"Yes," I responded.

"Heather Macy, I thought it was you. Come on in."

I was desperately trying to remember the man's name as he approached me with his hand extended. He was about my height and seemed to cover the ten or fifteen feet between us in one swift movement. The fact that he was not in uniform didn't help.

"I should know you…I think," I said, as we shook hands.

"John McGillivray. I used to drop by your house once in a while to try persuading your dad to go golfing."

"Yes, I remember now," I said. His grip was unusually strong. My guess was he still played a lot of golf.

"I'll never forget a pretty face like yours," he added, grinning. "Your hair is a bit longer and straighter, but it's still that beautiful auburn color."

"Well thank you," I responded, feeling a little embarrassed. "They tell me I take after my mother, as far as looks are concerned."

"I heard you were back in town. By the way, congratulations on becoming a lawyer."

"Thank you. I'm going to join Dad's practice."

"Yeah, I ran into your dad a few days ago. He couldn't wait to tell me, and anybody else within earshot, that you were coming back to town."

"Yeah, dads are sometimes funny that way."

"What brings you to our fair domain?"

"I'm working on the settlement of the General's Farm boundary dispute and I ran into Detective Turcot up there. I just wanted to check in with him on a couple of details."

"Oh, that." His dominant smile disappeared for a second.

There was a pause. The mention of the General's Farm seemed to bother Inspector McGillivray. I racked my brain to think of something to change the subject.

"I remember something you said one time when you and Dad went golfing."

"We've played golf a few times and I may have committed a faux pas or two."

"I was about ten and Dad brought me along as his caddy. We were on the golf course and I don't think you knew I could hear you."

"Uh oh. I know I'll probably regret this, but what did I say that you would remember after all these years?" he asked with a big grin.

"You were chipping onto the sixth green. Your ball hit and bounced right across into the long grass behind. Your comment was 'that green is as hard as hobo shit.'"

"I apologize my dear. I've heard that line many times, but I wasn't aware that I'd ever used it."

"That's okay. I haven't had the chance to use that expression until now. There are other things you said, but I think you've had enough for the moment," I said, as I moved toward Detective Turcot's door.

"Louis has been working on a body found at the General's Farm. I hope it doesn't affect your work on the boundary dispute," he said, as he knocked on Detective Turcot's door and stepped back.

A muted voice said, "Come in."

I nodded to Inspector McGillivray. He retreated into his own office and closed his door.

I opened Detective Turcot's door just far enough to poke my head between the jamb and the door. There was a filing cabinet against the common wall between the two offices, which meant if one wanted to enter Detective Turcot's office the door had to be almost fully open.

It was a small office with green and white tiled floor. A single fluorescent tube and one and a half windows lighted the room. The half window was shared with Deputy Chief McGillivray's office. A temporary wall bisected the window. Obviously, at one time the two offices used to be one.

You could tell Detective Turcot was not expecting visitors. He remained seated and kept his eyes concentrated on his task.

"I'm sorry to interrupt, Detective Turcot…" I started to say.

I expected him to at least look up and greet me in some fashion. When he didn't budge, I moved a step or two closer. I released the door and felt it move slowly toward the closed position by itself. I glanced back to see that it remained slightly ajar.

"Have a seat," Detective Turcot muttered, as he continued writing in a thick file. His left hand was holding up the upper sheets while he wrote on the page below. "I'll be with you in a minute."

On the temporary wall behind him, I noticed a city map dotted with colored pushpins. What intrigued me was a rectangle of red pins in the lower left-hand corner, about where I figured the General's Farm would be. Most of the rest of the pins were a mixture of various colors. I wondered what the different colors meant.

Through the windows you could see the weather had partially cleared up. The sun came out suddenly and the whole office brightened considerably.

Detective Turcot half stood, but continued to write. Still deep in thought, he finally put the file aside.

"Yes, what can I do for you...ah...ah...Heather. It took me a moment to remember your name. I've been so busy with this case. How are you? What brings you here?"

"I just came by to give you some information I think might be helpful regarding the body you found up at the General's Farm."

"By all means—information is something we can always use. Please, have a chair. Take the soft one." He moved a straight back chair out of the way allowing better access to padded chair at the far corner of his desk.

The overstuffed chair was too close to the desk for my comfort, so I gently pushed it back a few inches with the back of my legs. I hadn't noticed a parachute and a hard helmet leaning against the far side of the chair. The two pieces of flying gear tipped over as I sat down. The helmet made a loud noise as it fell on the floor and rolled away.

"I'm sorry. I didn't see your flying gear. Are you a pilot?"

"Yes, I am, but that's really my skydiving parachute and helmet." He stacked the two items in the corner underneath the half window behind his chair.

"An boyfriend of mine in Montreal was a pilot. He had a helmet much like yours."

"My interest is more in skydiving than flying. One of the main reasons I became a pilot was to earn some money by taking up other skydivers. Both hobbies beat working."

"I know how you feel. I only went flying to help my boyfriend qualify for his commercial licence. Every trip was like a free lesson for me."

"Have you ever tried skydiving?"

"No thank you. Why would anyone want to jump out of a perfectly safe aircraft, if you didn't have to?"

"You really should try it."

"I don't think so." I responded with enough emphasis to make sure there was no doubt about my lack of interest.

"But, that's not why you are here."

As Detective Turcot sat down, I could see the tab on the file cover he had been working on was labeled: "General's Farm Case." He opened his notepad and wrote my name after the last entry.

"Now then, what kind of information do you have for us?"

"Something occurred to me when you said the DNA analysis on the blood sample you retrieved didn't match the body. I don't know whether you know it or not, but Roger Wendelman used to live at the General's Farm until he disappeared about 30 years ago. I was wondering whether the blood sample you recovered might be his."

"Who's Roger Wendelman?" he asked, as he wrote the new name under mine.

"It's a little complicated, so I'll have to explain it to you in my own way."

"Okay, go ahead." The edge in his voice told me he would humor me only so long.

"Do you know Sergeant Woznica?"

"Yes, he's with the Maryland Police in Teasdale, I believe. Why do you ask?"

"I met Sergeant Woznica at the Old Stone Bridge near the General's Farm after I met you yesterday. He was investigating some human remains buried 30 years ago near the sixth green of the Hylands Golf Course."

"Human remains on the golf course—interesting."

"First, do you know my dad, Henry Macy?"

"Yes, I think so."

"When I mentioned your comment about the closeness of the DNA match, Dad remembered Roger Wendelman had disappeared about 30 years ago. And then, when I mentioned the human remains that Sergeant Woznica was investigating, I wondered whether the blood sample you had gathered might belong to Roger."

"But the body we found in the ravine almost certainly had to have been killed in or near the main building."

"I have a theory on that, too."

"Any theory is as good as the ones we have come up with so far. Let's hear yours." Detective Turcot was still being polite, but still sending a message that he was growing impatient.

"The way I figure it, Roger Wendelman was murdered in front of the fireplace and bled profusely all over the wooden floor…"

"Wait a minute. You say 'bled profusely.' How do you know this Wendelman fellow lost a lot of blood?"

"Sergeant Woznica said his victim probably died from a loss of blood. I think he said 'the bullet passed though the carotid artery in the victim's neck and it lodged inside the victim's skull.' I assumed, because it was an artery, the victim bled profusely."

"And how does Sergeant Woznica know all that from 30-year-old remains?"

"He sent the remains to the new forensic lab in Melcastle, The remains were wrapped in a hemp rug," I added.

"Okay, let's assume the victim 'bled profusely' as you say. Then what?" he asked, still skeptical. He started writing again, which made me feel better.

"The way I see it, Roger Wendelman's blood flooded into the cracks in the flooring and eventually formed a seal. When the second murder took place, the blood from the second victim couldn't follow the same path. The Javex you mentioned the other day when we met could also have contaminated the latest victim's blood. So the only usable sample would be from the first victim, which you gathered from underneath the main floor," I added.

"Hmmm, interesting theory. So now you're suggesting we compare our blood sample with a sample of the human remains found on the golf course."

"Exactly."

"I guess the first thing…I could do…is contact Sergeant Woznica. Perhaps, we could visit…the forensic lab together." He spoke in bursts, talking as he wrote.

"I'm sure he'll be more than willing to co-operate."

"I wonder why we weren't informed about the human remains?"

Detective Turcot mused in a barely audible voice as he continued to write.

As Detective Turcot recorded my information, I reflected on the body in the ravine. It suddenly occurred to me that the ravine victim could be Roger's son; assuming Ruby Wendelman's baby was safely delivered and was a boy. If that were true, then the "close enough to be a relative" comment would make sense. Besides, the now grown up "baby" would be about 30 years old last month—same as me.

As we continued to chat, I began to become uneasy with Detective Turcot's attitude. He didn't really give me the impression that my theory was as useful or important as I thought it was. My original idea was to tell him about Mr. McClelland's Diary and the licence plates, but I could only imagine how doubtful even a proactive police officer would be to a second-hand description of the drivers and a theory that I thought one of the drivers might be the chief. I quickly decided it would be best to hang on to that information for now.

We chatted for a few more minutes about my new assignment and the weather. As he was getting up to escort me to the door, he turned to his computer, pressed a few keys and waited a few seconds.

"There it is," he said. "Unidentified human remains—found on Hylands Golf Course, Teasdale County, Maryland—April 28, 2003—Cause of death—32-calibre bullet through the neck—lodged inside the skull."

"Sounds familiar," I said.

"There's a follow-up entry," he added. "The victim was a male, approximately 30 years of age, six feet tall and had a short beard."

The height and the beard was something new, I thought to myself. I didn't say anything. It made me think of Mom's dream.

"I sure wish our two computer systems were fully integrated. The operational exchange is fairly current, but Maryland's update just arrived this morning."

As I stood there, waiting for Detective Turcot to finish with his computer, all I wanted to do was leave that office. My mind was racing. How to make sense of all the pieces?—Mr. McClelland's Diary.—The licence plate numbers, especially SLE 360.—The newspaper article on the corridor wall. I made a mental note to follow up on the status of Mrs. Wendelman and what happened to the child she was carrying.

Detective Turcot rose and escorted me to the door.

"If there's anything else you would like to pass on please don't hesitate to drop in or give me a call at this number," he said as he handed me his business card.

For a moment, I had second thoughts about telling him about the ceremonial sword. I had wanted to suggest it as a possible murder weapon, but decided not to mention it until I had checked out the other ideas. First, I didn't know how to mention the sword without insulting him—to suggest that he had overlooked it as a possible murder weapon. Second, I was rapidly developing a serious distrust of this man.

Detective Turcot passed in front of me and grabbed the door and in a grand gesture, swung it open to let me out.

We were both startled to see Chief Parslow with his back to us, leaning against the common door casing between the two offices. The chief pretended to be engrossed in the message slips he held in his right hand. With his hat removed, I could see that the chief's head was mostly bald. The little hair he had around the sides was close cut and had turned white in patches.

At that moment, the chief hastily knocked on Inspector McGillivray's closed door.

"John, could I see you for a moment, please?" the chief asked, but remained partially blocking my exit.

"Certainly, sir," replied Deputy Chief McGillivray from inside his office. "I'll be right there."

As a polite way of warning the chief that we were behind him, Detective Turcot said in a raised voice, "Thanks again, Heather for stopping by. I'm sure your information will be of great help to us."

"You're welcome."

The chief turned to face us. While his features were familiar, he appeared to be a lot younger than a man whom I assumed would be about my father's age. The patchy white spots in his otherwise light brown hair weren't noticeable from the front.

"Oh Chief—this is Heather...Heather Macy," he stammered, struggling to say something meaningful to his commanding officer. "She's the lawyer assigned by Judge Sewchuk...to assist in settling the property dispute...at the General's Farm."

"Good afternoon, Heather. To what do we owe the honor of your visit?" said the chief. His composure, in light of the fact that he had probably been eavesdropping, was remarkable. Heaven knows how long he had been standing outside Detective Turcot's door.

"I was just visiting Detective Turcot," I replied obliquely, not wanting to become involved in any further discussions.

By then Deputy Chief McGillivray had arrived.

Detective Turcot, sensing my discomfort with Chief Parslow, asked, "Deputy Chief McGillivray, do you know Heather Macy?"

"Yes. As it turns out, we met a few years ago."

Detective Turcot returned to the chief's question, "Heather has come across some information that might help us identify the body found in the ravine behind the General's Farm and perhaps the human remains found on the golf course."

The chief stiffened noticeably at the end of the Detective's comments. He glared at Detective Turcot

"I don't know anything about any human remains found on the golf course," he snapped at Detective Turcot.

"The remains were found by the Teasdale detachment of the Maryland Police," Detective Turcot responded quickly. "I just found out myself. I'll be going over to see them immediately to check it out."

"Well, see that you do," retorted the chief, as he turned to his deputy. "John, I would like to go over the traffic study you've been working on. Do you have your copy handy?"

"Yes sir. Come on in while I find it."

Before I left the building, I sat underneath the donated cop car picture and made a few entries in my notebook:

Meeting with Detective Turcot at Police HQ

- *Decided not to mention Mr. McClelland's Diary and licence no's*
- *I don't think I could work for a sneaky man like Chief Parslow*
- *Check out (at Melcastle Journal) donated cop car picture*
- *Newspaper dated "Monday, 17 Sept, 1973"*
- *Ask Dennis O. to ask his sister at adoption agency,*
- *Who adopted Wendelman baby? What gender was it?*

On the way home, I spotted a fast food place where Dad used to take us when I was a kid. I thought a take-out for supper would be nice.

CHAPTER 22

Was There A Conspiracy?

Late Wednesday Afternoon

I left police headquarters full of ideas, questions and suspicions. I was convinced the body found in the ravine was the Wendelman "baby," who would have been about the right age. I was equally certain Roger Wendelman was murdered on the same spot 30 years ago.

The idea of a conspiracy connecting the two murders began to solidify in my mind. Not only were the two victims related, but also both could have been done in by the same killer or killers. My thoughts kept revolving around Chief Parslow and Judge Sewchuk. Detective Turcot couldn't possibly be involved in the first murder, but he could be part of a conspiracy or cover-up.

I didn't want to think about it, but Dad may also be involved somehow. Hopefully, Dad would be able to explain his presence at the farm three weeks ago. I thought the best approach would be to ask him about Chief Parslow first and Dad's involvement might come out naturally.

When I arrived home, Dad was sitting in the living room looking fresher than I expected he would be after his trip to Philadelphia. I thought my questions were more important than his trip, so I started first.

"Dad, how well do you know Chief Parslow?"

"Do you mean the Harvey Parslow I went to grade school with or his son?"

"The one you went to school with I guess."

"Harvey and I both grew up in Teasdale. It was a mystery how he ever became the chief of police in Melcastle. Before he went into the police force he was into all kinds of ventures, some of which didn't achieve very high moral or ethical standards. He even managed the Hylands golf course, until it went broke. Some say he ran it into the ground."

"Yes, but how close were you as friends...or...companions?" I asked, trying to suggest my real concern.

"I wasn't particularly a close friend. Your Uncle Arthur used to run around with the Parslow boys, Harvey Senior and Robert and their gang. Individually they weren't too bad, but as a gang they were into all kinds of trouble. Why do you ask?"

"I think Roger Wendelman may have been murdered and Chief Parslow may be involved," I stated and looked for a reaction.

Dad just sat stoically on the end of the chesterfield so I continued. "When I was speaking with Mr. McClelland yesterday, he mentioned licence number SLE 360 was on the scene in 1973 and the drivers' descriptions matched that of Chief Parslow."

Still there was no reaction from Dad.

"I believe Chief Parslow and Judge Sewchuk were the two drivers he described in last month's murder." I could feel a tremor in my voice and I couldn't control the tears welling up in my eyes. "And your truck in 1973...and your car...he says you were there...both times..."

"My, my, something really seems to be bothering you. What is it?"

I took a moment to compose myself.

"Mr. McClelland mentioned you were at the farm about the time of the murder three weeks ago. Judge Sewchuk and Chief Parslow match Mr. McClelland's descriptions…and I saw the chief and Judge Sewchuk in a picture in the judge's office…and the judge's jacket had spot marks on it…and that gun in the safe…"

"Whoa, whoa. Let's not get all heated up before we know all the facts."

"But Daddy, it all looks so bad and I can't believe you would have anything to do with those murders—especially the first one," I pleaded.

Dad put his arm around my shoulders. I felt more comfortable, but couldn't stop my tears.

"First of all, I can truthfully tell you that I had nothing to do with any murder up there or anywhere else. I visit up the General's Farm regularly. It must be a coincidence that I was there last month. As for Mr. McClelland being a witness, I'm sure any good lawyer would destroy his credibility on several counts."

"He sure convinced me," I said, wiping my tears.

"There must be some explanation. I would suggest we start with the most recent murder. There would likely be more facts available for that case and they would be fresher."

"Okay, I'll start with Detective Turcot. How well do you know him?" I looked at my notes for inspiration.

"I don't think I know Detective Turcot at all. Why are you so concerned about him?"

"I went to see Detective Turcot this afternoon and during our conversation something told me not to tell him everything I knew. I did tell him about the possible DNA match with the human remains found at the golf course, but I had planned to tell him about Mr. McClelland's diary…the licence numbers…the drivers descriptions and…"

"It was probably your gut feelings telling you something was wrong."

"I don't know. Maybe I should just read you my notes and you can tell me whether you come to the same conclusions."

"Okay, go ahead. Perhaps I'll pick up something I didn't pick up between what you told me yesterday and today."

"When I visited the General's Farm yesterday, I met Detective

Turcot. He was investigating a body found three weeks ago in the ravine. The body was a male, about 30 years old, stabbed seventeen times with a long instrument. He mentioned the DNA analysis on the blood found at the farmhouse was 'close enough to be a relative' to his victim. That's when you suggested it might be Roger Wendelman's blood."

"I don't remember the seventeen stabbings, especially the part about the long instrument. Did you find out whether it was Roger's blood from 30 years ago or not?"

"No, not yet. I just passed that idea on to Detective Turcot this afternoon. I presume he'll obtain a bone marrow sample from Sergeant Woznica and have the DNA comparison analysis done at the Melcastle lab today or tomorrow."

"Was the murder weapon found?"

"No, but that reminds me, I noticed there was a ceremonial sword hanging over the fireplace. That could be the weapon."

"It sure would be nice to clear up Roger's disappearance after all these years."

"Next, I met Mr. McClelland with his scribblers. He calls them his 'DIARY.' He even recorded what the weather was like 30 years ago. He was particularly excited about licence number SLE 360 and he said you were there when the 1973 murder happened."

"I don't recall you mentioning that Mr. McClelland kept a diary. All I remember is telling you about my paying for his cable TV. As for my being there at the time of the 1973 murder, Mr. McClelland probably saw Arthur and mistook him for me. Arthur practically lived at the farm about that time. Arthur left shortly after you were born."

If only I hadn't been on the phone when Mr. McClelland mentioned the two licence numbers associated with the murder last month. Then I remembered the partial licence number for the truck and made a note to visit Mr. McClelland again to check it out.

"Next, I met Sergeant Woznica. He was investigating some human remains found by the sixth green near the Old Stone Bridge. They had been buried for approximately 30 years. It was a male, about 30 years of age, wrapped in a hemp rug. A 32-calibre bullet was found inside the victim's skull after having passed through the carotid artery in his neck. And that's all I have, except a lot of nagging feelings and unanswered questions."

"You know finding a DNA match doesn't determine its identity," Dad suggested. "If the body found in the ravine is baby Wendelman, you may have to trace the DNA through the mother."

"You're right and I've been thinking about that."

"You'd best leave that up to the police."

"I suppose you're right, but I have an idea I want to explore before I give it up."

I hoped Dad wouldn't ask what my idea was. As I pretended to be searching through my notebook, another subject came to mind that was bothering me.

"By the way, Dad, those files stolen from your car, were they loose or in some kind of container?"

"They were in an expandable file folder. You know, the kind with accordion sides. Why do you ask? Have you found it?"

"No, I was just wondering—in case I ran across one and didn't know whose it was," I replied, hoping that would end discussion on that subject as well.

It seemed to work because Dad switched subjects.

"I know that your attendance at the heritage groups' joint meeting tonight is going to be critical to your assignment. I have a feeling I can help

"I'll take what ever help I is available."

"First of all, I suggest that we go early so that I can introduce you to some of the more significant members."

"Good. I read a number of the names in the minutes of their meetings. A few were prominent in the community when I was in high school, but I never really knew them. A few aren't familiar to me at all."

"I'm glad you've done some homework, because the six degrees of separation concept is very much alive in Melcastle."

"The six degrees of separation concept? What do you mean by that?"

"They made a movie about the concept a few years ago. In theory, everyone on earth is supposed to be connected to everyone else through six degrees of separation."

"I still don't understand."

"According to the theory, the first person is acquainted with another person, and that person knows another and so on until the sixth person is connected back to the first person."

"I think I have heard of that. As I understand it, the President of the United States could, through five other people, be connected to a dock worker in London, England, who went to grade-school with the president."

"That's the theory, only in Melcastle the connections are more intimate."

"How do you mean?"

"The first person is married into one family and that person's sister or brother is married to into another family and a daughter of that marriage is married to another family and so on until finally the sixth person is married to the son of the first married couple."

"I see. I think."

"Well, I don't pretend to know all the connections, but I can point out the ones I do know. The only thing to remember is no matter whom you are speaking to, that person is probably only six degrees or less away from the person you are speaking about."

"I'll keep that in mind."

"For example, Judge Sewchuk's wife Rose is the co-owner of the Melcastle Journal. The other co-owner, Lenore Andersen-Koop, is Rose's sister. Mrs. Andersen-Koop has two daughters, who are both employed at the Windemere Estates. You met one of the sisters yesterday, Mrs. Greisler. One of Mrs. Greisler's daughters runs the day-care center that Roma's son Alex attends. And you are the connection between Alex and the judge."

"Interesting. Would you mind repeating that so I can write it down? Things like that could be embarrassing. Some of the people on the Heritage Society might be connected that way and I should know whose ear I might be talking to."

Dad repeated what he had said and I copied it in abbreviated format.

After I finished, Dad continued.

"The twist gets even more complicated when an older person marries a younger person."

"A May and December wedding."

"Exactly."

"I'm sure there are many more human chains or "degrees of separation" as you call it, around here. Someday I suppose I'll be able to identify them for myself."

"I'd be happy to go over the names with you and tell you who to pay attention to and who to avoid, but that would take a little longer than we have right now."

"You're right. I can only absorb so much at one time."

"I know it would be rushing supper, but as I suggested, we should go to the meeting a little early."

"Fine by me, Dad. On the way home, I picked up a bucket of Kentucky Fried Chicken. I seem to remember that was a favorite of yours. I figured you'd be tired. By the way, how was your day in Philadelphia?"

"Fine, thank you. I ran into an old acquaintance who's now running the administration. We went over old times while she solved my problem."

"I'm glad that's settled," I said, as I opened the chicken bucket and poured a couple of glasses of water.

"By the way, I now know what the other Swiss passbook was for," Dad announced, triumphantly.

"Go ahead. I'm all ears."

"My father set up a scholarship fund in the name of William H Macy at the university using the same financial arrangements he used for the taxes on the General's Farm."

"There goes our trip to Switzerland."

"That's the reason for the mix-up on the addresses on my correspondence."

"Why would that cause the names to be confused?"

"It seems some clerk, probably about the time I graduated, put my student's file in Dad's sponsorship file."

"Thank goodness that mystery is cleared up."

"It just goes to show you that you shouldn't keep secrets from your family," Dad said, with a twinkle in his eye.

"I'll try to remember that."

We ate relatively quietly after that exchange.

"Shall we go?" Dad asked. "I'll drive."

"Yeah. Let's take PAW 6797," I said, wondering how Dad would react to that way of referring to his car.

"I see you've picked up a thing for licence plates."

"Yeah. Mr. McClelland gave me so many plate numbers today, including one for a truck."

"I noticed SLE 360 was a six-character number and most of today's plates are seven characters, if that's any help."

"When did they add the extra number or letter?"

"I don't know exactly—in the early eighties, I think."

"So the plates associated with last month's murder should all be seven characters?"

"That's correct. Unless they're from states other than Pennsylvania or Maryland."

"That's possible."

"Remembering licence plates seems to run in the family."

"What do you mean?"

"I remember watching a movie called 'Union Station' back in the early 1950s. The licence plate the police were looking for was 49R-280."

"Where would the world be without that information?"

CHAPTER 23

The Heritage Groups—Joint Meeting

Wednesday Evening

On the way to the city hall auditorium, I told Heather as much as I could about the General's Farm without giving away the secret about the impending sale. I knew that wasn't going to satisfy her for long. So I changed the subject.

"Which members of the heritage groups are you most interested in? I'm sure I know most of them."

"Just about all of them," she said, as she pulled a couple of files out of her briefcase and put them on her lap.

As Heather mentioned a name, I gave her a thumbnail sketch of each one as best I could. She wrote a short note in the margin beside each name. I wasn't sure she had named them all, but it seemed like quite a few.

As we entered city hall, I looked for the renovations that were supposed to have been done. The most notable change was a raised platform had been added, which extended the full width of the room at the far end.

The organizers of this meeting had set up the desks and chairs on the platform in a V-shape with a podium at the apex centered at the rear of the stage. The audience chairs, which took up half the room, were set in straight rows facing the stage.

It's unusual, in Melcastle, to see a large crowd out for a heritage meeting, especially a half hour before the scheduled start time. I pride myself on knowing most of the influential people in town, but I was astonished to see quite a few people I didn't know. For a moment, I wondered whether we were in the right meeting place. I felt better when I saw some of the heritage executive members from Teasdale.

I think Heather and I both spotted Judge Sewchuk about the same time. I knew he would be there, but I wanted to avoid starting off the evening speaking to him or rather having him talk at us.

I was deciding which way to go to avoid the judge, when Heather grabbed my arm and led me through the crowd. I nodded to a few people I knew, as we passed. It was my impression that Heather was leading me to where Mayor Logan was talking to another gentleman at the far corner of the room. That was good because I had something that I wanted to speak to the mayor about.

"Good evening Mister Mayor. I would like to introduce you to my daughter Heather."

"Good evening Henry," the mayor said. "Pleased to meet you Heather. I've heard a lot of good things about you from your friend Dennis, here."

"Good evening Your Worship," Heather responded. "Good evening Dennis. I hope you haven't given away our secret plan on how to solve the General's Farm issue. Dennis, this is my father, Henry Macy."

"Pleased to meet you Dennis. How do you happen to know Heather?" I asked.

"We met at my stepfather's car lot," Dennis answered.

"Of course, how could I forget? I have a senior's moment every now and then."

"Dennis and I had a chat after I found out he was the other lawyer involved with the General's Farm case," Heather explained. "Dennis was kind enough to make copies of the meeting minutes of both groups for me."

Heather made a thank-you-kind-of-nod toward Dennis.

"That's how you were able to obtain those minutes in such a short time," I concluded.

We chatted for a few moments until it seemed like a good time to address Dorothy Sparrow's financial problems with His Worship.

"Excuse me Mister Mayor, could I speak to you in private for a moment?" I nudged the mayor's elbow.

"Certainly Henry."

We moved to a corner a little distance away.

"I think I've found a lawyer for you regarding that financial matter we spoke about at the Baltimore airport."

"Yes, I spoke to Dorothy and she is interested in your recommendation."

"I think Carl Wickland is perfect for the job. He has been in town for about ten years and I've worked with him several times. He started out as an accountant for several years and then became a lawyer just before he arrived here."

"Thanks, Henry."

"Here's his card. I didn't tell him much about the case, except that it had to do with the disposition of Dorothy Sparrow's finances. He, of course, knows you are the mayor."

At that point, Judge Sewchuk approached carrying his bandaged hand like an imaginary sword to part the crowd. Fortunately, he had some business to discuss with the mayor, so I left the two of them and headed back toward Heather and Dennis.

Lenore Andersen-Koop had just entered the room. She grabbed my arm before I could take two steps.

"Aren't you going to say hello, Henry?"

"Hi Lennie."

"You're the only one who calls me Lennie anymore," Lenore said with an endearing smile.

Running into Lenore was fortunate; because she was one of the first persons I wanted to introduce to Heather. I've known her since the first grade; long before she and her sister Rose inherited the family fortune. In spite of their wealth, the Byrd family lived near us for many years in a modest house in Teasdale. Lenore was her usual bubbly self and whispered to me that she was looking forward to meeting Heather. As we approached Heather and Dennis, I introduced Lenore as Mrs. Andersen-Koop.

"Oh please, call me Lenore," she insisted.

"Pleased to meet you, Lenore," Heather responded. "Have you met Dennis Archard?"

"No, I haven't, but I've heard a lot about you, Dennis, from your stepfather. I understand you and Heather are going to help us through this General's Farm thing."

"I'm sure you folks in the heritage groups could figure it out all by yourselves," Dennis responded. "It's just that there seems to be some sort of urgency behind getting it done."

Lenore was pleased.

"A joint meeting seems to be a good idea," Heather interjected. "Have you ever had joint meetings before, Lenore?"

"No, we haven't and having legal counsel, especially with such young people, is a good idea too."

"That's one thing these young people have is new ideas," I put in.

"Personally I don't understand how a general could live in those quarters. Perhaps he was single and lived in the large room at the west end of the building. That veranda on top of the portico has the most gorgeous view."

"I was led to believe the general lived in the cottage," Heather suggested.

"Our research indicates the cottage was little more than a greenhouse," Lenore responded sharply.

There was a certain crustiness in Lenore's voice. Heather opened her mouth to say something, but at that point, Lenore spotted Judge Sewchuk and excused herself and moved in his direction. She waved to the judge as she left.

At that moment, I suddenly realized that the General in charge of "the Army of the Potomac," as President Lincoln used to call him, spelled his name without the letter "d" on the end. I didn't have time to ask Heather about it because out of the corner of my eye I noticed Val Albertson approaching.

Val Albertson was a hard person to miss. She was over six feet tall with the shoulders of a linebacker. Her thigh-length, leather sports jacket flared open as she walked. I haven't seen Val in a while and she seemed to have kept herself well, albeit having put on a few pounds around the middle. In recent years, she has been cutting her hair extremely short, almost a brush cut. I would bet that her short hairstyle was probably an attempt to disguise her changing hair color, which has gone from brunette to gray to almost white.

Val Albertson and her younger sister, Cynthia Leblond, also lived in Teasdale when we were kids. Both sisters married into families with money and both their husbands were considerably older. Charlie Leblond came from old money in Melcastle and Clint Albertson acquired his wealth in Teasdale. It seems he now owns most of the village. Clint tried to buy his way into Melcastle's society by acquiring one of the largest mansions on Coteau Avenue.

"Say, Henry, when are you going to introduce me to your charming daughter?" Val asked, in her usual bombastic style, as she approached our group.

"Hi Val. I didn't notice you come in."

"I came through the door by the stage. You can park right outside the door there." She looked Heather up and down as she spoke.

"By all means, let me introduce my daughter, Heather, this is Val Albertson, an old friend...I mean...a friend of mine I've known for some time."

"Pleased to meet you Heather. I understand you're the new lawyer in town."

"Pleased to meet you, Mrs. Albertson. Have you met Dennis Archard?"

"Certainly. Dennis and I are practically neighbors when I'm at my summer house in Teasdale," Val replied. "I still keep the old family home in Teasdale. The thick walls in that old stone house make it cooler in the summer."

"Just about everybody in Teasdale is a neighbor one way or another," I said.

"I understand you are the chairperson of the Teasdale Historical Foundation," Heather remarked to Val.

"Oh, I have an interest in our local heritage and none of the boys wanted to be the chairperson. I took on the title so they would let me attend their meetings."

"I'm sure you're being modest."

"Not really. Each of the members is an expert in some area. I just sit back and let them do their thing."

"I just skimmed through the papers attached to your meeting minutes," Heather commented. "I have a question. Can you tell me whether the general lived in the farm house or the cottage?"

"I believe he stayed in the cottage, but I'm not sure," Val said, looking around. "There's Bill Hird. Why don't we ask him? If any one knows for sure, he will."

Val took a couple of steps away, put a hand on Bill's shoulder and spoke to him for a few seconds. She soon returned with Bill in tow.

Bill has long been known as an intellectual. His appearance has hardly changed over the 50-odd years I've known him. Bill was head of the high school history department when I was growing up. He retired room teaching and went into the grocery business about 20 years ago. Running a store seemed to suit his personality better. He retired a second time a couple of years ago. Except for his white hair, you would never know he was at least seventy-five.

Bill and I are about the same height and build. A thin schlock of white hair stood up on his forehead. He had probably combed his hair before he left home, but the wind left it standing up at an odd angle. Over his standard blue jeans and denim shirt, he wore a tweed jacket. He approached us, his right hand grabbing a lapel as though he was wearing overalls, the other arm cradling a sheaf of papers.

Bill has always worn horn-rimmed glasses and had a habit of breaking into what looked like a smile when he finished a sentence.

After the introductions Bill commented, "Actually, I remember

Heather growing up, just down the road. You used to come by my store on your bicycle and buy candy and things."

"Bill," Val interjected, "Heather is the lawyer assigned to represent the State of Pennsylvania in the General's Farm dispute. Heather wants to know whether the general lived in the farmhouse or the cottage?"

"To answer your question as briefly as I can, the general lived in both places," Bill replied. "He stayed in the main building for a few months the first summer he was here, but moved into the cottage as soon as it was built. He stayed in the cottage most of the time his troops were located in this area. He used the whole compound as an observation post. The vegetation wasn't nearly as overgrown as it is today.

"The main building was occupied by his staff and they used the ravine out back as a sort of natural corral for their horses and cattle. The space under the house was used for feed storage and winter stalls for..."

"Thank you, Bill," Val interrupted. "There, you see. The boys do all the research and I just leave them alone."

There was no mistaking it, Val enjoyed being in control. As long as I've known her, she has tried to dominate everything she was involved in.

"Yes, thank you, Mr. Hird," Heather said.

"Actually the cottage is the only property that Teasdale Heritage Foundation is interested in because the main building is not within the state's boundary," Val added.

By the furrow on Bill's brow, you could see that he didn't entirely agree with Val. You could also tell Bill had wanted to finish the answer to Heather's question, but recognized Val's authority.

It was time to change the subject.

"Say Val, how did your grandson make out in the Little League baseball championships last year?" I asked, as though I didn't know the answer.

"He did very well, thank you." Val replied. "His team went all the way to the state final playoffs. The team received jackets and they presented me with one as honorary manager."

I didn't want to tell her the picture in the paper wasn't very flattering and made her look rather masculine.

"Of course…I remember. Your picture was in the paper," I added.

"Yeah, the picture was supposed to be me and Judge Sewchuk together," Val chuckled. "He was also an honorary executive, but he couldn't make the ceremony. He arranged a picture being presented with his jacket the next day, but Rose decided that it was old news and his picture never did appear in the paper."

"How come you didn't wear your jacket tonight?" I said as a joke.

"That's hardly an appropriate thing to wear on an evening like tonight," Val snapped. "Besides, I had to have it cleaned."

The organizers were getting ready to start the meeting. In the meantime, several other members of the Teasdale group had gathered around us. It was obvious that Val wanted to keep her group together. She pointed to a line of tables and chairs on the right of the stage and suggested it was time to head there.

As Val's group moved away, Heather pulled her notebook from her briefcase and wrote something down as we edged toward the audience chairs.

Heather and I hadn't ventured very far toward the only chairs left near the front row when the imposing figure of Victor Gabler approached. He obviously wanted to meet Heather.

"Heather, I would like you to meet Victor Gabler. He's with the United States Division of the Hal-Burton Property Development Corporation."

"Pleased to meet you, Heather," Victor said. "I understand you are providing some legal expertise to this situation."

"Pleased to meet you, Mr. Gabler. Yes, I hope to be of some service."

"I was saying to Heather earlier, I couldn't see what the problem was," I interjected. "It's obvious the main building is in Pennsylvania and the cottage is in Maryland. It seems to me they should just look after their own."

"On the other hand," Victor suggested, "if an invisible line had not been drawn between the two buildings, it could all be considered one historical site, couldn't it?"

"That's very perceptive, Mr. Gabler," Heather commented and reopened her notebook.

"Thank you. I must join my group. Again, nice to meet you, Heather."

"Nice to meet you too, Mr. Gabler," Heather responded, as she looked up from her writing and smiled.

As we sat, the noise in the room had become noticeably quieter, so we were obliged to talk in whispers.

"By the way Dad, were you aware that Hal-Burton has called a press conference for Friday concerning the General's Farm?"

"Yes, I received a card in the mail."

"I wonder whether they are the ones offering financial assistance to the heritage groups?" Heather asked, with a knowing look over imaginary glasses.

She is sharp, I thought, but didn't reply.

Judge Sewchuk, already standing at the podium, banged a gavel and called the meeting to order.

Judge Sewchuk started by explaining that he had accepted "with some reservations"—the appointment as chairperson of the "two state-joint commission" to settle the boundary dispute concerning the property known as the General's Farm. He didn't say what his reservations were, but you could tell he was proud of the appointment as recognition of his *status* in two states.

He acknowledged the presence of Judge Brothwell from Maryland seated at the back of the audience. There was no question; Judge Sewchuk was running the show.

Then he introduced the members of both heritage groups. He started with Lenore Andersen-Koop, the Pennsylvania chairperson. Lenore stood up, but instead of sitting down, moved directly to the podium. She obviously intended to introduce the members of her heritage society herself. Control of the introductions was probably what Lenore had spoken to the judge about before the meeting.

I could see Heather flipping to the minutes of the meetings and trying to put a face to a name as each was introduced. Sometimes

Heather made a comment as the names were mentioned.

After a few introductory remarks, Lenore introduced each member:
"Mrs. Doreine Pladsen—our Immediate Past Chairperson."
Doreine stood and nodded.
"Next, Mrs. Janet Fordham—our Secretary."
"Janet Fordham has really put on the weight. Rather 'Rubenesque' as they say," I whispered.
"I'll say," Heather whispered back.
"Next, Mrs. Dorothy Watkinson—our Treasurer."
She remained seated and waved to the crowd. I haven't seen Dorothy in a long time.
"Next, Mrs. Betty Galen—the Social Director, and...last but not least, Mrs. Shirley Posnick-Carswell our Fund-raising Director."
Both Betty and Shirley half-stood and waved to the crowd at the same time.

"This is more like a Society Club, all dressed in the latest fashions," Heather whispered, after all the Melcastle members had been introduced.

"Not exactly welfare candidates."

"The only one missing is Cynthia Leblond," Heather noted, running a finger down the meeting minutes.

"It must have been her chauffeur's night off," I added, assuming that Heather would pick up the inference that Cynthia had married into money.

At that moment, a fashionably dressed woman in a shiny brown suit entered the room through the door near the stage. The heavy door made a loud scraping noise, attracting everyone's attention. It wasn't until she turned around and headed toward the stage that I recognized the woman was Cynthia Leblond.

I knew Cynthia to be a shy person and had an affinity for the bottle, so it didn't surprise me she would come late to avoid talking to people. I was shocked to see how old she looked; yet she was a couple of years younger than me. She stumbled slightly, as she took the two steps up to the stage. Her composure was obviously shaken. She placed her hand on the back of each chair as awkwardly made her way to the last empty chair on the Pennsylvania tables which, unfortunately for her, was on the far side of the stage.

"You'd never guess, but Val Albertson and the lady who just walked in are sisters," I whispered.

"Did they have the same father?"

I didn't want to say any more, fearing who might overhear me. I just looked at Heather and rolled my eyes.

Lenore Andersen-Koop, obviously annoyed that one of her group had the temerity to be late, waited until Cynthia sat down before she introduced her:

"And, of course, Mrs. Cynthia Leblond, the Special   Projects Officer."

"What would those special projects be?" Heather asked quietly.

I put my thumb to my mouth as in a drinking motion.

Lenore remained at the podium. She launched into a speech full of platitudes and good intentions. She spoke mostly about the accomplishments her committee had achieved at several sites. It sounded hollow when she mentioned the difficulty she had in getting her executive together for an "extra…ordinary meeting" to consider the offer from Mr. Gabler to assist them in restoring the General's Farm. Her committee had agreed to study the matter.

"How nice of them," Heather whispered in mock disgust.

Lenore made a grand gesture of turning the podium back to Judge Sewchuk.

The judge then introduced Val Albertson, who in turn introduced the members of the Teasdale Heritage Foundation. As Val announced the names of her group members, each made a half-stand and casual wave.

"Tom Whiteside—our Foundation's Secretary."

"He must have been a handsome man in his younger days," Heather whispered and kept writing.

"Larry Scotten—our Finance Officer."

I could see Heather's notes: Larry Scotten—tall—thin—dresses casually—doesn't look like an accountant.

"And last, but certainly not least, Bill Hird—our Research

Director."

Val Albertson made an attempt to say a few words, obviously reacting to the fact that Lenore had made a speech. She said that Teasdale had also received a visit from Mr. Gabler and were only too happy to meet the conditions of his offer. She concluded her impromptu speech by introducing the speaker for the evening.

"Bill Hird will be making a short presentation complete with a chart."

Bill's chart turned out to be a large map of the Greater Melcastle Area, or GMA, as he kept referring to it. A dotted black line through the center of the map indicated the common border of Pennsylvania and Maryland. Various areas and former towns were identified using different colors. He had the Old Stone Bridge labeled as "OSB" on the map.

Most of what Bill had to say I already knew, but a few items toward the end caught my attention.

"Improvements to the Old Stone Bridge would involve state funding from Maryland and Pennsylvania and the municipal governments of GMA and Teasdale. Naturally, we would expect all four elected bodies to improve their respective roadways leading to the OSB before we start restorations on the bridge itself.

"That portion of Old Military Road above the Mason-Dixon Line and running past the farm house technically has no name. Since that roadway is now within the city of Melcastle, we are suggesting that Melcastle city council pass a bylaw to re-designate the roadway as 'Old Military Road—Private.'"

I doubt whether more than a handful of people caught the humor in the designation "Private" as a suffix to the General's Farm address. It was unusual, but Bill had actually made a joke. Nobody even cracked a smile. He continued.

"The Teasdale Property Management Office records indicate in 1903, the year the boundary was last surveyed, the general or one of his relatives acquired the cottage and the land for one dollar. The title included a 99-year, tax-free lease. This 'leased area' shown in light blue, is bounded by the Mason-Dixon Line on the north; Southgate

Road on the east; and by Old Military Road on the south and west.

"Please note the dark blue band within the 'leased area' follows the contours on the north side of Old Military Road. Our research indicates the houses on the north side of Old Military Road, were considered to be part of the lease. Technically, those houses were built illegally.

"That's the end of my presentation. Thank you."

With that, Bill left the podium. The audience was stunned by the abrupt ending and only began the applause about the time Bill had arrived at his chair.

While the judge was gathering his papers as well as his composure, I wondered, could Albert McClelland be the real owner of the cottage? Worse still, could Macy House actually be on Albert McClelland's land? The 99-year, tax-free lease was granted in 1903. What a coincidence that the lease should expire in 2003.

The judge thanked the two heritage groups for coming, the chairpersons for introducing their members, and especially Bill Hird.

Then the judge made a rather extraordinary closing statement, obviously prepared ahead of time.

"I'm sure both the Maryland and the Pennsylvania heritage people will agree with me that the time has come to stop the long-range sniping and settle on some future plans for the General's Farm. The Pennsylvania legislative executive has made it abundantly clear they are anxious to have this dispute settled as soon as possible."

Those remarks made me think there had been some lobbying going on at the state legislature level. I wondered if the SPA-KAL syndicate was behind the hurry-up action.

"The location of the property line between the main building and the cottage appears to be simple enough," the judge continued. "Surely, we can accept the 1903 ruling that the main building is in Pennsylvania and the cottage is located in Maryland."

The judge paused for a moment and grimaced as he placed his left elbow on the podium. He had obviously disturbed the bandaging because a distinct blood spot was evident near his wrist.

"The biggest problem, as I see it, is the determination of who owns the General's Farm, especially that portion on the Pennsylvania side of the border."

I smiled as I thought of public reaction when it soon would be revealed at the press conference that I was the owner.

The judge continued his closing remarks.

"Admittedly, the fire at the Land Records Office has caused some confusion, but the executive branch of the Pennsylvania legislature has given me six months to resolve the ownership on the Pennsylvania side. If ownership is not settled by that time, the state government intends to introduce legislation to expropriate the land."

Aha! That's the reason for the urgency to settle the heritage dispute.

The judge had probably planned to close the meeting with that speech. Then, as an apparent afterthought, he introduced Heather and Dennis.

"I'm sorry, I almost forgot to introduce the two legal representatives who have been appointed to expedite this case. First, I would like to call on Heather Macy to say a few words. She will represent the State of Pennsylvania."

I think he expected to catch Heather off-guard, but as I was beginning to realize, he didn't know Heather very well.

"Thank you Judge Sewchuk," Heather said as she stood up in place and opened her notebook. "For the purposes of this meeting, I would like to you to consider the buildings only and not the property. I agree there appears to be no problem with the boundary location. However, I would like to make a few suggestions to help resolve this situation.

"My first suggestion is to consider the two buildings as one entity as though there were no border. I would suggest a joint sub committee be established to manage this single heritage site, as it was originally designed. The sub committee need not be composed of more than three persons. Each of the state heritage groups would nominate one person and today's meeting would designate a third member as the chairperson. Mr. Hird seems to be a likely candidate as the chairperson. The sub committee thus formed would decide the future of the General's Farm.

"The sub committee's first priority would be to develop a five-year plan to rebuild and restore the main building and the cottage as one complex. Over the five-year period, tenders could be called for the main building only. The cottage would *not* be part of the initial 'rebuild and restore' process, because it is presently occupied.

"After the main site and upper Old Military Road has been rebuilt and restored, it could then be advertised as a tourist attraction. The tourist revenue would be considered joint income for both buildings. Half the funds from Hal-Burton would be held in escrow until such time as the cottage is no longer occupied.

"I would also suggest that the next joint meeting be held on site and approve the sub committee at that time.

"Thank you," Heather said and sat down.

Her statement was greeted with sustained applause. The audience instantly realized Heather's ideas could work and save face at the same time. I was impressed. Several people in front of us turned around for a better look at this young lady.

"I notice you didn't mention the small matter of a couple of bodies discovered nearby," I whispered, as the applause died down.

The judge wasn't about to put Heather's suggestions to a vote. He wanted control of his meeting.

"Next, I would like to call upon Dennis Archard to say a few words. Dennis has his own law firm in Teasdale. He has been appointed to represent the State of Maryland."

Dennis endorsed Heather's remarks and suggested an immediate vote be taken to establish the sub committee. He sat down to general applause.

The judge ignored both Heather's and Dennis' comments and reiterated most of his earlier remarks. He suggested each group meet separately and be prepared to make a joint decision by the next meeting. The next joint meeting would be held at the same time and place in four weeks time.

All of a sudden the meeting was over.

On the way out, Heather shook her head. "Was the judge at the same meeting we were at?" Heather asked plaintively.

"Don't worry about that. I was watching the heritage groups. They'll find a way around the judge."

Then Heather made an interesting comment.

"You know, I'm kind of glad this dispute took a hundred years to resolve. Had an agreement been arrived at earlier, I would never have found out half the things I have in the past three days. I wonder if resolution would have taken as long if the original general had been General Grant."

CHAPTER 24

Windemere Estates—The Other Half

Thursday Morning

Dad went off to Baltimore early the next morning and I took my time having breakfast. Between bites, I reasoned there were only two things I had to do for the rest of the day. The first was to check out Ruby Wendelman's status as a "guest of the state" at Windemere. The other was a revisit with Mr. McClelland and somehow persuade him repeat the licence numbers I had missed while I was on the phone. I wasn't looking forward to either task.

I reasoned that the longer trip to Windemere might give me some inspiration on how to approach Mr. McClelland. I'm sure in the old man's mind he knew he had already given me the licence numbers as well as the descriptions of the drivers. Would he be angry that it had taken somebody so long to take an interest? On the other hand, maybe he wouldn't even remember I was there.

As I left the driveway, I noticed the gas gauge in my "new" car was down to a quarter of a tank. Dennis may have used the car more than Mr. Barrigar knew about.

I stopped at Sylvie Spagnoli's Restaurant-Gas Bar for a fill-up. Sylvie came out to the pumps, just as Dad had said.

"Hi Sylvie. Long time no see."

"Heather! Long time no see, yourself. Your dad mentioned you were coming back to town," she said. We hugged, as though we were best of friends.

"Filler-up?" she asked, out of habit I'm sure.

"Sure," I replied. "Dad and I came here a couple of nights ago, but you weren't here. Dad comes here a lot. It must be the quality of the food."

I chattered on, as Sylvie started the gas flowing.

"Yes. Your dad is one of our best customers. You can credit the good food to our chef, Vito. He used to work at La Gondola until he had a major disagreement with the head chef and quit. Papa offered Vito a job here—even before this place opened."

"That was good luck. We really enjoyed our meal the other night. We were going to try the venison, but went for the hamburgers instead."

A metallic-green pick-up truck drove up and parked at the restaurant end of the parking lot. The young male driver waved in our direction as he made his way into the restaurant.

"That's my brother Dan," Sylvie commented. "Dad spoiled him with that truck."

"He was just a kid when I saw him last."

"Round it up to twenty-even?" Sylvie asked.

It took me a second to realize it was the amount of money for the gas she was talking about.

"Yeah, sure."

I scolded myself mentally for not getting the money out before hand. I went to the front of the car and put my purse on the fender. The money Dad had given me wasn't in my wallet. I frantically searched the various pockets in my purse.

"I'm glad you liked our food. When you mentioned the venison, it reminded me of an incident Dan had with a deer," Sylvie commented, while she waited for the money.

"Dan had an incident with a deer?" I asked absent-mindedly, while I continued my search.

"Yeah, shortly after we opened the restaurant—Dan showed up with a small deer on the front fender of his truck. It was a doe I think. Why he would strap the deer to the fender when the back was virtually empty, I don't know. Maybe he was pretending he was the last of the great white hunters. He claims he picked it up after another motorist ran into it."

"What was he planning to do with it?"

"He brought the deer here, thinking we would serve it in the restaurant. He carried the poor beast into the kitchen and put it in the freezer. When Vito found the hairy thing in his nice clean freezer and who had left it there, he was so angry he took the carcass across the street and dumped it on Dan's doorstep."

Sylvie could hardly keep from laughing.

"That must have been pretty funny."

"That really wasn't the best part of the story," Sylvie giggled. "Getting it off the fender was the funniest part. Dan didn't notice the deer wasn't really dead. It apparently had only been stunned and began to thrash around. Dan went into his glove compartment, pulled out an old revolver he had found and tried to shoot the scared little animal. When the revolver didn't work, he went back and selected one of his rifles and started shooting at the poor beast. The first shot missed and frightened it even more. By this time, the deer was nearly on its feet, but still tied to the bumper. Dan shot again and hit the window frame of the restaurant. Fortunately, there were no customers around at the time. Finally, on the third shot he killed it. His fellow members of the West Virginia Militia gave him the gears over that."

We had a good laugh, but the mention of an old revolver intrigued me.

"You say Dan found a revolver?"

"Yeah," Sylvie giggled. "He said he found it near the Old Stone Bridge. He told everybody it was a Civil War weapon."

"How do you know it wasn't?"

"It was a 32-calibre revolver. His militia buddies said that caliber wasn't in general use back then. They kidded him that it was a ladies' revolver."

"Does he still have it?"

"I think so. I know he had trouble buying ammunition. The only place he could find that caliber was through the militia. Why do you ask?"

"I ran into Sergeant Woznica when I was at the General's Farm and he was looking for some kind of hand gun near the Old Stone Bridge. That's all."

I was hoping she wouldn't become too interested and warn her brother.

Fortunately, another car pulled up for gas and Sylvie had to go. I gave her my last twenty-dollar bill. I had put it in an envelope the other day after paying the parking attendant. I was still shaken by the fact that it took twenty dollars for the fill-up. I had never paid to fill-up a car before.

I took a few moments to record the "found revolver" in my notebook. I noted the restaurant's address was 2117, so Dan's address would have be the duplex at 2116 or 2118. Then I remembered Judge Sewchuk said that Dennis Archard lived at 2118 Old Military Road. Dan probably lived at 2116.

I was glad Dad had driven the first time we went to the Windemere Estates. Even with that experience, the entrance to the driveway wasn't easy to find.

As I entered the lobby, I desperately hoped that because of Mrs. Wendelman's maternity condition at the time of her admission, she would be assigned to the east wing and I wouldn't have to go to the criminal side.

Perhaps I should have waited for Dad to accompany me. I hoped the desk clerk would accept my story about doing research on the General's Farm dispute. It was the only plausible excuse I had for seeing Mrs. Wendelman.

I produced my three pieces of identification and signed in. I expected to be referred to Mrs. Greisler. Instead, I was told to take a seat. I was close enough to hear the receptionist summon the Assistant Administrator on the phone.

"Mrs. MacInnis will be with you shortly," the receptionist advised after she hung up the phone.

After a few minutes, a woman in a pale green uniform appeared on the criminal side of the compound. She spoke to the guard as he unlocked the big iron gate.

The approaching woman was a tall, well-endowed blonde or at least she used to be blonde. She was obviously well along in her career. I wasn't sure someone at that administrator level would be as co-operative as Mrs. Greisler had been the other day. As she approached, I could see the pale blue background on the faded, embroidered nametag on her left breast identifying her as "Mrs. R MacInnis." The old identity tag didn't match the color of her new pastel green uniform dress. The new uniform also suggested a recent transfer from one side of the institution to the other.

"Hello, I'm Raylene MacInnis, Assistant Administrator for Windemere Estates," she announced. "I understand you asked to see Mrs. Wendelman."

"Yes, my name is Heather Macy. I'm a lawyer assigned to the land dispute at the General's Farm where Mrs. Wendelman was living before she was brought here. I'm doing some historical research and was wondering whether an interview with her was possible. I believe she's a patient here."

"Let's go back to my office and we can talk better there."

The guard unlocked the gate for us and Mrs. MacInnis made the register entries.

It was a long walk down several corridors to arrive at the Assistant Administrator's office, which was at the back of the building. I noted the distinct difference between the musty odors on the criminal side as opposed to the antiseptic smell of Mom's residence.

The view out the window behind Assistant Administrator's desk was absolutely bucolic. Behind the trees and rolling mounds of grass, I could see what I assumed was the western end of Candle Lake.

We spent the first few minutes chatting about the General's Farm. Mrs. MacInnis surprised me with her detailed knowledge about the farm. Her enthusiasm and willingness to talk made me think she must have some direct connection with one of the historical groups. It soon became apparent Mrs. MacInnis was familiar with Mrs. Wendelman's situation before she became a patient.

"I had just finished reviewing Mrs. Wendelman's file," Mrs. MacInnis said, "and was taking it back to central registry when the front desk paged me. Mrs. Wendelman was discharged two days ago. Perhaps you didn't know."

I was astonished and I guess it showed.

"You seem surprised."

As a knee-jerk reaction, I blurted out, "I don't even know why she was brought here in the first place."

I was trying to avoid the use of the word incarceration.

"I wasn't here at the time Mrs. Wendelman was admitted," Mrs. MacInnis said, as she opened a thick file. "I understand she was brought here as a result of her physical condition and the strange disappearance of her husband."

"Yes, I've heard that," I commented to keep the conversation going.

"The police were summoned by an anonymous caller," Mrs. MacInnis recited as she ran her finger over the hand written entry. "Mrs. Wendelman was living with her husband. The caller said 'something mysterious was going on at 3257 Old Military Road.' The unidentified caller wouldn't leave his name."

"Pardon me, you said earlier, 'as a result of her physical condition.' What was her physical condition exactly?"

I was hoping her reply would contain the word maternity or pregnant.

Mrs. MacInnis, read directly from the notes, "'Mrs. Wendelman was in a hypnotic state and had a deep cut on her forehead. She was on her hands and knees and repeatedly scrubbing the floor.'"

"A deep cut on her forehead?"

"Yes. Apparently whatever caused the cut was enough to cause a hairline fracture of her skull."

Mrs. MacInnis lifted up an X-ray, which was obviously of a human skull.

"And has she remained in a hypnotic condition all this time?"

"Not exactly," Mrs. MacInnis replied. "At first, her movements were robot-like, but after a few years she appeared to be relatively normal. By the time I arrived here, she responded well to directions, such as when to get dressed and when to go to the dining room. She could speak, but never spoke a word to the staff the entire time she was here."

"Was she ever charged or convicted of anything?" I asked casually. It was a leading question that I hoped didn't sound like it was based on prior knowledge.

"No, but we were instructed to keep her here until her husband was found or showed up—neither of which happened."

"Why was she released a couple of days ago?"

"A state policy was passed about five or six years ago. All inmates, not formally convicted and deemed fit to live on their own, are to be assessed every year by a staff doctor, with a panel review after five years."

"Obviously, Mrs. Wendelman had some communication skills before you would release her."

"We knew she could read because we tested her without her knowing it and she kept notes on a pad in her bedside table. It's just that she refused to talk to us."

"That was enough to release her a couple of days ago?"

I hoped the different form of the question would elicit a more enlightening answer.

"To be honest, we needed the bed. We traced her father though the visitation register. We suggested to him that she could be released if he would accept custody. He agreed."

"Did she have many visitors?"

"Let's see. I have her log right here."

Mrs. MacInnis flipped the file to the back cover. Several lined pages and forms with hand written entries were attached.

"It seems Mrs. Wendelman had quite a few visitors early on, but only a few over the past ten years or so. Mr. McClelland was the only consistent visitor throughout."

Mrs. MacInnis turned the file part way around to show me.

"Yes, I see."

"We were fairly certain he was related to her."

"Who were some of the others?" I asked casually, trying not to be too pushy.

"Well, in the beginning there was Corporal Parslow. That's natural because he was the one who brought her in. Yes, Corporal Parslow," Mrs. MacInnis confirmed by flipping back to the front cover of the file.

"Sounds logical."

"Next, we have Henry Macy. He visited regularly…it looks like for several months in a row," she read and stopped. She looked at me and realized his name was the same as mine.

"Yes, I understand Mrs. Wendelman and Dad were old friends."

"His visits seem to have stopped several years ago."

"I guess that's only natural."

"Also, we have Judge Sewchuk. He seems to have been a regular visitor for the first few months…and then…no record of visits by him for at least ten years…that I can see."

"Has Mrs. Wendelman had many visitors in the last few years?"

To my delight, Mrs. MacInnis continued to search.

"In the last few years, a young man by the name of Larry Leblond has visited quite a few times," she replied. "I remember him very well. A nice-looking young man, but he seemed to be distraught at first. We didn't really know whether we should let him visit her or not."

"Why's that?"

I concentrated on memorizing the name Larry Leblond. The Leblond part wasn't hard to remember because of Cynthia Leblond's memorable entrance at the joint heritage meeting. 'Larry Leblond— Larry Leblond,' I repeated to myself.

"We have to be conscious of the patient's welfare at all times."

"I suppose you're right."

"We escorted them on each of his visits at first. Later, we basically left them alone," Mrs. MacInnis said. "I'm convinced he was able to persuade her to talk. One of the nurses mentioned she heard them talking a few times. They certainly seemed happy together, but I don't recall seeing him for the last few weeks."

"Was the communication made known to the board?"

"Yes, I made a comment to the board myself. I don't know about nurse Coutts, but she did make the first observation and wrote a note on Ruby's file. My basic comments were simply that after each visit by Mr. Leblond, Ruby seemed to be more alive and walked about with more vigor and confidence."

"Thank you Mrs. MacInnis. Thank you very much for all your help."

"You're welcome," she responded. "I'll take you back to the front door."

"One more thing," I ventured as we stood up. "Could you tell me the exact date Mrs. Wendelman was admitted?"

It was a throw away question because I felt I already knew the answer. I was desperately trying to think of some way to press her for more information while she was in such a forthcoming mood.

She put the file on the corner of her desk and ran her finger down to the appropriate block on the admissions form.

"April 29, 1973."

"I understand there's a hospital on the other side of Windemere Estates. Do you have your own medical facilities over here?" I inquired, as we moved out into the hall.

"Yes, there's a first-class hospital and pharmacy accessible from both sides."

"Including a maternity ward?"

"Yes. We've had several maternity cases here."

"Was Mrs. Wendelman by any chance pregnant when she was brought here?"

"Why yes," she answered, evidently surprised by my question. "What makes you ask that?"

"My dad said that he thought Mrs. Wendelman was pregnant prior to the trauma and I wondered what happened to the baby."

"The baby was delivered here and then taken away by the Children and Family Services people."

"Do your records indicate the baby's date of birth?"

"I believe it was the same day that she was admitted...yes, 29 April 1973," she added, after a quick look at the inside of the front page of the file.

Then a strange look came over Mrs. MacInnis' face. I think she suddenly realized she had given away too much information. As we retraced the corridors back to the front entrance, I'm sure she was wondering how much information she had given out that she shouldn't have.

The guard recorded the time of my departure.

"Thanks again, Mrs. MacInnis," I said, as the gate clanged shut.

"You're welcome," she said mechanically.

Her previous enthusiasm was missing.

On my way out, I remembered Dad saying the two Andersen-Koop daughters worked at Windemere. I made a note to ask Dad whether Raylene MacInnis and Dawn Greisler were indeed the two sisters. Facially they looked alike, but they certainly were different sizes. Then a wild thought struck me. If Mrs. MacInnis' mother is Lenore Andersen-Koop and Lenore's sister Rose is married to Judge Sewchuk, I expect word of my visit would fall upon the judge's ear fairly quickly.

As a result of the chat with Mrs. MacInnis, the need to confirm the disposition of the Wendelman baby became paramount. Hopefully, Dennis Archard wouldn't mind doing me a favor and ask his sister to trace the adoption.

The phone booth in the Windemere parking lot was unbearably hot from the noonday sun. I wasn't sure whether Dennis was still making his regular lunch hour visits to Barrigar's Auto or not. To make matters worse, someone had ripped out all the pages of the phonebook under the letter "B." Fortunately, the yellow pages were still relatively intact.

After about five rings, Dennis came on the line. He apologized for taking so long to answer the phone. He had been out in the car lot.

I asked him if he would do me a favor and have his sister look up a file at the adoption agency. Specifically, I gave him the name of Larry Leblond—birth date 29 April 1973. Assuming baby Leblond was one of the agency's cases, I wanted to know who the birth mother was. I told him I thought the body found at the General's Farm might have been the adult Larry Leblond. I didn't go into any more details and Dennis didn't ask. He seemed to understand and said he would call back to me as soon as he could.

As I was leaving the Windemere parking lot, I remembered the newspaper clipping of the donated car and that the Melcastle Journal Building was on the way home. The newspaper plant was my main reference point before the turn into the Windemere Estates.

I asked at the front desk to speak to anyone who would have been with the newspaper before 1973.

"That would be Doreine," the receptionist responded politely. "She has been here more than 50 years."

I had no idea that the Doreine she referred to would be Doreine Pladsen, the past president of the Pennsylvania Heritage Society. As Doreine approached, she remembered me right away. Up close she looked more robust than when she appeared on stage at the heritage meeting. Her straight, white hair was done up in a shiny bun as usual. You could tell she was one of those people who craves company and loves to talk. She wanted to know how Dad was and did I enjoy being back.

When we eventually came around to the reason I was there, I said I had an interest in the evolution of communications and transportation in various police departments. I casually mentioned I had seen a picture at the Melcastle Police headquarters of a vintage police car that had been donated to a museum. The picture and story looked like good material for my research.

It took a few seconds, but Mrs. Pladsen thought she remembered the picture. She suggested we go to the microfiche archives and have a look. I told her on the way I thought the date was in 1973. Within minutes she had the picture on the screen.

"Ah yes, I remember it now," she said.

I examined the picture closely and licence plate SLE 360 was clearly visible. I asked whether I might have a copy. Mrs. Pladsen was only too pleased to comply. Since it was only one page, she offered it at no charge. She even asked whether I would like a copy of the article that went with it.

"You may have trouble reading the narrative because the page is reduced to 11 by 17 inches."

I thanked Doreine for her help. We discussed the historical societies' joint meeting for a few minutes. She again told me how much she was impressed with my remarks.

On my way out, I noticed some historical issues of the Melcastle Journal mounted on the wall. I was amused by the motto on the Journal masthead. It contained the expression "Covers the valley like the dew." I assumed they would change it to "Covers the valley like the snow," in the wintertime.

I stopped at the end of the Journal driveway. I could see an outline of the General's Mountain in the distance. To arrive at the General's Farm from that direction, I would have to go all the way around the mountain, through the western end of Melcastle, past Macy House and approach it from the other side.

I was probably less than five miles from the General's Farm, but I would travel about ten or twelve miles and take about 30 minutes to drive to the McClelland cottage.

CHAPTER 25

Mr. McClelland's Diary

Thursday Afternoon

At McClelland's cottage, I was careful not to drive near the wooden culvert that interrupted my previous visit. My main objective was to have the old man repeat the licence numbers of the vehicles that stopped at the General's Farm about the time of the murder three weeks ago. It seemed to me he had mentioned at least two numbers while I was on the phone. Another objective was to record the complete number of the truck involved in the murder 30 years ago. Dad had convinced me that Uncle Arthur drove the truck, so that wasn't as important.

I parked closer to the police tapes, so Mr. McClelland would be certain to see me arrive. I had hardly put both feet on the ground when he approached—scribbler in hand.

"Thought I might be seeing you again," he chuckled. "There were two men in suits sniffing around here early this morning."

"What did they want?"

"Don't know. Never talked to 'em. Just sat in my kitchen. They weren't from around here."

"How do you know that?"

"Just the way they looked...kinda big-city fellas. Besides their plates had a long legged bird and grass growing through the numbers."

"The Chesapeake Bay series plates."

"Chesapeake Bay series? What does that mean?"

"It's a project the state of Maryland started a few years ago to help clean up Chesapeake Bay."

I felt like an instant expert.

"The plates you have today aren't the same ones you had the other day," he said, as he wrote my licence numbers in his scribbler. "Can't say for sure because I just started a new book this morning."

"Yeah, I bought a car for myself."

"It must be nice having two cars in the same family."

At least he remembered my previous visit. I waited until I had his attention again.

"You know those diaries you keep, Mr. McClelland. Would you mind if I had a look at them?" I asked timidly.

He perked up noticeably at my question. His face broadened into a big smile. That was the first time I noticed he had only four teeth—two on top and two on the bottom. The warmth of his smile made me feel comfortable enough to venture another question.

"I'm particularly interested in who visited here about three weeks ago. You don't suppose I could see those numbers do you?"

"Sure. That's why I kept the recordings all these years. I figured they'd come in handy some day. We'll have to go back to my cottage. They're in another book."

I followed him and quietly took a seat at the kitchen table. The musty smell was still there, but didn't seem quite as overwhelming. He went straight to his safe.

"Let me see what my diary says," he said, as he withdrew the scribbler on top of the pile. "There hasn't been much traffic in the last month, if you don't count police cars."

After a few licks of his thumb and index finger, he arrived at the page he had been reading from the other day.

He looked at the calendar on the back of the scribbler. "Three weeks ago…would be 17 April," he said, as he confirmed the date. "The weather was clear and unusually warm for that early in the season. The first car was PAW 6797. That was late in the afternoon and he left after a few minutes. Of course, we know that was your father."

"Yes, that's the car I was driving last Tuesday."

He was about to continue, but stopped and gave me a sideways glance.

"Goodness gracious! I forgot my manners. Would you like a cup of tea?" he asked, staring at me like an owl.

"Yes, that would be nice."

I didn't really want a cup of tea, but I didn't want to offend him either. He promptly put his scribbler on the table and stepped toward the hotplate. He placed the kettle on one of the rimmers, turned up the heat and retrieve a small tin marked "TEA" seemingly all in one continuous motion. He deftly turned over two cups sitting on the shelf above and placed them beside the hot plate.

While he was doing that, I nudged his diary around slightly so I could see exactly what he had written on 17 April. His notes were childlike, printed in large capital letters. Each entry took up two full lines, plus a line for spacing. The only exception was the lower case "m" following PAW 6797. The narrative about time of day and weather conditions took up most of the page.

"Milk?" he asked without turning his head.

"No thanks. I take it black," I replied and quickly nudged the diary back to its original position.

He turned around, reached across the table and pulled the diary toward him.

"It'll take a few minutes for the water to boil," he said, as he picked up the scribbler. "Now, where were we?"

"You were looking up 17 April of this year and PAW 6797 had just arrived…late in the afternoon…the weather was warm."

As he ran his finger down the page, I casually reached into my briefcase and retrieve my own notebook, placed it on my lap and withdrew the pencil from the holder.

"Ah yes, 17 April...17 April...PAW 6797 came first, late in the afternoon and left after a few minutes."

He seemed to be in reflective thought for 10 or 15 seconds before he continued.

"The next car to arrive, about an hour later, was PEN 5055. The driver was a very tall man with short white hair. The PEN 5055 car stayed about 20 minutes...and left in a hurry."

He repeated the words "and left in a hurry" slowly and nodded his head in recollection at the same time. He wasn't looking at his diary any more.

I repeated PEN 5055 to myself and without looking down, except to see where to start, I carefully wrote:

$\mathcal{PEN} 5055$

The old man didn't say anything for a while and turned toward the window beside the door. It seemed as though he was reliving the events of three weeks ago before he spoke again.

"Then, another vehicle arrived about a half hour later...with two men in it. The speed at which they drove up raised a great cloud of dust. The two men rushed into the house. I couldn't see the numbers very well because of the dust and the sun was just above the horizon, right in my eyes. But, I was pretty sure it was HAR 2212."

As I listened to him describe the scene and the licence number, I carefully recorded in my notebook, the same way I had done before:

$HAR 2212$

My host seemed to be visualizing more than reading.

"I had just started my tea..." he said slowly, "...wanted to finish it...before I went to make sure HAR 2212 was the correct number. Besides, the hockey game was on and I wanted to go in between periods.

"It was about half an hour later and almost dark when I made it up to the driveway. Just as I arrived, the two men came down the stairs. One was carrying a plastic jug and a small pail. The other man was carrying a small shovel and a thick glass log. They didn't see me because I had stepped back into the bushes. They were definitely acting kinda suspicious. I clearly saw that the licence was HAR 2212 as they drove away."

I glanced down at my notebook to see whether I had recorded both licence numbers correctly. I felt it best to say nothing. I concentrated on the items they were carrying.

The pail seemed natural to hold water and cleaning equipment. The plastic jug was probably the source of the Javex smell. It took me a few moments to figure out the glass log item. Then it came to me. It was a role of plastic sheeting that they used to drag the body out to the ravine.

"I believe the passenger was the driver of the first car. What was its number…" He paused and looked back to find the entry in his diary.

"PEN 5055," I suggested, briefly glancing at my notebook.

"Yeah, that was it—PEN 5055. I particularly remember the PEN 5055 driver. Besides being very tall, he wore a red and white baseball jacket. I've seen his picture in the paper recently, I think."

I had the licence numbers I wanted so I wasn't too concerned any more whether my host saw me writing. I put my notebook on the table and, underneath the PEN 5055 number I had written earlier, I wrote the driver description he had just given me.

"What can you tell me about the driver of HAR 2212, Mr. McClelland?"

"The driver of HAR 2212 was much shorter and kinda stout. He wore a short deliveryman's jacket—but not as short as the big guy's baseball jacket. The short guy had a baseball cap on…with a crest on it. The crest looked like a bowl of cereal."

I immediately thought of the crest I'd seen mounted on the half-stair landing at the police headquarters.

"Was there a crest on the jacket as well?"

"Now that you mention it, yes there was. I couldn't see the crest on the cap very well. But, then I saw it on his jacket. I could see that one clearly."

I turned to a new page in my notebook and did my best to draw a design similar to the police crest about the size I figured would fit on a baseball cap. The English words stacked up in the middle were easy, but it took a little while to replicate the ribbon, especially how it curled up on either side.

"Yep, that's it. You see how it looks like a bowl of cereal," Mr. McClelland exclaimed proudly.

"I can see it might look like that.

The ribbon, curled up at both ends, would be the bowl and the pile of words would be the cereal."

While we were staring at the drawing, the kettle started to whistle. Mr. McClelland put his diary down, turned off the rimmer, poured the water into the teapot, all in a well practiced routine. He made a strange humming noise as he completed the chore. It was almost as though he had forgotten I was there.

"Do you like you tea weak or strong?"

"Weak," I replied.

"Me too."

He waited about 30 seconds and poured the tea into the cups and placed them in the middle of the table.

I didn't want to destroy the growing rapport that now existed between Mr. McClelland and myself, but I wanted him to return to the night of the first murder.

"Mr. McClelland, could we go back about 30 years, if you don't mind," I suggested quietly. "Can you tell me what the licence number was on the truck that visited the General's Farm on April 29, 1973?"

"How did you happen to pick that date?" he asked, blinking his eyes rapidly. It was obviously a date that had become etched in his memory.

"It's my birthday," I replied casually, as I picked up the closest cup of tea and took a sip.

He went back into the safe and took out the bottom scribbler.

"It shouldn't take long to find the answer because it's on the first page."

The teacup made a rattle as I nervously placed it back on the saucer. "Yup, the truck was licence number T 41973."

I paused for a few seconds and took another sip of tea. My mind was racing. I casually made a note:

$$T41973$$

"What else can you tell me about that night?"

"It was the afternoon actually. T 41973 arrived mid afternoon and the driver parked on the other side of the portico as usual," he said with a furtive glance at me.

I didn't understand that subtle movement for a moment. He was obviously trying to tell me something.

"Three or four hours later SLE 360 arrived," he said slowly.

Again, as he continued, I couldn't tell how much he was reading and how much was a description from memory.

"As I said the other day, it was just before dark. About a half hour had passed by the time I arrived at the driveway. I was in time to see the two of them lift a heavy, rolled-up rug into SLE 360. Then both men left in their own vehicles. That's when I made up my mind to record the numbers and hi-tail it down to the village to phone the police."

The old man spoke even more slowly and appeared to be playing the whole scene over in his mind. It took a few seconds for him to come back to the present. He turned slowly and looked directly at me. His gaze was serious and thoughtful. He looked away and lowered his head as though he was trying to soften what he had to say.

"Maybe you don't want to hear this, but I believe the man who drove that truck back in 1973 was your father."

"It could have been Dad's twin brother Arthur."

"No. It was Henry all right."

"How can you be sure?"

"I know Henry from when he used to date my daughter Ruby."

"Still, they were identical twins," I countered.

"That may be true, but I could tell it was Henry because he wore that T-shirt with the United States flag on it," he asserted. "Besides, Henry's the one with no space between his right ear and his head. I checked that out."

"How would you be able to see his right ear if you were standing in the bushes?"

"I had checked his deformed ear out earlier. I saw him coming down the stairs earlier in the afternoon."

"You're sure it was the same day?"

"Yes. It was the 29th of April," he stated emphatically. "I started my diary that same night. I hadn't paid my rent for March yet. I saw Henry coming down the stairs wearing that American flag T-shirt of his. So I asked Henry if he would mind passing the March rent money on to his father. At first he ignored me and kept heading toward his truck. Then he turned around and suggested that since it was so close to the end of April, why didn't I pay April's rent as well. I didn't really want to because that meant I'd have to go back to my cottage for more money."

"Did you go back for the money?"

"Yes, and he put the money in his baseball cap and put it back on his head. I'll always remember that funny look on his face as he went back up the stairs."

"And you're sure it was Henry and not Arthur?"

"Darn right I am. His right ear was definitely against his head. That was the last thing I checked before I gave him the money. That's the only way I know how to tell them apart."

I was in shock. I mumbled my thanks to the old man and left a little shaken. Could Dad really have been involved in the 1973 murder? Maybe the facts concerning Dad's possible involvement were more than I needed to know.

Back in my car, I recorded the information I had just learned. I added a few details to the descriptions of the drivers below the 2003 licence numbers.

PEN 5055

Driver: tall man—short white hair—wore red & white baseball jacket

HAR 2212

Driver: shorter man—big around

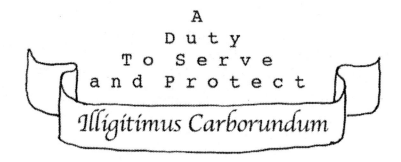

A
Duty
To Serve
and Protect

Illigitimus Carborundum

17 Apr 2003—body found in ravine

PAW 6797 arrived first—mid afternoon—stayed a few minutes & left
- Was Dad the driver? Mr. McC. pretty sure (ASK DAD)

PEN 5055 arrived—just before dark.

- Stayed 20 minutes—left in hurry.
- Driver: tall man—short white hair—wore red & white baseball jacket.

Could be Judge Sewchuk?

(MY OBSERVATION)

- Mr. McClelland has seen him on TV or in papers.
- 1/2 hour later, HAR 2212 arrives in a hurry
- Big man wit short white hair (from PEN 5055) is now passenger
- Stayed for about half an hour
- Both left in hurry—carrying a big jug & small pail with handle

- 2nd Driver—wore short, brown delivery-type jacket,
- Carried a shovel and thick glass log
- Wore baseball-cap with crest—looked like "bowl of cereal"

Could be Melcastle police crest

- Could be Chief Parslow?
(MY OBSERVATION)

April 29, 1973—body carried out in rug

TRUCK (Lic. no. T-41973)—arrived late in afternoon
- Mr. McC. says driver was dad?
(ASK DAD)
SLE 360 arrived after supper— (waited to finish tea)
- Put heavy rolled up rug in SLE 360
- Could be hemp rug Sgt W. was investigating
< (MY OBSERVATION)
- Driver was short and kind of stout—wore short brown jacket

No question, I had to talk to Dad about those revelations. I couldn't believe Dad was involved. The recorded visit of PAW 6797 last month had to be Dad, but in spite of Mr. McClelland's apparent certainty, how was I going to prove the truck driver wasn't Dad?

Meanwhile, knowing Dad wouldn't be back from his trip to Baltimore until late afternoon, I figured it was a good time to visit Sergeant Woznica and tell him about the donated police car and the revolver Dan Spagnoli had found. I could have phoned Sergeant Woznica about the revolver, but I wanted to show him the Journal photocopy of the police car and the SLE 360 licence plate. The photocopy was the link to Mr. McClelland's diary.

As I approached Sylvie's restaurant, I saw a Maryland police car in the parking lot. I figured the Teasdale Detachment wouldn't have too many squad cars, so it was probably Sergeant Woznica's. I waited as a metallic-green pickup truck pulled out of the parking lot entrance. The reflection of the sun gave the truck a sparkling glow that shimmered as it sped away. Preoccupied with the dazzling display of color, I didn't notice who the driver was.

I pulled into the vacated space and sat there for a few moments. How would I tell Sergeant Woznica what he needed to know without disclosing Dad's possible involvement? As I reflected, Sergeant Woznica rushed out of the restaurant. He was obviously in a hurry, but I was sure he would want to hear my exciting news. We met in the middle of the parking lot, but he kept on walking toward his car.

"Sergeant, I've traced the vehicle that was probably used to transport the human remains you found on the golf course."

"How in the world did you do that?"

"It's a long story. Bottom line—Mr. McClelland remembers a licence number—SLE 360. And I found a picture of it in the Melcastle Journal. It shows Chief Parslow donating the car to the Baltimore Police Museum."

"That's impressive, but an old man's memory about something that happened 30 years ago is kind of shaky evidence."

"That's the beauty of it. Mr. McClelland wrote it down in a diary he has been keeping all these years."

"Well, if that's true and the car is still at the Baltimore museum, we can have it tested for DNA."

"I have more good news."

"Fine, but can you make it quick? I have urgent business to take care of right now," he asserted, as he entered his car and started the engine.

"Dan Spagnoli found a 32-calibre revolver on the golf course."

"Dan found a 32-calibre revolver on the golf course?" he repeated, as he rolled the window all the way down and backed the patrol car out. "I must have a chat with young Dan about that."

"He lives in one of those houses across the street."

"Yes, I know where he lives. I'll check it out. Thanks very much," he said, as the car moved forward.

"I have several more things you should know about," I said, as I walked beside the moving car.

"I appreciate that, but could it wait until another time?"

"Sure. I'll stop by your office, first thing in the morning," I shouted.

"Thanks," he shouted back, as he exited the parking lot.

Different thoughts and emotions were leapfrogging over one another in my mind. I needed time to sort things out.

I wasn't sure what time Dad would be back from Baltimore, but I wanted to make sure he was home before me. I didn't want to appear to be sitting waiting for him to return. So I drove aimlessly around the city. Before I knew it, the sun was casting long shadows. It was time to go home, whether I wanted to or not.

CHAPTER 26

Arthur's Letter

Thursday Morning

The trip to Baltimore was a familiar one. When Bonnie and I were newly married, we used to make the trip three or four times a year, mostly for shopping and entertainment. Sometimes we combined business with personal visits. But, since Bonnie's illnesses became more severe and my business there tapered off, I had only made the trip about twice in the last five years.

Kirkland Street is in one of the older districts yet handy to the freeway. I stuck the address Ms Dietz had given me in the sunglasses holder on the dashboard.

There were a couple of misadventures caused by highway construction, new one-way streets and no parking spaces that delayed my arrival until after eleven o'clock. An ongoing funeral meant I had to park several blocks away. All told, I lost nearly an hour. Chances of catching Ms. Dietz between "sessions," as she so quaintly put it, would likely be slim.

At the funeral home, I asked for Andrea Dietz, as instructed. To my surprise, she appeared within seconds out of an office down the hall. I guess she wasn't involved in the session at eleven. Her warm and engaging smile also was unexpected as she introduced herself and led me to a storage room with a split door. The top half of the door was already open. Ms Dietz turned on the lights as she partially opened the bottom half and reached inside. While standing in the doorway, she placed a cardboard box, a little over one cubic foot in size, on the ledge on the half-door. While I was examining it, she placed a sign-off register on a clipboard beside the box. I signed for a cardboard box and a confidential letter.

A large envelope taped to the side was labeled 'Delivery Instructions.' Ms Dietz lifted the flap of the envelope and withdrew a white envelope and handed it to me. It was sealed with a huge gob of red wax and an embossing seal impressed into it. Whoever affixed that seal was careless or inexperienced; because the wax-impression was skewed so badly you could hardly read it.

There was also a single-page letter, which informed the McCosham Funeral Home the box contained an urn to be delivered to:

William Hector Macy and/or
William Henry Macy,
3155 Old Military Road,
Teasdale, Maryland.

Ms Dietz dutifully signed as a witness. It was a pleasant surprise to see her personality was totally different in person than the way she came across on the phone the other day. Besides being very attractive, she was pleasant and considerate.

Ms Dietz closed the half-door while I studied the white envelope. It bore the message:

"To be opened only by
WILLIAM HECTOR MACY

Or
WILLIAM Henry MACY"
CONFIDENTIAL

I took the word **CONFIDENTIAL** to mean I could open it in private. So I placed it in my briefcase and with the cardboard box under my arm, left the building.

On the return trip home, I glanced at the envelope every few minutes. What would Arthur have to say after all these years? I slowly realized I was feeling grief about his death for the first time. I rationalized my tardy lack of compassion as not really having considered Arthur a member of the family for so many years. On the other hand, why did I consider him the real owner of Macy House after 30 years absence? I certainly didn't have the same feeling about the ownership of the General's Farm.

As soon as I entered the house, I found the letter opener and nervously opened the envelope. In the envelope was a hand-written letter. I read it slowly, not knowing quite what to expect.

111 First Ave
Melfort, Sask
SOE 1A0

29 April 1993

Dear Dad and/or Henry:
I've never been much on letter writing, so
I'll get right to the purpose of this letter.

This is a voluntary statement to be delivered and opened only after my death. I'm writing this because I'm scheduled for open-heart surgery tomorrow morning and I want to leave some sort of record in case I don't survive. Should I manage to escape the grim reaper this time, I'll still leave this letter to be forwarded, at the appropriate time, by my lawyer.

What I have to say has been on my conscience for exactly twenty years. Today's date seems to me to be some kind of omen.

I will just tell my story like I remember it. I'm not proud of what I did, but others have done worse and should not be allowed to get away with it.

Init. WAM

Page 2

Twenty years ago, on the night of April 29, 1973, we had our usual gathering of what we called the "Mason-Dixon Club," at the General's Farm. Each member brought his or her own drugs or booze. Roger and Ruby Wendelman were permanent residents at the Farm and by then I was spending most of my time there as well. Other members of our club included Val Sparrow and her young sister Cynthia. Jack Sewchuk and Charlie Leblond were occasional guests. A couple of girls by the names of Rosie and Lennie attended once in a while. I can't remember their last names.

Before I say what happened, I must state two things. The first is that Roger W. had been in a disturbed mood all day.

Someone had hinted the night before that the child his wife Ruby was carrying might not be his. I believe it was Charlie Leblond who made the comment, but I wasn't there so I can't say for sure.

The second point is that Harvey Parslow worked for a syndicate that was trying to find out who was the owner of the General's Farm.

Init. WAM

Page 3

I believe they called the syndicate something that sounded like Sparkle. The Sparkle syndicate had apparently come to the conclusion, since Roger had been living at the Farm for ten years, that he either owned the property or knew who did. Roger refused even to tell Harvey P. who he paid the rent to. I had been with Harvey P.

several times when he visited other property owners in the area. His style was to try and intimidate the owners into selling. Because of their past friendship, Harvey P's attempts to pry the information out of Roger had always been gentle—until that day.

Late on the afternoon, April 29, 1973, I was with Val Sparrow in the second north bedroom and we had drifted off to sleep. I was awakened by loud, threatening voices. Then I heard what I thought was a gunshot. By the time I put my pants on and came out of the bedroom, Harvey Parslow was kneeling over Roger Wendelman's body and Roger's wife Ruby was kneeling on the floor a few feet away, holding her head and sobbing uncontrollably. She was trying to stop the bleeding from a bad cut on her forehead. The three of

them were on the wooden floor in front of the fireplace. I was certain I had heard at least two female voices screaming at one another prior to the gunshot, but only
Init. WAM

Page 4

Ruby was there. I saw Harvey pick up a small handgun that was lying beside Roger's body and put it in his pocket. Roger wasn't moving. I could see that the bullet had struck Roger in the neck and he was bleeding badly. After a few minutes, Harvey made up a plan. He suggested we bury Roger's body at the golf course.

Harvey was obviously concerned about his career. He was a Corporal in the Melcastle police force at the time and was due to be promoted to Sergeant. Harvey also mentioned something about not wanting his association with the syndicate to come out. He didn't want any evidence left around. He even went and found Val and suggested she leave and say nothing about what happened. He assumed I would go along with whatever he decided, and I did.

Ruby didn't say anything. She found a pail of water and soap and started cleaning up the blood. I could see she had a nasty gash over her right eye. Her own blood was dripping into the pail as she scrubbed. She must have hit her head on the edge of the stone apron in front of the fireplace during the struggle.
Init. WAM

Page 5
Meanwhile, Harvey and I gathered up a rug from the living room area and rolled up

Roger in it. Then, we carried him down to Harvey's car. We used Harvey's car because it was parked right at the bottom of the stairs. We put Roger across the back seat.

I followed Harvey to the golf course in my truck. Harvey knew the new owners kept a backhoe underneath the third arch of the Old Stone Bridge. The machine had lights on it. Harvey started it and dug a trench between the approach to the bridge and the sixth green. We removed the body out of Harvey's car and put it in the trench and then Harvey filled in the trench.

I didn't sleep for several nights. I still have nightmares. A couple of days later I gathered up my things and headed out to Saskatchewan where I've lived and worked ever since.

There's no way I can apologize enough

to Ruby and her unborn child. I can only hope they can forgive me and I wish them well in the future. The contents of this letter are unknown to

Init. WAM

Page 6

anyone else, including my lawyer. I told him it could be the admission of a crime and he advised me he would sign it as a witness and place it in a wax-sealed envelope in my presence. I have agreed to that.

Signed by
William Arthur Macy

Witnessed by:
Orest Nesturak
(Lawyer to W Arthur Macy)

P.S. We spent quite a while looking for the gun. We figured it must have fallen out of Harvey's pocket when he jumped out of the backhoe, but we never found it. Harvey said he would go back and look for it in the morning.

Init. WAM

Inside the cardboard box, I found a simple brass urn. I was surprised to find Arthur's will in with the urn as if it were just part of the packaging. The will was professionally written, folded and inserted in a plastic sleeve along with his lawyer's business card.

The contents of the will left everything to Arthur's wife and five children. I noticed he continued the Macy tradition of giving his boys the first name of William. I wondered whether Arthur ever mentioned the existence of relatives in Maryland to his family.

I fingered the business card. It seemed unusual for a business card to accompany a will and ashes. Was Arthur's lawyer trying to tell me something? What I was really searching for was a logical reason to make a phone call to find out the cause of Arthur's death. I've had regular medical check-ups, but I have been anxious ever since my father's sudden death.

I stared at Orest Nesturak's phone number, contemplating what I might say. Heather knew about Arthur, but I didn't want to make the call with her around. I didn't know when she'd be home, but it would probably be soon. I picked up the receiver and dialed before I could talk myself out of it.

"Mr. Nesturak, this is Henry Macy calling."

"Please call me Orest. My father is Mr. Nesturak," he replied, with a dry chuckle.

"Thank you, Orest. I'm calling about my brother Arthur's will and ashes you sent. I just wanted to thank you and let you know everything arrived okay."

"I'm glad," he replied. "Arthur and I were good friends. I was hoping everything would arrive all right. Was the letter useful?"

"Yes, the letter should be helpful in solving a 30-year-old murder."

"Wow! Isn't that something?"

There was a pause. Neither of us knew where to take the conversation from there.

"I just wanted to thank you personally for all your help, Orest."

"It was nice of you to call," Orest replied. "I think I'm the only one in Melfort who knew Arthur had any relatives. He didn't talk about you much. The fact that he wrote a letter gave me a clue that he was deeply remorseful about his part in an incident many years ago. It must be ten years since I witnessed that letter and frankly I can't remember whether I even read it."

"I can tell you this. It seems Arthur was a witness to a murder in 1973. They found the body last month. The arrival of Arthur's letter was good timing."

"That's good. I kind of wanted to find a way to tell you more about Arthur. He was very active in the community."

"That's what I thought when I saw your business card."

"I was pretty sure you were unaware of Arthur's health and you probably didn't know how well he was liked in the community."

"In his letter, Arthur said he had open heart surgery about ten years ago. I gather his health deteriorated after that."

"He had a lot of medical problems. His heart was just one of them. When I first met him, he alternated between a wheelchair and one of those canes with four legs. 'Four-on-the-floor' he used to call it. He had been a diabetic for years. I guess it was getting worse toward the end. He was gradually going blind as well."

"I had no idea."

"It didn't inhibit him much though. Even when he was forced to use the wheelchair full-time, he and his wife still went up to their cottage to fish—year 'round would you believe?"

"I don't recall him ever being interested in fishing."

"Even after he had to have his leg amputated, his wife and son Billy-Bob still took him up to the lake. Many times I saw them struggling to help him out of the truck or out of the cottage and onto a snowmobile and out to the hut on the lake."

"Sounds like quite a struggle."

"It sure was."

"You say Arthur was active in the community?"

"Yes. I met Arthur when I joined the Elks Lodge. We started talking and he mentioned he had a cottage. We discovered that not only did we have cottages at the same lake, we were practically next-door neighbors."

"That's quite the coincidence."

"I'll swear Arthur knew almost everybody in town and 20 miles around. Did you know he was a volunteer fireman?"

"No, I didn't."

"Yeah, 'Never lost a basement' he always used to say."

"That's pretty funny."

"Even in his job as a lineman, he would stop and talk to the customers and always left them laughing. As I said, he knew everybody and everybody liked him."

"I'm really glad to hear that."

"You should have seen the funeral. Everybody who was anybody was there. Mayor Philips said a few words and retired fire chief, Alyn Armstrong, added some very touching remarks. The duo of Joan and Bill Pain sang Arthur's favorite hymn. Which reminds me, I don't suppose you knew Arthur's wife's name was Grace Jameson before she was married.

"No I didn't, but that was nice of all those people to come out."

"Yeah. I spoke to Arthur's oldest son, Gene, after the service. The family was pleasantly surprised by the turnout. Originally the family wasn't going to have a funeral. They thought nobody would remember Arthur after so many years confined to a wheelchair and basically staying at home. The family was sad, of course, but very proud and pleased with the comments people made on the way out."

"Well, Orest, I'm glad I called. Thank you for your kind words," I said. "Oh, I almost forgot. As Arthur's twin brother, I'm interested in what was the cause of death?"

"I believe it was a heart attack, but I can't say for sure. He used to go to Saskatoon regularly for a check-up on his heart and his eyes. Sorry I can't be any more help."

"On the contrary, you've been a great help. Again, thanks for your efforts and kind words."

"No problem. Bye now."

After I hung up, I thought of several things I should have asked— perhaps another day. I was happy enough to know more about my brother. Dad would have been proud of the way Arthur turned out.

I also concluded that western Canadians' attitudes are much like their American counterparts are reputed to be.

CHAPTER 27

What About PAW 6797 and T 41973?

Late Thursday Afternoon

When Heather arrived home, she looked tired, but full of nervous energy. I didn't know where to start with my news, so I encouraged her to talk.

"How was your day, Heather?"

"Not too bad. I cleared up a lot of details about the two bodies at the General's Farm."

"Are the murder mysteries all solved?"

"Yes and no. You may be able to help me with a few of the details," Heather responded.

I detected a sharp tone in Heather's voice that I couldn't understand.

"Go ahead. I'll see whether I can help you."

"First of all, I've confirmed that a young man by the name of Larry Leblond has visited Ruby Wendelman regularly for the past several years. If I'm correct, Larry is Ruby's son. Hopefully, Dennis Archard's sister, who works at the state adoption agency in Melcastle, may be able to find out who adopted Ruby's baby. My theory is that he was born as Baby Wendelman and became Larry Leblond through adoption."

"Fascinating. How did you find out Larry Leblond visited Ruby?"

"I went up to Windemere and asked."

"Aren't you the adventurous one!"

"I also know your car has been up there regularly over the years and in particular, three weeks ago. I know in my heart you couldn't possibly have had anything to do with that murder whether it's Larry Leblond or not, but I need a better explanation, Dad," Heather declared. She sat down on the other end of the sofa, almost in tears.

"It's true," I replied. "I have visited the Farm many times over the years. I go up there to unwind and look at the valley."

"Okay, but what about the seventeenth of April, this year? It's pretty certain young Larry or some other male person was murdered around that date...Mr. McClelland's diary...indicates your car...PAW 6797,. was there on that day... That's your car,...Dad," Heather said. The edge in her voice was still there, but reduce to more of a sputter as she finished. There was also a pleading in her eyes.

"The truth is I discovered a young transient had been camping in the main building. I suspected someone had been living there for several years, but I never actually met him until about a year ago. I used to visit the Farm three or four times a year, but after I met him I started visiting more often."

"Why didn't you have him evicted? Oh, let me guess. You didn't want to let anyone know you owned the place. I forgot."

"I must admit, I was a bit afraid of him, because I could tell he was somewhat mentally challenged, as they say."

"Your frequent visits would account for why Mr. McClelland seems to know you fairly well," Heather commented, sounding a little less demanding.

"When you mentioned the police had found a body, I was afraid it might be my young squatter-friend. I didn't even know his name. All I can say is he lived like a hermit and didn't do any harm. I can see no reason why anybody would want to murder him."

As I was speaking, I looked at Heather for some sign of understanding, but she didn't appear to be listening. She was deep in thought and fixated on her notebook.

"Okay, but I have a question that really bothers me. There was a truck that used to visit the Farm regularly in 1973 and was involved in the first murder. Do you know anything about licence number - T - 4 - 1 - 9 - 7 - 3?" Heather stretched out the numbers as she read from her notebook. The edge had returned to her voice.

"How am I supposed to remember that far back?" I asked, plaintively.

"According to Mr. McClelland's diary, you drove a pickup truck on April 29, 1973. That was the day I was born," she snapped.

"Oh yes, your birthday...right...right. And that licence number...T4...whatever..." I sputtered, trying desperately to remember what there was about that number.

"T - 4 - 1 - 9 - 7 - 3," Heather spelled out curtly.

"T 4 1 9 7 3...T 4 1 9 7 3," I repeated, numbly.

Heather sighed impatiently.

"I remember now!" I exclaimed. "Arthur persuaded Dad to buy the used pickup truck. When they came back from the licence bureau, Arthur was more excited about the licence plates than the truck. He couldn't believe the numbers on the plates indicated the month and year of purchase. Arthur was sure it was an omen of some kind."

"What do you mean?"

"The "4" equals April and the "1-9-7-3" represents the year 1973," I explained. "Arthur was the only one who drove that truck. He was at the General's Farm because he was living with Roger and Ruby more or less full time the last few months before he left. If the truth were known, he was also fond of Ruby."

"But, Mr. McClelland was pretty certain it was you and not Arthur who drove the truck on that day. He even said he could tell you apart because you didn't have a space between the top of your right ear and your head."

"Hmmm, I didn't know Mr. McClelland knew that difference between us."

"If the two of you were identical twins, how did you happen to have different shaped ears?"

"That's easy. When I was a child, a bee stung me on my right ear. It swelled up so badly the doctor had to operate to relieve the pressure. The incision had become infected and he had to operate again. I guess the bandages were too tight or left on too long. In any case, that ear healed closer to my head."

"But, Mr. McClelland said he even checked the spacing on your ear when you took off your baseball cap, put in the rent-money for your dad and placed the cap back on your head."

"First of all, I have never worn a baseball cap in my life. Any kind of cap always irritates my right ear. Second, Arthur had a trick he used to use when he wanted to impersonate me. He would tuck his right ear under the edge of his cap. He would even answer to the name, Henry if he wanted to reinforce the deception."

"That's possible, I suppose," Heather nodded.

"My guess is Arthur's left side was toward Mr. McClelland when he called Arthur by my name. As soon as Arthur heard my name and there was money involved, he probably saw an opportunity and quietly slipped his ear under his cap while they were talking. And when he took his cap off to put the money in, he would have made sure his left side was facing Mr. McClelland. All he had to do was tuck his right ear under the edge as he was putting the cap back on."

"But why would Mr. McClelland call him Henry if he couldn't see his right ear when he first saw him?"

"I don't know," I replied. "Unless…"

"Unless what?"

"Unless Arthur was wearing something Mr. McClelland would only identify with me…"

"Such as?"

"Now that I think about it. Arthur took over ownership of a T-Shirt that I won in a high school essay contest. It had a large American flag on the front. I was proud of that T-shirt and wore it a lot when I was dating Ruby. It could be that Arthur 'borrowed' it. Maybe by 1973 Arthur was running short of clothes."

"Mr. McClelland did mention a T-shirt with a flag on it. I guess that could account for why he thought it was you back in 1973."

Heather seemed happy enough with my answers and much to my relief, changed the subject.

"How did your day go in Baltimore?" Heather asked.

"Fine, thank you," I replied. "I put the urn on the mantelpiece."

"That's what an urn looks like."

"Yes, but the more interesting part is the letter and the will that came with it."

"Who was the letter from?" Heather asked, with renewed interest.

I handed the letter to her. Her eyes widened as she read.

When she finished she said, "It seems like Mr. Parslow has a few questions to answer!"

"Seems that way to me."

"I guess there is no doubt Arthur was the driver of the truck."

"I should have thought of the letter earlier when I was trying to explain that Arthur was the driver of the truck."

"By the way, what does the 'Mason-Dixon Club' refer to?"

"That crowd was pretty heavy into the hippy culture back in the 1960s. I guess they couldn't let go. You might say they were a dissolute bunch."

"Dissolute bunch?"

"You know. Their morals weren't exactly their strongest character traits," I replied. "Let's just say I don't think any money changed hands for sexual favors."

"I see," Heather commented crisply and handed the letter back.

I realized that Heather was asking so many questions because I hadn't been totally open with her since her return from the Great White North. It was time for me to come clean and tell her about the meeting with Mr. Gabler from Hal-Burton. I made her promise not to disclose anything until after the press conference. I did hold a little back. I didn't tell her how much the sale would be worth.

When I finished talking, we were both silent for the longest time. Then Heather went back to her notebook.

"Dad, Mr. McClelland said two other licence numbers stopped at the Farm three weeks ago. I need to find out who the registered owners are. How does one go about finding out that information and how long will that take, would you say?"

"I have a contact at the Bureau of Motor Vehicles. I can have the names for you in no time."

"They're licence numbers HAR 2212 and PEN 5055. Here, I'll write them down for you."

"And what was that number Mr. McClelland first started his diary with, back in 1973?"

She added **SLE 360** to the sheet without looking at her notes. The characters were a little larger and darker than the others.

"You seemed to have memorized that number."

"Yes, and I'm pretty certain who the driver was."

She showed me a photocopy of the cop car donated to the museum. The photograph and the article made it pretty clear that Cpl Parslow was the driver of the car at the first murder. And the confessional letter confirmed that Arthur drove the truck.

"What are you going to do with Uncle Arthur's letter, Dad?"

"I think I'll turn it over to the FBI."

"Would you make a copy of it, please? I think I'll pay a visit to Sergeant Woznica in the morning. I'd like to tell him you have received it and he'll receive a copy eventually." She looked for my approval.

"That's a good idea. I want a copy for myself anyway."

"Could I see it again, please? I want to have some of the details from it for my notes."

I could see she wrote:
- Tell Sgt. Woznica about Arthur's letter—re night of Apr 29, 1973
- Indicates Corporal Parslow shot Roger W.—front of fireplace
- Body buried between O.S.B. and #6 hole
- Letter mentions lost gun

"I have an idea. Why don't you come with me to see Sergeant Woznica before you go to the FBI?"

"Can't. I have some urgent work to do. I've been neglecting it all week," I replied.

"What kind of work is so important that…?" she interrupted herself.

"Not another secret?"

I told her all about the contract for property research. I also tried to explain how I felt there was a connection somehow between the FBI and Hal-Burton. I wound up asking whether she was interested in sharing the work?

"I don't mind. If you were happy enough doing it, then why should I mind?" Heather commented, as she bobbed her head from side to side and puckered her lips.

"Good, perhaps we can buy another computer too," I added.

"Maybe we can buy four new computers, now that you're going to receive a bit of money from Hal-Burton for the General's Farm."

"Four new computers? Why four?" I gasped.

"One for the office here, a new one for Roma and portables for you and me."

"I see you've been giving this a little thought."

"A little," she chuckled.

"We'll see."

CHAPTER 28

How Wide Is The Conspiracy?

Friday Morning

When I came out of my bedroom Friday morning, Dad had finished his breakfast and was dressed for work. He said he wanted to run a few errands and do some property research in the downtown office. He must have been quite concerned about the Hal-Burton contract because he hadn't gone for his morning jog.

After finishing my breakfast, I took a few minutes to think about what to do with the evidence on the murder cases I had gathered. It would be hard to tell what would happen after the FBI received Arthur's letter. Things could develop quickly. I wanted to be ready.

My only real commitment was to see Sergeant Woznica this morning. It was comforting to know I had already given him the heads-up on the revolver Dan Spagnoli had found. My mind was pretty well made up that the only authorities I could trust were the Teasdale police. At least Sergeant Woznica didn't have any apparent ulterior motive.

The main thing I wanted to show him was how I had linked Chief Parslow to the SLE 360 licence plate and the newspaper photocopy was proof. That should impress him.

How was I going to talk about the other licence plates without revealing the existence of Mr. McClelland's diary? There was no way of avoiding it. The McClelland diary was the key to both murders. I must make an effort to convince Sergeant Woznica that any intrusion into Mr. McClelland's private life would have to he handled by somebody the old man trusted.

I didn't want to say my dad was already working on tracing the licence numbers, because I didn't want to expose his sources. On the other hand, I really wanted to tell Sergeant Woznica about my suspicions that the description of the first driver connected with last month's murder matched Judge Sewchuk and that I suspected PEN 5055 was his car. I was pretty sure that HAR 2212 would be Chief Parslow's current car. I based that on the driver description and the "bowl of cereal" crest on the jacket and cap.

I must mention the ceremonial sword as a possible murder weapon in the latest murder. I didn't want to forget that.

Then I thought it would be best to leave all the licence plate numbers and descriptions out of the meeting until I had confirmation. I convinced myself that anything beyond a casual meeting with Sergeant Woznica would be premature. The visit was to be low-key. I would tell him about my conspiracy theory later. After all, it was based mostly on evidence from Mr. McClelland and Uncle Arthur's letter. I really had to wait for a copy of the letter before saying anything.

Somehow, I had to make a point with Sergeant Woznica that I didn't really trust Detective Turcot. Louis was too close to Chief Parslow.

While I was mulling over my problem on how to proceed, the phone rang. Dennis Archard had news from his sister. I was right. Larry Leblond's natural mother was Ruby Wendelman and Charlie and Cynthia Leblond had adopted him. I thanked Dennis and said I would explain the reason for my request in a few days.

I wrote "Wendelman" after Larry Leblond in my notebook. Larry had obviously found out he was born as baby Wendelman and adopted by the Leblond's. It made my theory more plausible that Larry somehow had an attachment to the General's Farm.

The news from Dennis gave me the courage to confirm the blood sample Detective Turcot found matched the human remains at the golf course. If that were true, it would strengthen my theory that the body in the ravine was Larry Wendelman, cum Leblond, and the golf course human remains would undoubtedly be those of his father, Roger Wendelman. A casual phone call to Detective Turcot should be able to answer some of the unknowns.

"Good morning, Heather," Detective Turcot answered curtly.

"I was wondering how you were coming along regarding matching the DNA with the human remains found at the golf course."

When he didn't reply right away, I began to doubt my convictions for calling so soon.

"You were correct, Heather. The DNA analysis proved the blood sample we found matched the human remains in the Maryland case."

"Well, isn't that something."

"How did you happen to guess there would be a match?"

There was a sharp tone to his question. We both knew I had already explained that to him in his office. There was something else behind his question.

"Just luck I guess."

"There had to be more to it than that."

"As I said before, when I mentioned your expression 'close enough to be a relative' to my dad, he remembered Roger Wendelman disappearing many years ago."

"Well, that's quite a coincidence. The lab hasn't processed all the samples I gave them after my search last Tuesday. The match with the body we found in the ravine may be among them."

"You can always do a paternal DNA check with what you have and the ravine body, can't you?"

There was a long pause before he spoke again.

"You seem to know a lot about police work. I have a feeling you know more about this case than you are telling me."

"No, no. It's just my training as a lawyer coming out," I said and held my breath.

During the rest of the conversation, I was evasive, not wanting to disclose any more than I had to. There was something about Detective Turcot's attitude that really bothered me. I was even more convinced that he was involved or too close to the chief to trust. I certainly didn't want to tell him about the diary or the licence plates or the driver descriptions.

I was shaking like a leaf when I hung up the phone and waited a few minutes before phoning Sergeant Woznica. I took my time searching though my briefcase to find his business card. Sergeant Woznica answered the phone on the first ring. The mere sound of his voice was comforting as I suggested an appointment.

"As soon as you can make it," he replied. "I believe you know where my office is—number two, Old Military Road. Turn right at the traffic light at Wittig Street and immediately turn right again into the parking lot behind the Aalen Building."

"Ah yes, I can almost see it from here," I joked.

The pleasant nature of the phone call with Sergeant Woznica was in direct contrast to the Detective Turcot conversation. I could picture "Toley's" big, smiling face as we spoke.

As I grabbed my briefcase on the way out, it appeared to be awfully heavy. I left the heritage files behind. All I needed for this meeting was the newspaper photograph of the donated police car and, of course, my notebook.

They must have installed a traffic light at the corner of Old Military Road and Wittig Street sometime in the last 13 years. I didn't realize the building on that corner was called the Aalen Building. It was under construction when I left. I remember it as being a three-storey building. Apparently it was now a police station. No doubt it was still the center of the thriving metropolis (to quote Judge Sewchuk) of Teasdale with a burgeoning population of 500.

Just past Sylvie's restaurant and gas bar, I spotted a sign saying, "Welcome to Teasdale, Population 1,357." Such accuracy. Perhaps it was still small enough to count each individual. Even when I was a teenager, we drove all over the area, but we seldom went into Teasdale.

It was too bush-league for us. The place to be was Melcastle or Candle Lake during the summer.

The general appearance of downtown Teasdale was about the same as ever. There were a few new buildings and a few had obviously been torn down or destroyed by fire. The old brick and stone post office is still kitty-corner to the Aalen Building.

The parking lot behind the Aalen Building was nearly empty and still wet from an overnight rain. There was no evidence of rain at Macy House when I left.

A sign over a rear entrance indicated the Teasdale detachment of the Maryland Police was located on the second floor. The Commissionaire on the second floor directed me to Sergeant Woznica's office, but hardly looked up from his daily crossword puzzle.

"He's on the third floor. Turn left at the top of the stairs—last office on the right."

As soon as I reached the top of the stairs, I could hear Sergeant Woznica's familiar voice down the hall. He was on the phone. His door was open. He didn't notice me because he was leaning back in his chair and looking out the window as he spoke.

I waited at the doorway for him to finish. It gave me a chance to catch my breath from using the one-step-at-a-time elevator system. Most people call them stairs.

The Sergeant's office was somewhat lacking you might say: a desk, two chairs, one of which he was sitting on, and a computer. It was a corner office and because of its north-western field of view and being on the third floor, you could see the trees at the top of the General's Mountain, but not the farm house.

Sergeant Woznica hung up the phone and immediately started pecking at his computer. He still hadn't noticed me. My knock seemed to startle him. He jumped up and welcomed me—his big, friendly smile refreshing as usual.

I still didn't know how to start telling my story. I began by referring to my notes and randomly outlining facts. I soon became concerned that by not mentioning Mr. McClelland's diary, my delivery wasn't making sense. I presented everything in the order I had recorded them, not the chronological order in which the events had occurred. It was probably confusing to Sergeant Woznica. My McGill classmates would have been astonished at how ill prepared I was for this presentation. I must have sounded juvenile when I ended by suggesting all the Teasdale Police had to do was trace the two car licence plates.

Sergeant Woznica listened to my tale and made notes. When I finished, he had a few questions.

"You mentioned yesterday that Mr. McClelland had his data written down."

"I think I had better start over again."

I started with why and how Mr. McClelland kept his diary. I emphasized the date, April 29, 1973, the SLE 360 licence plate and description of the driver. I casually mentioned the truck, left out the licence number. I ended by reiterating yesterdays message that Dan Spagnoli had found a 32-calibre revolver on the golf course.

Sergeant Woznica continued to listen patiently and made some more notes, which made me feel better. He asked a few more questions which only led me deeper into my conspiracy theory.

When I switched to last month's murder, I made a point of calling it Detective Turcot's case.

I described the two drivers and their licence numbers and how Mr. McClelland thought the driver of the first car was the passenger in the second car. He was amused by the description of the Melcastle police crest looking like a bowl of cereal. I followed with the details of the things the two men were carrying. I decided that including Dad's car and why I eliminated him would have been too confusing.

While Sergeant Woznica was listening to the drivers' descriptions, he recorded them and made arrows to the two car licence numbers I had given him. I could see that below the description "very tall man with short white hair," he wrote Judge Sewchuk with a question mark after it. He also wrote "Parslow?" underneath the "short and kind of stout" description. He followed that by another arrow to the licence number SLE 360. Parslow was obvious from the jacket and crest reference, but I wasn't sure I had mentioned the judge's name.

Before I went any further, I needed to know whether what I was saying made any sense.

"What do you think, Sergeant?"

"To start with, your information sounds credible, especially if it can be substantiated by factual evidence and testimony."

That was a relief.

"I've known Mr. McClelland for many years—even before I was on the police force. I've always thought of him as an eccentric old man."

"But, you can't deny his diary," I interjected. "All we need to do is confirm the licence registrations and I'm sure other things will prove true as well."

"You didn't let me finish. I spoke to Mr. McClelland after we found the human remains near the Old Stone Bridge. I wasn't able to see his diary, but I had the distinct impression he knew more than he was telling me, including knowledge of the body in the ravine."

"I agree and I think if we approach him carefully, he would convince you his information is authentic."

Sergeant Woznica thought about my suggestion for a moment.

"You mentioned yesterday something about tracing a police car to a museum. What was that all about?"

"I nearly forgot about that," I said as I pulled out the photocopy of the newspaper article and handed it to him. "I noticed a framed picture of it hanging in the Melcastle Police Headquarters. The copy in your hand is from the Melcastle Journal."

"This is the kind of hard evidence we can use," he exclaimed. "This definitely connects SLE 360 to Chief Parslow, but not necessarily on that night because the car was only assigned to him, remember."

He glanced at the narrative and double underlined "Parslow" and add the words "see picture" beside SLE 360 plate number and the "short and kind of stout" driver description in his notepad.

"There's even more evidence, but I don't have it here," I added.

"What would that be?" he asked, still reading the newspaper article.

I waited for him to finish reading.

"Yesterday, my father received a deathbed letter from his twin brother, Arthur, along with his ashes. Uncle Arthur wrote that he was with then Corporal Parslow on the night of April 29, 1973. In the letter,

Uncle Arthur also said he helped Harvey Parslow bury Roger Wendelman's body between the approach to the Old Stone Bridge and the sixth green on the golf course."

Sergeant Woznica's eyes widened as I spoke.

"That's incredible!"

"It's a six page, notarized letter."

Sergeant Woznica was no longer smiling. He stood up slowly, turned and looked out the window. The raindrops that remained on the north window seemed appropriate for the solemn mood Sergeant Woznica had now entered. Neither of us spoke for several minutes.

"Where's that letter now?"

"My father has it. He said he was going to turn it over to a contact in the FBI. I didn't really expect to be talking about it this morning."

"Assuming the letter from Uncle Arthur has been received by the FBI, do they also have the rest of the story?"

"No, they don't, but I'm sure the letter will be in their hands sometime this morning," I said. "Dad had some other work to do at his office and I'm not sure whether he went to the FBI before going to the office or not."

"One thing I know for sure when you go after a chief of police, you'd better have your facts straight," said Sergeant Woznica. "This is way over my head. I wish I had a copy of that letter."

"I could always phone Dad to see whether he has given it to the FBI yet," I suggested.

"There's one way to find out whether the FBI has the letter and marry up your information at the same time," he pronounced, as he reached for the phone.

"I have a contact at the FBI I think would be just the right person to handle this situation."

He punched a quick series of numbers and asked to speak to Special Agent House.

While he waited, he cupped his hand over the mouthpiece.

"For your information, Heather, Detective Turcot called this morning to say Mr. and Mrs. Leblond had come in and confirmed the body found in the ravine was their son. They made a point of saying the boy was adopted and had left home about five or six years ago. They had hardly seen him since."

"I thought so," I said. I leafed through my notebook and recorded the information.

Sergeant Woznica took his hand off the mouthpiece.

"Special Agent House, this is Sergeant Woznica from the Teasdale detachment of the Maryland Police."

He waited for the person at the other end to recognize who was calling.

"I have some information I think you should have. It's about the human remains we found on the golf course and a possible connection with the body found in the ravine behind the General's Farm."

There was an even longer pause before Sergeant Woznica spoke.

"We would like to come over and show you what we have?"

Another pause. The agent probably wanted to know who the "we" was.

"Her name is Heather Macy. She's a lawyer working on the property dispute at the farm."

He listened for a few seconds.

"Okay, we'll be right over."

Agent House was interested. The presentation of my evidence was going to be tested again. How I wished I had a copy of Uncle Arthur's letter to help me out. What had I gotten myself into? So much for *"just a casual meeting"* with Sergeant Woznica.

On our way out, we passed the switchboard room. The operator was busy on the phone, so Sergeant Woznica wrote a note on the pad by her elbow. The operator waved at us as the sergeant and I left. Her face was familiar, but I couldn't remember her name. It wasn't until I left the building that her name came to me. Marilyn Hird had changed a lot since we were kids.

CHAPTER 29

Contacting Mr. Barnard

Friday Morning

I woke up early to go into the city to do some work on the property research contract which was due every Friday. Because of the Hal-Burton press conference at two o'clock, I only had about four working hours available. Fortunately, I had gathered enough data on several sites to do at least four or five of them without going outside the office. The cases I had been working on lately were taking much less time than usual.

Before getting started on the contract work, I wanted to ask Myrtle Barrigar at the Bureau of Motor Vehicles if she would trace the licence numbers Heather had given me. I also wanted to visit Hal-Burton to discuss the possibility of having Heather take on some of the contract work. If my hunches were correct, my visit with Mr. Barnard would be an opportunity to pass Arthur's letter to the FBI. I was reasonably certain of the Bureau's connection. It was mostly a matter of confirmation.

I parked in my usual parking spot and as I was about to press the elevator button, I remembered to make a couple of copies of Arthur's letter at Kinkos.

I continued to rehearse in my mind what I would tell the Hal-Burton receptionist. I worried about explaining why I wanted to arrange a face-to-face meeting with Mr. Barnard. My initial reasoning would be that I needed Heather to help me with the property research contract.

Sounding as businesslike as I could, I told the receptionist I wanted to see Mr. Barnard urgently. To my surprise, she accepted the request without any further explanation.

As I pressed the elevator button to go up to my office, I felt pretty good about how smoothly the meeting request had gone. Before the elevator had a chance to arrive, the Hal-Burton receptionist rushed out to instruct me to go down to the second floor and Mr. Barnard would meet me outside the glass doors.

While waiting for the elevator doors to open and close in the process of changing from up to down, I thought how silly it was to take an elevator to go down one floor.

Mr. Barnard was waiting at the elevator door when I stepped out and assisted me with the signing-in procedure. He directed me to a small conference room behind the glass doors bearing the familiar FBI crest. Once inside, I nervously started to tell Mr. Barnard that I was having trouble keeping up with my case quota, but before I could finish, he interrupted me.

"Before you go on, Henry, there's something I need to speak to you about. Hal-Burton has been analyzing the research data on this project and have come to some definitive conclusions."

He seemed as uncomfortable as I was curious.

"Hal-Burton has concluded that your services will no longer be required on the property research contract. Naturally, there's a severance clause, which Hal-Burton will honor."

I was stunned.

"That comes a bit of a shock after all these years. Would you mind telling me why, Mr. Barnard?"

"I'm not at liberty to say, except to tell you that your work has been of great use to the corporation. Whether the City of Melcastle wants to continue the research is up to them, but Hal-Burton has all the data it needs."

"That's fine with me. I was having trouble meeting the quota, anyway."

"Good. Then we're done here. I have briefed the receptionist upstairs on how to handle your severance package. Thank you very much for your services. Have a good day."

We stood up and shook hands.

Then I remembered Arthur's letter.

"Oh! I nearly forgot. I also wanted to talk to you about a letter I just received from my late brother."

I handed him the original.

"The letter came yesterday, along with my brother Arthur's ashes. I believe it is self explanatory."

I watched him as he read.

"This is very interesting. Do you know this lawyer in Melfort, Sask-at-che-wan?"

"No, I don't, but I have talked to him on the phone."

"We'll have it checked out. I'll see that it gets into the right hands."

"By *into the right hands*, do you mean the FBI's hands?"

"Of course."

Mr. Barnard escorted me back to the commissionaire's desk outside the glass doors.

The wind was chilly as I stepped out the back door of the Sparrow Building to make the short walk over to the Bureau of Motor Vehicles. The dampness in the air helped relieve the shock of the termination of the Hal-Burton contract.

It was pure luck on by part that Myrtle Barrigar was in before eight thirty that morning. It seems she has her own car now and doesn't need her husband John to drive her to work. That was good because I didn't want to run into John. It's not that John is the jealous type, but he can be like a dog with a bone when it comes to things like my asking Myrtle to trace licence plates. He would hound her until she gave him the names. Eventually, the owners of the plates would find out Heather was checking on them. John is a bit of a gossip, you might say.

I left the licence particulars with Myrtle and told her I needed the names as soon as possible. Myrtle said she would call me back as soon as she could.

CHAPTER 30

There It Was...Gone

A Newfoundlander was asked to describe how his fishing boat went missing.

"I went down to the wharf and there it was...gone."

After completing the two errands, I headed for my office in a bit of a daze. No more night work. No more transcribing notes. No more summary reports. All of a sudden, there it was...gone.

I kept wondering what the contract was really all about. I had my suspicions. I had to believe SPA-KAL was gathering property, but why the underhanded methods? Who were the SPA-KAL principals and what was their source of funds?

As the elevator arrived at the eighth floor, I thought about the first time I asked Myrtle to trace a licence plate registration for me. That was about 20 years ago. Myrtle was in charge of the old card oriented filing system and the request took her a couple of days. My only other request was made shortly after she became the supervisor of the computer system and that came back the same day. This time she estimated it would take her less than an hour. I headed to my office to wait.

Roma was startled to see me in so early. I had to tell her the Hal-Burton contract had been terminated, which upset her because she knew what the loss of income meant. I spent several minutes convincing Roma that her job was safe. Unfortunately, I was unable to tell her how much the severance check would be. Then I thought about the check from Mr. Gabler. Roma disposition brighten considerably when I told her I had received a $10,000 retainer for a future contract that had good income potential. I told her I had left it at Macy House and would give it to her on Monday.

The phone rang just as I entered my office. It was Myrtle and she not only had the identity of the owners of the plates, gave me more than I needed to know. I copied the information on a pad and thanked her for her efforts.

I was secretly pleased with the names Myrtle read to me, even though I didn't fully understand what it all meant. I cared only was that Jack Sewchuk owned one of the plates and Harvey Parslow the other one. She confirmed SLE 360 was a 1973 police vehicle. I knew from the photocopy of the donated police vehicle that Myrtle's information supported Heather's suspicions. Myrtle didn't ask, but I promised to tell her later why I wanted the data.

Now it was up to Heather to fit all the details together. I phoned home, but there was no answer. Then I remembered that she said something about visiting Sergeant Woznica. When I phoned the Teasdale police detachment and identified myself, I was greeted by a perky female voice, who asked:

"Hi Mr. Macy. Do you know who this is?"

"No. Should I?"

"I'm Bill Hird's granddaughter. I used to play with Heather when we were kids."

"Marilyn Hird?" I asked, hoping I had guessed the first name correctly.

"Yes, I'm glad you remembered, but it's Marilyn Swain now. I married Doug Swain. He was the tall kid who used to live near Grampa

Bill's store. He went into the Navy, but was too tall to be a pilot. He's out of the Navy and back in town. That's when we were married, you know."

"Congratulations Marilyn, but can you tell me whether Heather is still there?"

"No, she left about ten or fifteen minutes ago with Sergeant Woznica."

"Do you happen to know where they went?"

"He wrote me a note that says they went to see a Special Agent House at the FBI." Marilyn responded slowly at the end, as though she wasn't sure she should have given out that information.

I was fairly certain one of the FBI staff members in my building was named House. I dialed the Bureau number I found in the phone book and asked for Special Agent House. The raspy voice of Agent House came on the line. At first I wasn't sure whether it was male of female.

"Would Heather Macy happen to be there, please?"

"As a matter of fact, I think she just walked in. Hold one moment, please."

Heather come on the line, sounding a bit bewildered that anyone would know she was there.

"Hi Heather, this is Dad. I have the information on those licence numbers you wanted."

"Great! Give me a second…okay, go ahead."

"The first number—HAR 2212 is registered to Harvey Parslow."

"Okay," Heather said slowly.

"The second number, PEN 5055 is part of a series of Special Organization plate numbers assigned to Pennsylvania dignitaries such as legislators, judges, senators, handicapped persons, firemen, veterans, etc."

"That's great, Dad, but who is PEN 5055 registered to?"

"PEN 5055 is registered to Judge Jack Sewchuk," I replied.

"Thanks, Dad," she said "And please give my thanks to Mrs. Barrigar."

"How did you know it was Mrs. Barrigar?" I asked.

"Just a hunch, Dad. I'll tell you later. Bye and thanks again," she chuckled and hung up.

CHAPTER 31

Time To Visit The FBI

Friday Morning

It wasn't until Sergeant Woznica parked the car in the parkade behind the Sparrow Building that I realized the FBI office was in the same building as Dad's office...I mean, the Macy and Macy office.

We went up one flight and along a short hallway and signed in at a commissionaire station. Inside a set of glass doors, we approached the reception area. The main desk was staffed by a young lady who was sitting behind a large, multiple-desk arrangement equipped with an array of computers, telephones, a fax machine, a copy machine and Lord knows what all. The extravagance of the equipment made me feel embarrassed for the meager set-up in Roma's office.

Sergeant Woznica requested directions to Special Agent House's office.

"Her office is the other side of the water cooler. I'll buzz her and let her know you're here," the young lady replied.

The door beyond the water cooler was ajar as we arrived. A woman with bright red hair and dressed in a dark blue suit, held the door with one hand and a telephone receiver in the other. Obviously, we had interrupted a telephone conversation. She welcomed us and immediately excused herself and returned to her desk. She gestured for us to sit on the chairs on the other side of her desk. We went in, but we remained standing.

After a few minutes, she terminated the conversation, but before we could introduce ourselves the phone rang. Agent House excused herself and after a few words turned the phone over to me.

The caller was Dad with the news from his contact at the BMV. He gave me the news on the licence numbers he had traced. I copied the names beside the three numbers in my notebook and told him to give my thanks to Mrs. Barrigar. He seemed surprised.

Sergeant Woznica had introduced himself while I was on the phone. When I rejoined them, he introduced me as the other Macy in the law firm of Macy and Macy."

"Pleased to meet you, Heather" Agent House responded, as we shook hands. "I haven't actually met your father, but I've heard his name mentioned while I was doing some work with Hal-Burton."

"It's my pleasure. I'm anxious to get this off my chest, so to speak. I didn't expect to see anyone so soon."

"From what Sergeant Woznica told me over the phone, the FBI could be interested in what you have to say," she replied.

"Heather has a theory on how the two victims might be related."

"Okay Heather. Let's hear your story," Agent House said and gestured for us to sit down. At the same time, she pulled out a well-worn file from a desk drawer.

"Special Agent House, are you familiar with a man named Albert McClelland?"

"Yes, he lives in the cottage beside what is commonly called the General's Farm at the upper end of Old Military Road."

"Are you aware Mr. McClelland has been keeping a diary for the past 30 years of all vehicle traffic at the General's Farm?"

"No, I'm not aware of any diary."

Agent House looked at Sergeant Woznica who was nodding his head. She started writing on a blank notepad.

"It's a detailed diary and in my opinion Mr. McClelland has an excellent memory to back it up," I added, feeling more confident than during my previous presentation.

"We need all the factual evidence possible. Continue please, Heather."

"According to Mr. McClelland's diary, on the afternoon of April 29, 1973, a pickup truck—licence plate number T41973—arrived at the General's Farm and stayed for several hours. The truck was driven by William *Arthur* Macy, my father's twin brother. As an aside, William *Arthur* Macy is now deceased. His ashes arrived yesterday. Included with his ashes was a letter, which connects several local people to the 1973 murder, which took place at the General's Farm and the body buried on the golf course. My father is handing over the letter to someone in the FBI this morning."

I looked at Sergeant Woznica. I realized I had just given Agent House information about the truck I had not given him. He nodded his head and recorded it in his notepad.

"And your father's full name is...?" she paused, waiting for me to fill in Dad's name.

"William *Henry* Macy," I replied, emphasizing the Henry.

"I'll check on the letter while we continue."

On her intercom, Agent House asked for someone to check on the receipt of a letter signed by a—William Arthur Macy. While she was using the intercom, the light from the window exposed an iridescent sheen on the dark blue ripples on the arm of her suit coat. I wondered whether it would go well with my hair color.

"Do you have anything else, Heather?" she asked.

I was startled back into reality.

"Yes I do. Just before dark, on the afternoon of April 29, 1973, a car licence number S L E 3 6 0 arrived and stayed for a few minutes. I've since discovered that licence SLE 360 was assigned to Corporal Harvey Parslow of the Melcastle Police."

Agent House kept writing, but her eyes flashed up as sign of recognition of the name Parslow. I continued.

"Mr. McClelland noticed a car that afternoon. It was not a regular visitor to the house next door. He kept an eye on the place because his daughter lived there. He couldn't see the licence plate because the sun was in his eyes. After he finished his tea, he went to check on the car. It was getting dark. As he approached the farmhouse, he heard two men coming down the stairs. He hid behind some bushes and watched two men load a rolled-up rug, into the back seat of SLE 360."

I paused to make sure I wasn't going to fast.

"Continue please, Heather," Agent House said.

"My theory is that on that date in 1973, the then Corporal Parslow went to the General's Farm to shakedown Roger Wendelman to persuade him to sell the property to the SPA-KAL syndicate."

At the mention of SPA-KAL syndicate, I noticed House and Woznica looked at one another, but said nothing.

"The way I see it, Corporal Parslow probably threatened Roger Wendelman with a gun, they struggled and the gun went off. The bullet severed the carotid artery in Mr. Wendelman's neck and the bullet lodged inside his skull. Corporal Parslow probably panicked. According to Uncle Arthur's letter, Corporal Parslow engaged Uncle Arthur to help him wrap the body in a hemp rug, drive it to the nearby golf course and bury it near the Old Stone Bridge using a golf course backhoe. Sergeant Woznica and Detective Turcot have confirmed the blood found in front of the fireplace at the farm was that of Roger Wendelman. The area was flooded with his blood as he died."

Agent House looked questioningly at Sergeant Woznica who nodded his agreement.

"During the fatal struggle, Mrs. Wendelman, nine months pregnant, was probably knocked down and hit her head on the edge of the stone apron. After Corporal Parslow and Uncle Arthur had taken her husband's body away, she managed to recover enough to cleanup the area. Am I going too fast?"

"That's okay," the agent answered. She kept on writing.

"Mr. McClelland didn't have a phone at that time, so it took him an hour or so to go down to the village to phone the police. Presumably, this can be confirmed by the Teasdale Police."

Sergeant Woznica picked up the cue.

"Yes," Sergeant Woznica said, consulting his notepad. "Our police log shows: 'something mysterious is going on at 3279 Old Military Road.' The call was made by a male person at 21:09 hours."

"Did your log record anything else, Sergeant?" asked Agent House.

"A cruiser was dispatched," he continued. "They found a woman scrubbing the wooden floor in front of the fireplace. The log indicates whatever happened took place on the Pennsylvania side of the border. The dispatcher called the Melcastle Police. Corporal Parslow arrived shortly afterwards and took charge."

"Okay, anything else, Sergeant?"

"The caller didn't leave his name, but I believe it was Mr. McClelland."

"Heather, anything else you would like to add?"

"Yes. Mrs. Wendelman was unable to speak and the police soon discovered she was in labor. She was taken to Windemere. After her baby was delivered she was held in custody. I suggest a little pressure from the 'office-in-charge' may have had something to do with her disposition."

Agent House paused for a second and flipped through a few pages in the file on the side of her desk. I waited until she went back to making notes before I continued.

"We know a car bearing licence plate SLE 360, as recorded in Mr. McClelland's diary, almost certainly driven by Corporal Parslow, visited the murder scene on April 29, 1973. The letter from my late uncle will corroborate the fact he and Corporal Parslow buried Roger's body on the golf course, 30 years ago."

I paused to make sure there was no confusion between the murder 30 years ago and the one last month.

"Is that it?" she asked, without looking up.

"That's all I have for the 1973 murder."

"Does that mean you have something on the murder last month?"

"Yes."

"Go ahead."

301

"I've confirmed Baby Wendelman was put up for adoption. His adopted name became Larry Leblond. The Windemere log shows young Larry visited Mrs. Wendelman often over the past few years. My theory is that when Larry discovered his real mother was being kept at Windemere and his father was probably dead, he became depressed. It could be Mrs. Wendelman told her son about the General's Farm and perhaps what happened to his father."

"Is there any evidence Larry Leblond visited or lived at 3279 Old Military Road?" Agent House asked.

"I believe there is. My father met a young man who took up residence at the farm several times over the last few years."

"And you think that young man was Larry Leblond."

"Yes," I said. "My assumption is that when Larry Leblond went to the farm, he found it vacant and moved in. Presumably police patrols saw evidence of someone living there. Eventually, that information came to the attention Harvey Parslow—later to become Chief of Police—and his fellow syndicate members."

"And according to your theory, what happened next?"

"As of last month, Larry Leblanc would have been 30 years old. It's my contention he was murdered on the same spot, i.e. on the wooden floor in front of the fireplace."

"That would be the body found in the ravine behind the farm," Sergeant Woznica interjected.

"Exactly," I said. "Detective Turcot obtained a blood sample by scraping between the cracks on the underside of the flooring. The DNA didn't match the body found in the ravine. When I met Detective Turcot, he said the blood sample was 'close enough to be a relative.' When I mentioned that expression to my father, he recalled Roger Wendelman's disappearance 30 years ago. The next day, I suggested to Detective Turcot that he try matching the DNA from the blood found at the farm with the human remains found on the golf course."

"That's why Detective Turcot requested a bone sample to check against the DNA he found at the farm," Sergeant Woznica mused.

"Yes and this morning Detective Turcot confirmed the DNA does match the human remains, which I believe are those of Roger

Wendelman," I said. "Detective Turcot is now attempting to prove the body found in the ravine last month is, in fact, related to the golf course remains."

I paused, looking for confirmation that my theory was believable. I also recognized that I was becoming very thirsty.

"I think Roger's blood, from 30 years ago, formed a barrier and stopped Larry's blood from passing through the flooring. More digging might produce evidence of Larry's blood. I was also thinking that since Larry was stabbed to death, you might check for traces of blood on the ceremonial sword that hangs above the mantelpiece."

My throat was getting raspy.

"Could I have a glass of water, please?"

"Oh! Of course," Agent House said. "I'm sorry, I was so caught up in what you were saying I completely forgot to offer something to drink. How about you Sergeant?"

"No thanks, I haven't been doing the talking."

Sergeant Woznica winked at me as Agent House took two mugs from a cabinet behind her desk and filled them with water from the cooler outside the door.

"Continue please, Heather," Agent House said, as she handed me a mug of water.

"I believe Judge Sewchuk was involved in the murder last month."

"Judge Sewchuk?" Agent House asked in astonishment. She looked at Sergeant Woznica for confirmation. He nodded.

"Yes. We know the judge was there because, according to Mr. McClelland's diary, licence number PEN 5055 was on the scene on 17 April of this year. That was my father on the phone a few minutes ago and he confirmed PEN 5055 is registered to Judge Jack Sewchuk. It is my belief Judge Sewchuk went to the farm on behalf of SPA-KAL. My theory is the syndicate was desperate to find out who owned the property."

"The 17th of April, does that co-ordinate with the forensic lab's estimated date of last month's murder?" Agent House asked Sergeant Woznica.

"That's smack in the middle of the range of dates the Melcastle

Police registered on their analysis sheet," he replied, checking his notes.

"Anything else, Heather?" she asked.

"Yes. Obviously there was a violent confrontation between the judge and Larry Leblond. Someone grabbed the sword from over the fireplace. The judge's hands were cut in the struggle."

"Can anyone confirm the judge's hands showed signs of injury three weeks ago?" Agent House asked.

"As a matter of fact, I saw a bandage on his left hand a few days ago," Sergeant Woznica replied.

"And I can confirm the judge also has band-aids on his right hand as well," I interjected.

"Okay, let's assume the judge has two injured hands about that time," Agent House said. "Is there more to your theory, Heather?"

"After the judge killed Larry, he panicked and left. A half hour later, he and another man returned in a car licence number HAR 2212, as recorded in Mr. McClelland's diary. Again, my father's sources confirm that HAR 2212 is registered to Harvey Parslow."

"Harvey Parslow was the driver and the judge was a passenger?" Agent House asked as a point of clarification.

"Yes. The two men buried the body in the ravine. The body was found on 28 April and had been dead for 10 to 12 days according to the forensic lab. Mr. McClelland's descriptions of the two drivers matches Judge Sewchuk and Chief Parslow."

Sergeant Woznica, sensing I had pretty well finished my presentation, to my relief, took over the conversation. He produced the photocopy of the donated car and the write-up I had given him earlier. He pointed out the SLE 360 plate as he handed the document across the desk.

"I can add a few points," he said. "First, the photocopy proves the involvement of Chief Parslow in the 1973 murder."

Agent House examined the picture and scanned the narrative. She circled 1973 date at the top of the page.

"Second, I'll try to make a suggestion to Detective Turcot to test for DNA on the sword, if he hasn't already done so, without arousing suspicion."

"Good," commented Agent House.

"Third, I have already used FBI resources in Baltimore to check whether the revolver found on the golf course was the one used to murder Roger Wendelman in 1973."

"You found a revolver on the golf course?" Agent House asked incredulously.

"Actually, Heather located it. She learned a young man by the name of Daniel Spagnoli found a revolver and she told me. I persuaded Daniel to hand the gun over as evidence in a murder case."

"Interesting," Agent House commented and continued to write.

"In some states it is mandatory that ballistics profiles of all weapons issued to police officers and public official be kept on file," he said.

"What's are ballistics profiles?" I asked.

"It's a record of the markings on a bullet after it has been fired by a specific gun," he replied.

"Thank you."

"I'm reasonably certain all Pennsylvania judges were issued 32-calibre revolvers in the past," he stated, looking at Agent House. "It could be Judge Sewchuk was issued with one. Do you know whether a ballistics profile requirement exists in Pennsylvania?"

"I don't really know, but I'll check it out," Agent House responded.

"I also sent a fax to the Philadelphia Police asking them to do a forensic sweep of the 1955 Ford, licence SLE 360, donated to the Police Museum in 1973," Sergeant Woznica continued. "I also sent an electronic copy of the DNA of Roger Wendelman's blood and the fibers the body was wrapped in. I asked for top priority. Their response should be back in a day or two."

"Okay, please keep me informed on that," Agent House said as she opened another file on her desk. "Now I think it's time I gave you some of the information the FBI is working on."

"Excuse me. There are a couple more things I would like to add," I interjected.

"Sorry, Heather, I thought you were finished."

"Mr. McClelland also described one of the persons visiting the

General's Farm three weeks ago wore a red and white baseball jacket."

"Thank you, Heather." Agent House wrote a short note.

"The judge has a red and white baseball jacket. I saw it in his office and it has some splatter spots on the one of the sleeves," I declared.

At that point there was a light knock at the door.

Agent House stepped away and returned with a thin file. She sat at her desk as she read the contents.

"This is the letter from your uncle. It appears to support your theory," she said, as she handed the file to me. I confirmed it was Uncle Arthur's letter and passed it to Sergeant Woznica.

"As I said earlier, I owe you some information," Agent House said quietly.

Sergeant Woznica became engrossed in reading the letter.

"I must ask you to treat what I'm about to say in the strictest of confidence."

"Of course," I said.

Sergeant Woznica nodded his head as he continued to read.

"The FBI has had Chief Parslow and several others under surveillance for some time. We are concerned someone has been using intimidation tactics to buy strategic parcels of land, particularly in the east end of the city for several years. And now, the General's Farm is a prime target."

"Why would anyone think that rocky piece of land was worth anything?" I asked.

"We're talking about the land north of the ridge. That land is relatively flat," Agent House explained.

"That area is included in the General's Farm?" I asked.

"Yes and the buyers appeared to be a team led by Chief Parslow. From what has been uncovered, it appears the money might be coming from SPA-KAL, whose members are unknown at this time. The various parcels of land they have acquired are relatively small individually, but collectively make up a sizeable percentage of land area in the city of Melcastle."

"So that's why they wanted the farm," I interjected.

"Our agents will be out to contact Mr. McClelland later today with some mug shots, including Chief Parslow and Judge Sewchuk. From what you tell me, Mr. McClelland's diary is pretty important. Did he write down the suspect's descriptions or did he describe them from memory?"

"I can't be sure the descriptions were written down, but he seemed to be looking at his notes as he spoke," I replied. "Almost certainly the comments about the weather were written down. So the suspect's descriptions probably were too."

"Our agents will also arrange to make photocopies of Mr. McClelland's diary. On behalf of the FBI, I would like to thank you both for your help," said Agent House.

"Only too happy to help," I replied.

"Yes, I wasn't looking forward to taking on a chief of police and possibly even a judge," said Sergeant Woznica.

As we approached the door, I couldn't resist inquiring about a picture by the door of two identical looking females holding certificates.

"That's my sister, Sharon, on the left. We attended the FBI Academy together. We called it the *Full Blown Idiot's* course. Sharon was posted to the Embassy in Ottawa. She may have the high-profile job, but I have the real cases."

"Let me know if I can be of any further help," I offered.

"Will do."

Out of earshot, I said to Sergeant Woznica, "We know her sister's first name is Sharon, what is her name? I gather it isn't proper to use your first name in the FBI."

"I think it's Shirley."

As we left, it was pretty clear the FBI was on the case. Two men in suits virtually bounced out of an office down the hall and headed towards "Shirley's" office.

"Do you think we have time to catch a quick lunch, Toley?" I asked, intentionally using his nickname.

"Sounds great to me, but on one condition. It's my treat." He gave no sign of recognition that I had used his nickname.

"Why your treat?"

"Without your help, we—meaning my Maryland detachment, the Melcastle Police and the FBI—might never have solved these two cases."

"Let's not use the word 'solved' yet. Besides, I was a bit lucky."

"'Solved' may be premature," Sergeant Woznica replied.

"Agreed."

"How about La Gondola?" he gestured to his left as we reached the bottom of the stairs. "It's right over there."

"Perfect. I expect Dad will be there and I can hitch a ride to the Hal-Burton press conference at two o'clock."

"Haven't you heard? The press conference has been postponed to Sunday at noon."

"I didn't know. I wonder whether Dad knows?"

As we entered the restaurant, I could see Dad seated in his usual spot. He had finished his lunch and was about to leave. He was looking at his watch.

"May we join you for lunch, Dad?"

"I'd love to, but I have to see Roma before she leaves. She sometimes brings her son with her on Fridays."

"Before you go, I'd like to introduce Sergeant Woznica. He's with the Teasdale Police. Sergeant Woznica, this is my father Henry Macy."

"Pleased to meet you Sergeant. How did your meeting with the FBI go?

"It went very well," I said. "Special Agent House seemed to appreciate all the facts we were able to pass on to her. I think she even liked the 'Wendelman father and son' theory."

"Don't forget about your uncle's letter. That carried a lot of weight," Sergeant Woznica added.

"That's great and I'd love to hear more about it, but I have to leave some things with my secretary, so she can sort them out over the weekend," Dad said. "Nice meeting you Sergeant. I'll see you at the press conference in about 15 minutes, Heather?"

"I guess you haven't heard, Dad. Sergeant Woznica tells me the Hal-Burton press conference has been postponed until Sunday at noon."

"The venue has also been changed to the high school gymnasium,"

Sergeant Woznica added.

"Sunday?" Dad asked. "Why on earth would they hold a press conference on a Sunday?"

"I think I know the reason, but I'm afraid the answer is classified," Sergeant Woznica said. "I believe it'll all become clear on Sunday."

"In that case, Roma and I will have more time to work on the company tax return. Lots of fun," Dad responded as he moved away.

"I'll still need a ride home," I said, in a raised voice so Dad could hear me at the cashier's stand.

"Okay. Come up when you're finished," he said and disappeared.

As we sat at Dad's table, I quickly made up my mind what I was going to do with the now open afternoon.

"I must go shopping this afternoon," I announced, "but this time it'll be with that dull old American money."

"You Canadians are all alike," Sergeant Woznica joked.

"Not really, but I do like money that has colors."

"Since the press conference has been postponed we can have a long lunch," Toley suggested.

"That's good because now I'm thirsty and hungry."

CHAPTER 32

At Loose Ends

Later Friday Morning

I was in my office still trying to figure out what to do next, when an old friend, Norm Olshin, walked in. I hadn't seen him since he retired from teaching high school several years ago. He wanted to discuss the possibility of hiring a lawyer. I'd never seen him so nervous. Even in high school and later as a teacher, Norm was always the cool one.

It took Norm a while to bring up what was bothering him. He wanted to know whether I would represent him should he have to go to court concerning his part in certain SPA-KAL property acquisition tactics. Norm's involvement began when Doug Bockington, a fellow retired teacher, tried to recruit him into the SPA-KAL real estate business. Doug knew Norm was having difficulty living on his teacher's pension. Norm was pretty sure the job was illegal when Doug first suggested it. Norm said even though he could use the extra money, he turned Doug's offer down.

Norm confided that a few days after he declined the offer, Chief Parslow paid him a visit. The chief hadn't stopped by Norm's house because they were old friends. The chief offered to drop the drug possession charges against Norm's daughter, Ardin, if Norm would join the, "SPA-KAL property acquisition team."

I told Norm his case depended on exactly how he was instructed to carry out the "property acquisitions" and whether any of the instructions were in writing. Norm said that not only was everything verbal, but all commissions were paid in cash.

Then I suggested that a large part of Norm's case would depend on whether Doug Bockington would back him. Norm was sure Doug would support him because Doug had been "recruited" in much the same way. He and Doug both began to worry about six months ago when they stopped getting paid.

I was curious as to whether Norm knew who any of the principals of SPA-KAL were. Unfortunately, Norm hadn't seen or heard from anybody other than Chief Parslow.

Norm said he would talk the situation over with Doug Bockington and call me back.

I picked up a Request for Proposal (RFP) I had been neglecting for several weeks. The RFP preparation proved to be a little more work than I thought it would be. Initially, the contract coming from the RFP was to be a small job, but one that could easily lead to further opportunities. The prospect of more work seemed a little more enticing now that Heather was on board.

I couldn't concentrate on the RFP so I decided I would venture down to the restaurant for lunch even though it was a little early.

Just as I was finishing lunch, Heather entered La Gondola and introduced Sgt Woznica to me. It was during that conversation that I was informed that the Hal Burton press conference had been postponed to Sunday. I guess I was flustered because I found myself making a silly excuse that I had to go back to my office to finish my tax returns.

I was still in my office, when Heather dropped by to announce she was going shopping. She left her briefcase and said she would pick it up after she finished.

I put the finishing touches on the RFP and wrote out the address on the envelope by hand (Roma hasn't shown me how she does envelopes on the Mac yet). The deadline for the RFP bid was today and if I left it for Roma, it wouldn't go out until Monday. Considering it was Friday, I dropped the envelop in the mail box outside the building.

I took Heather's briefcase with me and locked it in the trunk of my car. I wedged it in beside the plastic gas can for the lawn mower. Perhaps that would remind me, on arrival home, to also remove the can that I had filled several days ago. After mailing the letter and dropping off the briefcase, a visit with Bonnie at Windemere seemed like a good plan.

Bonnie was smiling and walking around quite sprightly when I arrived. She had traded in her walker-with-wheels for a cane and I was surprised that she only needed to use it casually. She suggested we go outside for a walk around the grounds. Mrs. Greisler happened to be passing by and I advised her that Bonnie and I would be going for a walk outside. In the past, Bonnie was usually tired out by the time we reached the back door. Unfortunately, the wind was up and it had turned chilly. So we came back in after a few minutes.

On the way back to her room, Bonnie surprised me by asking how Heather was getting along. She even wanted to know whether I had left everything in her room the way it was when Heather left. I told her nothing had been moved. I added that Heather was looking forward to another visit next week.

"Me too, I enjoyed her last visit," Bonnie said.

I was elated.

Mrs. Greisler noticed how well Bonnie was getting along. I made sure she heard enough of our conversation to note Bonnie's progress in her charts. I asked about Dr Hammersmyth's whereabouts. Mrs. Greisler said that the doctor wasn't in, but she would inform him that we had asked.

The Windemere trip had been satisfying. It was refreshing to see Bonnie's tremendous progress since Tuesday. I couldn't wait to tell Heather.

On my way back to the city, I remembered Heather had asked me to give her a ride to pick up her car. I parked in my usual spot and went up to my office. Heather wasn't there so I went looking for her. How many ladies or linen shops could there be? Then again, I suppose she had been in Montreal long enough to have earned her black-belt in shopping and any outing wouldn't necessarily be just for ladies wear and linen.

After searching several stores, I saw her through the window of Linens & Things, the last commercial building on Taylor Street north. By the time she hit the street with all her purchases, it was nearly five o'clock.

At my car, I discovered it had been broken into. This was the second time I had to report a break-in to the police in less than a month. The damage was minor and I wouldn't necessarily have reported it, except Heather's briefcase was stolen.

I helped Heather put the boxes and bags in the trunk and tied the lid down with some bungee cords. Then we drove the two blocks to the Melcastle Police Station. We were immediately referred to the duty Corporal's office. He pulled out a file from a pile on his desk. He confirmed it was the same car I had previously reported the bullet-hole in the window. Heather described her briefcase and contents and that was about it. The duty Corporal thanked us for reporting the break-in; which he said was the latest in a series, and offered us some hope that it might help catch the guy.

We took the new highway home and we were approaching the one and only traffic light in Teasdale, when Heather remembered she had left her car in the police parking lot.

"Oh yeah...I forgot. My car is in the parking lot...over there...behind the police station," she sputtered out and pointed in the direction of the Aalen Building.

In her exited outburst, she forgot I was very familiar with the Teasdale police parking lot. Fortunately, the light was green and there was no traffic, which allowed me to make a casual left and then right turn into the parking lot.

After seeing Heather had managed to start her car, I made a giant U-turn out of the parking lot, a left turn to the traffic light and left again around the Aalen Building. I looked in the rear view mirror to see whether Heather had made it through the light okay. She had. I wondered how she learned to drive so well without her father around to help.

CHAPTER 33

Warning Signs

Friday Afternoon

After lunch with Sergeant Woznica, I set out on my shopping trip. My briefcase seemed a tad inappropriate, so I went up to Dad's office to leave it there. Dad barely acknowledged my presence. I left my case conspicuously in his way so he wouldn't miss it should he decide to leave before I returned. I didn't have many things to pick up so I didn't expect to be long.

The first thing I had to do was go to the bank and change my money and see whether my blank checks were in.

After a while, the long shadows of the parking meters on the sidewalk were my best indication that several hours had passed. Besides, my clutch of purchases had become too big and heavy to carry around much longer.

I had bought most of the items on my mental list, but my last objective was to find a place that sold linens. I had to buy something for the house because I didn't want it to appear as though I had spent the whole afternoon shopping for myself.

I braved the traffic and headed for a place across the street called Linens & Things. They had an excellent selection of Irish linens, but a tad expensive.

I was standing in the checkout line when I looked up and saw Dad peering in the window. The clock behind the counter showed the time was well after five o'clock. It was hard to believe that over three hours had passed. The shoe stores would have to wait for another day. Dad graciously helped me with my parcels.

I hadn't sat down since lunch and Dad's car was a welcome sight. Dad put the bags he was carrying in the back seat and hung the dresses behind the driver's side window. While he was doing that, I tried to open the rear door on my side, but it wouldn't budge. Dad tried to open it with the buttons on his door. That didn't work either. Fortunately, the front door on my side worked.

"I guess the car is trying to tell me it's getting old. Better put your stuff in the trunk," Dad suggested. "That is if I can open it. The button for the trunk doesn't seem to work either."

"Maybe the window wasn't all that was damaged when that guy broke into your car last month."

"That's odd."

"What's the problem, Dad?"

"The lock appears to be broken," he said, as he lifted up the lid revealing a mess of bags and boxes, a gas can, loose chains, to say nothing of the mud and dirt.

"Looks like you've been using your car for construction storage," I commented.

"No, no. Someone's broken into it! I think the lock has been broken. Sure it has. Look!"

"Yes, I see the jimmy marks."

"Damn!" he said. "Your briefcase, I put it in here before I went looking for you. It's gone."

"Damn is right. That was an expensive briefcase. It was a farewell gift from Thelma. Fortunately, there wasn't much in it, just my notebook and a few legal pads."

"I'm sorry."

"I'll miss my briefcase, but the contents of the notebook should be easy enough to recover from memory," I offered, hoping to ease his concern.

"The police are going to think I'm some kind of nut. The last time it was some lost files. Now it's a briefcase."

Dad undid some bungee cords he had strung on the underside of the trunk lid and tied the lid to the bumper. Then we drove to the Melcastle Police Station. The biggest part of the report was the description of my briefcase.

On the way home, Dad dropped me off at the Teasdale Police parking lot where I picked up my car.

When we arrived at Macy House, we discovered someone had tried to break-in the front door. The handle was loose and the doorjamb had some chisel marks on it, but the door was still locked. Dad inserted his key and the door opened. I stepped inside with my shopping bags. As I was putting my purchases on the desk beside the door, Mrs. Griffin, a long-time neighbor, came over. Dad was still outside opening and closing the door.

"Good afternoon, Henry," Mrs. Griffin shouted, all out of breath. I could see and hear just enough of her through the opening in the door to tell she was upset over something. Her arms were gesturing wildly.

"I'm not so sure it's such a good afternoon, Mrs. Griffin," Dad shouted. That was a clue Mrs. Griffin's hearing loss was more serious than it was when I was a teenager.

"I just wanted to let you know the strangest thing happened this afternoon. I've been sitting on my front porch since four o'clock waiting for you to come home."

"Did you see what happened, Mrs. Griffin?" Dad asked.

I opened the door to be polite. Besides, I was curious.

"Yes, I did...oh, hello Heather," she interrupted herself. The volume in her voice was noticeably lower, but no less agitated. I said hello.

"As I was saying, this young man drove up in one of them trucks with the big wheels. The first thing he did was to start fooling around with your front door. I asked him what he was up to, but he pretended he didn't hear me. He jumped back in his truck and left. The truck was that funny green color, all shiny-like. He drove off like it was his everyday business."

When she finished talking she heaved a big sigh and raised her arms and dropped them to her side in a gesture of futility.

"Did you happen to catch the licence plate number?" I asked.

I was starting to develop a thing for licence numbers.

"What?" she asked, and looked at me as though I hadn't heard anything she had said.

I repeated the licence plate question in a louder voice.

"No, just a young man in blue jeans and a T-shirt."

"Was he tall or short? What color was his hair?" I persisted.

"Can't rightly tell. He was bent over fooling with the doorknob by the time I really noticed him. He did have long, curly black hair—not real long like a girl's, but it hung down close to his shoulders." She made a chopping action on her neck above her shoulders.

"Well thank you, Mrs. Griffin. It looks as though you may have scared him off."

"Your car wasn't here, so I knew you weren't home and it certainly was odd seeing a strange man at your place doing something like that. Just thought I'd let you know," Mrs. Griffin said, as she backed away to her property.

"Thanks again, Mrs. Griffin," Dad shouted.

"We don't need a burglar alarm system," Dad whispered as Mrs. Griffin left. "She keeps a pretty good eye on things around here."

"We should give her a telescope and a scribbler."

Dad shook his head and rolled his eyes.

"I see old Albert McClelland has really gotten to you."

"That reminds me, do you have a notebook around here I could used until I can replaced mine?"

"I suppose I could find something," Dad replied. "Come to think of it, I did pick up a pad and pencil set from an Intellectual Properties convention I attended in San Francisco a few years ago. I'm not sure where the set is now though."

"San Francisco. I wonder whether any of those conventions will ever be held in Montreal?"

"Wouldn't be surprised. The association I belong to is an international organization and they try to spread the sites around."

CHAPTER 34

An Emergency Meeting

Saturday Morning

I awoke the next morning to the unmistakable sound of a nylon jacket being slipped on and zipped up, which meant Dad was preparing for his morning jog. Soon, all I could hear was the kitchen radio. It seemed louder than usual. Maybe it was because I was trying to sleep in.

I snuggled up in the covers and thought about the weather. It didn't really matter. This was Saturday and staying in bed was my prime ambition for the day. Even what to wear was already decided. The selection would be my favorite blue jeans and a color-matching, long-sleeved cotton sweater. My thoughts shifted to breakfast, which gradually overcame my desire for more sleep.

I already knew what breakfast was going to be as well. Even before I opened my eyes, I could picture Canadian back-bacon and scrambled eggs on toast. Mmmm…Always a good thought.

I put frying pan on the stove and was about to turn it on when the phone rang. The ring wasn't coming from its usual place on the end of the kitchen counter. Misplacing cordless phones can be a problem. The phone was on its third ring when I located it on the chesterfield. Dad must have left it there yesterday.

Detective Turcot wanted me to meet him at Sergeant Woznica's office in Teasdale, to witness some evidence they had found. He asked me to come right away. There was a kind of high-pitched tone in his voice as though he was anxious about something.

I checked the stove to make sure it was off and looked for something to eat during the drive into the village.

I had no idea how long I would be at the police station, so I wrote a note to Dad on one of those Post-It pads he keeps on the kitchen counter near the fridge:

> "Gone to meet Det. Turcot at
> Sgt. Woznica's office in Teasdale.
> Shouldn't be long.
> Love Heather."

I stuck the note on the fridge door and left it sticking halfway out so Dad would be sure to notice it.

The weather outside looked beautiful, but as I picked up a banana, I heard the weather forecast on the radio. The announcer said that a storm front was moving in and current wind speeds were 15 to 20 miles per hour and would be increasing to 40 and gusting to 50 later in the day.

The sun was bright, but there was a chill crispness in the air, as I stepped out of the house. A line of fair-weather cumulus clouds could already be seen on the southeast horizon.

When I opened the car door, the hot air rushing out felt like a sauna.

Before I entered, I lowered the driver's side window all the way down and cracked the passenger side down an inch or so. I figured when the interior temperature cooled off I could roll my window up as needed. Electric windows do have their advantages.

As I pulled away from the parking area, I became aware of two men at the other end of the driveway—on the median between the In and Out lanes. One of the men was tall and thin, the other short and heavy-set. The shorter man, wearing a raincoat, seemed to be staggering backwards away from the other man. The short guy held what looked like a bottle in a twisted, brown paper bag, in his outstretched arm. The taller man looked like he was trying to persuade the other one to hand over the bottle. As I neared the end of the driveway, it appeared to me that the taller man, the one facing me, was wearing fake glasses—the Groucho Marx kind with a large nose. Something was drastically wrong with this picture.

Suddenly, the tall man moved fully into my path. By that time, I thought I was going to hit the both of them. I slammed on the brakes and groped for the horn. Suddenly, the guy waving the bottle turned around, lunged at me through the open window and covered my face with a damp cloth. The last thing I remember seeing was his amber-tinted sunglasses. I slowly slipped into the "Arms of Morpheus"—the God of Dreams.

CHAPTER 35

Where Could Heather Be ???

Saturday Morning

On weekends, I usually take my morning jog around eight and return about nine. This morning I returned about nine-fifteen. It was a beautiful day for jogging. As I entered the house, I was puzzled why Heather wasn't up yet. This was our first Saturday together. Perhaps she was in the habit of sleeping in late on weekends.

After my shower, Heather still wasn't out of her room, so I called outside her door. No response. I knocked. Still no response. I knocked again, and then opened the door. She wasn't in her bed, but I was pleased to see that Coco-Bear had resumed his place on her pillow.

I checked all the possible places she might be, including the back yard, the offices and the conference room.

I was standing in the kitchen and had just come to the realization that Heather's car was gone too. At that same moment, the phone rang. It was Mrs. Griffin. There was no mistaking her voice.

"Mr. Macy. I'm glad I finally caught you. I've been calling your number for half an hour and nobody answered," she said, all exited, almost angry.

"I guess I must have been in the shower, Mrs. Griffin. What can I do for you?"

"It's Heather. I didn't see it all, but two men jumped into her car at the end of your driveway…I mean, one man got in, but they both moved her out of the driver's seat…and then one of them drove her off…" Mrs. Griffin was all out of breath.

"Slow down, Mrs. Griffin. Start from the beginning and tell me what happened," I said calmly, trying not to reveal how anxious I was myself.

"I don't know what happened, except it was at the end of your driveway. When I looked out my front window, I saw Heather's new car and both front doors were open and two guys were moving her across the front seat like she had a heart attack or something. Then one guy drove off with her toward town. And the other guy ran over to his car and followed them…and…" Mrs. Griffin stopped to catch her breath.

While Mrs. Griffin was talking, I spotted a note sticking out on the fridge door. I was trying to read the note and listen to Mrs. Griffin at the same time.

"It's okay, Mrs. Griffin. Heather left me a note. It says she has gone to meet Detective Turcot and Sergeant Woznica in Teasdale."

"But, what about those two guys at the end of your driveway?"

"I don't know. Perhaps she was car-jacked," I offered, but not convinced it was a viable answer.

"But, why would they be moving her around in her car?"

"I don't know, Mrs. Griffin. I'll do some phoning around and see whether I can make some sense out of it. Thanks very much for calling, Mrs. Griffin."

After I hung up, I stood in the kitchen for a few seconds trying to think of what I could do. My first thought was Heather must have had a medical problem and somebody tried to help her. I looked up the number of the Melcastle hospital in the phone book. The receptionist said she was sorry, but they had had no new patients in the past few hours.

I sat down at the kitchen table and tried to imagine what possible scenario could explain what Mrs. Griffin's had seen. I looked at the note again. Obviously, Heather was in her car and heading out to a meeting with Turcot and Woznica in Sergeant Woznica's office in Teasdale.

It took me a while to find the Teasdale Detachment phone number. I eventually found it in the emergency pages in the Melcastle phone book.

I was hoping the person answering the phone would be Bill Hird's granddaughter. No such luck. All the duty officer would tell me was Sergeant Woznica was not available. The officer didn't know when the Sergeant would be back.

Next, the idea came to me to phone Detective Turcot's office in Melcastle. The switchboard operator said the detective was not on duty that morning. "Could anyone else be of assistance?" When I insisted it had to be Detective Turcot personally, she suggested he was probably at home, but wouldn't give me his home phone number.

Fuddle duddle! I screamed silently to myself, as I hung up.

By that time, it was after ten o'clock. I phoned the Teasdale detachment again to report Heather as a missing person. The duty officer gave me the standard response that they needed to have evidence the person was really missing. Somehow, taking Mrs. Griffin down to the police station didn't seem like a good move.

I tried the hospital again. Same reply.

Panic had started to set in. I paced around the kitchen for a while and finally came up with the idea of phoning the FBI office in the Sparrow Building. The operator was no more helpful than the Melcastle or Teasdale Police.

Then I remembered the 1-800 number on Pierre Barnard's card. As I dialed, I didn't know whether to expect an FBI Agent or a Real Estate salesperson. The person answering the phone greeted me with a mixture of unintelligible words only the speaker could understand. That was a good indication I was connected to some branch of the government. I knew his card said Mr. Barnard, but, on a hunch, I asked for Special Agent Barnard.

"Special Agent Barnard is out on assignment. Would you like to leave your name and number?"

My little trick worked, but somehow I didn't think he would return my call as quickly as I needed on a Saturday morning.

As I was about to hang up, an inspiration came to me. I asked if I could speak to Special Agent House. The operator's response was more encouraging this time.

"Special Agent House is on another line and will call you as soon as she is available. Would you please leave your name and phone number."

Waiting for Special Agent House to return my call, I wondered what else I could do. Where could Heather be???

CHAPTER 36

The Thrill Of Skydiving

Mid Saturday Morning

My return to consciousness was slow and painful. Body aches and nausea were minor compared to a throbbing headache. I was half-sitting, half-lying and tilted to one side on the end of a canvas-covered bench in the corner of a small room. The sun shone on my face through one of three small, round windows along the wall opposite me. The warmth felt pleasant on my face, but the glare was hard on my eyes. I moved my head slightly so my sunglasses would shield my eyes from the direct sunlight. I was groggy and confused. I felt nauseous, but instinctively resisted the urge to vomit.

I could see the brim of what appeared to be a baseball cap perched on my head. I soon came to realize that my forearms were overlapped and bound in front of me, as though I was in some sort of straitjacket. I could see my arms were tightly held in place by several strips of duct tape from elbows to wrists. Underneath the duct tape, my forearms had been wrapped in wool padding-like material. It looked like strips ripped from a blanket.

My body movements were also restricted by some thick, strap-like material, which I soon came to recognize as part of a parachute harness. It was the backpack that held me away from the wall behind me. My knees and ankles were also bound together by the same strips of wool and duct tape arrangement.

The slightest attempt at movement caused pain all over, especially my neck. I kept my body still and straightened my neck for a more level view. The pain was sharp for a second, which brought on momentary panic. I talked myself into lying still and observing my surroundings. I needed to focus—to think clearly.

Another canvas-covered bench took up most of the space along the opposite wall. There was a low door with a curtain strung across it at the other end of the room with daylight visible beyond. The floor sloped upwards toward it. The wall behind me on the right contained another small door with a round window in it. I slowly realized this room was the inside of a small airplane. Through the windows behind me, I could see the unmistakable edge of a large hangar door.

My thoughts returned to the sunglasses. The ones I was wearing were amber-tinted, which meant they were somebody else's. Mine were the green wrap-around kind, which I hadn't been able to find since leaving Montreal. Whoever tied me up, also added the glasses and the baseball cap.

I slowly became aware of two male voices outside the plane. One person was doing most of the talking in a voice that sounded familiar. He was saying reassuring words like: "You know the drill. You're the best student we have."

The second voice would say the occasional "okay" but he didn't really sound convinced.

Then a third male voice was added. It was much deeper than the other two. The authoritative voice said, "You've made seven jumps so far—jump number eight qualifies you for a discount."

The third voice seemed to be familiar as well. I didn't know which voice to concentrate on. The word "jump" seemed important.

Suddenly, it became clear. A student was being prepared for a parachute jump. The first voice had to be the instructor and the second had to be a student.

Then I realized why I was wearing a parachute. Could it be that my captors had a planned "accident" in mind? Were they planning to dump me out as part of a skydiving caper? My mind was racing. They had bound me up with wool strips to ensure no residue from the tape was left on my skin or clothing. Once in flight, they would remove the bindings, give me another shot of whatever was on that damp cloth and shove me out the door.

I decided to concentrate on what the voices were saying.

Instructor: "Okay, you're all set."

Student: "But, why today? I was planning on going golfing."

Instructor: "Today is perfect—no clouds anywhere near us. Just enough wind to control where you land. You'll see."

I desperately wanted to shout that the winds were really too strong for a training jump and likely to become worse. But, I decided it was best to pretend I was still unconscious.

Student: "Okay, if you say so," came the weak reply.

Instructor: "By the way, we have another student with us today. This is her first jump and she's kind of nervous, so don't pay any attention to her."

"Okay, Lou."

The name "Lou" still wasn't enough to fill in the voice recognition puzzle.

Third voice: "She's already on board. She's a celebrity and doesn't want anybody to know who she is. She's wearing a disguise and would appreciate it if you didn't look at her. So, in you go and sit in the jump seat, as usual."

Student: "Okay gramps."

Gramps? That voice! It was Ronald Spagnoli! Now I understood. They were setting him up as a witness.

Instructor: "Ronald, you and I can do the external inspection while Harv checks out the other student."

I didn't have long to reflect on who "Harv" was. Within seconds, a big hand grabbed the doorframe. A bowed head appeared. He couldn't see me, but as soon as I saw the round face and balding head and patchy white hair, I close my eyes. It couldn't be anybody but Chief Parslow! He must have been the shorter of the two guys who jumped me at the end of the driveway. He had discarded his raincoat, but he carried the same bottle in a twisted, brown paper bag.

I pretended I was still unconscious. In seconds, I could feel his presence in front of me. He put a hand on my right hip and another behind my left shoulder and jostled me into an upright position. Then he spread a light blanket over me and tucked it behind my shoulders.

I listened for the telltale swish of liquid in a bottle, which I suspected was chloroform. Then, without warning, he pressed a cloth firmly to my nose and mouth. The cloth was much drier than the first time. Obviously he hadn't reloaded the chloroform, but I wasn't in a position to hold my breath. I resisted as long as I could, but finally I had to inhale. I passed out again.

The next thing I was conscious of was the roar of the engine and the airplane bumping along. I felt groggy and sick again. I opened my eyes just enough to see two figures, facing forward, sitting near the entrance door. My cap had been pulled down tight to the top of the sunglasses. That gave me confidence that Chief Parslow would find it difficult to see whether my eyes were open.

I could see Chief Parslow was looking out the window to his left. I remember thinking it strange that the bright sunshine coming through the window made his hair look all white and not brown with white patches. Ronald Spagnoli was seated half-on and half-off the other end of my bench beside the exit door. He was wearing a light blue flying-suit and red parachute pack and nervously jerking his hands and arms around. After a while, I figured out he was going through his skydiving routine.

I wished I had paid more attention to the parachute inspections Robert Hiebert had me go though. If I could find the D-Ring and release the parachute inside the plane, Ronald Spagnoli would have to notice. At least, he would be able to say at the inquest that I shouldn't have made the jump.

I knew the D-Ring was on the left and was designed to be pulled with the right hand.

It was hot under the blanket. Sweat was running into my eyes. I had the irrational thought that I hadn't put any deodorant on this morning. I forced myself to think about what to do.

I realized the blanket would disguise my arm movements and the plane's motion would also help cover my actions.

My wrists and forearms were bound tightly to one another, but I could lift them together. My hands were relatively free, the left arm on top and the right underneath. I felt the hard outline of the D-Ring under the canvas safety cover with my right hand. I knew the D-Ring had to be pulled out about six inches to activate the spring mechanism. I was going to have to move both arms at least that far.

Another irrational thought came to me: Smaller breasts would probably have been an advantage in this situation, but who's measuring at a time like this?

Concentrate! Concentrate!

I figured the only way to move the D-Ring six inches would be to squeeze it out of the safety cover a few inches with my right hand and then try and snare it with my left thumb and pull it the rest of the way.

I checked again to see whether I was being watched. The chief turned his head and looked for a few seconds at Ronald Spagnoli and then out the window on his side.

As I moved my arms to the right, I slowly squeezed the D-Ring out of its safety cover until it stopped. It had come to the end of the wire that physically removes the pins holding the spring release in the parachute pack. Another inch and the chute would pop.

When I moved my arms back to the left, I couldn't feel the D-Ring at first. I repeated the action with my right hand and squeezed the D-Ring as far as I dare. Finally, I was able to feel the edge of the ring with my left thumb, but getting my thumb back far enough and down far enough to grab it was going to be difficult.

I checked up front again to see whether my movements had been noticed. Chief Parslow seemed to be enjoying the view out the portside window.

My next thought was to exhale and arch my shoulders forward to see whether that would help. After a few tries, I was finally able to grasp the D-Ring securely on my left thumb. I didn't want to move it any farther, until I was ready to make the big move.

By now, I was fully conscious.

Suddenly, the plane came to an unexpected stop and at the same time I heard what sounded like several cars screeching to a halt in rapid succession.

"*STOP. THIS IS THE FBI*," blared a familiar raspy voice over a loudhailer.

The airplane engine was still running at taxi speed.

"*COME OUT WITH YOUR HANDS IN THE AIR*," came the unmistakable voice of Special Agent House. Man, was I glad to hear that voice.

Chief Parslow and Ronald Spagnoli were both in complete shock, albeit for different reasons, I suspect. They quickly opened the door, put down the fold-up ladder and exited the airplane. The pilot took his time shutting off the engine. When the propeller had come to a complete stop, the pilot pulled the curtain fully to one side and exited the cockpit. Of course, it was "the instructor"—Detective Turcot.

He stood at the door and looked at me blankly, but said nothing. Then he put his hands on top of his head and stepped down the short ladder. There were a few moments of scurrying around outside and then it was quiet.

Deputy Chief McGillivray was the first to enter the plane. He was in uniform and had his gun drawn. When was the last time the deputy chief had drawn his gun, I wondered? He glanced at me, checked to see there was no one else in the cockpit, and put his gun away. He gently took my hat and sunglasses off. I looked at him, but was lost for words. Instead, I concentrated on gently unhooking my thumb from the D-Ring.

"I'm sorry you had to go through all that," he said.

"That's okay," I mumbled.

Deputy Chief McGillivray cut the duct tape from around my arms with a pocketknife. I could see that removing the duct tape from the other areas was going to be a little delicate for him, so I took the knife and finished the job. I stood up and bumped my head on the ceiling and sat down again.

"We thought we had pretty tight surveillance on the chief, but he gave us the slip early this morning," said the deputy chief. "Fortunately, we had Detective Turcot's cell phone under surveillance and we followed the directions the chief was giving him. They met at 3155 Old Military Road and you know the rest."

"Yes, I recognized the address."

"We used Mr. Gabler's communications gear to arrange for the FBI plane to circle the area and capture your kidnapping on film."

"Why the FBI?"

"We had to call in the FBI because the kidnapping took place in Maryland, out of the Melcastle jurisdiction."

I staggered to my feet again.

"We had to wait until the plane crossed the state line. The hangar is in Maryland and the runway starts in Pennsylvania."

"It's a good thing the wind is from the southeast, isn't it?"

"By golly, you're right...I'm not sure whether the other runways cross the state line," he admitted. "Anyway, the plane would never have left the ground. You know that! Special Agent House instructed the control tower to deny takeoff clearance."

"It's okay Chief. These things happen," I said.

"I suppose so."

"Are you all right?" I asked, trying to add a little humor.

"Me? Sure, I'm fine. Yeah, let's get out of here."

"Where's Special Agent House?" I asked, as we stepped into the brilliant sunshine. "I recognized her voice over the loud-hailer."

"Right here," said Agent House stepping out of the van parked in front of the plane. "How are you feeling?"

Agent House put an arm around my shoulder.

"Man, am I glad to see you."

"I understand you've inhaled some gas. You should be okay in an hour or so. You may have a minor headache for a while. Would you like a Tylenol?"

"Yes, I do feel kind of groggy and I certainly do have a headache."

Agent House produced a bottle of Tylenol and a paper cup of water from an impressive medical cabinet in the van.

"Here, help yourself."

I struggled with the bottle. She helped me open it and poured a couple of pills into my hand. When I bent my head back to swallow the pills, I felt dizzy. I was glad she had resumed her hold on my upper arm.

"Do you feel well enough to provide a statement now?" she asked. "I can arrange for you to give it later, if you like."

"No, I think I'll write it down now while it's fresh."

Agent House guided me to a chair inside the back of the van, past several monitors and other equipment. There was a small space on the desk in front of the last screen. She leaned over my shoulder and pulled out a pad of paper and pointed to a selection of pens and pencils in a holder.

"Take your time. Don't worry about the grammar or spelling. I'll go over it with you when you're finished. The important thing is to record the details as you saw them. I'm going to phone your father now. He phoned about half an hour ago."

"Thanks," I said, as I focused on the blank pad.

"By the way, your car is over by the hangar. We'll be dusting it for fingerprints and such. I'd suggest your father drive you home."

As I began to write, I could hear Agent House on the phone. I couldn't hear what she was saying, but I assumed she was talking to Dad.

CHAPTER 37

Worry Time

Later Saturday Morning

The return call from Special Agent House seemed to take forever, but in reality was only a few minutes. I never noticed before, but the phone seems to have a different ring when it's held in your hand. The vibration didn't help my nerves.

"Hello, Mr. Macy. This is Special Agent House."

"Special Agent House—thanks for calling back. I have a problem with my daughter's disappearance…"

"Before you go any further, Mr. Macy, let me tell you your daughter is all right. She was involved in one of our operations and is unable to come to the phone at this time."

"I don't understand."

"Heather became part of one of our operations at the Melcastle and Teasdale Airport and we're just wrapping it up."

"She's all right then. Can I talk to her?"

"She's writing up a statement right now and we would like her to finish that while it's still fresh in her memory. She should be finished that in a few minutes."

"Okay, I'll be right over," I said.

As I was getting into my car, Mrs. Griffin came through the hole in the fence between our two properties.

"Have you found Heather?"

"Yes. Heather's all right. She's out at the airport. It was just a misunderstanding."

"Out at the airport?" she asked, with a bewildered look on her face. "What's Heather doing out there?"

"She's working on something with the Teasdale Police," I said. I didn't dare mention the FBI for fear Mrs. Griffin would flip out and then I'd have another problem to handle.

CHAPTER 38

The Paperwork

The task of making my statement wasn't going to be easy because my handwriting was noticeably shaky. Hopefully, that would wear off soon. A few minutes later, Agent House poked her head in the sliding door behind me.

"As a matter of interest, Heather, I checked the bottle Chief Parslow was carrying. He used ether on you, not chloroform. Ether is much easier to administer and has fewer side effects."

"Thanks. I hope you're right."

It didn't take me long to write up my statement. There wasn't much to tell really. When I was finished, Agent House went over it. She was able to help me with a few of the details because she had seen the "alleged" kidnapping on film.

"By the way, Heather," said Agent House. "Please put the outer garments and footwear you were wearing in a plastic bag. We already have the sunglasses and hat. We'll pick the bag up later today or tomorrow."

"Will do."

We stepped out of the van to face a strong wind. The weather had begun to cloud over.

I noticed several policemen and men in plain clothes swarming around the plane and my car. Sergeant Woznica was among them. I felt satisfaction knowing I had chosen the right police officer.

CHAPTER 39

Glad To Have You Back

Still Later Saturday Morning

The traffic was heavy and seemed to be moving slower than usual. Then again, I don't usually do much driving on Saturday mornings.

I recognized the Hal-Burton van parked nose to nose with a small plane out on the runways. There were several police cars surrounding the plane, so I parked behind them. As I was getting out of my car, I recognized the bright red hair of the woman getting out of the rear door of the van. She was probably the same woman who accompanied Mr. Gabler last Monday morning. Heather followed immediately behind her. Heather's slouched posture and the way she walked gave me concern for her health.

"Heather, are you all right?" I asked.

When we embraced, I could feel she was weak and shaking.

"I'm fine. Just a little groggy and a headache, which Special Agent House has taken care of," Heather replied. She gestured toward Ms

House as a kind of introduction.

"Thank you…I mean, pleased to meet you…Special Agent House."

"It's my pleasure, Mr. Macy."

"What happened?" I asked, looking back and forth between the two of them.

"I'll tell you all about it in the car, Dad."

"You're sure you're all right, Heather?"

"Yeah, I'm okay, but I think you should drive."

"Heather may not feel like eating for a while, Mr. Macy, but that symptom should go away in a few hours as well."

I was reluctant to leave until I was sure Heather was okay. Her voice sounded hollow and weak. The wind caused her hair to fly around. She stood with her feet spread apart as though making an extra effort to maintain her balance. Her complexion was pale in the bright sun.

Agent House convinced me Heather was all right, so we headed for my car. As we approached Macy House, I suggested to Heather that she should take it easy and lie down for a while.

"It's only eleven-thirty," she said, glancing at my watch.

"We might as well go directly to the press conference."

"But, that isn't until tomorrow at noon, dear," I replied in complete astonishment.

"Right," Heather responded, and smiled wanly. "Just checking to see if you remembered."

At that point, I wasn't so sure my daughter was in complete command of her faculties. I felt a little better on the way home when she started to tell me all about her ordeal. The excitement came back into her voice and I could only imagine the terror she had been through. I mostly just listened and shook my head.

CHAPTER 40

Keep The Home Fires Burning

Saturday Afternoon

On the way home, I told Dad all about the "alleged" kidnapping. I sugar coated it a bit to make it sound like a casual affair that could happen to anyone. In particular, I mentioned I was fortunate that the liquid Chief Parslow had used to render me unconscious was ether and not chloroform. I told him Special Agent House described ether as much safer, with fewer side effects.

When I finished my tale, somehow I felt better and the furrows in Dad's forehead were less pronounced the more I spoke.

Then Dad told me about how he tracked me down. I was impressed with his sleuthing techniques.

"Anyway, you're safe. What you need now is peace and quiet. I'm going to make you a light lunch and put you to bed."

"I agree with the peace and quiet part, but as far as the light lunch is concerned, haven't I had enough frightening experiences for one day?

Just kidding, Dad."

I was pleased with myself on how I finessed telling the story about the skydiving affair. Dad didn't press me for more details, and I was happy not to offer.

But, our adventures weren't over.

As Dad and I approached Macy House, we could see several fire trucks in our driveway with hoses leading around to the back of the house. Mr. and Mrs. Griffin were out in front of their house and she approached us as we were forced to park in their driveway.

"Hi Henry, hi Heather. You missed most of the excitement."

"What's going on, Mrs. Griffin?" Dad asked. "Hope you don't mind us using your driveway."

"No, not at all. There was a grass fire, but I think they have it under control."

"How did it start?" Dad shouted. He had to shout extra loud to be heard over the noise of the pumper truck. Just as Dad finished, the pumper part of the fire truck shut down and the only noise that remained was the relative quiet of the truck's motor.

"Don't know," Mrs. Griffin replied. "All I can tell you is we saw smoke coming up from behind your house. Lester went over to see where the smoke was coming from while I called 911. There were flames all along the split rail fences outback."

"It looks like you've come to our rescue again," Dad shouted.

"Yeah, Chief Jessum told us it's a good thing I phoned while Lester was having a look. If I'd waited a minute or two longer, your house might have gone up in flames."

"I always thought a stone house was pretty safe from a grass fire," I commented.

"Chief Jessum said the wooden columns on your back porch had caught fire and in no time it would have burned up into your attic."

"I guess we'll have to go and see," Dad commented and waved, as we drifted toward our backyard. "Thanks again, Mrs. Griffin and thanks to you Lester." Lester just nodded.

As we left the Griffins, Dad whispered in my ear.

"I guess Mrs. Griffin has forgotten about your unusual departure this morning. I thought that would be the first thing she would want to hear about."

"I can just imagine how she reacted."

"Who knows? Maybe by tomorrow, she will have forgotten all about it."

We stepped over several fire hoses and made our way around the house. Four or five firemen in the common grass areas were hopping over the split rail fences and putting out flames on some of the rails. Behind our house, one fireman was pumping a hand-held canister and applying water to the underside of the porch ceiling. The fire had scorched one of the wooden pillars holding up the back porch. He was making sure fire had not passed through the soffit and into the attic.

"It came pretty close eh, Dad?" For a moment, I was back in Canada, eh.

"Yeah, a couple more minutes and it would have been in your attic," the fireman said, with a satisfied grim.

"Well, thanks a lot," Dad added. "We appreciate your help."

"I'm afraid there was a little more damage to your tool shed," the fireman said, pointing at the shed a few feet away.

"That wouldn't have been much of a loss. There isn't much in there besides an old lawn mower," Dad commented.

The shed looked relatively untouched until we walked around behind. Then we could see what the fireman meant. The far side was blackened and still glistened from the water he had applied.

"Yeah, we were surprised by the 911 phone call. We thought the woman was kidding at first, because of the big thunderstorm we had in town last night. How could there be a grass fire with all that rain? The storm obviously never hit this area."

"I guess all the rain we've had in the past week didn't hit here either," I added.

"You're right. Chief Jessum figures it started in the yard behind the Farrow house, up the street. I dare say they are looking for cigarette butts. He's with the inspector over there along the fences."

"Ah, yes I see them…behind the old Merrick place," Dad confirmed. "It's a good thing Cindy is away right now. She would be panic-stricken by now."

"Yeah, that's them, only that's the Wootten place now," he responded, as he gathered up the hose by the shed.

"They're looking at something pretty closely," I said. "I wonder whether they've found the source?"

"Can't rightly tell," he grunted, pulling on the hose.

We decided not to venture over the two or three fences to join the fire chief and his inspector. We concluded they would eventually have to return to their vehicles. We followed the fireman as he pulled the hose to the front yard.

"I would recommend you check your attic to make sure there's nothing smoldering up there," the fireman suggested.

"I appreciate the advice," Dad replied.

"You're welcome," he responded, as he swung his gear into the back of the fire truck nearest the house.

The Griffins were still overlooking the scene.

"Well, Mrs. Griffin, you were certainly right. The fire came awfully close to getting into our house."

"What did he say?" Mr. Griffin asked his wife.

"He said, 'Thank you,'" she shouted in his ear.

Both Dad and Mrs. Griffin looked at one another and grinned.

We stood watching the remaining firemen checking out little wisps of smoke. Conversation with the Griffins started to become forced, so we casually drifted toward our front yard. The Griffins turned and went through the hole in the fence and eventually inside their house.

As we waited for the firemen to come back to their vehicles, the smell of the burned grass made me think of Uncle Arthur's ashes.

"I have an idea," I offered.

"What exciting idea have you come up with now? I'm open to any suggestion at this point."

"In Uncle Arthur's letter, he asked that his ashes be buried by the flag pole."

"That sounds like something we could do. You bring out the urn and I'll see if the shovel survived the fire in the shed shovel."

The fire chief and inspector came back to the chief's car as we finished burying Uncle Arthur's ashes. Dad and the chief chatted for a few minutes while I tidied up the ground around the flagpole. I shouldn't have been, but I was surprised that Chief Jessum and Arthur had been good friends.

After everyone had left, Dad and I went inside. I still wasn't hungry, but agreed to have a bowl of soup. I went to bed much earlier than usual. I don't think Dad stayed up much later.

I never told anyone, but I had several dreams that night about flying and skydiving. I was glad when morning came.

Even though I had nothing to do until the Hal-Burton press conference at noon, I forced myself out of bed early. The morning went by ever so slowly. After breakfast, I watched TV and did some reading. Dad went for his usual jog, had his shower and read the morning paper. Wasting time didn't suit Dad either. He even examined the front door handle again, but ended up concluding it probably should be replaced.

After a while, Dad joined me to watch a movie on TV. We kept an eye on the time by watching the clock in the kitchen. It wasn't until the TV station broke away for one of their periodic fund-raising pitches and announced that the next movie would start a noon that we realized the time was eleven-thirty and not ten-thirty as the cuckoo clock showed.

It seems the days of the old clock was finally coming to an end.

CHAPTER 41

The Press Conference

Sunday Noon

Heather and I scrambled into the car and drove quickly to the press conference. The new highway was definitely the fastest way to go.

The weather had cooled off considerably. Dark clouds had moved in and it looked as though the heavy rain forecast for today was going to happen at any minute.

The Sunday midday traffic was relatively light. Consequently, we were able to make it to the high school with about five minutes to spare.

I expected the front parking lot to be full. The plan was to drop Heather off at the front door and I would park out back. Just as we approached the front door, somebody was backing his car out of a choice spot.

"That's Charlie Leblond," I said. "Wonder where he's going?"

I waved as I waited for him to drive away and then pulled into the vacated spot.

"The old school brings back a lot of memories," Heather said.

"Don't forget I attended this high school as well, dear."

"I didn't realized it was that old," Heather responded and gave me a nudge on the elbow.

As we entered the gymnasium, lightening could be seen through the little windows high on the walls. It had grown even darker outside. The lights in the ceiling went off for about ten seconds. An eerie light came from the back-up lights behind the temporary panels positioned along the outside wall on the right. Other back-up lights on the stage highlighted the podium with two easels on either side, which had obviously been specially arranged for the press conference.

"I guess today wouldn't be such a good day for skydiving, either," Heather commented.

"Yeah, I don't know how you let them talk you into such a crazy idea, yesterday."

"Good afternoon, folks," Sergeant Woznica said, as he approached and the main lights came back on. "I trust you have recovered from yesterday's ordeal, Heather?"

"Yes," Heather agreed. "Just a slight headache last night."

"I guess it's okay to tell you why the press conference was postponed," Sergeant Woznica suggested.

"Yes, do tell," I said.

"Perhaps you don't know sir, but Heather informed me that young Dan Spagnoli found a 32-calibre revolver near the Old Stone Bridge."

"No, I didn't know," I acknowledged, looking sideways at Heather with my eyebrows raised.

"I suspected, as I'm sure Heather did, the gun may have been the murder weapon related to the human remains we found near the Old Stone Bridge."

"That could be tricky after that many years."

"I sent the gun to Baltimore Thursday night to be tested by the new Hand Gun Laboratory at Johns Hopkins University. We needed the ballistics confirmation before we could make any arrests. That's one of the reasons why the press conference was postponed."

"That was quick, Sergeant. I only told you about Dan Spagnoli finding the gun on Thursday afternoon."

"We can move quickly when we have to."

"How come you didn't send it to the Forensic Centre in Melcastle?" Heather inquired.

"Melcastle doesn't have a dedicated gun lab. The equipment and software at Johns Hopkins costs nearly a million dollars. That was part of a recent POTUS announcement of $40 million to provide every state with the latest diagnostic equipment as far as hand and long guns are concerned."

"Didn't they use that equipment to match the slugs to the rifle in the D.C. area sniper case last year?" Heather asked.

"Yes, it was. Even the fragmentary bullets the police had in each separate case were traced using the new equipment."

"It's too bad so many people had to die to prove its worth," I added.

"How does it work?" I asked.

"A massive computer is linked to a high-powered microscope. It matches a bullet to the gun it was fired from. The shell casing is matched to the weapon through microscopic examination of the firing pin and the imprint the pin leaves on the casing. The beauty of this set-up is that they can do this with 100% accuracy in about two hours."

"I can see how that would be useful in your business," I suggested.

"We're really looking forward to the implementation of the same equipment across the country," the Sergeant said. "Old crimes are being solved every day and the evidence is kept in a ballistics data bank. Eventually, every gun made or sold in the United States will have a ballistics profile making it possible to link the projectile to the casing, to the gun, and to the owner. It was developed in Montreal by a guy whose name sounds like the author Robert Walsh. His invention is in competition with a system built in the States. There's some national loyalty to the American one, but there's no question the Canadian product is the best system available."

"Of course. What else would you expect from Montreal?" Heather chimed in.

"You mentioned something called "potus" earlier? What is that?" I asked.

"I'm sorry. That's an acronym we use to refer to the President Of The United States."

"You started to tell us about the gun Dan Spagnoli found," Heather suggested.

"When I picked up the gun from Dan Spagnoli, I found it still contained a spent cartridge in the firing chamber. I sent the gun and the slug from the skull to Baltimore Thursday night by special courier. We already knew the gun had been registered to Judge Sewchuk."

"And my brother's letter confirms Harvey Parslow lost a small gun at the golf course. Still, it has to be proved that Harvey pulled the trigger."

"And the results of the Baltimore tests were…?" Heather asked.

"A perfect match. The people at Johns Hopkins even test-fired one of the new bullets that Dan Spagnoli obtained and confirmed the match that way as well."

"You said the gun was one of the reasons why the press conference was postponed, Sergeant. What were the other reasons?" I asked.

"Maybe the donated cop car—SLE 360?" Heather quickly added.

"Right on, Heather. We originally asked Hal-Burton for the postponement, until we were able to obtain the results of the FBI tests for fibers and blood samples on the car. We expected the results today. Hal-Burton wouldn't wait beyond Sunday because to them time is money."

"And do you have those results?" Heather asked.

"Yes, we do," Sergeant Woznica replied. "The FBI people confirmed an identical match with human remains and the blood sample that Detective Turcot originally gathered. An FBI team also found hemp fibers in the SLE 360 car at the museum which matched the hemp rug the human remains were wrapped in."

"I guess that wraps up your case, so to speak," Heather said, looking to see whether Sgt Woznica had noticed the pun.

Sergeant Woznica smiled and continued his explanation of the background information.

"As you know, the Leblonds confirmed Detective Turcot's victim as their son, Larry. You probably didn't know that Detective Turcot confirmed a DNA paternity match with the golf course human remains which is therefore, Roger Wendelman."

As Sergeant Woznica finished speaking, Mr. Gabler approached and led me off to one side.

"Henry, I can handle this press conference one of three ways. I can leave your identity out altogether. Or I can include your name as part of the announcement. Or I can turn the podium over to you and you can make your own announcement."

"I'm sure you're much more skilled at that sort of thing than I am. Just don't make too big a deal about my part in it."

"Fine. I think I know just how to deal with it."

Mr. Gabler strode to the podium and raised his arms indicating he was ready to start.

"Ladies and gentlemen, may I have your attention please?"

The well-dressed crowd, of about 75, fell silent. Those still standing found a seat quickly and sat down.

Mr. Gabler pulled out a thin folder from his briefcase, shuffled some papers and paused for effect. Then he stated in a matter-of-fact tone:

"The United States Division of the Hal-Burton Property Development Corporation wishes to announce the purchase the land area hitherto known as the General's Farm. The sale was arranged through a numbered Swiss bank account. Henry Macy is the administrator of the account.

In addition," he followed quickly, in a raised voice, "Hal-Burton has taken action to ensure, as of this announcement, all assets and property units identified as being owned by the SPA-KAL syndicate are hereby frozen, pending further investigation."

Mr. Gabler then nodded to Deputy Chief McGillivray standing to the left and rear of the podium. The Deputy Chief in turn signaled to two other points around the room. Nothing seemed to happen for a few seconds, that we could see. Mr. Gabler took a sip of water.

A low buzz came from the crowd as they struggled to take in the announcement. I was probably the only person in the room who realized that Mr. Gabler had sandwiched my name between the purchase of the General's Farm and the bombshell announcement freezing SPA-KAL's assets.

After a short pause, he began again, "The Hal-Burton purchase of the General's Farm also includes our concurrence in the preservation of the main building and the cottage. The offer includes one acre of land occupied by the two buildings."

The buzz in the crowd was now quite loud. Mr. Gabler calmly continued his presentation over the din.

"The current occupants of the cottage will be allowed to remain in situ indefinitely or at least until such time as alternate arrangements can be made."

In addition to the growing noise from the crowd, there were some people moving behind the curtains at the back of the stage. You could also see movement through the tiny spaces between the temporary panels along the side of the room. Mr. Gabler was losing his audience.

Thunder and lightening echoed and flashed outside, punctuated Mr. Gabler's speech.

"The former owner of the farm will be entitled to one half acre of land anywhere on the property, at his choosing."

I could see Heather was excited, because she knew who the "former owner" was. I must admit the half-acre of property had completely escaped me last Monday.

"Agreement has also been reached with the two local heritage groups. Each will be given a developmental grant of $15,000 over a five-year period. In addition, each will receive matching dollars for each dollar raised through their own fund-raising activities."

Bill Hird was particularly excited about the grant item. His face literally beamed as he looked around for his fellow foundation members.

Probably the only people listening to Mr. Gabler, at that point, were the finance members of each heritage group.

Meanwhile, at the front of the room, Deputy Chief McGillivray quietly approach Judge Sewchuk who was standing slightly off center stage behind Mr. Gabler. The deputy chief, in his well-pressed uniform, leaned toward the judge and whispered in his ear. Obviously confused, the judge's posture stiffened. He turned slowly and left with the deputy chief.

Some people behind the panels were being moved to the back of the room. Through the cracks between the panels, I could see that at least one of the individuals being escorted out was a female.

A uniformed officer approached two gentlemen, seated in the row behind us and spoke quietly to them. I could see them bend over out of the corner of my eye. The two, seated gentlemen seemed initially to protest, but then submitted to a tight grip on the nearest arm. As they left by a side door, I recognized the duo as the well known Terry Andersen-Koop and Clint Albertson.

The thunder could still be heard in the distance, but had abated considerably.

Mr. Gabler interrupted his presentation to take another sip of water and then continued. The noise from the crowd was much lower by this time.

"And finally, Hal-Burton is interested in the redevelopment of the Old Stone Bridge as an extension of the Old Military Road." He pointed to a close-up map on the easel on his right, "As you can see the Pennsylvania-Maryland border, the Mason-Dixon Line, passes right through the middle of the bridge."

The audience became politely quiet. The mention of the familiar Old Stone Bridge had caught their attention.

"Our engineers have examined the structure, and while it was well built in its day, it would not stand the rigors of today's traffic. We are proposing a further study by the respective states and municipal officials to determine the viability of completing this heritage link around the General's Mountain. Our financial contribution to the reconstruction of the Old Stone Bridge would be subject to a joint study attended by appropriate municipal and state representatives."

Mr. Gabler gripped the podium and looked out at the crowd.

"That concludes the formal presentation. Are there any questions?"

A stylish young woman stood up in the front row.

"Sir, one question, if I may?"

"By all means, go ahead, ma'am."

"Sir, Colette Gayner, representing the Melcastle Journal. I would like to know what you meant by," she paused to read from her notes, "'all assets and property units identified as being owned by the SPA-

KAL syndicate are hereby frozen, pending further investigation.'"

"All I can say at this time is that an investigation has been going on in the Melcastle-Teasdale area for several years concerning the SPA-KAL syndicate and their methods of acquiring various pieces of property that that group presently owns."

"Could you be more specific as to the location of those 'various pieces of property,' sir?" Ms Gayner asked.

By this time, the crowd had developed a keen interest in the SPA-KAL subject.

"Only that the areas marked in red on this map are the properties of interest to Hal-Burton," Mr. Gabler replied, pointing to the second easel. "Some of the properties identified as belonging to the SPA-KAL syndicate are within those areas."

"Can you tell us who are the principal members involved in the SPA-KAL syndicate?" some one else asked.

"That will all come out in due course. We at Hal-Burton are satisfied that the SPA-KAL principals have been identified and are being questioned as we speak."

The noise from the crowd began to rise again. They probably thought, as I did, that Murdock Sparrow and Ben Kalloway originally organized SPA-KAL. My bet was that Judge Sewchuk headed the present management. Nobody I knew seemed to know for sure, but somebody had to have been managing the multi-million dollar organization for at least the past five years.

"Are there any more questions?" Mr. Gabler asked again. "If not, thank you all for coming."

Mr. Gabler quickly left the podium before more questions formed among the curious in the audience. I was glad no one asked about my "administration" role, as Mr. Gabler had put it.

Several groups formed to discuss what they thought they had just seen and heard. Heather and I left quietly. Fortunately, the rain had stopped. We had just opened the car doors when Mr. Gabler came rushing up. He was waving an envelope.

"Your first settlement check, Mr. Macy. I trust you will find everything satisfactory. If not, I can be reached at the 1-800 number on the letterhead. Nice doing business with you. Good evening, sir. Good evening, Heather."

I handed the envelope to Heather as we drove out of the parking lot.

"Do you want me to open it?" Heather asked.

"Make that your first official act as partner of Macy and Macy."

Heather extracted a one-page letter.

"Oh my gosh, Dad. This letter is a promissory note."

She read:

"Dear Mr. Macy:

The Hal-Burton Property Development Corporation, U.S.A. agrees to purchase the property known as the "General's Farm" from William Henry Macy. The terms of the agreement are: five hundred and fifty dollars for each acre of land officially zoned as residential (estimated at 2,000 acres) and one hundred dollars for each acre for the remainder of said property (estimated at 13 acres)."

"Is there a check attached?" I asked.

"The attached check of **one hundred and ten thousand, one hundred and thirty dollars,**" she read, emphasizing the dollar amount in a raised and excited voice "**represents approximately ten percent of the total settlement offered on Monday, May 5, 2003.**"

"I guess that's about right," I said casually, waiting for her to do the arithmetic.

"Ten percent…that means the General's Farm is worth over **a million dollars**," she shrieked.

"That's nice," I said, nonchalantly.

"**That's nice**? **That's *all* you have to say**?" she said incredulously.

"I told you about selling the land to Mr. Gabler," I replied, with a straight face.

"Yes, but you didn't say it would be worth over a **million dollars**."

She kept looking at the check and then at me and shaking her head.

With our newfound wealth, we decided to eat out for lunch. We chose the most expensive restaurant in the area—the Hylands Golf and Curling Club. At the same time, I checked out the membership and initiation fees. Who knows? Some day it could only be a short drive across the Old Stone Bridge.

CHAPTER 42

What's Next?

Later Sunday Afternoon

Dad and I took our time at the restaurant. It was nice to relax and let all the recent events sink in. The past week had been quite traumatic for both of us.

We traded comments on how we each reacted to the press conference.

"I was thinking about how efficiently the police did their jobs in the background. Who were those two elderly gentlemen that were arrested in the row behind us, Dad?"

"The short one was Senator Terry Andersen-Koop and the tall, thinner one was Clint Albertson. Before the two of them retired a few years ago, they used to dominate the business community for most of Melcastle and Teasdale. No doubt you saw the deputy chief take Judge Sewchuk away."

"Yes. I thought the judge handled his departure about as well as could be expected. From what little I know about the judge, he seemed genuinely surprised."

"Terry and Clint seemed more angry than surprised, if you ask me," Dad commented.

"Would Andersen-Koop and Albertson be part of the SPA-KAL syndicate?"

"I suppose they could," Dad mused. "Somebody had to be taking care of business after Murdock Sparrow died and Ben Kalloway retired."

"I wonder how all the arrests will affect the business community? Even as a teenager, I recognized that Andersen-Koop and Albertson were pretty big names."

"Any scandal with those two involved would certainly change the operation of the Melcastle Journal," Dad suggested.

"What do you mean?"

"You remember the other night I was telling you about the six degrees of separation?"

"Yes."

"As you know, the judge's wife, Rose Sewchuk, and her sister, Lenore Andersen-Koop are the co-owners of the Journal. Val Albertson is highly involved on the advertising and sales side of the paper. If their husbands all go to jail, they may have a serious conflict of interest problem. The Journal won't be able to ignore or cover up the involvement of two former prominent businessmen and a judge of long-standing."

"Don't forget the arrest of Chief Parslow and Detective Turcot Saturday morning," I added.

"And whomever else the police and FBI arrested behind the screens," dad suggested.

"Yeah, I wonder how many there were? The noise they made sounded like quite a few."

"Working at the Journal should be interesting for a while. We'll have to read between the lines, as they say," Dad noted.

"By the way, are Mrs. Greisler and Mrs. MacInnis sisters?"

"Why, yes! How did you figure that out?"

"Just a guess."

"You're such a wealth of knowledge."

"Speaking of wealth—if Mrs. Greisler and Mrs. MacInnis are supposed to be wealthy, why are they working at Windemere?"

"As I understand it, the two daughters won't receive their inheritances until they reach the age of 55."

"Never heard of that kind of arrangement. It must be nice to know you always have an inheritance to fall back on."

"My guess is those were the original conditions under which Rose and Lenore received their inheritances. Their parents wanted to ensure their kids worked for a living before the unearned income had a chance to spoil them. You never know. It could happen to you."

"Daddy! You wouldn't."

Dad let a few seconds pass before saying, "Just kidding."

On our way out of the restaurant, we met Sylvie Spagnoli on her way in. She was surprised to see us and had been obviously caught off guard.

"Hi Sylvie. Fancy meeting you here," I exclaimed.

"Hi Heather, Mr. Macy. I'm just here visiting Beryl Delgat. She's Dan's girlfriend. She works here," Sylvie added, nervously. "I need to talk to her about something."

Sylvie was obviously upset. After a little prompting, she confided that her brother Dan had borrowed some money and had left town. Sylvie wondered whether Beryl knew anything about Dan's plans. I don't think Beryl really believed Dad when he told her he understood. We did our best to comfort Sylvie, but we knew she would have to deal with Dan's departure in her own way.

The conversation with Sylvie left both Dad and me in a somber mood as we headed out to the car. The rain had been over for a couple of hours. Hopefully, the rain had hit Macy House this time.

"You know, Dad. I've been here nearly a week and other than the General's Farm contract, which I still think was a set-up, I haven't contributed much to the firm of Macy and Macy."

"On the contrary, my dear, your efforts have been priceless in establishing a reputation for the firm. We may never know what kind of opportunities will come out of the heritage dispute. You can rest assured it will be substantial—enough to last your career. I can see the slogan now—'From The General's Farm To The White House.'"

"Thanks, Dad. I needed that."

The phone rang as we entered Macy House. I was closest, so I answered it. The caller began to speak even before I put the receiver to my ear.

"Where have you been?" Roma demanded.

"Hello Roma. What's up?"

"I've been dialing your number for hours."

"We were at the Hal-Burton press conference and then we had a long lunch. Why? What is it Roma?"

"I was in the office at noon finishing off some work for your dad and there was a message on the answering machine. The time was 11:35. The man said his name with a French accent. It sounded like Row-ber Zee-ber."

"Row-Bear E-Bear," I corrected her, giving Robert Hiebert's name in phonetic French.

"That's it!" Roma exclaimed. "He said he was in Philadelphia for a two-hour stopover and wanted to speak to you. He left the number for Qantas Airlines. He had something important to tell you."

"That's all?"

"Do you want the Qantas number?"

"Okay, but 11:35 was over three hours ago. He has probably taken off by now."

"He said he obtained your phone number from your roommate in Montreal. Is that any help?"

"I guess so," I replied, still a bit nonplussed.

"I don't mind telling you I was starting to become worried when you didn't answer."

"Thanks Roma. We'll tell you all about our adventures on Monday."

"What adventures?"

"Let's just say I was tied up on Saturday and things were heated up around Macy House after that. We also received some good news at the

Hal-Burton press conference."

"What's the good news from the press conference?"

"It means more money coming in. We'll tell you everything on Monday, Roma."

"Okay...bye. See you tomorrow."

I phoned the Qantas number right after Roma hung up. While I waited, I asked Dad if he knew why there was no "U" Qantas.

"Qantas is an anagram that stands for Queensland And Northern Territories Air Services," I grinned.

"A regular fountain of information, aren't you."

The Qantas operator finally came on the line. She had some difficulty finding Robert's name until I convinced her his last name started with an "H" not an "E." I think I confused her even more when I told her the "H" was silent as "P" in swimming.

Unfortunately, Robert was already in the air on his way to Mexico City.

Dad, of course, was curious about what was going on. After I explained the call, we had a genuine father-daughter talk about my social life. I enjoyed that. During the conversation, I suddenly realized I should phone Thelma in Montreal and see whether Robert had left any clue with her what that "something important" was.

I had barely finished dialing the number when Thelma answered the phone. I could tell she was expecting my call. The message Robert had left with her was that he had finally found his birth mother. He was actually born an American and the people who adopted him moved to Canada when Robert was very young. Thelma said he sounded all excited and was seriously thinking of changing his name to MacNeil-Heibert. The reason he went to Philadelphia was because his birth mother worked at a university there.

I was surprised because I didn't know Robert had been adopted. It wasn't the "something important" I was expecting.

I gave Dad a summary of the message from Thelma and did my best to hide my disappointment. I didn't think Dad would be interested in Robert's finding his birth mother so I left that part out.

As a way of getting myself out of my somber mood, I thought a new subject might help. The conversation with Thelma made me think about the "play" I had started.

"You know, Dad, I think I'll write a novel."

"That's nice," he said, while absent-mindedly looking at the flyers he had collected from the mailbox.

"Yes, my novel will be a murder mystery, but it won't be one that ends on the back page. Two different characters, starting from opposite ends of the book, will tell the story. I want the story to end in the middle of the book. I call it the 'tumble-read' concept. That format will make it more difficult for lazy readers to sneak a peek to find out how the mystery ends."

"A novel like that should make the New York Times Wet Cellar List, for sure."

"Daddy! That's not very nice."

"I'm sorry. I've been waiting to use that expression for years. Good luck finding someone adventurous enough to publish your novel, my dear."

CHAPTER 43

Hair Apparent

Late Monday Afternoon

Heather and I spent the rest of Sunday quietly at Macy House. We rehashed the events of the week, particularly the skydiving adventure; the various arrests; and the sale of the General's Farm. We talked about what we were going to do with the money. The only conclusion we came to was to take the Hal-Burton check to the bank Monday morning and discuss our options with the manager. I'm not sure about Heather, but I didn't sleep well Sunday night. Monday morning I felt like staying in bed all day, but once I started my jogging routine, I was back to reality.

Roma was startled to see us early Monday morning. She was used to seeing me arrive at the downtown office around noon. I let Heather tell Roma about the murders and arrests. Roma was excited because she knew most of the people involved and asked all kinds of questions. I was impressed with the way my new partner laid out the episodic drama, in a complete and logical pattern.

While Heather was talking to Roma, I phoned Dorothy Gallows, the manager where I keep my personal account. Dorothy was able to make an appointment for us right away. I've known Dorothy since high school. We used to call her "Giggles" because of her name and peculiar sense of humor. I don't imagine they call her that today.

The time was near noon, when we finished our financial discussions at the bank. We ended up depositing the check and Dorothy gave us the name of a financial advisor in which she had the utmost trust.

Heather and I returned to the office to discuss Roma's future with us. In the elevator, we had decided on a healthy raise for Roma and a similar increase in the partners' weekly allowances.

Although we told Roma about her raise and extend her hours to full time, I'm sure she knew something else was going on. She was delighted, of course, but clearly puzzled at our generosity. We ended up taking her to lunch. She was eager to start full time, but still needed to take care of Alex in the afternoons for several weeks. Heather and I agreed Roma could increase her hours, whenever she could make alternative arrangements for Alex.

After lunch, Roma went to pick up her son and Heather and I went back to office. We spent the rest of the afternoon discussing renovations to the downtown office and Macy House. We left for home about four o'clock.

At Macy House, Sergeant Woznica was waiting in his patrol car and munching on the remnants of a sandwich. As we parked beside him, he discarded a brown paper bag and took a swig from a water bottle. Sergeant Woznica left his patrol car and greeted us. He looked like his day had already been a long one. As he approached, he continued to clean between his lips and his gums with his tongue.

"Little late for lunch isn't it, Toley?" Heather commented.

"Good afternoon, Sergeant. Haven't seen you in a long time," I remarked.

"Good afternoon, Mr. Macy. Hi Heather. Yeah, it's been at least 24 hours," the sergeant said, as he touched the brim of his hat with two fingers as a casual salute.

"My, how time flies," I said.

"By the way, Heather, they haven't finished with your car yet. The FBI wanted to have a separate look at it today."

"That's okay, but I would like to have it for tomorrow."

Sergeant Woznica reached into his uniform jacket pocket and pulled out his notepad and made a quick note.

"What's up Sergeant?" Heather asked, as she noticed Sergeant Woznica continued to stare at his notepad.

"Just routine stuff."

"Hope it's not too serious," I offered.

"No, not really, sir," he replied, but was still searching for a way to express himself.

"Is there any thing we can help you with, Toley?" Heather asked.

"It has to do with your old boyfriend, Heather, Casey Clarkin." Sergeant Woznica waited for Heather to recognize the name.

"Yes, what about him?" Heather asked cautiously. Her ever-present smile disappeared.

"His real name is Ken Clarkin. He apparently used Casey as an alias. It has to do with his initials KC sounding like the name Casey."

"What brings that up?" Heather asked.

"There's a Canada-wide warrant out for his arrest. It seems Mr. Clarkin's parents and their housekeeper were found dead in their house in Montreal. Ken or Casey's wanted for questioning. Our detachment was notified because he lived for a while with relatives in Teasdale, as you know."

"That's terrible," Heather exclaimed. "I can't believe he would be involved."

"Unfortunately, the warrant from Montreal didn't include a photograph. We first tried looking for him in the high school yearbook, but there was no picture of him opposite his biography. Would you happen to have one, Heather?"

"I'll look through my old photo album to see whether I have any of him."

"I'd appreciate that."

Sergeant Woznica kept looking at his notepad, as though there was something else he wanted to say.

"Is there something else we should know about?" Heather asked.

"I thought you'd like to know some additional details we've uncovered on the 'Mason-Dixon Murders,' as we have taken to calling them. We owe you something for helping us break these two cases."

"We were lucky," Heather said. "I like the title 'Mason-Dixon Murders'—it has a nice ring to it."

"I really didn't have much to contribute," I added. "But we would be interested in finding out all the names of the people who were rounded up at the press conference."

"As you know, we arrested former Chief Parslow and Detective Turcot at the airport. We're holding them on several charges."

"You said 'former Chief Parslow,' doesn't he have to be found guilty first?" Heather suggested.

"No. That was Harvey Parslow senior, the retired chief of police that we picked up at the airport. As far as we know, his son, the new police chief, Harvey Junior, isn't involved," the Sergeant replied.

"Well I'll be," Heather exclaimed while shaking her head. "I didn't even know he had a son. When…how did all this happen?"

"Come to think of it Harvey was married and had Harvey Junior before leaving high school. His wife Marsha left school and went to live with her parents in New York somewhere. Harvey Junior apparently spent most of his time growing up at a military academy and then became a police officer and returned to Melcastle and eventually won the chief's job."

"They do look a lot alike both facially and physically. We call the son "patches" because of his hair or "junior"—behind his back, of course," Sergeant Woznica added.

"What about Mr. McClelland's description of the driver wearing a short brown jacket and baseball cap with crests on them?" Heather asked.

"The old man still wears the jacket and baseball cap as if he were still on the job. It was his way of telling the city council he didn't like being retired a year early."

Nobody spoke for a few seconds as we thought about the oddity of it all.

"Where do Dan Spagnoli and his pickup truck fit in all this?" I asked as a way of keeping the information coming.

"That's a good question. Our detachment and the Melcastle police have been tracking him for several months and so far we haven't been able to link him to anything serious. We suspect he fired the shot through your car window, Mr. Macy. We would dearly love to test those guns he keeps in his truck. I've been looking for him all day."

"Have you checked with Dan's sister, Sylvie?" I suggested.

"Yes, but she couldn't or wouldn't tell us anything."

"How about Ronald Spagnoli?" Heather asked.

"We had to let young Ronald go. He appears to be innocent and was just being used as a witness in the skydiving caper. The young lad was shaking like a leaf when he left."

"That's good. I mean that he was innocent," Heather added.

"As a matter of fact, we think the skydiving set-up was mostly a test for Detective Turcot to see whether he would actually go through with it."

"What makes you think that?" Heather asked.

"When we subjected 'retired' Chief Parslow," Sergeant Woznica responded with emphasis on the word retired, "to interrogation including playing the video and telephone tapes, he started singing like a canary, as they say. The FBI checked out his confession before the press conference started. That's why we took so many people into custody."

"Can you tell us more about Harvey's confession?" I asked.

"Only parts of it. Chief Parslow quickly realized he had to make a deal. I can't tell you everything he confessed to, which I'm sure you can appreciate."

"Of course," Heather and I responded simultaneously.

"Well, he confessed to the kidnapping just as we all know it happened. He said the kidnapping wasn't really his idea—the order came from SPA-KAL. The syndicate met the previous evening and decided they had to test Detective Turcot. They felt the detective knew too much and it looked as though one Heather Macy knew too much as well. They knew that from your notebook, Heather."

"Which was stolen Friday afternoon," Heather added.

"According to the chief," Sergeant Woznica explained, "the SPA-KAL plan was only to proceed with the skydiving plan up to the drop time. If Detective Turcot showed no signs of backing off, the chief would order the detective to land. The assumption was, by going that far, Detective Turcot was committed. The two of them would then put your unconscious body back in your car, Heather, and push it over an embankment. Detective Turcot's car would be the convenient police vehicle in the area to take care of the anticipated accident report."

"How convenient," I commented.

"The chief even tried to convince us that Detective Turcot had suggested that your car be rigged with an incendiary device to set the car on fire on the way down. He said the detective suggested the spare gas can from the trunk be strapped to your leg with rubber bands so that there would be no evidence left."

"Very clever," Heather commented sarcastically.

"By the way, your "car accident" was going to go off the road on the way up to the General's Farm and end up on the Pennsylvania side of the Old Stone Bridge," Sergeant Woznica added.

"Appropriate, I suppose," Heather commented, dryly.

"Did the chief have anything more to say?" I asked.

"Indeed. He implicated several prominent citizens."

"Are you at liberty to say who they are?" I asked.

"I'm sure you saw us pick up Mr. Andersen-Koop and Mr. Albertson at the press conference. We also directed some people to wait behind the screens before the press conference started. That was done to minimize disruption."

"Was one of them Mr. Leblond?" Heather asked.

"Why, yes," said Sergeant Woznica and smiled. "Why am I not surprised you knew that?"

"We saw Deputy Chief McGillivray lead Judge Sewchuk away. Can we assume Jack was involved?" I asked.

"That's what we thought too, but he has a different story."

"I thought he would."

"He denied any involvement with either of the murders."

"But surely he couldn't deny his part in the syndicate." I said.

"Not really. He said his wife had money invested in some sort of financial group, which could have been SPA-KAL, but the money was all hers from her inheritance. He claims he had no part in any plans or operations."

"How about Detective Turcot?" Heather inquired.

"Other than the kidnapping charges, we know of no other involvement with the syndicate or the murder last month. He says he was just asked to fly the plane and persuade young Spagnoli to make a jump. But, there are a few details to be cleared up."

"Obviously he was involved before getting me into the plane. Surely, he had to be one of the two men at the end of our driveway."

"Detective Turcot claims he knew the syndicate was testing him," grimaced Sergeant Woznica, "to see how far he would go with the kidnapping. Detective Turcot claims he was doing some undercover work on his own and was never going to complete the skydiving caper. He says he was going to declare that the winds were too strong for skydiving and abort the mission before they left the ground. Detective Turcot thought his testimony would be useful when it came time to prosecute his mentor, the former chief, and the members of SPA-KAL. Unfortunately, Detective Turcot's actions were unauthorized."

"You said there were a few details yet to be cleared up in Detective Turcot's case. What kind of details are you talking about?" I asked.

"We know there were at least two people involved in the shakedown of the various property owners. Detective Turcot may have been one of the 'buying team' members. We need to obtain more accurate descriptions from one or two more owners. From the latest descriptions on file, we have our eyes on a couple of retired high school teachers."

"Is there anything else you can tell us, Sergeant?" I asked, hurriedly. I didn't want to pursue the retired schoolteachers subject for the time being. One of them might me a client.

"Where does Deputy Chief McGillivray fit in all this?" Heather asked.

"He was the FBI's inside man, but he swears he didn't know what

Detective Turcot was up to."

"What about my friend the judge? What have you charged him with?"

"The only thing we have against him, at present, are possible conspiracy charges. As for his injured hands, he claims he cut them trying to repair a broken window at his cottage. That part of his story checks out with the emergency room at the hospital."

"What about the evidence against Judge Sewchuk in the Larry Wendelman murder last month?" Heather asked.

"When we interrogated Judge Sewchuk, he said he and his wife were attending a Newspaper Owners' Convention in Baltimore the week that murder was supposed to have been committed. Specifically, they were at an awards luncheon on 17 April, the day Mr. McClelland recorded PEN 5055 at the General's Farm."

"Sounds like a pretty convenient alibi," I commented, skeptically.

"We're still checking out the judge's story. Rose Sewchuk was the only one officially required to attend any of the seminars or the luncheon. In theory, he could have slipped away, come back to Melcastle and returned to Baltimore without his wife knowing about it."

"What about the splatter marks on the judge's baseball jacket?" Heather asked.

"The judge had an answer for that as well. According to him, he was wearing the jacket when he cut his hands. When he tried to remove the blood spots later that day, the spot remover took the color out as well."

"It sounds like Jack is going to escape this whole thing."

"It now depends on whether any of the other accused parties squeal on him. We'll have to let the prosecutor determine that."

"What about the gun?" Heather asked, "You proved it was the murder weapon and that it belonged to the judge, right?"

"The judge says his 32-calibre revolver was either lost or stolen right after it was issued to him over 30 years ago."

"Is there any record of the judge reporting the gun's disappearance?" Heather asked.

"We're still checking that."

"Do you suppose the judge signed my letter of recommendation before he was arrested?" Heather mused.

We all realized the absurdity of the question and had a good laugh.

Sergeant Woznica had been using his notepad to pass along the details. I could see that he spelled the names out in full of all the people arrested except Terry Andersen-Koop. He listed Terry by the initials "A-K" only. Then it hit me. That was why the SPA-KAL logo had that peculiar hyphen in the middle.

"You know, Sergeant, the membership of the SPA-KAL syndicate still bothers me," I said. "I notice you wrote all the names you mentioned in full, but for Andersen-Koop you just used the initials 'A-K.' I'll bet the 'A-K' represents the two letters in the middle of SPA-KAL."

"You could be right."

"The 'S' could be for Sewchuk," Heather suggested.

"That sounds like him—always had to be first," I said.

"The Sewchuk part is correct, but according to Judge Sewchuk, the 'S' would be Rose Sewchuk and not the judge."

"Okay, I can go along with that and the 'P' would be for Parslow?" I guessed.

"Actually, from Chief Parslow's statements, we have reason to believe the 'P' stands for Doreine Pladsen," Sergeant Woznica stated.

"Doreine Pladsen? Why would Chief Parslow implicate her?" Heather asked.

"Mrs. Pladsen apparently was more than just a financial adviser. It seems, back in the beginning, the Byrd sisters were looking for someone to give them advice on how to manage the family estate they had inherited. Mrs. Pladsen was a guidance counselor for the girls and is quite wealthy in her own right."

"Bird sisters? Who are the Bird sisters?" Heather asked.

"Of course! You wouldn't recognize the Byrd family name," I explained. "When old Morley Byrd died and the two daughters married, the name 'Byrd' kind of disappeared. Rose Byrd married Jack Sewchuk and Lenore Byrd married Terry Andersen-Koop."

"I see," said Heather.

"You remember in Arthur's letter, he referred to Rosie and Lennie as casual members of the Mason-Dixon Club. Well, Rose used to be called Rosie and Lenore was called Lennie…when they were younger, of course."

"I thought 'Lennie' would be a male."

"Sergeant, my guess is that the second 'A' and the 'L' would be Albertson and Leblond," I suggested.

Sergeant Woznica nodded and wrote the names out in the SPA-KAL sequence at the bottom of his notepad. He then circled the first letter of each name.

"After all the years of the syndicate trying to find out who was the owner of the General's Farm, it's ironic that they should be forced to reveal their identity at the same time," I commented.

"You know, being a member of a syndicate isn't illegal," Heather observed, "unless we can prove they conspired to commit the murders—to further the interests of the syndicate.

"Or used illegal tactics to acquire property," Sergeant Woznica added.

"All of which may be hard to prove," Heather suggested.

"But, I was sure that Chief Parslow was a member of the syndicate," I insisted.

"That's an interesting story according to the chief as well. Back in 1973, membership in SPA-KAL cost a minimum of $200,000, which Harvey didn't have. Harvey obviously resented not being considered. That's why he revealed their names. The chief admitted he tried to work his way into becoming a member by conducting 'interviews' with property owners."

"To say nothing of taking care of the occasional dead body," Heather added, "which Uncle Arthur's letter confirms he did."

"What about my friend Ben Kalloway? I always kind of assumed he was the last three letters of SPA-KAL."

"No, as far as we know, his role was strictly as a legal adviser."

"That's good. I've always liked Ben and he seems to be a capable enough lawyer."

"It also depends on whether others squeal on him or not. So far, no one has."

"Let's hope that's the end of it," I commented.

"We'll have to wait and see whether the syndicate's current lawyer follows the same pattern. Perhaps she might not be as careful as Mr. Kalloway was."

"You mentioned 'she'—can you tell us who she is?"

"Not really, but assuming you lawyers have a pretty close communications network, all I will say is she may well become a judge in the near future."

"Crowsfoot!" exclaimed Heather.

"H-e-a-t-h-e-r," I admonished my daughter, with a stern look.

"I don't know what 'Crowsfoot' means, but I assume he or she is a fellow lawyer. In any case, I should be off."

Sergeant Woznica turned and grabbed the handle of his car door.

"Before you go," I said. "I noticed one of the people you arrested at the press conference was a female. Would that be Rose Sewchuk or Doreine Pladsen perhaps?"

"I really can't comment on that, at this time," Sergeant Woznica replied, with a look that said he wanted to tell us more.

"Come on Toley. You know anything you say is safe with us," Heather urged.

"Oh, what the heck. Because they are well known people, it'll become common knowledge in a few days anyway," Sergeant Woznica replied. "But you'll have to swear what I tell you will be kept in strict confidence."

We agreed.

"We arrested Cynthia Leblond on site. Chief Parslow named her. According to the chief, Cynthia fired the gun that killed Roger Wendelman 30 years ago. As near as we can tell, the bullet glanced off Ruby's forehead and then hit Roger, killing him and sending Ruby to the hospital. It appears Cynthia had 'borrowed' the gun from Judge Sewchuk on one of his earlier 'social' visits to the General's Farm."

"A gun theft would support the judge's story," I suggested.

"When we interrogated Cynthia Leblond, she claimed she was trying to stop the fight between Harvey Parslow and Roger. She claims she stuck the gun in the faces of the two men as they wrestled. Then Ruby joined in. It seems Ruby grabbed Cynthia's arm and the gun went off. Afterwards, Harvey told Cynthia to leave and he would take care of everything. So Cynthia jumped on her bicycle and went home."

"That's why there was no record in Mr. McClelland's Diary of Cynthia being there," Heather commented. "She rode a bicycle."

"Yes," Sergeant Woznica said. "She and her sister Val used to live near the fifth tee on Old Military Road and it was a short walk or bicycle ride."

"Well, isn't that something! I never would have guessed little Cynthia being involved in a murder. It must have been weighing on her conscience all these years."

"What about the murder of Larry Leblond last month?" Heather asked. "Did Cynthia Leblond murder her own adopted son?"

"No. We now believe Val Albertson killed Larry."

"What?" Heather and I said in unison.

"Chief Parslow put us on to her, too," Sergeant Woznica said. "According to the chief, Val visited Larry at the farm to try to persuade him to return home to his adopted parents—the Leblonds. Val's suggestion to Larry was apparently enough to provoke a violent outburst and he attacked her. Cynthia told us that Charlie Leblond was a wife beater and child molester. It seems the mere mention of Charlie's name, and the thought of going back to the Leblond house, released years of pent up anger in Larry."

"Well, I'll be. I've known Charlie since we were kids and I never would have suspected him of anything like that. Poor Cynthia, first she was involved in a murder 30 years ago and then being married to a wife beater. No wonder she turned to the bottle."

"Remember Uncle Arthur's letter?" Heather asked. "He mentioned something about Roger not being the father of the child Ruby was carrying. Perhaps Charlie thought Larry really was his son. Maybe Charlie felt he was forced to marry Cynthia and that's why they adopted Larry."

"Come to think of it, Charlie and Cynthia were married about that time," I said. "It's too bad paternal DNA tests weren't available back

372

then. I wonder whether things would have been different if Charlie had known Larry wasn't his son?"

"In any case," Sergeant Woznica continued. "When we interviewed Val Albertson, her story is that she was able to fend Larry off from his first lunge. Larry's attack threw her up against the mantelpiece. When Val reached up to prevent herself from falling, she knocked the sword onto the floor. She grabbed the sword and accidentally stabbed him as he lunged toward her."

"Accidentally seventeen times?" questioned Heather.

"He kept coming back at her. So she pushed him away with the sword several more times—to 'defend herself' according to Val," Sergeant Woznica added.

"Imagine! The Sparrow sisters! Who would have guessed that they could be involved in something as distasteful as murder?" I commented.

"The Sparrow sisters! That's it!" Heather exclaimed. "That's what Mr. McClelland was talking about when he said the sparrows and birds were always around. He was talking about family names."

Suddenly, the old man's seemingly meaningless comments fitted into this complicated mystery.

"The Sparrows and the Byrds, never thought of it that way," I commented.

"After Val Albertson killed young Larry Leblond," Sgt Woznica continued, "Val panicked and drove over and picked up Chief Parslow and had him help her dispose of the body. That's the body that was found in the ravine."

"Why would Val call on the chief of police?" Heather asked.

"The chief claims he was originally trapped into working for SPA-KAL because they caught their accountant, Harvey's brother Bob Parslow, embezzling syndicate funds. Bob repaid the money but was never charged. I guess the deal was Harvey would owe an allegiance to SPA-KAL forever."

"Seems like quite a stretch from embezzling to disposing of body," I suggested.

"That's true," Sergeant Woznica said. "But more importantly, Val

Albertson was now the SPA-KAL leader. Val knew, through her sister's involvement with the first murder, that Chief Parslow had taken care of the Roger Wendelman's body 30 years ago. Who knows? Perhaps she offered Chief Parslow membership in the SPA-KAL syndicate to do the most recent body disposal service."

"Val Albertson is the leader of the syndicate?" I asked.

"Yes. She freely admits that."

"Let me guess," Heather said. "Val Albertson was the other 'A' and Cynthia Leblond was the 'L' in SPA-KAL and not their husbands."

"Apparently so. As far as we know, there were only five members and all five were female," Sergeant Woznica commented. "Mrs Pladsen and two sets of sisters with too much money."

"Wow! Whoda thunk it?" I added, in my less-than-best courtroom English.

Heather still seemed to be bothered by something.

"But Mr. McClelland clearly described the other person as a big man, with short white hair, like Judge Sewchuk...and we confirmed that the licence plates belonged to the judge."

"Yes, we thought that too," Sgt Woznica said. "But when Mr. McClelland failed to identify the judge from the mug shots the FBI took with them, we had to rethink the whole process. Because of the information passed on to us by Chief Parslow, we suggested the FBI include pictures of members of the syndicate and make another visit. We suggested Val Albertson in particular because of her size and hairstyle. Bingo! She was the person Mr. McClelland had seen in the papers being presented with a team baseball jacket. It seems Mr. McClelland assumed the person receiving the jacket was a man."

"Come to think of it, in the fading evening light under the portico, one could easily mistake Val Albertson for a man," I added. "She is big and Mr. McClelland would expect a person with short hair to be a man, wouldn't he?"

"But what was Val Albertson doing driving Judge Sewchuk's car?" Heather asked.

"That's a weird one, too," Sergeant Wozniak said. "It turns out the car was actually Val's. It was a stroke of luck how we found that out.

When we looked at the photocopy of Mr. McClelland's diary, we noticed the letter "m" in lower case, following licence number PEN 5055, meaning it was a Maryland plate. We had been predisposed from your BMV check that it was a Pennsylvania licence. When PEN 5055 checked out to be his number, we thought we had him. As it turns out, Val Albertson still has her family home in Teasdale, Maryland. She requested 'PEN 5055' as a Maryland vanity plate."

"Well I'll be. I wonder why she would do a thing like that?" Heather mused.

"I think I know," I said.

They both turned to me in anticipation.

"Val Albertson was the "other woman" Jack Sewchuk was having an affair with many years ago. My guess is she wanted to maintain some sort of connection to Jack and that was her way of demonstrating it, without anyone else knowing about it."

"A vanity plate became her undoing," Sergeant Woznica concluded, as he folded his notepad and put it back in his jacket pocket.

"Well that should make it interesting when it comes to court," Heather predicted.

"You've made our day, Sergeant," I said.

"The pleasure is all mine. We appreciate your help. Thanks again, but please remember, the identities of the suspects I just mentioned are confidential."

"You have our word," I pledged.

"Someday we will have to have you over for supper...being neighbors and all," suggested Heather, as the Sergeant rolled down the drivers side window and slid behind the wheel.

"That would be nice, thank you."

He held Heather in his gaze a little longer as he backed his patrol car out of the parking space.

We stood in front of Macy House and watched the police car leave the driveway.

CHAPTER 44

Life Goes On

I was awakened from my flashback trip down memory lane by Dad's voice.

"What did you say, Dad? I must have drifted off."

"I asked you whether you had found a picture of Casey."

I showed Dad the blurred graduation party picture and he suggested that, apart from Casey's red eyes, Sergeant Woznica probably would accept it.

I removed the picture and folded up the photo album while Dad put Uncle Arthur's letter in the center drawer of his desk. We stood up and left the office together.

"If we're going to have Sergeant Woznica over for supper, I guess one of us is going to have to learn how to cook," Dad suggested, as we entered the kitchen.

"What do you mean? I learned to cook a pretty mean Kraft Dinner and Montreal steak at McGill."

"Montreal Steak?"

"Sliced bologna."

"Oh no."

"Gotcha, for the tube steaks."

"Kraft Dinner and bologna. I assume you're kidding."

As we went inside, Dad lingered in the doorway for a moment.

"What is it, Dad?"

"You know, as much as I hate to admit it, I do believe Jack Sewchuk could be innocent."

"I agree. All the clues that pointed toward him were obviously misleading," I said. "Perhaps we misjudged him—no pun intended."

The phone rang as I passed by the kitchen table. It was Dr. Hammersmyth and he wanted to speak to Dad. I handed over the phone.

"Hello doctor. Is everything all right?" Dad asked.

Dad listened for a moment.

"External day visits. Sure, if you think it's okay. When would you suggest we start?"

There was another pause.

"One moment please, doctor, I should consult with Heather."

Dad put his hand over the receiver.

"Heather, Dr. Hammersmyth wants to know whether we are interested having your mother come here for external day visits. He's suggesting a couple of hours once or twice a week would be very helpful."

"Sure, fine with me," I replied.

Dad made no effort to hide the excitement in his voice as he communicated our decision to the doctor.

After Dad hung up the phone, he just stood by the kitchen sink staring out the window.

The radio was on and a news bulletin caught my attention.

"Dad, did you hear that?"

"No. What is it?"

"The radio just announced the Melcastle police found an elderly couple murdered in a barn on the south side of Melcastle. I didn't pay much attention to it until I heard the announcer mentioned the barn was in Pennsylvania and the house was in Teasdale. He referred to the location as being on the Mason-Dixon line."

"A lot of people still refer to the border that way."

Dad and I stood by the radio as the on-scene reporter completed his coverage of the gruesome discovery.

"Neighbors have just identified the couple as Chat and Emma Clarkin," the reporter commented.

"Oh my gosh!" I screamed.

"Who would want to harm a nice couple like Chat and Emma?"

"That's not the point, Dad. The Clarkins were the relatives Casey stayed with after Casey's parents returned to Montreal."

"That means we could be in danger, right?" Dad suggested.

"Obviously Sergeant Woznica didn't know about the Clarkin murders when he was here," I said.

"We can debate the lack of communications between police forces later. You call the police and I'll get the gun."

No sooner had Dad finished speaking, when the doorbell rang.

"Maybe that's Sergeant Woznica," I commented.

"**The**n again, it could be Casey," Dad cont**end**ed.

Printed in the United States
45698LVS00003B/181-183

9 781413 786798